THE MIDDLE-AGED VIRGIN IN ITALY

FROM HOLIDAY ROMANCE TO RELATIONSHIP

OLIVIA SPRING

HARTLEY PUBLISHING

First Edition: July 2020

www.oliviaspring.com

Follow Olivia on Facebook/Twitter/Instagram: @ospringauthor

Dedicated to my darling PD.

CHAPTER ONE

Coco?
    Notto de coco?

No. That's not right. What on earth was coconut—or rather, *desiccated coconut*—in Italian?

I was in the cramped aisle of the local supermarket, and for the life of me, I couldn't remember.

Anyway, I didn't have time to stand here guessing. There was only two and a half hours before Marta, aka the mother-in-law from hell, would be round for dinner. Which meant that somehow I needed to whip up a restaurant-standard dessert and clean the house before she arrived and no doubt started criticising everything.

The only dessert I knew was fail-safe was my mum's apple crumble. I'd made it a couple of times before, and as long as I followed everything to the letter, it was *guaranteed* to taste delicious. But, I repeat, only *if* I followed the recipe precisely. No deviations or omissions allowed.

I had the flour, butter, sugar and apples. Miraculously,

I'd even managed to track down some cinnamon—or *cannella* as I'd just discovered it was called. But the one thing I couldn't seem to find was the coconut and I *needed it*. Coconut was the secret ingredient my mum added to give it extra flavour. Sweetness. It took the dish from ordinary to *extraordinary*. And after my last disastrous attempt at cooking for Marta, I needed a miracle. I *had* to show her that I wasn't completely useless in the kitchen. The crumble *had* to be perfect.

Jesus. That sounded so bloody antiquated. Never did I think I'd be scrambling around a supermarket, desperate to find an ingredient so I could 'prove my domestic worth'. I thought we'd moved on from the Dark Ages and stereotypical traditional roles. But food was important to Lorenzo's mother and his mother was important to him. So as much as it grated on me, I was determined to make a good impression. I would win her over. Show her that Brits didn't just eat fish and chips and drink tea. We could cook up a storm in the kitchen too. Tonight's dessert was critical. Not just for the culinary reputation of the United Kingdom, but for my relationship with my mother-in-law. I *had* to find the coconut.

Sod it. I'd tried to remember the Italian, but I couldn't, so I'd just have to ask my new best friend and all-round lifesaver, Google Translate, what the magic words were and then little Leo and I would be on our way.

I unzipped my bag and reached in for my phone.

No, no, no…

Not again.

I put the basket on the floor and rooted through my bag frantically.

I vaguely remember taking my mobile out to answer a call just before we left...and...*oh yes*. Then Leo started screaming and I put it on the table so I could pick him up.

Dammit.

This forgetting-my-phone thing was becoming a habit. There had been too much going on in my head lately.

Don't worry. Keep calm.

Lorenzo did the food shopping, so I hadn't been to this store before, but perhaps someone would speak English.

Fat chance.

Ever since I'd arrived here in Chiorno, a small town in Tuscany three months ago, I could count on one hand the number of people I'd met who *parla inglese*, so I wasn't holding out much hope. Still, it was worth a shot.

I picked up the basket and approached a cashier who was unpacking a box at the till.

Here goes nothing.

'*Scusi, per favore... dov'è ... dov'è ...coco...de...notto de coco? Coco de notto poco?*'

Christ.

The moment the jumble of words fell from my mouth, even *I* could tell they weren't right.

I'd hoped that adding the word *little* at the end might convey that I needed the coconut to be desiccated, but something told me it hadn't made a blind bit of difference.

The lady glared at me like I was a five-legged purple alien who'd just landed from the moon. Then she started speaking at a hundred miles an hour, waving her hands in the air. I didn't have a clue what she was saying, but something along the lines of *stupid English lady* was probably accurate.

Two other women in their late fifties joined her and started talking loudly. Suddenly they began sneering, holding their noses and making choking sounds.

Then the smell hit me.

Oh, Leo.

Of all of the times to drop a stink bomb, this wasn't one of them. But what could you do? *When you have to go, you have to go.* He was only a baby, for goodness' sake.

Probably sensing that they were talking about him, Leo started wailing like he was being tortured. I pushed his pram back and forth to calm him down, but his screams grew louder.

The women started pointing wildly towards the door. I might not have understood the words shooting from their mouths, but their expressions said it all: I was a bad mother who needed to take Leo home immediately and change his dirty nappy.

And of course, learn how to speak Italian, as they had no intention of talking English anytime this century.

As Leo's cries became more high-pitched, one of the women stormed over to the door and flung it open, flapping her arms and ushering me outside. '*Vattene! Vattene!*' she shouted.

I got the message loud and clear. She wanted us to leave. I dropped the basket angrily on the counter and wheeled the pram outside as fast as I could.

You'd think I'd insulted them or been caught shoplifting. Since when was not speaking the native language or a baby answering the call of nature a crime?

Ever since I'd moved here, *that's when*.

Don't get me wrong. It wasn't all bad. I couldn't deny

Chiorno had character. It was a medieval hilltop town, with pretty red-roofed houses and buildings. Very easy on the eye. That was one of the things I'd loved when I'd first visited.

When Lorenzo had turned up at my fortieth birthday party in London last year and invited me over to see if I'd like to live here with him permanently once Leo was born, I'd jumped at the chance. And from the moment I arrived, I thought I'd been transported to a fairy-tale town. It looked like a picture-perfect Italian postcard.

The cute, winding cobbled streets were a million miles away from the grey, dreary pavements in London. The views of lush greenery and clear blue sunny skies were so different to the clouds and cold weather I was used to back home. And on the rare occasions that we left the house (or shall I say, the bedroom) to go for a stroll or eat at the local restaurants, the people seemed fine. But it wasn't real. Everything was fresh and exciting. I wasn't thinking clearly. I was in a bubble. High on love. Giddy about the new chapter in my life. Little did I know what I was letting myself in for…

My bottom lip began to quiver.

Get a grip. Don't let those bullies upset you. You're stronger than that.

As the tears started rolling down my cheeks, it became clear that I wasn't. Then, to make things worse, it started to rain.

What was I doing here?

Trying to be a domestic goddess and getting kicked out of a shop wasn't my idea of a happily-ever-after.

What happened to the idyllic life I'd dreamt of? Where I'd spend my days basking in the Italian sunshine with my perfect baby and the love of my life by my side, whilst eating delicious pizza, pasta and gelato?

I knew moving to another country where I didn't speak the language would be difficult, but I didn't realise it would be this hard.

Was leaving London to be with Lorenzo a big mistake?

CHAPTER TWO

'*Cocco disidratato*,' said Lorenzo as he stroked my hair. Leo had finally got off to sleep and we were tucked up in bed.

'Huh?' I said, passing him a mug of lavender herbal tea. He'd slept badly last night, so I thought it might help.

'*Grazie. Cocco disidratato* is how you say desiccated or dried coconut in *italiano*. So you were almost right.' He kissed me gently on my forehead.

'Well, I'd said *coco* instead of *cocco* and I had no idea about that last word you just mentioned, but *yeah*. Apart from that, I was spot on,' I sighed, still feeling deflated about my rubbish Italian skills.

'*Tranquilla*. Don't worry,' he purred in his beautiful accent. 'You can do it. You just need time.'

'It's been three months!' I mean, I wasn't expecting to be an expert, but definitely thought I should be doing a lot better than I was.

'And *patience*. Took me many years to learn English.

And still is not perfect. I think you should try some lessons. Will make everything easier.'

'I know I should, but when? *How?* I barely have time to scratch my head, never mind study.'

'Can you try to continue with Duolingo? For few minutes each day? You did well with that before, no? Practising when Leo is on the breast?'

'I *was*, and I *used to* be able to squeeze in a couple of lessons on my phone, but now because of all the extra stuff I'm doing for the business, *breastfeeding and Duolingo time* has become *replying to emails and making calls time*, because apart from when Leo's asleep, during the day it's usually the only chance I get to do anything else.'

After turning down the offers to buy BeCome, my beauty PR agency, I'd promoted my associate director, Robyn, to acting managing director and put her in charge. I trusted her implicitly. We'd worked side-by-side for a decade and as she knew the business inside out, she was the obvious choice to head up the company. Robyn had always been reliable, but lately I got the feeling she was overwhelmed. There'd been a few forgotten emails and deadlines missed, which wasn't like her at all. I raised my concerns and she said she was fine, but I decided that even though I was still supposed to be on maternity leave, I'd start taking on more work to help out, just in case.

So when you added the extra workload to trying to cope with the whirlwind of becoming a new mum and living in a foreign county, it was easy to understand why learning to count to twenty in Italian hadn't been my highest priority.

'*Amore*.' Lorenzo took my hand. 'I know it is difficult, but it will be more difficult for life here to get better if we cannot find time for you to learn. It is not tourist town and many people are older, so will be easier if you speak the language. I can ask the restaurant to reduce my hours so I can help more, or Mamma can—'

'You've already cut your hours, so I know you can't reduce them any more. Thanks'—I kissed him on the cheek—'but I don't need your mum's help. I can manage by myself.'

The mamma conversation. *Again.*

It felt like her name was mentioned fifty times a day. At least I'd escaped her coming around for dinner this evening. As soon as I'd called Lorenzo and told him about my nightmare in the supermarket, he'd phoned Marta and said we'd need to reschedule dinner for tomorrow instead. He'd even brought some desiccated coconut home. Such a sweetie.

Whilst I had been saved from Marta for twenty-four hours, I'd still have to face her tomorrow. And probably the next day and the next. She only lived ten minutes away, so she liked to visit often.

Before I met Lorenzo, I'd heard a lot about Italian men and their mothers. That the mums doted on their sons— even when they were grown—and that in the man's eyes, their mamma was perfection personified. But I'd never really believed it. Surely it was just a stereotype. Just because he was Italian, it didn't mean Lorenzo automatically idolised his mother, right?

Wrong.

Can't get the kitchen clean enough? Mamma would know how to make it sparkle. Coffee not tasting right? Mamma used to make the perfect cup, whilst simultaneously cooking the perfect meal for a family of forty people *and* negotiating world peace.

That was the impression I got from the way he raved about his childhood.

I wasn't saying respecting and loving your mother was a bad thing. After all, they did so much for us. I adored my mum and I hoped I'd raise Leo well enough that he'd feel the same about me too. But please, God, don't let me become a helicopter mother who hovered over her son constantly like Marta did.

Don't get me wrong. Lorenzo wasn't one of those guys who was tied to his mum's apron strings. After all, he'd left this town many times to go and work abroad and develop his career. He was perfectly capable of cleaning up after himself, and naturally, being a chef, he didn't need mummy to do his cooking. Thankfully, Lorenzo was an independent man. However, there was no doubt about it. They came as a package deal. Love him, love his mamma. We *had* to get along.

But it wasn't easy. For starters, she didn't speak any English and I could tell she didn't like me. I just sensed it. I didn't know why exactly. Maybe she didn't approve of Lorenzo having an English girlfriend. Or perhaps she didn't like how we'd agreed to bring up Leo.

As his grandmother, I couldn't stop Marta from seeing Leo, but this was *our* baby, so Lorenzo and I would share the responsibility. I'd worked hard to get Leo into a routine and the last thing I wanted was to start letting her have extended babysitting sessions so that she could disrupt it.

'*Va bene*. Okay,' replied Lorenzo. 'But remember, we have the option and Mamma wants to help. Think about it.'

'Okay,' I said, switching off the lamp, knowing that I wasn't going to change my mind. I'd manage without her.

Lorenzo shuffled up and held me.

I shut my eyes. My mind was racing. On the one hand, being here in his arms felt like the best place in the world. I felt secure and happy. I'd finally found the man of my dreams and had the baby I'd always wanted. We were a family. When Leo was calm and Lorenzo was by my side, I was convinced I was the luckiest woman on the planet. But on the other, during the day, whilst Lorenzo was at work, when Leo wouldn't stop crying, when I missed my friends, when I had nobody nearby to talk to and nothing interesting to do in this town, I hated living here. I felt completely isolated and would dream of being back in London, surrounded by familiarity.

Lorenzo pulled me closer into him.

Uh-oh…

And then there was *that*.

Sex.

That was another thing I was worried about.

I felt his hard-on pressing against my bum and froze.

What was wrong with me?

Before Leo was born, just looking at Lorenzo was enough to give me the tingles. The slightest sensation of him touching me would have sent shockwaves through my body and I'd be on top of him faster than you can say *nookie*. It was like I was constantly on heat. But now? *Forget it*. That was the last thing on my mind. I had zero desire. *None*. It was like Leo arrived and my sex drive instantly evaporated.

The idea of getting jiggy again made me want to run

for the hills. Or join a convent. It worried me. No. *Scrap that*. It actually *terrified* me.

It was crazy. When I was with my ex, Rich, for fifteen years, existing in a dead-end, sexless relationship, I'd craved nothing more than swinging from the chandeliers with a hot man. I would have killed for the chance to go at it all night. Then I'd met Lorenzo and after a few false starts, when we'd finally got together, we had an amazing sex life—even during the final stages of my pregnancy. And yet now, here I was: on the cusp of regaining my MARGIN status. *Yep.* After not having *relations* for almost six months, I was about to become a Middle-Aged Virgin.

Again.

At my six-week check-up in London, my doctor said it was fine to get back on the saddle. Not that I'd asked. He'd just assumed that I wanted to. Although the birth was relatively straightforward and physically, he'd said, I was all healed down there, mentally, I didn't feel ready.

For a start, I was constantly tired. Like, *all the time*. I loved Leo dearly. But after a long day working, breastfeeding, wiping up poo, dribble and snot and trying to keep on top of the housework, I just wanted to sleep. I couldn't even begin to imagine how I'd even find the energy to bounce up and down on Lorenzo like I used to.

To me, it only felt like five minutes ago that I'd pushed Leo out. It was too soon. I thought maybe I'd be ready after two months. Then I convinced myself it'd be three. Then four…

Now here I was, *five* months later and still nothing got my fire burning. There wasn't even a flicker.

I just didn't get it. I had the sexy man, he had the perfect equipment to get the job done and was ready and willing to use it, but my mind and my body had somehow checked out.

Don't get me wrong. I still fancied him. He was a god. Six foot two, dark wavy hair, with flecks of grey sprinkled through (I *loved* that salt-and-pepper look), beautiful thick beard you just wanted to stroke, a killer smile, hypnotic, deep come-to-bed eyes and the most magnificent muscular, golden chest. Lorenzo was still as drop-dead gorgeous, kind and funny as ever. I loved him so much. But yet, in moments like these, when he was resting against me, I felt nothing down below. It was like the sex switch had been turned off.

Lorenzo had been really understanding. He hadn't pressured me or become impatient. He said he could wait until I was ready. But I couldn't expect him to be patient forever. It wasn't fair. And knowing that I wasn't satisfying him made me feel shitty.

So on top of everything else, I also had to find a way to get my sexual mojo back.

The million-dollar question was, *how*?

CHAPTER THREE

*R*ight. *What to do first?*

My schedule was a bit out of sync today. It was 12.37 and Leo had just started the first of his afternoon naps, so that was when I usually exercised for half an hour, had lunch, then did some washing or tidying up. But because I was busy working on some amends to a proposal Robyn had sent me when Leo was sleeping this morning, I'd missed my normal 8.30 a.m. expressing milk session, so needed to fit that in. Plus, I had to call Viktor at Purity Skincare, who was one of our biggest clients. With Leo due to wake up at around 2 p.m. and the house to prepare for tonight, it was going to be tight, but I could do it. I'd find a way.

I warmed up the leftover tagliatelle with king prawns that Lorenzo had cooked to cheer me up last night, wolfed it down, loaded the dishwasher, then headed to the living room. My phone chimed. It was a message from Bella, checking I was okay. *Dammit.* I forgot to reply to the text she sent two days ago. I missed her and Roxy, my other best friend, so much, but had been terrible at keeping up with messages. *Must do that later.* Maybe during Leo's nap at four? Then again, that was when I was supposed to be baking and checking over the social media strategy for another client. *Mmm.* Messaging tomorrow was more realistic. *No, no. I can send Bella and Roxy a quick voice note in the group chat when Leo and I go for our walk at three. Yes. Sorted. Good plan.*

How was it five to one already?

I needed to express some milk. I tried to do it no later than an hour before the next feed, so if I was quick, I'd still be fine to give Leo the breast at two. As I'd invested in the quietest pump I could find, I could do it whilst I was on the phone. Multitasking at its finest. After I quickly washed my hands and attached the pump, I dialled the number.

'Viktor, hi!'

'Sophia, long time no speak.' That was true. Robyn had been liaising with him and sending me weekly updates, so although I'd sent him the odd email here and there, we hadn't actually spoken for months.

'Well, technically it's earlier than anticipated, because I'm still on maternity leave for another month or so, but I'm just starting to make myself available for my extra special clients…'

'Glad to hear it. Listen, I'm in London in a few weeks, so I'd like to meet. Thought we could discuss the new body care line we'll be launching later this year.'

When I said I was making myself *available*, I meant on the phone, not by jumping on a plane.

'Sounds exciting, and I would have *loved* to have met with you, but remember I'm living in Italy now and—'

'Oh! You're still there?' He sounded surprised. Like I'd just revealed I had four nipples or something. 'I thought that was just a fling with that guy. Y'know, a holiday romance thing? I was sure you'd be back in London by now, getting ready to return to work.'

Bloody cheek.

I knew that was what a lot of people thought. They were convinced it wouldn't last. Just because I ran my own business, they didn't think I'd be happy going out with someone who was 'just a chef'. Even my best friend Roxy took a while to get used to the idea of me leaving London to live with Lorenzo. I'd prove them all wrong, though. I was in Italy to stay. I wouldn't fail.

'Yes, I'm still here and everything's going great actually. Couldn't be better!' *If only.* I deserved an Oscar for that performance. 'Like I said, I'm still on maternity leave, but as you know, Robyn is heading up your account and she'd be *more* than happy to clear her schedule to meet with you.'

'What? Like she did when I was over two weeks ago and she cancelled at the last minute?' he snarled.

She did what?

How did I not know this?

When I'd asked Robyn how everything had gone, she'd said it was fine. Even sent me a summary of the points that were discussed in her weekly report.

'I'm very sorry about that,' I replied quickly, trying to keep my cool and not let on that this was the first I'd heard of it. 'Extenuating circumstances, I believe. You did still manage to catch up, though, and cover all the important points?' I was half making a statement, half asking.

'Yes, a day later, on a conference call, but that wasn't the point.'

'I totally agree and I can assure you that it will not happen again. Robyn will make meeting you her absolute priority. In fact, she can take you to your favourite restaurant in The Shard for dinner too, by way of an apology. It'd be our treat. And then of course, if there's anything else you'd like to discuss, we can all have a conference call, together.'

Hopefully that would do the trick. I needed him to understand that things were different now and for him to continue seeing Robyn as the first point of contact. Much harder to do so now I'd discovered she'd committed the cardinal sin of cancelling on a client. I'd have to deal with her later…

'Fine.' Viktor sighed heavily. 'Get Robyn to call my assistant to set things up. We'll speak afterwards.'

'Will do.'

'Look, I've got a meeting now, so I'd better go, but I have some initial ideas for the ambassador I was thinking could head up the campaign, and I want you to take a look and send me your thoughts. Naturally I'm sure you'll have your own ideas—after all, that's what I'm paying you for. Anyway, I'll email you later.'

Clients. Give them an inch and they'll take a yard. Now it was my turn to sigh. I'd already told him to go directly to Robyn, so really she should deal with it, but because Robyn had already let him down once, we couldn't afford any more fuck-ups. Especially since he was our biggest account. Plus, I'd worked on lots of ambassador-led campaigns, so hopefully it wouldn't take me long…

'Okay. I'll take a look and get back to you.'

As soon as the call ended, I dialled Robyn's number. It was engaged. Damn. I'd have words with her later and find out what the hell had happened.

Back to my schedule. I looked down at the pump. Not quite enough milk yet. I'd give it a few more minutes. Whilst I was waiting, I switched on my laptop and pulled up the YouTube page so that I was ready to start my workout as soon as I finished.

I tried to exercise every afternoon. Well, not *every* afternoon. Occasionally I gave myself Sundays off. It wasn't fun, but with the weight I'd gained since having Leo and moving here and indulging in lots of delicious food, courtesy of Lorenzo, it was the only way I stood any chance of getting back in shape.

I switched off the pump, put it down on the side, pulled on my bra and T-shirt, rolled my exercise mat on the floor, then pressed play. I watched this postpartum workout video on YouTube so often I knew it off by heart.

I lay on my back with my arms along my sides, bent my knees, keeping my feet on the floor, then lifted my head and shoulders. Then it was curl-ups, followed by criss-cross abdominal exercises. This was hard. But no pain, no gain, right? These torturous moves were all supposed to tone my stomach and burn calories. So far, I'd seen no evidence that they helped with either. But I had to persevere.

I was just about to do the leg raises to help firm my

bum and thighs when the phone rang. Video call from Mum? *That's advanced for her.* Normally my brother Harrison would set it up or I'd have to call and sit patiently whilst she figured out that FaceTiming tended to work best when you didn't hold the phone to your ear or up at the ceiling. Technology was not my mother's friend.

'Hey, Aunty!'

'Jasmine? Hi!' I said, as her cute face and curly hair filled the screen. Wasn't expecting my niece to appear. 'Good to see you! What are you doing there?'

'I just came round to see nana on my way to uni and she asked me to FaceTime you, 'cos she couldn't remember how to do it.'

'Makes sense,' I laughed. 'I have shown her a million times, though.'

'Not *quite* a million.' Mum's face suddenly appeared on the screen. Well, I say her face, but she had the phone resting on her lap, so I had a bird's-eye view of her nostrils. *Nice.*

'Hold the phone up, Mum. That's not a flattering angle. Hold it with the phone pointing towards your face…'

'Yes, yes, darling,' she said, bringing it up so close that her face now filled the screen. 'Say bye-bye to Jasmine. She has to go now.'

'Laters, Aunty,' she said, pulling my mum's hand back so it was at a more appropriate distance, ducking in front of the screen and waving.

'Bye, niecey. Talk soon and say hello to Marilyn for me. Promise to call you both soon.' Note to self: to call my sister and niece tomorrow. *Hopefully.* Just needed to find a spare half an hour…

'You look tired.'

'Thanks, Mum. Hello to you too. In case you've forgotten, I have a five-month-old baby. Bags and dark circles are standard.'

Mum looked lovely as usual, her brown hair tied back neatly and her skin glowing like she'd just had a facial. Despite being in her mid-sixties, she barely had any wrinkles. I hoped I looked as good at her age.

'I do have three children of my own, you know. Yes, it's tiring, but that's why it's important that you take naps when Leo does.'

Chance would be a fine thing.

'I can't. I use that time to get house stuff done, exercise and work. There's a lot going on with the business and—'

'Darling, I know the business has always been a big part of your life, but don't you think it's time to sell up and move on? You're a mother now. You have bigger priorities.'

'I don't have to sell the business just because I'm a mum.' I rolled my eyes. 'Women manage a career and having children all the time. I'm fine.'

My mother was so old-school. Although she'd worked when we were younger, it was just a means to an end. A way to pay the bills. It was never her passion. Her focus was always firmly on family. She didn't get the whole career thing. Unlike her, I believed that women *could* have it all. We shouldn't have to choose. I knew single mothers who worked full-time *and* raised a child. And I had the support of Lorenzo, so there really was no excuse. I just needed to improve my routine.

'But you're not. You're doing too much. Harrison said

you had some really good offers to buy the company. I'm sure it's not too late to accept them.'

'It's not that simple, Mum. I told you. They either wanted to offer me peanuts or tie me in to work for them for two years. *Two years!*'

'Well, that is a long time. Leo will be almost ready for school by then.'

'Slight exaggeration, but yeah. They said they'd need me to drive the company in a new direction first before they brought in my replacement. I'd just be a puppet, slogging my guts out for them with no real control.' I shuddered at the thought of some strangers ordering me around in a company I'd built from scratch. 'No, thank you.'

'But surely there's another way. Couldn't you have compromised?'

I'd been over this with her a hundred times before.

'*No.* I tried. And they were against me working from Italy. They said after my maternity leave—which, by the way, they wanted me to reduce to just two months—they'd expect me to be in the office for at least four days a week. And because I wanted to be at home with Leo for at least six months and would only consider coming back to London once a month at most, it was never going to work.'

That was when I'd told them all to stick their offers where the sun didn't shine. I didn't need them. I wasn't going to let them control my destiny. I'd decided I would keep the business and work remotely.

So that was that. Soon after, I'd given birth to Leo and Robyn had stepped in with running the company, and for the first few months I'd checked in once or twice a week to see how it was all going and give advice. I'd thought it was working okay, but this past month, things seemed to have changed…

'I see. Well, think about it, darling. There must be a way to get someone to take it off your hands. Little ones grow up so fast, and I wouldn't want you to miss Leo's first steps or first words because you're wrapped up in sending emails.' My heart sank. I definitely didn't want that to happen. I wouldn't let it.

'Don't worry. I've got it under control. It'll be fine. I just need to organise my time better. Any news on when you and Dad might come over to visit?'

'Oh, darling, you know I'm not keen on flying. Maybe in a couple of months? We'll see…'

There went my heart again. It was so hard not having my mum just a few miles away like I used to. Especially now I had Leo and was still trying to get my head around all this motherhood stuff. I thought my friends and family would be jumping at the chance to come over to visit me, but everyone had been busy. Roxy and Bella both had a lot on with work, Harrison was stacked, heading up the digital division of my business, Marilyn couldn't get the time off from her job and Jasmine was at uni. I missed everyone so much. But I guess, thanks to technology, we had other ways to stay in touch, so it wasn't too bad. FaceTime had become invaluable.

Speaking of time… *shit*. It was twenty to two. Leo would be waking up soon and I hadn't got half of the things done that were on my list.

'Sorry, Mum, I better go. Marta is coming round for dinner tonight, so I've got to start tidying up and make the crumble.' Plus fit in the daily walk, look over the strategy document for one of our perfume clients, work on the ambassador stuff and reply to Viktor and call Robyn…

It'll be fine. I'll manage.

'Okay, darling. Glad to hear you're doing your own cleaning…'

'Yes, Mum.' I rolled my eyes again. She hated the fact that I used to have a cleaner once a week when I lived in London because I was always so busy at work. She said it was too *la-di-da*. She needn't worry now, though. The days of having hired help were over. I could do it myself.

'Oh, and don't forget to sprinkle the top of the crumble with some granulated sugar before you put it in the oven to give it that extra crunch. And to add the coconut.'

'Yes, Mum.'

'And I've been experimenting with using oats too. A teeny tiny bit less flour and more oats. Gives it a nice texture.'

Dear God. It was hard enough getting hold of bloody coconut. I didn't need another new ingredient to add to the list.

'Maybe I'll try that next time. I'll call you soon, okay? Say hello to Dad.'

'Will do. And give my little pumpkin a big kiss from his nana. You sure you can't wake him up a bit early just so I can give him a little wave?'

No way. There was now only fifteen minutes until he woke up and I was already behind. I had to stick to the schedule before things got even more out of control.

'Um, maybe we can speak tomorrow or later in the week and you can say hello properly then?'

'Okay. I'll do the Face video thingy when Harrison comes round next and sets it up for me.'

'It's really not that difficult, Mum... you just press... yeah, okay,' I said, deciding I didn't have time to go over it with her again right now. 'Speak then. Love you.'

Just as I hung up, Leo started crying.

Great. It wasn't even two yet.

That was the thing with babies. As much as you wanted them to stick to the schedule, sometimes they had other plans...

CHAPTER FOUR

*P*erfect.

Even if I did say so myself. Mum would be proud. The apple crumble had turned out just how I wanted it to. Leo had been bathed, fed and the house was tidy.

In the end, despite trying to fit everything in, I reluctantly had to accept defeat and switch things up in my schedule. I couldn't risk not having the house looking spotless, so I'd decided to skip our afternoon walk and swept and mopped instead, which took ages. That was the thing with this place. All the floors were tiled, so just running a vacuum around wouldn't cut the mustard. As Marta was visiting, I had to make it sparkle.

The house wasn't like the others in the main part of town, which were mostly on two floors. Our bungalow, which was about a fifteen-minute walk from the centre, was on one level. It kind of reminded me of a rustic farmhouse. It was a traditional stone building, with pretty green shutters on the windows and large potted plants next to the wooden front door.

As soon as you stepped into the house, you were inside the open-plan living room and dining area. It was fairly large, with terracotta tiles, original wooden beams and a fireplace. The furniture was simple: just a pair of red patterned sofas, an armchair, coffee table, TV and dark wooden dining table. I was happy to see everything was in its place. All the cushions were lined up neatly. Yep. Looking good.

I walked towards the two double doors either side of the fireplace, which led out to a terrace and huge garden. As always, the views of the rolling hills in the distance were stunning.

When I first came to visit, I'd imagined having lunch on the terrace against the breathtaking backdrop. I'd pictured our baby playing out on the lush green grass. Running into our arms, being free to enjoy the outdoors and breathe in the fresh country air. When it got a bit warmer, maybe we could sit out here on a Sunday afternoon as a family. That would be something nice to look forward to.

I put Leo in his chair and quickly walked from the living room into the hallway which led to the main bedroom. The tiled floors were sparkling too. Even though Marta should have no need to come in here, I *had* to make sure it was up to scratch.

Our bedroom was simple in terms of style. Lemon walls, a double bed with an orange patterned duvet, Leo's cot, rustic wooden wardrobe and bedside tables. Very different to the sleek, modern design of my place in London, but I liked it. It was authentic, practical and child-proof. The cream-and-white colour scheme I had in my townhouse definitely wasn't ideal for raising a baby.

Next door to ours was Leo's room, the kitchen was opposite the bedrooms and the bathroom was at the end of the hall. I'd given those rooms the once-over too, so everything was in order and ready for a visit from the mother-in-law. I challenged her to fault anything. Then again, saying that out loud was probably asking for trouble…

I checked the time. They'd be here any minute. Thankfully, Lorenzo would be bringing dinner. If I'd had to make that *and* the dessert, today would have been even more challenging. One of the many perks of having a chef as a boyfriend was that Lorenzo would often bring food home, which was a massive help.

It was Lorenzo's idea for me to cook something for Marta. He said the way to an Italian's heart was through food, so introducing her to more British dishes would help us build a relationship. Knowing how important it was for us to get on, I thought it was worth another try.

I say *another*, because on my first attempt last month, I'd cooked another classic British dish: shepherd's pie. Trouble was, I'd accidentally sprinkled sugar onto the mince instead of salt. In my defence, it was in a little white bowl beside the stove, so I just thought Lorenzo had put it there to season the food whilst cooking. How was I to know it was some sugar he'd left after experimenting with some new cake recipes and he'd forgotten to tip it back into the bag?

To make matters worse, because I wanted to warm the oven up quickly, I put it on fan rather than normal. I'd then got sidetracked on a call to Robyn, so rather than the potato on top looking nice and golden, by the time I'd got off the phone and rushed back to the kitchen, it was pretty much chargrilled. A polite way of saying burnt to a crisp. I did a good job of scraping off most of the worst bits, but it still tasted awful.

Whilst Lorenzo tried to be nice about it and managed a few mouthfuls, Marta lifted her napkin to her mouth and spat it out. If I was being honest, I couldn't blame her. So I was relieved the crumble had turned out much better. Hopefully Marta would like it and I would have redeemed myself.

In fact, maybe I was exaggerating and being oversensitive about her. I mean, Lorenzo thought she was amazing and I trusted his opinion. She clearly adored him and his last girlfriend was a psycho, so was it any wonder she was a bit wary of me? Perhaps I was being too hard on her. I mean, maybe she was lonely. Lorenzo's dad had left her a couple of years ago, and with his brother in Singapore, it was understandable that she wanted to spend time with Lorenzo and her only grandchild. *Yeah.* I just needed to make more of an effort, that was all.

I heard the key in the door.

'Look, Leo!' I picked him up and carried him towards it. 'It's Daddy and Nana—*Papà e Nonna!*' I was pleased that I'd managed to use two whole words of Italian. Hopefully that'd impress Marta.

'*Piccolino!*' Lorenzo opened his arms and lifted Leo from me, kissing him on the head before leaning forward to give me a kiss on the lips.

'*Buonasera, Marta.*' I smiled.

'*Buonasera.*' Marta frowned, looking me up and down. That was not an expression of approval. More of disappointment. *Gosh.* And I'd even put on lipstick and eyeliner rather than my standard tinted moisturiser, mascara and lip gloss. I was wearing my thick, dark shoulder-length hair down instead of in my usual undone ponytail and had dressed up in a loose pink-and-black zebra-print maxi dress rather than my normal T-shirt, leggings and jumper uniform. What was her problem?

'Leonardo!' Marta's expression completely changed the moment she laid eyes on him. Her stone-cold face melted into a smile and her eyes lit up. '*Amore di Nonna*!'

Marta looked immaculate as always. She was dressed in a perfectly pressed navy blouse and long patterned navy skirt with her dark hair neatly tied up into a bun. *That used to be me.* Not the hairstyle or clothes, obviously, but well turned out. Nothing out of place. I'd scrubbed up okay this evening. Not as polished as the old Sophia, but no matter how tired I was, I always made an effort to shower, do my hair and try to make myself look presentable in the morning whilst Lorenzo watched Leo. Some days were better than others, though, and it was much easier to look good when you didn't have a small human to run around after. Then again, if Lorenzo's tales of Marta were to be believed, Mrs Supermum here could probably run the whole of Italy *and* raise twenty kids without breaking a sweat.

She took Leo from Lorenzo's arms, kissed him on his forehead, then lifted him above her head and sniffed his bottom. Marta turned up her nose and then babbled something in Italian to Lorenzo.

'Mamma asked if Leo needs to be changed?'

Oh, here we go. She'd only been here two seconds and had started her critiquing already.

'No, he's fine. He's had a bath and I just changed him fifteen minutes ago.'

Lorenzo translated for Marta and she raised her eyebrow as if to say I was wrong. It was unlikely he'd done another poo, but babies were unpredictable. I supposed it wouldn't do any harm to check again…

'Here,' I said, holding out my arms. 'If you give him back to me, I can have another look before I put him to bed.'

Marta ignored me and lifted Leo up in the air and then back down again to her face, showering him with a thousand kisses. I'd let her blanking me go. Language barrier and all that.

She handed Leo back to Lorenzo and then took off her coat. Marta shivered, rubbed her hands together and then said something else to Lorenzo.

'You're cold?' I asked.

'Mamma asked if you could put the heating on, for Leo.'

For God's sake.

There was nothing wrong with the temperature. Yes, it was the beginning of February and still quite chilly outside, but not in here. I glanced over at the thermostat on the wall and it was twenty-one degrees. *Honestly.*

Before I'd had a chance to reply, Marta picked up a giant bag filled with food containers and waltzed straight past me into the kitchen.

Although I knew she'd probably find her way in here at some point, I hadn't realised it would be so soon. It was fine. I'd scrubbed everything.

Except the windowsill, so it would seem…

I walked in to see Marta running her finger along it, holding her finger up and shaking her head.

Jesus. Did she have some sort of cleanliness radar? Trust her to pick up on the one thing I hadn't done. I should have checked better. I scanned the room, looking for other potential pitfalls.

The kitchen was pretty big. Like most of the rooms here, wood featured heavily, so the cupboards followed the same theme, but they were a lighter shade and more modern: oak with sleek silver handles. Like the bedrooms, Lorenzo had given the kitchen a makeover before Leo and I came to live here. The ceilings still had the original wooden beams, though, so kept some character.

There was a large stove and two ovens, as Lorenzo liked to try out new recipes on his days off, plus a tiled island in the centre, with a couple of stools in front of it. I'd often sit there with Leo on a Sunday and watch Lorenzo cooking up a feast.

Marta started unpacking the bags.

'What's with all the food?' I asked Lorenzo as he stood beside me.

'Mamma has made some *wonderful* dishes for us to enjoy tonight, including some of her amazing homemade pasta.' He wrapped one arm around me whilst bouncing up Leo in the other.

'Oh…right.' My face fell. 'I thought you were bringing home dinner tonight. From the restaurant?'

'I had planned to do that, but when I spoke to Mamma, she said she would make it and—well, I could not let you miss the chance to try her homemade pasta. I cannot believe you have been here this long and not tasted it yet. You wait. It is not in this world!'

I loved it when Lorenzo didn't get English sayings quite right. Especially in his gorgeous accent. Everything he said sounded sexy.

Twenty minutes later I'd put Leo to bed and dinner was ready. We sat down at the table. Marta had certainly cooked up a feast. The first course in Italy, or *primo piatti*, was often pasta. It looked so professional too. Each tube was shaped to perfection. I took a large helping along with some of the sauce. *Mmm*. Lorenzo was right. Mamma's pasta was indeed out of this world. Perfectly al dente. Tender but still with a slightly firm texture. It was some of the best pasta I'd ever tasted. Truly.

Even though she'd annoyed me earlier by implying Leo's nappy needed changing (which I'd checked and—surprise, surprise—it hadn't), I was a believer that credit should be given when credit was due. This dish was amazing. I should tell Marta so too. A compliment was always a good way to endear yourself to someone. Better still, what better way to win over your *Italian* mother-in-law than complimenting her in *Italian*. Great idea!

I'd done a few food lessons on the Duolingo language app. I knew that *mi piace* meant *I like* and delicious was *delizioso*. *Yep*. The Italian was starting to fall into place. I just needed to practise. And now was the perfect time.

'*Mmmm*,' I said, facing Marta. '*Mi piace pene*,' I closed my eyes, then licked my lips to emphasise my enjoyment. '*Delizioso*!'

There! How's that for progress?

Marta almost choked on her food and Lorenzo let out a loud snort.

Oh. That wasn't *quite* the reaction I was hoping for. Maybe my accent was too British?

Marta's face turned to stone, whilst Lorenzo was now bent over in a fit of giggles.

'What?' I frowned, now turning to face him. 'What's so funny?'

'Sorry… I should not laugh,' he said, doing exactly that. 'Is just you say, you said…' Lorenzo lowered his voice, almost whispering in my ear. 'You told my mamma that you like *penis* and that it is delicious!'

Shit.

'I…what? No! I said *mi piace pene*!' I protested. Marta slammed her hand on the table, tutted and stormed into the kitchen. 'I don't understand. I was complimenting her pasta. Why is she upset?'

'Yes…' He snorted again. 'I know what you meant, but you pronounced it *pen-eh* with one *n*, which is *penis*. If you want to say *penne* with two letter *n* for *pasta*, then you must say: *pehhh-neh*.' He chuckled again.

Great.

I couldn't believe I'd just told Lorenzo's mother—the woman who seemed to hate my guts—that I not only loved dick, but I also found it delicious.

Cringe.

And I closed my eyes and licked my lips, which made it ten times worse.

Bollocks.

Ooops. Poor choice of words once again…

Now Marta probably thought I was a raving nympho. If only she knew that right now, *pene* was the last thing on my mind…

Surely she'd see the funny side, though. It was an easy mistake to make.

'Oh God!' I buried my head in my hands. 'How was I supposed to know that? The words sound so similar!'

'*Tranquilla*. Don't worry, *amore*. Is normal to make mistakes. I remember I said many bad things when I was learning English.'

'But English is so much easier!'

'Of course you will say that.' He waved his hands in the air. 'You are English!' *Obviously*. Then again, even learning French came more naturally to me. 'But words like *beach* and *bitch*, *beer* and *beard*, *ankle* and *uncle* or *fanny* and *funny* sound similar. I remember once on holiday I met a captain and told him he had a very big *shit* instead of *ship*.' He shook his head.

'You *didn't*!' I chuckled.

'*Sì!*'

'Still. Not as bad as what I just said, though. At least you said it to a stranger you were never going to see again. I said it to your mother!'

'Is okay. Mamma knows you are learning. But as I said before, the best way to avoid this type of mistake is to study. One of the customers at the restaurant today is starting Italian lessons in the town.'

'Oh?' That surprised me. I didn't think there would be much demand for it here.

'Yes. I took her number.' He reached in his pocket for his mobile. 'I will send it to you now.' I heard my phone ping. 'Call her tomorrow.'

'I'll think about it.'

'Please.'

Marta came back in the room holding a large dish with steak and vegetables. I didn't really eat a lot of red meat, but it did smell good. She gave me a dirty look. No doubt because I'd committed the terrible sin of pronouncing something wrong (I know, shoot me, right? Most normal people would have just laughed it off). She dished out the food and annoyingly, it was just as amazing as the pasta. But I'd learnt my lesson. This time I would *not* be attempting to compliment her. Knowing my luck I'd end up saying something like *I love a nice bit of rump*, rather than *I like this beef. Sigh.*

'Mamma,' said Lorenzo as he cleaned his plate. 'For dessert, Sophia has made a crumble for us all. Is a traditional British dish.' He translated in Italian, then Marta raised her eyebrow.

My heart started beating. That was my cue. It was time to bring out what I hoped would be the *pièce de résistance*. No idea how that was said in Italian. I felt like I was a contestant on *Come Dine with Me* about to serve up my food after slaving away in the kitchen all day. Okay, it hadn't taken *that* long, but you catch my drift. If this was a competition, I wasn't sure I would be declared the winner, as Marta's cooking was a tough act to follow, but I was still feeling confident.

I went to the kitchen and removed the foil from the dish. *Looking good.* I warmed the homemade custard I'd whipped up earlier. Lorenzo had taught me how to make it and it tasted much better than the shop-bought ones. It had been a long time since I'd felt like I was winning, but I'd been pretty productive today: with work, as a mum and in the home. Not so much on the Italian language front, but the crumble would be my saviour. Even Marta would have to give me a thumbs-up after having a mouthful of this.

Done.

I poured the custard into a jug, took it out with the

crumble to the table and began scooping it out into the bowls, starting with Marta's.

'*Bene?*' I said in a poor attempt to ask if one spoon was okay. She didn't respond, so I went ahead and was about to add a second helping when she raised her hand in protest and shook her head vigorously like I was about to sprinkle poison on top.

'Mamma will just start with one spoon,' said Lorenzo, 'but I will have three, please. Looks very delicious!' God, I loved him. He was always enthusiastic whenever I tried to cook.

I served myself, poured the custard over everyone's helpings, then took a spoonful.

Thank goodness. It tasted as good as it looked.

'*Mmm.*' Lorenzo smiled. '*Deliziosa!*'

Phew. One satisfied customer down, one to go…

I turned to Marta. She moved the tiny portion from one side of the bowl to the other, like a child who'd been asked to eat spinach when all they wanted was ice cream. Her face crumpled. For some reason, bringing herself to push even a sliver of apple onto the spoon and lift it towards her mouth was a monumental task. She muttered something in Italian, got up and went to the kitchen.

What the hell?

All that effort.

All the stress of getting the ingredients, rushing around to make it for her and she wasn't even going to try it?

Bad form.

If this really was an episode of *Come Dine with Me*, behaviour like that would make the other contestants give her an earbashing.

So rude.

I felt the anger rise inside me.

'Mamma said it looked nice, but after dinner she was very full.'

Kind of Lorenzo to try and spare my feelings, but I was pretty sure Marta didn't say that. 'Perhaps you'd like to ask *Mamma* if she would like some to take home?'

I'd like to ask Marta a lot of things right now, but offering her a doggy bag definitely wasn't one of them…

I bit my tongue.

'Nice idea, but I wouldn't know how to.'

'Another reason to try the Italian lessons, *si*? Will be good for you.'

Of course it would be helpful, but I'd have to look into it later. Possibly next week. Things might be calmer at the office by then, and I'd have more time. Better still, Mum and Dad might change their minds and finally visit next month, and if they did, perhaps I could consider taking some lessons then.

Yes. I'd been here three months, so waiting a few more weeks wouldn't make any difference.

Like Lorenzo said, these things took time. I just needed to be patient…

CHAPTER FIVE

P lease pick up.

Please, please, please.

I was trying to reach Lorenzo, but his phone was just ringing.

He'd left at the crack of dawn to drive to Florence, so he was probably still in a meeting with the supplier.

Shit.

I called again then left a message.

'It's okay, darling.' I stroked Leo's back, trying to calm him down. He'd been crying all morning.

I put my hand on his forehead again. He was burning up.

I sat down on the edge of the bed and tried to give Leo my breast, but he wouldn't take it. It was probably the fourth or fifth time I'd attempted it, and each time he'd refused. Normally he'd jump straight on it as soon as he woke up, but today he seemed to have completely lost his appetite.

My heart was racing. I knew he was sick but had no idea how to help him.

I stood up again and tried singing. I was definitely no Mariah Carey. If I auditioned for *The Voice*, I was pretty sure not a single judge would turn their chair round for me, but strangely, when I sang to Leo, it often stopped him from crying. He was particularly fond of 'Happy' by Pharrell Williams and 'Head Over Heels' from the Eclectic Detectives, probably because Lorenzo and I played it so much when I was pregnant. Leo also liked 'You Are My Sunshine' and 'Twinkle Twinkle Little Star,' but this morning, even my best crooning attempts weren't helping. Today, Leo was impersonating Simon Cowell and his screams were telling me I definitely *didn't* have the *X-Factor*.

I had no clue what to do.

I was tempted to ask Google. But whilst it'd been invaluable helping me with my Italian, I was afraid that if I typed in his symptoms, it would tell me he was dying and I was already freaking out.

Mum.

She'd know what was best.

I dialled her number.

The phone rang out.

Don't know why I bothered. She rarely answered her mobile straightaway. The house phone was always a better bet.

Answerphone.

'Mum, it's me. Please can you call me back ASAP? Leo's burning up and isn't eating. I'm really worried. Ring me, please.'

Leo's cries became more high-pitched. How could

something so small make so much noise? He seemed to be getting hotter. I carried him to the bathroom, reached for a towel, ran it under some cold water and rested it across his forehead. He started kicking in protest. I held him tighter to stop him from falling. Poor thing. If I'd been screaming as long as he had, my lungs and throat would be killing me.

Bella! She was a mum, so might have some advice.

Aaaarggh. Another voicemail.

Of course. She'd be teaching.

I tried Lorenzo again. Still ringing. Maybe he was back at the restaurant by now? Even if he was, it would take fifteen minutes to walk there. It wasn't like I had a car or could just jump in a taxi or even on a bus. This wasn't London. It was at times like these that I wished I had a friend or family member close by.

Who else could I call?

Think.

I knew there was one person I *should* be able to ask, but I really didn't want to.

Marta.

Considering how she reacted to last night's *pene* vs *penne* mix-up, she probably wouldn't even take my call. And after she'd rudely rejected my crumble (even when Lorenzo asked if she wanted some to take home), she was the last person I wanted to call right now. But this wasn't about me. This was about Leo's health, so I had to put my feelings to one side, suck it up and phone her.

I jigged up and down on the spot, still trying to calm Leo, then dialled Marta's number.

It was ringing.

Still ringing.

Voicemail.

Where was everyone today?

This was hopeless. As scared as I was about what I might find, I had to see if there was any useful advice online.

I launched the browser on my phone and started typing in the search bar, which wasn't easy to do with just one hand and a screaming little person wriggling around, but I managed it. As I suspected, what felt like a million results appeared. The first article to pop up was entitled:

***Is your baby seriously ill*?**

Great.

Some articles suggested it could be a fever. They recommended I gave Leo fluids. That was easy enough. I could give him some water. And paracetamol? Wasn't he too young for that? I needed to check the box first.

I read on.

Oh no!

Do not sponge the child down to cool them. A fever is a natural response to infection.

What? Were they saying Leo had an infection? And I'd just put a cold wet towel on him.

Shit.

I clicked onto another article.

Meningitis?

Oh my God. This article said fever and lack of appetite were two of the symptoms.

I quickly laid Leo down on the bed and scanned his body for rashes or blotches.

I glanced over at the rest of the article.

Someone with meningitis can get a lot worse very quickly.

Fuck, shit, bollocks…

If a child isn't eating and isn't their normal self, get an urgent appointment with your GP.

That was the only sensible option left. I had to try the doctors. But I knew they wouldn't speak English. That was why I was trying to get hold of Lorenzo. If I wasn't even capable of getting a supermarket cashier to understand me asking for bloody coconut in Italian, how on earth was I going to explain my sick baby's symptoms?

I had no choice.

Thankfully, I'd saved the local doctor's number in my phone, not long after I'd moved here. Just in case. I'd only been a handful of times for Leo's check-ups, but Lorenzo was always with me and translated everything. I wouldn't feel confident communicating with him if I had to go by myself.

Time to put on my big girl pants and try.

I Googled some phrases, wrote them down quickly, then called the doctor's.

Come on. Pick up.

'Er, *buongiorno. Il mio bambino è malato,*' I said, reading from the piece of paper. The lady on the other end of the line started babbling away. '*Parla inglese?*' I added desperately.

The only word I understood was that she didn't.

She babbled some more, at 100 miles per hour, I think asking me questions, but my mind went blank. She could have been speaking Japanese for all I knew.

'Hello? I mean, *Ciao? Ciao?*'

Then I heard the dialling tone. She'd put the phone down on me.

So rude. What was with some of the people in this

town? I'd been to many cities in Italy and everyone had been nice. But here, they seemed really unfriendly.

I was fuming.

And then it hit me.

I'd let things get out of control. Become too dependent. Without knowing the language, I needed Lorenzo for everything. Along with Google Translate, he'd become my crutch. I couldn't read a local newspaper, watch the national news or buy basic things in the supermarket without them.

Well, this time I had no choice. I had to stand on my own two feet. I dressed Leo, put him in his buggy, dragged on my coat and rushed out of the door. I was going to the doctor's and would try to explain with miming or sign language, whatever it took, what was wrong with him. I'd just have to hope I could understand them and that he'd be okay.

Then I needed to make this taking lessons thing a top priority. It wasn't the receptionist's fault that she didn't speak English. It was mine. We were in Italy, so the onus was on *me* to learn Italian.

It was ridiculous that I'd let it get this far. I'd heard that sometimes it was easy to feel like you'd lost some of your identity after becoming a mum, but this was out of hand. Where had fiercely independent Sophia Huntingdon gone? She would never have become so reliant on other people. Even with a million balls to juggle, she would have found a way to get to grips with the language. And she'd address all of her other issues too.

Finally!

Reasanna, the voice of reason who often came into my head, suddenly piped up.

I was wondering how long it would take for you to wake up and smell the coffee. Should have been a lot sooner considering you're living in Italy.

Yep. I'd buried my head in the sand for too long. No more of this half-hearted wishy-washyness.

If I could learn a language and go and live in France by myself when I was twenty, I must be able to learn another language in my forties. My mind wasn't as fresh, so it would be a challenge, but I had to at least try.

I'd made a commitment to living here, so I needed to go all in. Really make an effort to make it work.

My relationship, my sanity, my happiness and little Leo's health depended on it.

CHAPTER SIX

I rushed through the surgery doors. Leo was still crying. As soon as we entered, everyone stared. I wasn't surprised. His high-pitched screams weren't something you could ignore.

There were a few people queuing up at reception. I pushed the buggy into a corner, took Leo out and held him against my chest.

'It's okay, darling. It's going to be okay. We're at the doctor's now. They're going to make you better.'

I really hoped they could. I steadied him in one arm and used the other to fish my phone out from my bag. Although it hadn't worked earlier, I still needed to try and have some sort of phrasing prepped to attempt to communicate. Hopefully now that we were here in person, it would be easier for the receptionist to understand how ill Leo was.

This was taking ages. There was an elderly lady at the front, deep in conversation. Naturally I had no idea what she was saying. The man behind her huffed. He was either frustrated about her holding up the queue or annoyed at Leo crying. *Tough.* It wasn't his fault; Mr Grumpy would have to deal with it.

I quickly typed in *My baby is hot. He has a temperature. Please can I see a doctor urgently?* into Google Translate. The translation flashed up on the screen. I stroked Leo's back as I read the words out quietly to practise. I had to pronounce it properly so that I could get Leo the help he needed.

One more person in front of us.

'Won't be long now. All we need to do is hold on a bit longer.' I kissed Leo on the forehead to try and soothe him, but he started kicking. He'd grown tired of waiting. Just as we got to the front of the queue, Leo kicked again and almost slipped out of my arms. I caught him just in time, but my phone crashed to the floor.

Dammit.

The receptionist greeted me and I think asked how she could help. What I wanted to say was on my phone, which was still on the floor and Leo was now wriggling around so violently, I needed both hands to steady him. I tried to remember what was on the screen.

'*Bambino…caldo…temperatura…*' *Fuck.* How did you say *doctor* again? I could remember the French, but not the Italian, which wasn't helpful. Sweat started rolling down my forehead. Why was it so hot in here?

Come on, Soph. Think, think, think.

'*Medico? Per favore…* urgent,' I couldn't think what *urgently* was, but I remembered it being similar to the English.

The receptionist frowned, looked at Leo and said something.

'*Caldo!*' I said, touching his forehead and fanning him. She must bloody understand that? There wasn't anything else I could mime to get the message across.

Leo worked himself up so much with the crying that now he was coughing.

'Please! *Please!* I really need you to help my baby!'

'Soph?'

I turned around and saw Lorenzo rushing towards me.

Thank God.

He scooped Leo from my arms and started talking to the receptionist at a hundred miles an hour. She nodded, immediately picked up the phone and started speaking to someone. Seconds later, she hung up, then said something else to Lorenzo.

'What's happening? What did she say?'

'Is okay. She asked the doctor to see Leo. We just have to wait until he finish seeing a patient.'

What a relief.

I didn't know if Leo somehow understood or if it was Lorenzo's soothing presence, but he started to calm down a little and his cries turned into a whimper. I felt the same. As terrified as I was about Leo, having Lorenzo here just instantly made me feel like we were safe. Like he'd do whatever he could to take care of us.

I picked my phone up off the floor and we sat down in the waiting area.

'Sorry I could not get here sooner.' Lorenzo stroked Leo gently on his back. 'I was driving from *Firenze* when you called. I come as quick as I could.'

'I'm just relieved you got my message. You have no idea how happy we are to see you.' I wrapped my arm around him and gave him a big squeeze. 'I am *so* glad you're here now.'

The receptionist called Lorenzo's name and we got up to go and see the doctor. Pretty sure we'd jumped the queue, but I'm sure the others would understand.

We opened the door to the office, stepped inside and took a seat at the table. It was a different doctor to the one we'd seen last time, but Lorenzo seemed to recognise him. In a small town like this, most people knew each other.

Lorenzo asked me to explain what had happened. As I ran through Leo's symptoms, the doctor frowned, peering over his glasses and tapping the table impatiently. Clearly he wasn't used to waiting for a translation. Lorenzo relayed our conversation. The doctor nodded, then got up to take a look at Leo.

As he took Leo's temperature and spoke to Lorenzo, I desperately wanted to scream, *What the hell are you saying? How bad is it?* But I knew I had to let him finish. Never had I felt so helpless. So out of control. I was supposed to be Leo's mother. To protect him from harm. Take care of him at all times. Yet right now, I was about as helpful as a chocolate teapot.

The doctor went back to his desk, prepared a prescription, gave it to Lorenzo and then he stood up, signalling that it was time to go.

'The doctor says is just fever and Leo's temperature will be normal again in a few days. No need to worry.'

It felt like a thousand bricks had just been lifted from my shoulders.

Leo was okay. Our son was going to be okay.

I flung my arms around Lorenzo and Leo, then turned to the doctor, relief written over my face. '*Grazie.*'

'*Prego*.' He nodded with a smile.

'Come, let us go to pharmacy and then take Leo home,' said Lorenzo.

It didn't take us long to get back. I gave Leo some water and medicine like the doctor had apparently advised, then put Leo down in his cot.

'I reckon he'll sleep for ages now, poor thing.' I pulled the blanket up to his shoulders.

'*Sì*. I have never seen him so bad before.'

'Tell me about it. I was so scared.'

'Is okay, *mi amore*. I was too. But is fine now. Leo will be fine. I will stay with you. I will call work and tell them I cannot come in today.'

'No, no, it's okay. You don't need to.'

'But I want to make sure Leo is fine. That you are both fine.'

'We are. We will be.' I stroked his shoulder. 'Don't worry. I've got it covered. You go.'

'Okay. But you call me if you need me, *sì*?'

'Will do.' I hugged him. 'Thank you for saving the day.'

'I did not do anything.' He shrugged his shoulders like it was no big deal. 'Is our son. Of course we both want him to be safe. *Ciao, bella*.'

'*Ciao*.'

I watched him leave, flopped onto the bed, then let out a loud sigh. Even though I'd told Lorenzo I'd be fine and that I had it covered, the truth was, I wasn't sure I did at all. Give me a PR campaign to manage and I could do it with my eyes closed, but when it came to this motherhood stuff, most days I felt clueless. Like I was winging it. Today was a prime example. Although I was trying my best, it wasn't good enough. I had to do better.

Sitting there and not understanding what the doctor was saying about our little boy was a huge wake-up call. We were lucky today, but this dependence could have had much more serious consequences.

What if Leo had got worse and I still couldn't get hold of Lorenzo? Who would have rescued us then? What would happen if I was out one day and I forgot my phone again? I'd heard stories of people dying abroad because they couldn't explain their symptoms in the native language. How would I have communicated with the doctors if I had to go to the hospital?

Last time I'd been in a mess like this, I had been a workaholic in a dead-end relationship with my ex and was deeply unhappy. Back then, it had taken the death of my dearest friend and mentor, Albert, who was like my second dad, for me to take a long, hard look at the sorry state of my life. I didn't want another tragedy to be the catalyst for me taking action. No matter how much I had to do, I needed to get my shit together. I needed to make changes. And I needed to make them now.

CHAPTER SEVEN

I picked up a pen and notepad then opened up a fresh page. Just as I'd made my MAP (*Make Albert Proud*) plan two years ago, when I'd vowed to end my last relationship, work less and live more, it was time to set some more goals to make my new life in Italy a success.

I believed that if there was something you weren't happy about, it was important to do something to change it, and in my experience, making a list was always the best way to sort things out. Once I'd written everything down, my mind would be clearer. I'd have a road map of what I had to achieve, and like I had before, if I tackled each task, I could get my life back under control again.

I didn't have time to think of a name for it. Even though Leo was exhausted from all the drama this morning, his schedule was out of sync, so it was difficult to predict how long he'd be asleep. And I'd already procrastinated for too long. I had to do this now before I found another excuse not to.

Right. First and foremost:

1) Learn Italian

Priority number one. My Italian language skills were abysmal. How was it that I had managed to get a first-class degree in French and yet was doing so badly with Italian? It was pathetic. I'd fully intended to take lessons in London before I came here so I'd be well prepared, but with the business, getting ready for the birth and one thing and another, I hadn't had time. But there could be no more excuses. I needed to apply myself more. Study harder. Just like I did at uni.

I'd start by researching that Italian teacher Lorenzo had mentioned and find out when her earliest available lesson was. There was no reason I couldn't learn another language. This was not beyond my capabilities. I just needed to structure my days better and pull my bloody finger out.

Next up…this one was definitely needed:

2) Make Some New Friends

I'd always felt isolated here, but this morning really brought home how much. Without Lorenzo, I had no one. I needed to get new friends. It would be nice to have someone else to talk to so my life didn't solely revolve around my boyfriend, baby and work. Although I still messaged and spoke to Bella and Roxy, it wasn't the same. They were hundreds of miles away and we were all busy. I missed them so much. Especially our monthly Food, Therapy and Alcohol catch-ups (or FTA sessions as Roxy,

Queen of the Acronyms, preferred to call them), but I couldn't spend time pining and feeling lonely. This was the life I'd chosen, so I had to make it work.

I knew it would be tricky because most people I'd seen seemed to be pensioners, but there must be other mums here? Or some sort of organised mother and baby group? Maybe that was a bit of a stretch as it was such a small town, but I had to at least look into it.

The whole language barrier thing was another issue, but maybe we could do a little exchange: I help them learn English and they help me with my Italian? It was worth a shot…

3) Be More Independent

Sometimes living here felt like being a kid again. I couldn't do anything without asking for someone else's help. I couldn't go to the supermarket by myself or explain basic things to a doctor. For someone who had been used to being independent for so long, it was hard to depend on other people to help me do the things I'd been doing for decades on my own in London.

I didn't want to keep having to ask Lorenzo or have to rely on Marta. I needed to be stronger.

4) Sort Out My Sex Life

Here we go again… I was only a few weeks away from reaching the *six months without sex* status—in other words, becoming a Middle-Aged Virgin.

When Lorenzo and I had finally got together, I'd thought my sexless days were over. *Pff.*

On the one hand, I knew I'd just birthed a small human, which was no small feat, but surely I should be back in the game by now. I needed to figure out a way to revive my sexual mojo and, in the meantime, make more of an effort to keep Lorenzo satisfied in the bedroom. Not because he expected me to. He didn't. Thankfully, he wasn't someone who saw sex as a duty that a woman *owed* to her man. I wanted to do it because I loved him and I also remembered how frustrating it felt to have a partner who didn't want to be intimate. And whilst Lorenzo had been patient so far, even the kindest, most reasonable guy would have his limits. He couldn't wait forever.

If I wasn't ready for full-blown nookie, maybe I could try and start with something easier. A hand job or a BJ? Can't say the prospect of exercising my right hand or giving my mouth a workout was remotely appealing, as like the names suggested, it did sound like another *job* to add to my massive to-do list and I could use those five minutes to sleep, but I was going to *try* and give it a go. Lorenzo was more than worth it. There must be books or articles on getting it on again after having kids. I couldn't be the only woman in the world who had experienced a post-partum sexual slump.

5) Get Back Into Shape

If I was going to be swinging from the chandeliers (not that we had any, but you catch my drift), then I needed to get my body back into shape. I'd been doing online classes and going for walks every day, but the weight just wasn't shifting. I couldn't let myself go. Not just because it was affecting my confidence, but also because I needed to be healthy for Leo, so that when he was older, I'd be able to run around with him in the garden without doubling-over and panting like a hippo attempting a 100-metre sprint. Loads of mums got back into shape after having a baby, so I should too.

And as well as upping the ante on the exercise front, I

needed to be more disciplined with food. Just because Lorenzo baked multiple times a week and was always feeding me delicious pasta, it didn't mean I had to shovel it down in such large quantities. It was ridiculous. Especially the sponge addiction. One minute there was a large slab of my favourite crushed Florentine orange cake in front of me and the next, I'd glance down and wonder where it had all gone. *In my gut, that's where*. I know his cakes were always so tasty, but I had to learn to resist having that second, third and usually fourth slice. As the saying goes, *a moment on the lips, a lifetime on the hips*. Or in my case, hips, thighs, stomach, arse…

Yep. I definitely needed to get my fitness and healthy eating regime in check, lose these extra pounds and get my body back under control.

6) Have a Good Relationship with Lorenzo's Mum

Oh boy. I already knew that *this* was going to be painful. I was trying. I really was. At times I felt like I was sucking up to Marta so much that my head was going to disappear up her butt (now, *that's* a horrible thought). But although it grated on me, it had to be done, right? If she was anyone else, I wouldn't even give her the time of day, but Marta was Lorenzo's beloved *mamma* and it would make him happy, so I needed to try harder and find a way for her to like me and for us to get along.

Ugh.

Can you believe she didn't even phone me back after seeing my missed call when Leo was sick? Lorenzo said she'd thought I'd phoned her by mistake, so she didn't see the point. But that's *exactly* why she should have known it was an emergency. She should have realised that I'd only ever put myself through the pain of dialling her number if I was desperate.

I knew she thought I was a rubbish mum and girlfriend because my cooking and domestic skills weren't as world-class as hers. And on the home front, she was right. I was no Martha Stewart or Mrs Hinch, but I'd show her that I could do better. I *would* be a great mum and girlfriend.

Just watch me.

I also had to play nice with Marta because as much as I hated to admit it, I needed her. If I was going to do these language lessons and try and rebuild my sex life, we'd need someone to look after Leo that we could trust. And whatever I thought of her, I knew Marta adored her grand-son, so with her, he'd be in safe hands. She'd just better not mess with his routine, or there'd be trouble…

7) Get the Business Back Under Control

Ever since that phone call with Viktor yesterday, I'd been annoyed, not just at Robyn, but also at myself for not keeping on top of things. I'd dropped the ball. I should have known about that meeting getting cancelled, so clearly I needed to do more. Be more involved. If I'd implemented more regular updates, kept a closer eye on things and was more in control, it wouldn't have happened.

I refused to believe what Mum and other people said. Selling up wasn't the answer. I'd considered it before. I'd even thought about alternative careers, but nothing grabbed me. Then I decided that with Robyn running things, I didn't have to. I could still be a business owner, earn an income so I wasn't relying on Lorenzo's salary (I'd always been financially independent and that was *exactly* how I wanted to stay) and keep my hand in the game.

The company had been part of my identity since I was

twenty-five. I'd built it from scratch, so I wasn't going to give it up or let things go down the toilet just because I'd had a child. Millions of women held down careers and had kids—some did it with two, three or more. I only had one, so it *could* be done if I organised my working day better and managed the team more closely.

I'd start by returning Robyn's call this afternoon to get to the bottom of what had happened (she'd tried phoning this morning, but with Leo being ill, I couldn't answer), then I'd create a plan to get things back on track.

8) Enjoy My Life in Italy

And like I'd included on my MAP list, I needed to find a way to embrace my new life. With all of the frustrations that came with the move like missing my friends and family and the language barrier, it was easy to lose sight of what I *did* have. Lorenzo was amazing. I'd never been more in love. And Leo was the miracle baby I'd thought I'd never have. Yes, this town wasn't London. Yes, life here wasn't what I'd expected and the people might not have welcomed me with open arms, but the scenery was beautiful. The lush rolling hills and vineyards were straight from a *Visit Tuscany* brochure. I was living in bloody Italy! So many people would *love* to trade places with me. I had a lot to be thankful for.

I had all the right ingredients for an idyllic life. I could be living the dream. I could prove the doubters wrong and make my life here a huge success, if I tried a little harder. Stepped out of my comfort zone. *Again*. It wouldn't be easy, but I was sure it'd be worthwhile. After all, when I'd taken control of my life and created my MAP plan before, it had helped me find happiness and gave me Lorenzo and Leo. What could creating a list bring this time?

Yes.

Done.

I put down my pen, read over the points again and instantly felt more positive. I finally had a plan. Direction. Goals. And just like before, I was determined to do whatever it took to achieve each and every one of them.

CHAPTER EIGHT

I couldn't find her anywhere. I'd tried Google and searched on social media, but nothing came up.

Now more than ever, I'd realised how important it was for me to take proper lessons, so I needed to know who I was dealing with first. Do my thorough checks to find out what her credentials were. I couldn't afford to waste any time. I had to get up to speed as quickly as possible.

The language barrier definitely made everything harder. It was at times like this morning that I wished I was back home. I could have sorted Leo out in seconds if all I had to do was speak English. Plus in London I had friends. Family. A doctor who understood me. Everything was so much easier. But London didn't have Lorenzo. And I didn't want to be without him again.

Once I'd got back from my first trip to Chiorno after my birthday last year, Lorenzo and I had done the long-distance thing. He'd try and fly over for two or three days a month, so we'd never spent more than a few weeks apart.

We'd decided early on that I would have the baby in

London. I'd felt more comfortable having the familiarity of my midwife, a hospital I knew and my mum close by.

Lorenzo had wanted to be there for the birth. So a week before I was due, he'd quit his job as a chef at Taste Holidays and come to live with me in London.

It had been great to share those special moments with him, like taking Leo home from the hospital for the first time, feeding and bathing him. You know, to give us both the chance to bond. And let's get real. I also needed Lorenzo there to change nappies and take over when I was too tired to keep my eyes open. Mum and Dad popped over regularly to help out too, which was a godsend.

In mid-October, when Leo was six weeks old, Lorenzo had gone back to start a modest chef job he'd secured in the restaurant in town. We both knew that with his experience, he could do much better. He'd been head chef at some of the top restaurants in Florence and any one of them would have welcomed him back with open arms. But working in the city would mean more time travelling back and forth, longer hours and more stress. And Lorenzo had insisted that being closer to me and Leo was more important.

I'd followed Lorenzo a couple of weeks later at the beginning of November, excited to start what I thought would be my idyllic new life in Italy with the man I loved and our little boy. And the rest, as they say, was history.

I crept into the bedroom to check on Leo. He'd been asleep for a couple of hours and looked so peaceful. Such a contrast to how distraught he had been earlier. But hopefully he was on the mend now. Today only highlighted the importance of protecting him.

I was tempted to pick him up for a cuddle. He was so

fragile. So precious. And so beautiful, with his thick mass of dark curly hair. It was still hard to tell who Leo resembled the most. I felt like he changed every day. Lorenzo was convinced he had his dark eyes, but actually, I thought they were quite similar to mine. There wasn't much in it, I supposed. I could definitely see both of us in him, though. I had seen his resemblance to Lorenzo the moment he was born. I just knew.

After breaking up with Charlie, who I'd dated for a few months, and then hooking up with Lorenzo shortly afterwards when he'd unexpectedly come to work in London, there had been a question mark hanging over who the father could be. I know, right? Sounded like something from a soap opera or the *Jerry Springer Show*. *What can I say…?*

Anyway, originally, when I was pregnant I'd said I wanted to know, but then when Leo had been born I'd changed my mind and decided not to bother doing the paternity test thing. Lorenzo had said that either way, he'd raise Leo as his own. But after some pressure from Charlie, who was desperate for a son and an heir to his family empire (he was loaded), Lorenzo and I had discussed it and decided to go ahead. To get confirmation and Charlie off our backs.

Somehow, though, during the time we had to wait for the results, I hadn't been nervous. I'd just *sensed* that he was the father. And thankfully I'd been right. Leonardo Rossi-Huntingdon was Lorenzo's biological son.

Leo began to stir a little. He might wake up soon, so I had to get on with calling this Italian teacher. I went back to the living room and picked up my phone. I didn't have time to search online anymore. I just had to call her and get info the old-fashioned way.

I launched WhatsApp and scrolled through Lorenzo's messages to find the number. *There we go*. It started ringing.

'*Pronto*.'

'*Ciao*…is this Angelica?'

'*Sì*.'

'*Bene*. Good. I'm calling to find out about your Italian lessons. I couldn't seem to find your website—'

'Website?' Angelica let out a raucous laugh. I wasn't sure exactly what was so funny… 'Not my style. First lesson starts tomorrow. Six p.m.'

'Tomorrow?' I repeated. That didn't give me much time to ask Marta.

'We will meet at Casini. You know it?'

'Is that the bar near the supermarket?' I shuddered, remembering my nightmare visit there a few days ago.

'*Sì*.'

'Well, then, yes. I know it.'

'See you then.'

'Wait!' I needed to know a lot more about her and the lessons before I agreed. 'I have some questions to ask you first…'

'You want to know the cost?'

Well, that may have been one of the questions, but it wasn't my biggest priority. Before we got to price, I wanted to know things like how long the lessons lasted, the format, the number of students, what sort of things we'd learn, the examination and grading process, her experience…

'Fifteen euros for two hours, plus expenses,' she replied.

That's cheap. Maybe she'd make up for it with some extortionate expenses.

'Are the expenses for the textbooks and study guides we'll be using?' Hopefully she'd even bring some along, so I could buy a selection to go through at home.

'Ha! Textbooks!' She laughed again. '*Come ti chiami*?'

'*Mi chiamo Sophia*,' I replied confidently. At least I knew how to say my name.

'See you tomorrow at six, Sophia. *Ciao*.' She put the phone down.

Huh?

What about all my questions? And what was so funny about textbooks? Everyone knew they were the corner-stones of learning a language properly. I'd had shelves of them when I learnt French. Maybe because the world is digital now, she had some sort of high-tech online portal or app that we could access instead? Then again, if she didn't appear to have a website or any form of social media presence, that might be unlikely…

Oh well. I guessed I'd have to go along tomorrow and find out. But first, time to work on point number six: attempting to build a relationship with Marta. Starting with finding the words to ask her to babysit…

CHAPTER NINE

Marta had turned up twenty minutes late (probably deliberately), so I now found myself sprinting down the road, to try and make it to my first Italian class on time.

Asking Marta to babysit was just as painful as I'd thought it would be. I'd spoken slowly and kept my language simple—'You, stay with Leo tomorrow 5.30?'—but she'd kept on saying '*non capisco*'—that she couldn't understand. I'd hoped she had a basic knowledge of English and would get the gist of what I was saying, but clearly she didn't, which was fair enough. Even if someone spoke to me in Italian at one mile per hour, if I wasn't familiar with the vocab, I couldn't be expected to know what they were talking about.

So, once again I had to rely on my two crutches: Google and Lorenzo. I messaged him a translation I'd found online and asked if that was the correct thing to say. He replied with some corrections and said he could speak to Marta if I preferred, but I was determined to try. So I called her back and relayed the phrase. She still claimed not to understand, but eventually after repeating it several times, she'd said yes. I decided to send her a WhatsApp message, though, just so that I had it in writing. Couldn't risk her saying I hadn't asked…

Asking Marta was only stage one of the process, though. As much as I wanted to stop depending on Lorenzo, in the end, because of the language barrier, I still needed him to help me with stage two: briefing Marta on Leo's routine.

Lorenzo assured me that she understood. Not too much stimulation in the evenings, bottle of the milk I'd expressed and left in the fridge as soon as she arrived, bath at seven, another bottle at seven-thirty, song or story at eight, followed by putting Leo to bed at eight-fifteen whilst he was sleepy but still awake. No picking him up after that, unless there was something really wrong.

Marta would probably ignore everything, but I had to *try* not to worry. For the next two hours, I was going to focus on learning. Developing myself. Regaining some level of independence and control. If these lessons went well, then I'd be able to explain things to Marta all by myself.

Being outside on my own felt really weird. I could count on one hand the number of occasions I'd been away from Leo since he was born. And this was the first time we'd been apart and he wasn't with Lorenzo.

It was fine. *Totally fine…*

I burst into the bar, mopping the sweat from my forehead.

Inside was pretty small. It had tiled terracotta flooring and wooden beams across the ceiling. As well as the dozens of bottles of wine and alcohol on display in multiple old-fashioned wooden shelves around the bar, the walls were lined with framed black-and-white photos of various people I assumed were important to the town in some way and posters which looked like they spanned decades.

A bar wasn't a normal place to have a lesson, but I guessed that this was just the central meeting point and she'd take us somewhere else afterwards. Or maybe as it was our first meet-up, she thought a quick drink would help break the ice before we got down to the nitty-gritty.

Wow. That must be her.

A woman with vibrant blue hair cut into a sharp bob, with one side shaved and the other long, was sat at the head of the dark wooden table. She certainly stood out. I'd not seen anyone like that in this town. There were two other women sat with her. I went over.

'*Ciao*. Are you Angelica?'

'How did you guess? Was it my earrings?' She chuckled, touching the sparkly red hoops dangling from her ears.

'Well, actually…'

'I'm pulling your foot,' she replied. Pulling my *foot*? Now *that* made *me* chuckle. Clearly she meant pulling my *leg*. Crazy for me to find her minor English mistake amusing. Just wait until she heard my horrendous Italian. That would have her rolling on the floor.

'You must be Sophia. *Siediti, per favore*. Sit down, please.' I pulled out the rustic wood-and-straw chair, then took off my coat. '*Va bene*. We are ready to start. First I want each of you to tell me why you are here. And I do not want boring answers about improving yourself, saying is for hobby or other garbage. I want to know what *really* happened. What was the moment that made you say, *merda*! I need to learn Italian? Was it when you heard the old ladies laugh at you at post office and you want to know what they say? When a creepy guy try to hit on you and you wish you could tell him to leave you alone, or because you want to know when your mother-in-law talk shit about you?'

Everyone's eyes popped out.

Yes! I found myself screaming in my head. She was spot-on. I'd *love* to know what Marta said about me. Then again, I knew it wasn't good, so maybe ignorance was bliss...

'Come on, ladies. Must not be shy.'

'Well,' chimed in a very prim-looking posh woman with short brown hair who was smartly dressed in a grey trouser suit. 'We're just here visiting my new husband's parents for a few months and I simply wanted to keep myself occupied. Broaden the mind, so to speak.'

Angelica rolled her eyes. 'We will come back to you... Holly?' She glared at a girl with long wavy blond hair who was maybe in her late teens or early twenties. 'What is your story?'

'*Oh gosh…*' She winced. 'This is like, *so* embarrassing. Well, basically, I'm like, an au pair. I'm here because it's where my *amazing* boyfriend Umberto lives, he's like, *so* hot! Anyway, so, when I arrived, I might have told the host dad that I had twenty assholes instead of saying I was twenty years old…'

I snorted. I didn't mean to. It just came out. Holly buried her face in her hands.

'Sorry,' I said.

'No worries,' she shook her head.

'Ah, the famous confusion between *anni* and *ani*... *Years* is easily mistaken for *anuses* if not pronounced correctly...and you, Sophia?'

'Where do I start?' I sighed, thinking about the dozens of awkward incidents I'd had since I'd arrived here. 'If we're talking about recent events, there was the time I was chased out of the supermarket by the unfriendly cashiers, and then when my baby was sick and I couldn't communicate with the doctor and...erm, similar to Holly, I may have also told my mother-in-law that I liked *penis*, instead of *penne*...'

Angelica and Holly erupted in laughter. Mrs Snooty raised her eyebrow.

'Now, *that* is what I am talking about!' Angelica grinned. 'Yes, we all want to improve by learning new language and *find something to make broader your minds*, but often it is those embarrassing moments that make us take action. The things that happen in real life. So, my lessons are not about sitting in a classroom with textbooks.' She glared at me. 'They are going to be *authentic*. I will teach you things you *really* need to know, like how to ask for more wine in a restaurant or ask for condoms in the pharmacy. And of course I will give you words to defend yourself.'

WTF?

Did she say *no textbooks*? I *definitely* didn't like the sound of that. How were we supposed to learn Italian properly without books or something to refer to in between lessons?

'But what about grammar?' the posh lady chimed in. 'Verbs, tenses and sentence construction?'

Exactly what I was thinking.

Angelica rolled her eyes. 'We can worry about that later.'

Later? Oh great. As much as I hated it, understanding grammar was the basis of learning any language. How was I supposed to sort out my bloody Italian if the so-called 'teacher' wasn't even taking this seriously?

'As I said, these lessons will be about how to survive. If you think it will not be for you, then you can leave now and pay only for your wine. Then go home and study from books and the internet. It is up to you.'

Everyone looked at each other and back at Angelica.

Hmmm…

I'd been trying to study by myself with the app, and although it was helpful, I needed more than that. Maybe I could try a couple of these lessons, but order some proper grammar books to use at home. As far as I knew, there weren't any other teachers in Chiorno, and when I'd made my list, I'd said I'd step out of my comfort zone, so I should be more open.

Although it went against the way I'd successfully learnt French at uni, I had to admit I was a teeny bit intrigued by Angelica's unconventional approach. And anyone who promised to help me stop embarrassing myself in front of my mother-in-law was worth listening to.

Okay. I'll give it a try.

'Count me in,' I said, attempting to sound enthusiastic.

'I'm *totally* up for it too!' said Holly.

Angelica smiled and then turned to Mrs Snooty Pants.

'Well, I'm not entirely convinced that you can offer me what I'm looking for, but as I'm aware that the options for language lessons are somewhat limited in this town, I'm willing to give you a chance for a week or two…'

How embarrassing. Once again, that was exactly what I was thinking. I *definitely* had to give this a go. I did *not* want to become a Mrs Snooty Pants…

'Oh, thank you so very much, Your Highness. I am ever so grateful!' replied Angelica sarcastically, putting on a posh British accent.

'There's no need to be rude!' snapped the woman.

'Ha! If you think I am rude, you will be very shocked when you find out what the other people in this town think of you. Please do not believe you are helping me by staying. I want only to teach people who want to be here. *Anyway*. We have much to get through today. First I need to see exactly how much Italian you know…'

The two hours flew by. We began with the basics, which was good. Introducing ourselves, what we were doing here. That sort of thing.

Most of us had only been here a little while. Shamefully, I'd been in Chiorno the longest but seemed to know the least. Everything I'd learnt on Duolingo and from Lorenzo evaporated from my brain the moment Angelica asked me a question. I managed to remember how to say stuff like where I was from, but that was about it. Explaining what job I did before—*blank*. Remembering how to pronounce the letters of the alphabet —*disappeared*. Counting past ten? *Forget it.*

Jeez.

Holly had been in Chiorno for a month and Daphne, aka Mrs Snooty Pants (who is *absolutely*, *definitely*, *nothing at all like me*…), had only arrived last week, and whilst their skills were still at the beginner's stage, they still seemed to have a better grasp of Italian than me.

And the worst thing was that even when Angelica told me the Italian for something, I'd remember for a second, but when she asked me the same question two minutes later, it was gone.

I thought that, having studied another language before, it would be much easier for me to learn Italian now, but so far, that wasn't happening. At least, not for me anyway. Maybe it was because I was older. But, no, I reckoned Angelica and Daphne were in their forties and they seemed to be doing just fine with speaking multiple languages. So clearly I'd developed some kind of new language block.

Great.

Whatever the reason, one thing was clear: If things were going to get better, I had a *lot* of work to do.

CHAPTER TEN

I launched WhatsApp. If I didn't send Bella and Roxy a voice note now, I didn't know when I'd get to reply to let them know how I was. So I decided to kill two birds with one stone and send a message in our group chat whilst I cleaned the kitchen and hallway floors. I pressed record, then held my phone up in my left hand and the mop in the other.

Hey, ladies! Sorry for being a stranger. It's all go at the moment... lots on with work and Leo and, you know, stuff. But it's all good! Lorenzo is amazing and constantly feeding me amazing food. By the time I see you in London, I'm going to be the size of an elephant, I swear! But everything's great. It's so pretty here. Like a postcard. I'll have to send you some new pics. And some more photos of Leo. I've taken hundreds. He's adorable. I can't wait for you guys to see him again. I miss you both so much. Feels like ages since I've seen you. Maybe we should FaceTime soon?

Anyway, how's everything with you, Bella? Hope Paul

and Mike are well. And Roxy, how's work and your love life? Sorry, what am I saying? You don't do love. How are the fuckbuddies? Any new ones on the scene? Anyway, better go. Got to do some exercise and studying before Leo wakes up. Did I tell you I'd started taking Italian lessons? It's going well. Before I came here, I could only count to ten. Now I reckon I can count to at least eleven! Only joking! I've made a lot more progress than that. I'll tell you all about it next time.

Right, I really am going now. Love you guys!

Hopefully I sounded upbeat. Normally I shared everything with them. The ups and downs, highs and lows—but I didn't want to tell them that I was finding some things hard. Partly because of the distance and not wanting to worry them when they were too far away to help. And, yeah, I admit I didn't want to hear the *I told you so* speech.

Roxy had always been sceptical about me coming here. Although these days she was much warmer towards Lorenzo because she'd seen he was a great partner and father, she still thought I was taking on too much with trying to run a business from over here.

In Roxy's mind, I would have been better off staying in London. To her, moving to Italy meant having to get to grips with a new country, culture and learning a new language (all true), which added unnecessary stress where it wasn't needed. She couldn't see why Lorenzo didn't just move to London. So if I told her I was struggling with Italian, didn't really have anybody else to call on for help and was juggling a million balls like she'd predicted, I'd have to admit I was failing.

I'd tell them about the reality at some point, of course, but it'd be better to do it at one of our catch-ups next time I was in London. Hopefully by then I'd have things more under control.

The doorbell rang, snapping me out of my thoughts. Part of me asked, *Who could that be?* But the other already knew the answer.

Marta.

I sighed. She was the only one who visited unannounced. I was tempted to pretend I wasn't in (I *may* or may not have done that before…), but seeing as the kitchen window was wide open, she'd know we were here. She might have even heard me speaking on the phone. Dammit.

Now *really* wasn't a good time. As well as the studying and exercise I'd mentioned I had to do in my message, whilst Leo was having his last afternoon nap, I also had to reply to some emails and had a pile of washing to put on. Lorenzo was off today, but he'd gone to do a big shop and run some errands and I didn't know when he'd be back. Plus the floors were still wet, so now I'd have to walk over the damp tiles just to let her in.

Great.

'*Ciao, Marta*,' I said through gritted teeth as I opened the door and tried my best to be welcoming.

'*Ciao. Sono venuta a vedere Leo.*'

Right now? That was all I needed.

Well, at least I understood what she said for a change, which was a major miracle. Think I'd learnt something similar on Duolingo. She'd come to see Leo.

'*Leo dort.*' Oops. No. That was the *French* way to say Leo was sleeping. Pretty sure the Italian was something similar, though…

Being similar isn't going to help right now, though, is it? Seeing as Marta speaks Italian...

Yes, Reasanna. Thanks for highlighting the obvious.

Marta breezed straight past me, leaving a trail of footprints on the wet floor.

Grrr.

'Leonardo!' she cried out excitedly.

Oh no, she didn't...

I raced into the bedroom to see Marta picking Leo up out of his cot and kissing him.

'Leo has to sleep!' I snapped. She didn't need to understand English to see that he was in his cot for a reason. This was his designated naptime. He was tired. If he stayed awake now, that would mess up his feed and sleep schedule and then he'd probably be up all night. She couldn't just waltz in here with zero notice because she felt like having a cuddle.

This woman!

She had no respect for routine.

Leo started crying. Didn't blame him. How would she like it if someone just interrupted her sleep like that?

'I'll take him,' I snapped, lifting Leo out of her arms. It wasn't a request. She huffed and left the room.

It took me almost half an hour to settle him again. Twenty-seven minutes wasted unnecessarily because she'd just decided to rock up.

I gently shut the door and headed to the living room to see what she was doing now, but I found her in the hallway. Mopping. *Too bloody right she should clean up her dirty footprints.* I heard the key in the door. Thank God Lorenzo was back. Now he could deal with his mother. I'd already had enough of her.

'Lorenzo!' Marta gushed, rushing towards him, mop still in hand. She rested it against the wall and squeezed his cheeks like he was a baby.

'*Mamma!*' he said as Marta threw her arms around him like they hadn't seen each other in years. *Good grief.*

They started babbling away in Italian and then Marta picked up the mop, started pushing it up and down the floor and wiping her brow like she'd been scrubbing for hours. Then she gestured towards the kitchen solemnly.

'*Grazie!*' He squeezed her hands, then came over to give me a hug and a kiss. 'Mamma is so kind! She tell me that she come to help clean the house. She put washing on and now she clean the floors. *So kind!*'

What?

I cleaned the bloody floors! The only thing *she*'d done was mop up her own mess and now Lorenzo thought Marta was Mother Teresa. And she put on the washing? I walked into the kitchen and sure enough, the machine was on. I was just about to do that myself when *somebody* decided to invite themselves over without warning, wake our son up and screw with his schedule in the process. Then she had the audacity to make out like *she* was doing *me* a favour. If I bit my tongue anymore, it would fall out of my mouth. Lorenzo was grinning, eager to hear my response.

Suck it up, Sophia. Play nice. It's Lorenzo's mum. Do it for him.

'*Grazie,*' I said, putting on my best fake smile.

'Mamma, after all of your help, you *must* stay for dinner!'

Oh, great.

I was hoping that after Leo woke up and Lorenzo gave

him his bath, then fed and put him to bed, we could just relax on the sofa. Together. *Just the two of us.* But whenever Marta came for dinner, she often didn't leave until late. Lorenzo would drive her home and even though it wouldn't take him long, by the time he got back, I was usually fast asleep.

And what was I going to make for dinner now that she was here? I always liked to cook for Lorenzo on his days off, so thought I'd do something simple like a chicken pie, using the puff pastry sheets I had in the freezer, with mashed potatoes and a bit of veg. But if I did, Marta would make some snide remark about the fact that I hadn't made the pastry from scratch.

God help me.

'I'll go and get started on the dinner.'

'No need, *amore.* Mamma is going to cook for us. *So kind.*'

Mamma, mamma, bloody mamma.

To Lorenzo, Marta was just a sweet mother who had innocently popped round to be helpful and do some housework. But I couldn't help but think sometimes her kind gestures were for show. Just to make herself look good and to make me look lazy and hopeless in the process.

Still, if I didn't have to cook or put the washing on, I could recoup the time she'd cost me earlier. That was the least she could do. But if she pulled a stunt like disrupting our day again, I'd need to ask Lorenzo to have words with his precious *mamma...*

CHAPTER ELEVEN

Y*es.*
   That could work…
   I was on the sofa with my iPad, trawling the internet for tips on how to help me address goal number four: sorting out my sex life.

   I should really be using Leo's afternoon naptime to get some rest myself because I was knackered. But, my relationship was also important, so I *had* to make time to do this research.

   After reading only a handful of articles, I started to feel a bit better. I was not alone. Although there were stories of women having sex again after a few weeks (how they even had the energy, never mind managing to do it after everything that happened *down there*, was beyond me), there were also examples of women who waited months and some even a year or more before bedroom business resumed.

   And like me, lots of women still fancied their partners, but just didn't have *the urge*. Whilst I'd guessed it was down to hormones, I hadn't realised that breastfeeding also caused you to lose your libido. Did that mean I had to stop doing it if I wanted to get my sex life back on track? As painful as it could be at times, I'd said that I was going to try and continue for at least six months. Until Leo could start eating solids. Although I could give him formula instead and he'd be fine, I wanted to see if there was another way to ease myself back into the game.

I kept on reading. But then it started to get depressing. There were various horror stories from mums about the first time post-partum. I crossed my legs tightly as I skimmed the study that said one in five women continued to have painful sex up to a year and a half after giving birth. *Yikes*. Then there was talk of bleeding, dryness... If I read any more of this, I'd never do it again.

I clicked back to the search page, then stumbled upon an article that seemed more up my street. It was all about warming up to sex again *without* having intercourse. It talked about trying massage, oral sex or mutual masturbation. One mum who'd been interviewed said she had eased her way back into being intimate with her husband by setting aside *sexy time*. She'd planned a date night and got a babysitter so they could be more relaxed. That would definitely be needed as rather than fretting about Leo waking up, I could lie back and rest for ten minutes. *Oops*. I meant I could lie back and enjoy Lorenzo's hands all over me. *Yes, of course*. I was sure that would be nice too.

Oh God. This was worse than I thought. The objective of Lorenzo massaging me was to relight my fire, not to use the opportunity to have a nap. I needed to get back my desire and fast. Before it disappeared permanently.

Time to message Lorenzo to find out when he'd be free, before I lost my nerve.

~

Tonight was the night. Lorenzo would be home soon. Because the restaurant owners knew how lucky they were to have a chef of his calibre working for them, as well as Sundays and either a Monday or Tuesday off, Lorenzo had also negotiated at least one evening off during the week. That meant he could help out more with Leo and on nights like tonight, he was able to come home early so we could spend some quality time together…

Marta would be arriving in ten minutes to pick up Leo and it had been a rush to get everything ready for her. It was the first time he was going to be away from home without me, so I wasn't used to packing an overnight bag.

There were dozens of things to remember and prepare. I'd expressed enough milk to last until he was back in the morning, so those bottles were chilling in the fridge. Then there were the nappies, his blanket, his favourite cuddly toy, change of clothes, bubble bath, creams… I'd tried to think of everything.

I'd also attempted to prepare the house to make it more romantic. The mum in that article online recommended doing things outside of the bedroom to help spice things up a bit, which was a great idea. When Lorenzo and I were reunited in London after we'd first met months earlier in Italy, we'd had sex all over his flat. On the kitchen counter, in the shower, against the wall, on the floor… *those were the days*. So tonight, whilst I wasn't ready to be *that* adventurous, I thought we could at least have our massages on the sofa rather than on the bed.

I found some oil I'd used to help with my stretch marks, which, as far as I could tell, wasn't making a blind bit of difference but smelt quite nice, so that should do the trick. Once Leo and Marta left, I'd light some candles to try and set the mood, then when Lorenzo came home in half an hour, we could take a shower together and head back to the living room.

Sounded like a plan.

But first, coffee. I wouldn't normally drink it so late, but I needed to be as alert as possible if I was going to get through tonight…

～

'*Ciao, bella*,' said Lorenzo as he stepped through the door. He looked exhausted too, but his smile still lit up the room.

'*Ciao*, handsome.' I kissed him on the lips. 'How was your day?'

'Tiring. Everything okay with Leo and Mamma?'

'Yes, all fine.' Luckily she seemed to be in a hurry and had even arrived ten minutes early, so I'd literally put Leo in the pram, quickly given her his overnight bag and off they went.

'*Bene*. Thank you for trusting her with Leo. I know it is difficult for you to let him go, but Mamma is very happy to spend more time with him.'

I'm doing it for us, I said to myself. For the sake of our relationship, so it wasn't all for Marta's benefit.

'So…' He wrapped his arms around me. 'We have the

night to ourselves. What would you like to do? Have you eaten? You want me to cook for you?'

'Thanks, but you've been cooking all day! I thought maybe we could take a shower together and then…and then…' It was important to manage his expectations. I didn't want to get his hopes up and make him think that full nookie was on offer. But at the same time, I wanted to get him in the mood for *something* at least. 'And then maybe we can just relax, y'know. Chill on the sofa with a glass of Prosecco…'

I'd checked with my doctor back in London, and having alcohol occasionally was fine as long as I didn't breastfeed for a few hours afterwards. And seeing as Marta wouldn't be back until tomorrow morning, I had a clear pass for the night.

'Mmm, sounds good.' He smiled. 'Let's go…'

'Great! I'll be there in a sec.'

I quickly lit the candles, as I'd forgotten to do it earlier (my memory was like a sieve these days), then headed to the bathroom. Lorenzo had already stripped off and was about to step into the shower.

God, he looked good. I took in his broad chest and shoulders, solid thighs and toned stomach. Despite spending most of the day surrounded by food, he still kept himself in shape, mainly by going running three times a week. Unlike my attempts at exercising, his had certainly paid off. Lorenzo's body was like a perfectly sculptured statue. Why was my undercarriage failing to appreciate this gorgeous specimen?

I was about to take my clothes off (always a good idea before getting into the shower), but then I froze.

It had been a while since Lorenzo had seen me fully

naked. Whereas I used to sleep without anything on when we'd first got together, these days I always wore a loose nightdress to bed so he couldn't see what lay beneath. Thinking about it, Lorenzo probably hadn't seen me in the buff since before I'd given birth. And a *lot* had changed since then…

Lorenzo had loved my body and my bump whilst I was pregnant. But now, that firm, blossoming stomach was flabby, saggy and covered in stretch marks. Five months on, I hadn't lost my baby weight. If anything, I was carrying all of that plus 'relationship and living in Italy with a chef' weight too. Lorenzo was always concerned that I wasn't eating enough. So him feeding me lots of lovely food (and my lack of self-control) meant my days of having a toned figure were long gone.

I knew Lorenzo was with me for more than how I looked, but I still felt self-conscious. Suddenly the idea of standing in the shower with him naked and him running his hands all over my body whilst I lay on the sofa scared the shit out of me.

I wasn't ready. I didn't want to see his face fall when he saw what I'd become. Even *I* tried to avoid looking at myself as much as possible.

'Do you need some help?' Lorenzo stepped forward and went to lift up my top. I jumped back. 'Sorry… I did not mean to…'

And now I've just made him feel bad.

'It's okay.' I rested my hand on his. 'I just… I think I'm leaking. Why don't you go ahead and take a shower whilst I sort myself out? I'll shower later. Just meet me in the living room when you've finished.'

'*Va bene.*' He kissed me on the forehead and turned on the shower.

I stepped out into the hallway, shutting the bathroom door behind me.

Jeez. I couldn't even get naked in front of my own boyfriend. And even when I pushed him away, he was still so nice. Patient. Understanding. I was so disappointed in myself. I wanted tonight to be about getting my mojo back. Dipping my toe back in the water. But I'd blown it before even getting off the starting block.

It wouldn't be forever, though. Now I'd started upping the ante on my exercise regime and tackling my pasta and cake addiction, we could do the showering together thing once I'd lost weight and I was feeling more confident. And we'd need to save the massage thing for another night too. Preferably in the dark, when he couldn't see my stretch marks and cellulite… Viktor said Purity would be bringing out a new bodycare range soon, so maybe I'd ask him to send me some early samples that might make them less noticeable. Yep. That was a much better plan.

I thought back to the article. Maybe all wasn't lost. It said to take things slow. Not to rush. To begin with doing intimate, small things.

Okay. So maybe I wasn't ready for him to touch me, but I could try touching *him*. Or actually, perhaps a BJ was in order? *Yeah*. That would make him happy and maybe satisfying Lorenzo could give me a buzz too.

I rummaged through my bedroom drawers and found a black silk dressing gown. That would cover my stomach and my thighs but still look a little bit sexy.

I went into the living room, pushed the coffee table to

the side, pulled the big armchair into the centre, then put a cushion on the floor in front. *That will protect my knees.*

I poured two glasses of Prosecco, moved the candles on the coffee table, then switched off the lights. That way, he could see my face as I went down on him, which I knew he'd like, but it wouldn't be light enough for him to see the rest of my body.

Good plan.

Lorenzo strutted into the living room naked. As he got closer to the candlelight, I could see his manhood swinging as he walked. He'd always been comfortable without his clothes on.

'This looks…nice,' Lorenzo said cautiously, stepping towards me. I could tell from his expression that he wasn't quite sure what to make of it all. One minute I was suggesting we shower together, then I'd literally run out of the bathroom and now here I was, making the living room look all romantic. 'Do you want to find a film for us to watch while I get dressed?'

I took a large gulp of Prosecco. Was I sure I was up for this? *Yes, yes.* It was important. If I was going to do it, though, I needed to get it over and done with before I lost my nerve. Then once I'd finished him off, we could have a nice early night. It had been ages since I'd had a full night of uninterrupted sleep. I couldn't wait to have a proper rest.

'No need…' I took his hand and gently pulled him in front of the armchair. Lorenzo's eyes popped out of his head, and that wasn't the only thing that sprung up… 'If you sit down, there's something I'd like to do… to *try*…'

He sat down, still looking confused, but also excited.

Christ. I'd almost forgotten how big he got when he was hard.

I knocked back the rest of my drink, slamming the glass on the table. It was time to get down to business. I spread his legs, kneeled on the cushion between them, leant forward, then slid him inside my mouth. Lorenzo groaned loudly. That was a good start. He'd probably thought his days of getting BJs from me were over.

I moved my head up and down. It wasn't so bad. For a start, I was still awake, which was an achievement in itself. The way I was feeling earlier, I thought I'd need matchsticks to keep my eyes open.

I glanced up at him. Lorenzo looked like all of his Christmases had come at once. His eyes were rolling with pleasure and his expression flipped between delight and gentle moans. The mission was swiftly being accomplished. At least in terms of making him happy.

Normally the thought that I was satisfying him would be enough to get my juices flowing, but still nothing was happening. I just couldn't find a way to relax my mind and let go. Instead of fantasising about all the things we could do to each other, a million other thoughts were racing through my head.

First I started worrying whether I'd tied my dressing gown tight enough. I didn't want Lorenzo to see the state of me.

Next I started thinking about the mountain of things I had to do tomorrow, including finally having a conference call with Robyn. I'd been trying to speak to her since last week, but we kept missing each other. She'd call me back when I was busy. Then when I returned her call, she was speaking to clients or out of the office, and it wasn't something I wanted to do over email. I needed to do a video call so I could look her in the eyes.

I hadn't chased as much as I would have normally because I knew she was extra busy overseeing a big make-up launch we had this morning and I needed her to be focused. But when I'd called the office at lunchtime to find out how it had gone, they'd said she'd left early because she didn't feel well. I texted her to see if we could speak. She'd eventually replied hours later saying she was too ill and promised to call first thing. I wanted to be sympathetic —after all, she couldn't help being sick—but I really couldn't wait any longer. By hook or by crook we'd *have* to speak tomorrow. My gut said something was off, but Robyn had always been so reliable and competent. It just didn't make sense.

Lorenzo groaned again.

I continued sliding him in and out.

He seemed to be enjoying it, which was a relief. It'd been a while since I'd done this, so I was bound to be rusty.

How was Leo? I hoped he was okay. Fingers crossed Marta had found everything he needed. *Did I pack enough milk?*

Lorenzo's body began to tremble and he raised his hips, pushing himself deeper in my mouth.

Jesus.

I couldn't be thinking about our son's overnight bag when Lorenzo was on the verge of coming. That was just wrong. On so many levels. I needed to focus.

'Sophia…' Lorenzo gasped. I knew what he was going to say. He was about to explode. He wanted to ask if it was okay if he did it in my mouth or if he should release elsewhere. I nodded, giving him the green light to continue.

Hmmm. In hindsight, that probably wasn't the best idea. I'd no idea if there was weeks or months of build-up that was about to erupt.

Actually, I was being silly. That would be impossible. Lorenzo wouldn't have been able to survive that long. He would have relieved himself. I'd imagine it would be uncomfortable otherwise. Surely that wouldn't be healthy.

It'd be fine.

Lorenzo squeezed his eyes shut. Yep. It was going to happen any second now.

Just as he let out a loud groan, I heard a bang, then the room lit up.

Something must have fallen in here, or in the kitchen.

The kitchen.

Like a flash of light, it hit me.

Milk!

I'd forgotten to pack Leo's milk.

I hadn't taken it out of the fridge.

Bollocks.

How could I forget something so bloody important? That should have been the first thing I'd checked.

Fuck.

I had to take it to Marta's. Leo couldn't miss his feed. Lorenzo would have to come in his hands or something.

Just as I slid Lorenzo out of my mouth, he exploded all over me.

Whoa.

I stand corrected. Maybe Lorenzo *hadn't* been doing himself. It went on my face, on my dressing gown... I knew it'd been a while, but I don't remember him *ever* ejaculating this much. It was like a missile had sprayed a round of bullets.

Just as I wiped my right cheek and some drops of spunk fell on the floor, there was a loud scream. It was too high-pitched to be Lorenzo. It was also so bright. As I came to my senses and brought my mind fully back into the room, I realised the flash of light wasn't in my head. The lights were actually on.

Because someone had turned them on.

But it wasn't me and it certainly wasn't Lorenzo.

So who…?

His eyes popped out of his head.

'*Mamma!*'

I span around and saw Marta standing at the doorway, holding Leo and shielding his eyes.

Double fuck.

The noise I heard wasn't something that had fallen in another room.

That was the sound of the door opening.

And my mother-in-law stepping through it.

This could not be happening.

Whilst I was rooted to the spot, hoping this was a big nightmare, Lorenzo jumped up. But just as he surged forwards towards his mum, he slipped on his cum and landed on his back, legs akimbo.

'*Mio Dio!*' screamed Marta, slapping her head.

I understood that she was calling the Lord's name, but even God himself couldn't help us out of this sticky situation.

Oops. Poor choice of words.

Lorenzo got back on his feet, attempting to shield his crown jewels with his hands before realising they weren't big enough to cover everything and grabbing a cushion from the sofa instead.

They were both screaming at each other and of course, I was only understanding about one word in every fifty. Lorenzo was throwing the hand that wasn't gripping the cushion wildly in the air. I think he asked Marta what she was doing here. I heard the word *tomorrow* and *morning*, so he must have been saying she wasn't supposed to come back until 8 a.m. *Yes, that's right.* That was the time we'd agreed. Marta then scowled at me like I was the world's biggest whore and was shouting a load of stuff back at him. The only word I understood was *latte*. From that I gathered she must have gone in the bag to give Leo his bottle, realised that terrible mother Sophia hadn't even packed it and so decided to come back. But how did she even get in?

Frankly, that was the least of my problems right now.

What a shitstorm.

With all of the commotion, it wasn't long before Leo started crying, and instinctively, I rushed over to take him from Marta. She quickly stepped back like she was shielding him from a leper. She shooed me away angrily, brushing her shoulders with disgust and pointing at me.

Oh yes. I forgot about that.

I glanced down at my dressing gown. The thick, creamy substance stood out even more against the shiny black silk.

I *had* to get out of here.

I rushed to the bathroom, locked the door, then caught myself in the mirror.

O. M. G.

It was worse than I imagined. I thought it had only got

on my right cheek, but there was some stuck in my hair and a little bit was even hanging from my chin…

Mortified.

I quickly rinsed off my face, wishing that I could erase what had happened just as easily, then buried my head in my hands.

How would I ever be able to look Marta in the eyes again after this?

First I made her think I was a nympho by telling her I loved penis at the dinner table, then as if I was on a mission to prove just how much, she walked in to find me sucking her darling son's cock like a lollipop. And of course saw me covered in his love juice as if I really couldn't get enough.

Oh God.

I could bounce back from a lot of things, but *this*? I would never be able to live this down.

I'd better pack my suitcase right now and leave town.

CHAPTER TWELVE

'Soph! So good to see you!'

After several attempts, I was finally on a video call with Robyn. We were supposed to speak at 8.30 a.m. when Leo had his nap, but she didn't get to the office on time and when she finally arrived after ten, it was time for his feed. Robyn said she'd call this afternoon at 12.45, but when I chased at 1.30, she said 'something had come up.' So now, here we were at 5.35 p.m. UK time, 6.35 in Italy, getting to speak at long last. It wasn't ideal, as I'd planned to give Leo his bath half an hour early so I could have a proper chat with Lorenzo about what had happened last night…

After Marta had left, Leo had taken ages to get to sleep and by the time he had, I'd been too exhausted to talk and then Lorenzo had gone to the restaurant extra early this morning.

Oh well. I guess that discussion would have to wait as this conversation was long overdue.

'Good to finally see you too, Robyn…'

'How's life in Italy?' she added quickly.

'Great! Idyllic. *Wonderful*!' *Ugh*. I felt bad putting on an act with Robyn, but it was important for the team to believe everything was fine. 'How are you feeling now?' She looked pretty ill to be honest. Pale with dark circles. Her rich chocolate hair wasn't as vibrant and her green eyes had lost their normal sparkle. It seemed like I wasn't the only one who hadn't been getting enough sleep.

'Better. *Sooo* much better. Thank you. I'm really sorry about taking time off and being late this morning. I think I must have been struck down by some bug or something,' she added, avoiding eye contact. 'Lots of people have had it. Really floored me, but I should be back on track now.'

Hmmm.

I hated to say it, but I didn't believe her.

'Really glad to hear you're feeling better. Look, are you sure you can still handle it all? Running the business?'

'Yes! Of course! Absolutely!'

'It's just, had a very concerning conversation with Viktor, who said that you cancelled a meeting at the last minute. And I received an email from MIKA Cosmetics this morning that seemed to imply the number of features secured for them has been dwindling. Then there were those missed emails and phone calls from a couple of other clients…'

'I still don't know what happened with those emails. Maybe they went to spam or something or I didn't get the messages…' She glanced down on the floor, then looked back at the screen again. 'I normally always reply. And I'll talk to the team about getting more coverage. Give them a bit of a push. I mean, with so many big magazines closing, it's been tricky… and, um…sorry about the meeting with

Viktor. I had food poisoning and so… I cancelled as soon as I knew I couldn't make it in. I made sure we had a conference call the next day, though. We spoke for a good hour and got all the key points covered.'

The old spam excuse. There's no reason the clients' emails would suddenly start going to spam. Harrison always kept on top of those things. Yes, magazines have been folding, but there should still be plenty of opportunities online. And someone else could have taken the meetings.

'Why didn't Gail step in and meet Viktor instead? As a senior account manager, she'd have been more than capable. I know you couldn't help being ill, but we never cancel meetings on the day. Unless it's an extreme emergency. It's unprofessional.'

'I'm sorry'. She winced. 'I should have asked her. I just wasn't thinking straight… it won't happen again. I promise. Everything's under control. I'll call a meeting with the team tomorrow. Check everything's running smoothly with the accounts, that the results are on track for this month. I set up that meeting with Viktor's PA for when he's coming over in a couple of weeks and have booked a table at The Shard to take him out for dinner as an apology.' *Glad she'd arranged that.* 'I can fix this.'

'Good. It really can't happen again, Robyn.'

'Understood. Look, I know it's getting late there, so I'll let you go. I'll keep you posted.'

'Okay. Goodnight…' I'd barely got the words out before she hung up.

Hmmm…

She was saying all the right things and had obviously been in touch with Viktor since I'd last spoken to him, but somehow this didn't seem like the reliable Robyn I knew. The one that I had trained and could always trust.

I'd give her the benefit of the doubt for now, but my gut was telling me that I needed to keep an even closer eye on things. On my list, I'd vowed to get the business back under control, so now I had to get round to actually doing it. I needed to draw up a plan of action.

And fast.

CHAPTER THIRTEEN

'*Ciao, amore!*' Lorenzo came in the living room with our favourite band, the Eclectic Detectives, blaring from the portable speaker.

OMG.

I slapped my forehead. He looked ridiculous! He was swinging his hips in time to the music whilst pouting, trying to balance spaghetti above his top lip like a moustache and making funny faces...

'*Piccolino!*' he shouted, lifting Leo from my arms into the air and blowing raspberries on his stomach as he brought him back down. Leo let out his little laugh, clearly enjoying the show. Unsurprisingly, the spaghetti didn't stay on Lorenzo's face and tumbled onto the floor after a few seconds. *Honestly.* He'd become a real clown since Leo was born. Always trying to find some way to entertain him. It was so funny to watch.

The song switched to the "Macarena." Lorenzo must be playing the "Fun with Leo" playlist he'd created.

'Come on, *mamma*!' said Lorenzo, doing a terrible impression of a baby voice and grinning at me. 'Dance!'

Juggling Leo in his left arm, Lorenzo brought his right arm out in front of him, turned his palm upward, then put it on his left shoulder.

'Come on, Soph!'

Oh, what the hell. After my conversation with Robyn, I needed cheering up.

I put my hands on the back of my head, down on to my hips one at a time, then both Lorenzo and I moved our hips around in a circle three times before jumping to the left and clapping. Funny how I still remembered the moves after all these years. Or maybe it was because I'd seen Lorenzo perform it for Leo a few times. I loved that he didn't take himself too seriously. He'd do anything to make me and Leo smile.

'*Bene!*' cheered Lorenzo. 'Again!'

Lorenzo kept us dancing for twenty minutes. I didn't know how he had the energy after working and then going for a run straight afterwards. It was exhausting, but great fun. Good exercise too. It was typical of him. Whenever Lorenzo saw me looking down, he'd always do a silly dance until I burst out laughing. Normally I preferred Leo not to have too much stimulation before bed, but we all needed a bit of fun sometimes, and I was sure that once Lorenzo gave him his bath and bottle, Leo would be nice and calm.

≈

'I forget to say thanks for fix my sweater.' Lorenzo smiled, picking up the jumper and holding it close to his chest.

He'd just put Leo to sleep and was sitting beside me on the sofa.

'You're welcome!'

I'd noticed Lorenzo had a hole in his blue jumper when I was doing the washing, so thought I'd attempt to sew it up. I say *attempt*, because the last time I'd done any kind of sewing was when I was fourteen and had to make an apron at school. I always took things straight to the dry cleaners, so if someone had suggested before that I sit down and sew myself, I would've laughed. But love does funny things to you. It makes you want to do stuff you wouldn't normally, just because you enjoy seeing the man you adore happy.

I knew this was Lorenzo's favourite jumper (it was mine too, because it was the one he had worn the morning after our first steamy night together), so I *wanted* to mend it for him. I remembered stashing one of those mini sewing kits you get in hotel rooms in my make-up bag ages ago (not because I had any intention of using it, mainly because it was free), so I used that. It probably took me longer to thread the needle than it did to sew up the hole, but I got it done and it looked pretty good. *Who knows?* This could be the start of something. Today I fixed clothes. Maybe one day I could be making them. *Ha!* Although with the state of my towering to-do list, I wouldn't hold my breath...

'So, how it go with Robyn?'

I filled him in on our conversation and my concerns.

'Is difficult,' he said, taking my hand in his, 'but you will have to trust Robyn and see what happens. Hope everything will be fine.'

'I really hope so.'

'Try not to worry or push yourself too hard. Remember we are human. People get sick. People make mistakes. Is normal. Everything cannot always be perfect.'

I heard what he was saying, but pushing myself was important. If I hadn't pushed myself before, I wouldn't have gone on the cookery holiday and I wouldn't have met Lorenzo. And if I didn't push myself to keep the business running smoothly, then we'd lose clients.

'I know I can do better, so I have to try.'

'I understand, but is important to also be kind to your-self and not work too hard again, *si*? Especially as you have to find more time to study.'

I know he was worried about me slipping back into my old workaholic ways, but I was fine. I wasn't working anywhere near as much as I used to. Those days were long gone. My life was much more balanced and thanks to my list, I was already making progress. I'd ordered a load of Italian textbooks and study guides, and strangely enough, I was even looking forward to my next class. There was just one problem…

'Yeah…I wanted to speak to you about that. I've got a lesson tomorrow evening, but I know you're working, so…'

'Is fine. Mamma can stay with Leo? No?'

I cringed.

There was no way I could face Marta after last night. It was too soon. Sometime next century might be more bear-able. *Just.*

'After what happened? You must be joking!' It wasn't just the BJ disaster. Marta already thought I was a shit mother and I'd proved her right. I mean, what kind of mum sent her son away without checking that she'd packed the bloody milk?

'*Amore.*' He pulled me in to him and looked into my eyes. '*Tranquilla.* Is easy to forget the milk. Was the first time Leo stay overnight somewhere. And do not worry. Is natural for a man and woman, for us to do these things. There is nothing wrong with this.'

'It may be natural *in private*, but it's definitely *not* natural for your mother to see me doing the deed in front of her and then talking to her with a face covered in spunk. So embarrassing!'

'It was not something I would choose do in front of her either, but things happen, no?' He shrugged his shoulders.

Easy for him to be so calm. He was his mother's golden boy. The apple of her eye. Marta would forgive him even if he committed murder.

'Mamma should have called or knocked the door first,' Lorenzo continued. 'But because there were no lights on, she thought we had gone out. And I had not remembered that she still had the key to my place to check on when I was living in London. I am sorry. But you must not worry. Mamma will be fine.'

'Fine for *you*, maybe. Your mother loves you, but she hates me.'

'She does not hate you.' He rubbed my shoulders reassuringly. 'Is just… you need to know each other better, that is all. That is why will be good for you to spend more time together.'

More time? Five minutes with Marta was enough to last me a lifetime. If I didn't see her for another decade or two, it would suit me just fine. The way she sneered and looked down on me. Didn't she know it was hard enough being a first-time mum and trying to figure stuff out without someone scrutinising every move, willing you to make a mistake and then giving me the evils when I eventually did? I guessed she didn't. She was probably always perfect at everything to do with motherhood.

I was torn. I didn't want to miss my lesson tomorrow, but I didn't want to face Marta either…

Fuck it.

I'd just have to suck it up and swallow humble pie. Puns *not* intended.

'Okay. But could you ask her this time?' I felt weak for asking Lorenzo to do it, especially when I was supposed to start being more independent, but given the circumstances, it was for the best. 'When I call her, the way I ask her to look after Leo is correct. I say it exactly how you taught me—well, close enough—but she says she doesn't understand and makes me repeat it several times.' I was sure she did it on purpose. Just to make me sweat. Marta knew babysitting Leo would be the main reason I'd call, but yet she always played dumb and made me feel like I had to beg.

'*Bene.* I will call her tonight. From five-thirty until nine, *sì?*'

'Yes. The class should finish by eight, eight-thirty, but say nine, just in case.'

'*Perfetto.*'

I cringed, just thinking about how awkward it would be to see her face-to-face again.

'I better make sure I don't eat anything creamy before she gets here.'

'I do not understand?' said Lorenzo.

'If I have anything like that on my face when your mum sees me, I think she might faint. Or book me into some sort of sex addiction clinic…'

'I am sorry…' He slapped his forehead. 'It is my fault… I was excited and I made a lot of mess…'

'There was a *lot* of build-up…'

'There was…' He winced.

'I was surprised. I mean, obviously I know I haven't been ready to… *you know*, but I thought maybe you were self-servicing…'

'Self-*what*?' He frowned before realising what I was saying. 'Oh… well, sometimes if I need, but not very often. I prefer do it with you. I know sounds crazy, but I feel if I use my hands, I will be disloyal to you, so I wait for as long as I can before do that.'

Now I felt *really* bad.

'Oh, darling.' I wrapped my arms around his waist. 'Please don't worry. I know you have needs and I wish I could help you with them right now, but…'

'Is okay. I understand. And thank you for last night. I know has not been easy for you, so I appreciate. I was enjoying a lot until…'

'Yeah… *until* we were interrupted,' I laughed, desperately trying to see the funny side, but still feeling mortified. 'Honestly, though, it's fine. If you need to use your hands, go for it. As long as you don't develop some sort of wanking addiction and never want to sleep with me again!'

'*Impossible*.' He squeezed me tighter. 'And remember, no need to rush do anything. You have given me a son. Your body has done a wonderful thing and gone through many changes. *Ti amo.* I love you. I can wait. We have the rest of our lives to have sex and when you are ready for us to be together again, will be worth it. *Certo*. I know it will.'

As I rested my head on his shoulder, I hoped to God he was right.

CHAPTER FOURTEEN

'Right,' said Angelica as she took a sip of her wine. 'Now for the things you have been excited to learn!'

'Grammar?' replied Daphne.

'*No…*' Angelica rolled her eyes. '*Parolacce*. Swear words.'

'Is that *really* necessary?' sighed Daphne.

'*Sì*. Remember, these lessons are about real life. And in real life, people get angry and sometimes they swear. *A lot*. You need to know if locals are saying bad things about you.'

'Sometimes ignorance is bliss…,' said Daphne.

Exactly what I'd thought before. Was this woman reading my mind or something? Unlike Daphne, I wasn't too fussed about learning grammar today (and, no, it didn't have anything to do with the fact that my textbooks had arrived. Honest…). This time I agreed with Angelica. I swore in English, so if I was learning Italian, it was important to know some rude lingo. That way if someone pissed me off, I'd be able to express myself, *authentically…*

I'd arrived at the lesson nice and early this evening. And thankfully I hadn't had to face Marta. Lorenzo said it was quiet at the restaurant, so he'd popped home just before five-thirty and did the handover with Mamma whilst I hid—I mean, *got ready*—in the bathroom and then he went back to work. He said he'd come home around nine too, which meant I should also be able to avoid Marta after the lesson.

I suspected it wasn't really that quiet at the restaurant but that Lorenzo had made an effort to come home to spare my blushes because he knew I was still embarrassed about seeing Marta. *So thoughtful.* I knew I'd have to face her again eventually, but I wasn't in any hurry…

'How many of you want to learn cuss words?' asked Angelica.

Holly and I both raised our hands enthusiastically. 'That's what I thought. It is normally the first thing that students want to know. I am afraid, Daphne, that you are the exception.'

Daphne crossed her arms like a sulking teenager.

First Angelica went through the many ways to call someone an idiot, which I was sure I'd been called several times by some people in this town. Then she gave us vocab for expressing our disappointment.

'If you are upset about something and want to say *damn* or *what the hell?*, you say *che cavolo.*'

Holly giggled. '*Cavolo?* Isn't that the word for cauliflower? No, I mean cabbage?'

'*Sì! Bene.* You are correct. The literal translation is: *what cabbage!* In fact, this is not a very rude word, so could be good for you, Daphne, as it will not offend. Another gentle word is *che palle*—which means *what the heck*. But, if you need something stronger, you can say *porca miseria!*'

That would certainly come in handy. I imagined myself waving my hands in the air and saying it like a real Italian.

'What about if you want to tell someone to sod off?' asked Holly.

'Ah. There are many ways. Daphne, cover your ears: *vaffanculo* is the strongest. It means to go and fuck yourself.'

'Oooh! Okay!' Holly typed the phrase in her iPhone. 'Think I'll be using that one a lot…' Her voice trailed off.

After Angelica reeled off enough rude words to fill a small dictionary, she then taught us different phrases to express our feelings.

'In traditional language lessons, normally you learn robot responses. If someone asks you how you are, they teach you how to say *good*, *fine*, *okay* or just *bad*. This is acceptable for the stranger in the street who you do not want to know about your life. But you are not a machine. If you are communicating with your friends or your lover, you need to be able to talk about how you are *really* feeling. To say that you are exhausted because the baby was crying all night.' Angelica smiled at me. 'To say I hate my job and my boss is getting on my nerves.' She turned to Holly. 'So this is what we will study now…'

Once again time went quickly. I was starting to get into these lessons. And Angelica was right. Although I still believed in the value of textbooks, you'd never get to learn this sort of stuff just using those.

'Goodbye, Sophia, Holly, Angelica,' said Daphne

formally as she walked out the door. I wasn't sure that we'd be seeing her again. She'd spent most of the lesson cringing.

'Bye!' I replied. 'And see you next week, Holly.'

'Can't wait!' Holly squealed. 'Actually, we should *totally* connect in between lessons. What's your Insta?'

'Um, I don't really have a personal Instagram account…' *These youngsters.* Always on social media. *Gosh.* I sounded like a dinosaur. 'How about we message on WhatsApp instead?'

'Cool! What's your number?'

I read it out to her. It would be great to finally have someone local to chat to, and especially an English speaker too. But then it dawned on me that I probably wouldn't get time to respond to lots of texts. It was already hard enough keeping in touch with Bella and Roxy. What I'd *really* like, though, would be to have a friend to meet for coffee. To get me out of the house. I know that I was supposed to be making friends with an Italian to improve my language skills, so meeting Holly was kind of cheating, but maybe we could also study together?

'Actually, chatting on WhatsApp is cool, but I was thinking it would great to meet up—you know, *hang out* too,' I said using her style of lingo. Now I really did sound like a dinosaur trying and failing to be *down with the kids*.

'*Totally!* We could create our own little study group!' She clapped her hands with excitement. 'How about coffee at my place tomorrow morning?'

'Great!'

'Cool! I'll message you with the deets. *Ciao, Sophia*!'

'*Ciao!*' I waved.

Brilliant! That would give me something to look

forward to. Angelica finished chatting to the woman behind the bar, then put on her bright orange coat. She certainly liked a lot of colour. It went well with her vibrant hair. I followed her as she stepped outside.

'Thanks for today's session, Angelica.'

'*Prego*. And please. Call me Geli.'

'Jelly?'

'*Sì*. Pronounced like you English say *jelly* but spelt like *Geri* but with *l* not *r*: *Geli*. Angelica does not suit my personality. When you know me, you will see that I am definitely *not* an angel...' She let out a raucous laugh.

'Oh, right! Okay, then. *Geli* it is!'

As soon as I saw her, I got the feeling that she was probably a bit of a rebel. Someone who didn't play by the rules. That was also clear from the format of her lessons. And she certainly didn't seem like someone who 'belonged' here. Geli seemed too adventurous—too big for such a small town.

We started walking home.

'So what do you think of life here, Sophia?'

'Honestly?'

'Of course! That was what the lesson tonight was all about. Remember, you are not a robot. Express your true feelings.'

'Difficult,' I sighed. 'My boyfriend is fantastic and I love when we're alone with our son, Leo. When we're a family. And this town is beautiful. I love things like these cute cobbled streets and the amazing views, but there's not much to do here. The people in this town—well, present company excepted—aren't as nice as other Italians I've met either. Then of course there's the overbearing mother-in-law and the language barrier… but at least your lessons I think will help.'

'*Sì*. But I cannot perform miracles! Especially when it comes to mother-in-laws!' She laughed again.

'And you? What brings you here? This town doesn't seem very, well, *you*.'

'Correct.' Geli smiled. 'I prefer to be a free spirit. I enjoy travelling the world. I never stay in one place for too long. Just three weeks ago I was in Rio de Janeiro, hiking in the Tijuca rainforest, showering under waterfalls, partying and drinking with the local people. Having the time of my life. But then Mamma got sick and had an operation. She will need to stay in bed to recover, so I come back to take care of her. I love my mamma, but I cannot stay in that house all day. I need to do something for me. So when I hear some horrible woman in the super-market cursing the *stupid English lady*, I ask around and found out that there were a few new English people in town, so thought I could give lessons, so you would know how to defend yourself against people like that.'

'She was probably talking about me!' I slapped my forehead. 'Chased me and my son out of the shop. Just because I couldn't speak Italian. And possibly because he'd dropped a big one in his nappy and she didn't like the smell.'

'*Puttana*! I cannot stand fools like that. Do not worry, Sophia. She will get her, how you say? *Just deserts*?'

'Yes, that's the one!' I smiled. Her English was really good. 'I hope so.'

'Well, Mamma's house is this way, so I will see you at the next lesson, *sì*?'

Looked like she didn't live too far away from me. Just a five-minute walk. That was handy.

'Definitely! Looking forward to it already. *Ciao*, Geli.'

'*Ciao*, Sophia.'

That was probably one of the most enjoyable evenings I'd had in this town since I'd arrived. I'd received an invitation to coffee tomorrow with Holly and had a lovely chat with Geli. I really liked her. She had character. A quirky personality. Spunk. Actually, might be best not to use that word after recent events…

Although I was old enough to be Holly's mother and we were unlikely to have much in common socially, I reckoned Geli would be a lot of fun to *hang out* with. In a town that had been so cold and unwelcoming towards me, I hoped that I'd finally found one, possibly even *two* new friends. I was on my way to tackling multiple points on my list.

Maybe, just maybe, things were beginning to look up after all.

CHAPTER FIFTEEN

I was on my way to Holly's for coffee and as crazy as it sounded, I was really excited.

When we'd messaged last night, she'd said to come anytime after eight-thirty because by then the kids would be at school and the host parents at work. That was ideal as Leo would be ready for his nap, so we'd be able to chat freely.

Holly only lived five minutes from the centre, so about a fifteen-minute walk from home. To be honest, it didn't really take more than twenty minutes to walk anywhere here. The only reason Lorenzo had a car was to pick up supplies for the restaurant if he wanted something special from Florence or anywhere out of town.

Leo and I had plenty of time to walk there, so I took the scenic route, weaving through the narrow, winding cobbled streets towards the centre. I loved looking down the secret passageways and staircases. One day I'd have to explore all of them properly and see where they led.

I passed the quaint red-tiled pastel houses with green

shutters and colourful hanging baskets. Everything was so peaceful here. Even though some people were on their way to work, there was no big rush hour. You could stroll through the streets without having to fight your way through the crowds like in London. There were no big traffic jams. No honking horns, road rage or exhaust fumes. Despite being in authentic Italy, it wasn't like wandering through a big tourist trap. *Nope.* As far as I knew, they didn't get many visitors here. This was a sleepy town with real Italians living real, quiet, simple lives.

But all those qualities were also what made being here more challenging for me. The peace and quiet had been nice for a while, but after living in a big city like London for so long, it was easy for that to become boring. No tourists also meant no need for residents to speak English. And why should they? *Yep.* If I wanted to make things work here, I'd need to continue with my lessons and fit in with their way of life.

As I approached the town centre I passed the super-market (yes, that awful one), the cobbler and a little shop that sold some local beer, honey and cheese. I passed through the main square or *piazza* where Casini's, the bar we met at for our Italian lesson, was based, along with a couple of cafés. Even though there was still a chill in the air, people were gathered outside enjoying coffees and pastries as they read their newspapers or just watched the world go by.

The grand limestone cathedral was also in the piazza. I'd only been inside it briefly when I'd first visited. As it was right at the summit of the town, the views were stunning. The landscape was lush and green, with rolling hills, picture-perfect valleys and mountains in the background.

Apparently they also had an antique fair in the square every other Sunday and dozens of stands would be filled with second-hand and vintage stuff. Sundays were when Lorenzo, Leo and I liked to spend time together at home or go for long walks, so I hadn't been yet. To be honest, I wasn't that interested in antiques, but as it seemed to be one of the highlights of the Chiorno social calendar, in the spirit of trying to make the most of my time here, I should at least make an effort to check it out. *At some point...*

It wasn't much further to get to Holly's now. I passed a few more streets and then I spotted the one I needed.

There it is.

I'd barely knocked on the wooden door when it flung open.

'Hey!!' said Holly. Looked like I wasn't the only one who was excited to have coffee and a catch-up with a fellow Brit.

'Hi!'

'OMG! Is this your son? He's *totally* gorge! Oops. Sorry, I shouldn't shout! Don't want to wake him.'

I glanced down at Leo. No worries there. He was out like a light. The fresh air and having a good feed earlier must have helped.

'He's fine. He should sleep for at least an hour and a half now, so all good!'

'Come in, come in!' said Holly, ushering us into the tiled hallway, then through to the kitchen. 'Coffee and croissants good for you?'

'Sounds perfect!'

～

'More coffee?' said Holly.

'Mmm, yes, please.' For the past hour we'd sat and chatted about our Italian lessons, how we were finding life in Chiorno, etc., but now Holly had to start preparing the lunch so it'd be ready to put in the oven later before the family came back. 'You sure I'm not distracting you?'

'Nah, it's cool.' Holly grated some cheese into a bowl. 'It's nice to have company and speak English. And I'm only making a quiche. I could do this in my sleep.'

I'd never made a quiche before. Would be good to learn so I could make it for Lorenzo.

'Do you have to do a lot of cooking for the family?'

'Usually just brekkie for the kids and lunch. Sometimes Ilaria, the mum, makes dinner so that I can focus on giving extra lessons.'

Holly explained earlier that she taught English to eight-year-old Aurora and ten-year-old Tommaso, the two children of her host family, for about an hour a day. She also had to take them to and collect them from school, cook and help out around the house. In exchange, she got free accommodation, food and a tiny weekly allowance. But for her, it was all worth it because it meant she could live in the same town as her boyfriend.

'So,' I said, quickly checking Leo was still okay in his pram. He was due his next feed soon. I was sure once he was hungry, he'd wake up and let me know... 'Tell me all about Umberto.'

'Oh. My. *God*, Sophia! He's, like, *sooo* hot! I mean, sometimes I just look at him and want to melt, you know? He is *lush*!' She reached for her phone, scrolled and tapped the screen rapidly, then thrust it in my face. 'Look-at-him!' Holly squealed. 'I mean, isn't he *gorge*?'

He was sweet. Dark hair, stubble, nice eyes. I could see the appeal.

'He is! How long have you guys been dating?'

'Um, well, just a few months. We met when he was on holiday in London and we were, like, inseparable. We tried the whole long-distance thing, but *y'know*, we just couldn't bear to be apart. So I looked for a job over here, which wasn't easy. But if you want something in life, you've got to just go for it, right?'

'Right!'

'I mean, some people go through their whole lives never finding *the one*. And after he'd been sent to me, I couldn't just let him slip through my fingers. Could I?'

'No!' I said, trying to keep up with her enthusiasm and the speed of the words shooting from her mouth. Maybe it was the five cups of coffee she'd had since I'd arrived that was making her speak at five hundred miles an hour. Didn't know how she drank so much so quickly. And without having to go to the toilet either. I was bursting, but was enjoying the conversation. I crossed my legs tightly.

'*Totally!* So I spent six weeks looking for something here and *voilà*! My hard work paid off! I couldn't believe it when the job came up in Chiorno. I mean, talk about fate! So when they told me I got it, I quit uni and jumped straight on a plane. Just goes to show you, if things are meant to be, they're meant to be, right?'

'Yeah…' I hadn't realised she'd quit uni to come here. The mother in me heard myself saying that maybe she should have finished her education first, but who knows? Maybe she hated her course and would have left anyway. Uni wasn't for everyone and having a degree didn't guarantee anything. There were loads of people who achieved success without one. Plus, Holly was only twenty, so she'd have time to go back to studying later if she wanted to.

'I mean, it's early days but, seriously, I think this is *it*. He's, like, totally *the one*!'

Holly's face lit up brighter than Christmas lights. Not too long ago, if I'd heard someone her age gushing about a guy like that, I would have said *ah, young love*, making myself sound like I was about ninety-five in the process. But now I knew those butterflies and feelings of happiness weren't just for twenty-somethings. Like me, Holly had thrown caution to the wind and chosen love. Maybe we had more in common than I thought.

'I get it. It's exactly how I feel about Lorenzo.'

'*Totally!* I mean, what is it with these Italian guys? They're just dripping with sex appeal, aren't they? I mean, like, most of them are anyway. Not the old fogey ones, *obvs*. And Umberto is, like, *totally* into me. I mean, when he picks me up on a Saturday night and we go for a drive, he can't keep his hands off me. And *oh my God*! He has got *skills*. He deffo knows his way around my body. You know what I'm saying…?' she winked.

I did indeed know what she was saying. Those early days of passion with Lorenzo were epic. *Oh, to have a fully functioning libido again...* I sighed in my head.

'Yeah, there's definitely something in the water with Italians. I remember when I came to Florence a couple of years ago, thinking that the ratio of hot guys there was much higher than in London.'

'*Totally!*'

I chuckled to myself. Holly was *totally* a fan of that word.

'Sounds like you're really enjoying yourself here,

then?'

'I mean, the whole language thing is a bit of a ball-ache and the clubbing scene is nonexistent, but life isn't a bed of roses, is it? Things can't always be hunky-dory. At the end of the day, I'm, like, *totally* in love with Umberto and I'm in freaking Italy, baby! All my mates are well jel! Compared to my life in London, I'm living the dream!'

I loved Holly's positivity. What she was saying was just like what I'd written on my list. We were lucky to be here and to be in love.

'And how are your host family?'

'The kids are cool. We have a laugh. And the parents are…alright. Really, um…*friendly*.'

'That's good, so how—'

Suddenly the kitchen door opened and short, round man appeared.

'*Ciao!*' He smiled at Holly and then his eyes widened as he spotted me on the other side of the kitchen counter. '*Ciao…*' He took my hand and kissed it slowly.

'Sophia, this is Silvestro. The host dad.'

'*Ciao.*' I smiled politely. '*Mi chiamo Sophia.*'

'*Piacere,*' he said, kissing my hand again.

Alright, mister, that's quite enough, agreed Reasanna.

He babbled something in Italian and then left the room.

'He's a bit of a charmer, isn't he?'

'Um, yeah, a bit,' Holly said sheepishly. 'He only works around the corner, so sometimes he pops back early before lunch.'

'Oh, right, okay,' I said. Holly turned on the tap to rinse out our mugs. The sound of the water reminded me I needed the loo. I really couldn't hold on any longer. 'Can I use your bathroom, please?'

'Course! It's upstairs on the left at the end of the hall. I'll keep an eye on Leo.'

'Thanks.'

I raced upstairs. *Yep. There it is.* I could see the bathroom door was ajar. I pushed it open.

Oh shit.

'Sorry! *Spiacente!*' I winced.

Silvestro was butt naked, shaking himself off after taking a wee. *How embarrassing.*

I quickly turned on my heels and rushed back out to the hallway.

He casually followed me out.

'*Va bene. Ho finito.*'

I was rooted to the spot. I understood that he'd finished so I could use the bathroom, but I was pretty sure he was still starkers. He hadn't washed his hands, which was gross enough, and if he hadn't done that, I doubted that he'd had time to get dressed either. But I was *bursting*. Ever since I had Leo—well, in fact, even when I was pregnant—my bladder seemed to have shrunk to the size of a pea.

Was it really a big deal? At the end of the day, he was just a naked man. Granted, I wasn't used to seeing a guy in the buff two minutes after meeting him, but this was his home and I had to respect that some people preferred walking around their house in their birthday suits.

Exactly, added Reasanna. *He wasn't to know you were going to come upstairs, was he? He was just answering the call of nature.*

I'd just ignore his lack of clothing, go to the loo, then head back downstairs. It was either that or wet myself, which would be much worse.

I turned around and saw Silvestro standing in front of

the bathroom door. As suspected, everything was hanging out. And I mean *everything*. His beach ball belly, his wiry grey pubes and his meat and two veg. *Oh God*. I couldn't look. He casually ran his hand over his bald head and through the straggly pieces of greying hair at the back which skimmed his shoulders, like he was a male model posing at a photoshoot. He definitely wasn't lacking confidence. His stance was so cocksure (poor choice of words) that you'd think there was a Chippendale standing in front of me.

'*Scusa*,' I said as I approached the doorway. He smiled and remained rooted to the spot.

This is awkward.

'*Scusa*,' I repeated. Louder this time, to make it clear that I needed to get past him.

He stepped back inside the bathroom, giving me a full view of his big hairy backside in the process. He then pulled a brown patterned silk dressing gown from the back of the door, put it on, then walked off.

Why didn't he do that earlier?

Weird.

I stepped into the bathroom and shut the door. I should really lock it too. After that run-in, didn't want to risk *him* walking in on *me* mid-flow.

I jigged up and down like a million ants were in my knickers. I *really* needed to go.

Shit. There was no lock.

I scanned the top, middle and even the bottom of the door frame again and nothing.

But if I waited ten seconds longer, I was going to piss myself.

I'd just have to risk it.

I pulled down my leggings and knickers, then perched over the toilet.

Aaaaahhh.

Oh my goodness. That felt like absolute heaven.

It had been a while since I'd had sex, but right now, I couldn't imagine it comparing to the relief of finally going to the loo after holding it for so long.

Jeez, Soph! Things must be really bad if your greatest pleasure in life these days is emptying your bladder.

True, Reasanna. I'd been doing some pelvic floor exercises to make my muscles stronger down there, but maybe I needed to do more…

I washed my hands and went downstairs.

As I returned to the kitchen, I saw Leo slowly opening his eyes. It was if he knew I was coming. He looked so cute as he stretched out his little arms. *What a hard life, eh?* Sleeping, eating, pooing and crying all day long must be *so* exhausting. Still, that's what babies did. I'm sure I wasn't any different. Maybe he'd be good and just go back to sleep.

Ha.

As if.

Just as the thought left my head, he started crying. I picked him up and tried to soothe him, but he wasn't having it.

Silvestro came in the kitchen, wearing his dressing gown, thankfully, and raised his eyebrow. That look told me everything. Whilst he didn't appear to be embarrassed about the awkward bathroom encounter, he was *not* a fan of noisy babies. Was anyone? I got the hint.

'I'd better go.' I attempted to put Leo back in his pram as he wriggled and kicked his legs in protest.

'Oh no!' said Holly. 'Stay!'

'Best that I take Leo home. It's time for his feed and you've got to finish preparing lunch.' Normally I used Leo's naptime to do emails and express milk, so I'd also have a lot to catch up on when I got back. It was worth it, though. In fact, maybe we could stop off to see Lorenzo at the restaurant quickly too. It was in the town centre, so only five minutes from here. That would make Lorenzo's day. *Yeah. Good idea.*

'No, honestly! It's totally cool! *Please stay*. Can't you feed Leo here? Breastfeed him in my room.' She looked at Silvestro nervously. I wasn't sure if he approved of her having friends round. 'I could come up with you, once I'm done.'

'Don't worry. You've got things to do. I'll leave you to it. Thanks again for coffee.'

'Okay,' she said reluctantly.

Holly's hands were covered in pastry, so after saying bye to Silvestro, I told her I'd see myself out. I could tell she was disappointed, but I didn't want to get her in any trouble. If she invited me round for coffee again, I could come a bit earlier to give us more time to talk alone in case Silvestro turned up.

Better still, I'd invite her round to my place. It'd be more relaxed. Zero chance of bumping into anyone naked, and the lock on our bathroom door was solid too.

Either way, whether we met at her house or mine, I was just happy to finally be making friends. And of course, I liked getting the goss on her steamy romance with Umberto. With my own sex life rapidly disappearing down the toilet, hearing about her blossoming relationship could be just the kind of escapism I needed.

CHAPTER SIXTEEN

I t had been a rough few days.

Leo hadn't been sleeping, which meant *I* hadn't been sleeping. And because he was tired, he'd been crying. *A lot.* I was exhausted.

My schedule was completely out of sync. Normally after feeding Leo, I'd take a shower and make myself look decent whilst Lorenzo held the fort, then we'd have breakfast together. But today I just didn't have the energy. After I'd given Leo the breast, I'd collapsed back on the bed and stayed there until Lorenzo had woken me up to tell me he was going to work.

Even though Leo had finally fallen asleep, that didn't mean I'd be able to continue catching forty winks. I had work to do.

Despite the fact that it was only 8.45 a.m., our client Viktor had already sent me three emails. *Three.* I wanted to reply, but my brain was too fuzzy to string a coherent sentence together, so I needed to wait until I'd at least had a coffee or a shower first. Preferably, both.

I checked Leo in his cot. If I was really quiet, hopefully he'd sleep until ten-thirty so I could go through those emails after breakfast. I really needed to express some milk before he woke up too. But first, shower.

Just as I was about to go into the bathroom, my mobile rang.

Dammit.

I raced to answer before it woke Leo up.

'Hello?'

'Sophia?' I looked down at the phone screen to see who it was.

Oh great. It was Viktor. Talk about persistent. And *jeez.* What time must it be in Canada right now? Pretty sure they're nine hours behind Italy, which means it's almost midnight. *What the hell?*

Well, I'd answered now, so I needed to speak to him.

'Yes, hi, Viktor… I was going to reply to your emails, I just—'

'Can you call me back on this number. *Right now.*'

'Yes. Of course. Will do.'

He *always* did this. I think he was worried about calling me in Italy because he thought it would cost a lot for an international call. He was worth millions and yet sometimes could be so tight. That was probably why he was so rich.

I wondered how long the call would last. If it went on for ages I wouldn't get everything done. Actually, I could multitask and use my pump whilst I was speaking to him like I did before. I grabbed it quickly, attached it, propped a pillow up behind me and sat up in bed. That was the benefit of working from home. You could be in your night-dress, with your boob out whilst writing an email or making calls, and the person on the other end would be none the wiser.

Anyway, best call him back quickly. I launched Whats-App, clicked on his name, tapped on the call button, then rested the phone on my knees in front of me. I needed my hands to be free for the pump.

'Hi…er, what the hell is *that*?'

'Oh shit!' I grabbed my phone quickly. I'd stupidly hit the video call button instead of the call button, so he'd just got an eyeful of my breast with the pump attached. Why were the buttons so close together? 'Um, sorry about that,' I said, holding the phone up to my face instead.

'*Jesus*, Sophia!' He winced like he'd just eaten a bowl of live maggots.

For crying out loud. Why were people still so offended by breastfeeding? Okay, technically Leo wasn't on my breast, but it was an honest mistake. And it was only a boob. He always went to a 'gentleman's club' whenever he came to London, so I was sure he'd seen plenty of those before.

Let's not dwell…

'My God. It can't be?' He recoiled from the screen with disgust. 'What *on earth* has happened to you? You look a mess!'

Oh.

I'd just realised. I was holding the phone up to my face. Standard practise for video calling, as I'd told my mum so many times. But definitely *not* a sensible idea when you haven't washed your face, combed your hair or slept properly for days and had bags the size of giant spaceships under your eyes.

It would have been bad enough for a friend to see me

like this. But for a client, the president of one of the largest beauty brands in the world, to get a close-up when he'd only ever seen me looking like I'd just stepped out of a salon, it wasn't ideal…

'Sorry. As you know, I'm on maternity leave right now and, well, Leo, *my son*, he hasn't been sleeping, so… anyway, I'm sure you remember what it's like,' I chuckled, attempting to lighten the mood. 'You have two young boys of your own, don't you?'

His eyes widened and his jaw was still on the floor.

Oh, come on. I know I was no oil painting right now, but he must have been able to understand.

'That's what nannies are for,' he sneered. 'To deal with those things. Why don't you have a nanny? *Everyone* has a nanny. I'm very concerned, Sophia. *Very* concerned. First Robyn and her flakiness, the poor results, the slow replies to emails and now *this*.'

'Well, I'm sure we can–'

'I've got to go, Sophia. *Eugh*…' He hung up.

What the hell? Did he really just hang up because he couldn't bear to look at me? Was I really that repulsive?

I jumped up and looked at myself in the mirror.

Oh dear.

My hair was tangled and sticking up in different directions. I had some dried dribble on the side of my mouth, sleep crust in the corners of my eyes, as well as the enormous bags and, oh—*how lovely*. A giant angry spot, smack-bang in the middle of my forehead.

Brilliant. *Bloody brilliant.*

I flopped back down on the bed.

It's okay. I'm overreacting.

Viktor was an intelligent man. He might work in

beauty, but he knew that there was more to me than just how I looked. It was my brain and my experience, the work that the team did, that was most important. We'd generated amazing results for his company in the past. Helped to establish the brand in the UK. Gone above and beyond.

And anyway, it wasn't like he was a new client. We'd known each other for years. Surely I was allowed to have one off day? It would be fine.

My phone chimed. I really needed to put it on silent whilst Leo was asleep.

It was an email from Viktor. I read the subject line.

What the…?

Termination.

He can't have…

I clicked on the email.

Sophia,

Please take this email as written notice that Purity Skincare wishes to end our contract with BeCome with immediate effect.

It's clear that you and your team are no longer capable of representing our brand.

Regards,

Viktor

'*Vaffanculo!*' I screamed. '*Testa di cazzo!*'

I shouted, thinking of all of the rudest Italian swear words Geli had taught us. I was so annoyed I wasn't even thinking about waking Leo up.

What a giant dickhead.

I'd always worried that if clients ever saw me looking less than immaculate, they wouldn't want to work with me. That's why I used to always wear designer clothes and four-inch heels, have my hair swooshing around like I was auditioning for a shampoo advert and my nails and make-up looking flawless. Roxy always said I was a glamour puss who preened more religiously than a Christian went to church. It was true. But I didn't want that life anymore. I had known that as soon as I'd come back from the cookery holiday two years ago, and I'd been trying to relax my style and dial down my image ever since.

Yeah, I still used to glam up for meetings and events, just in case, but day-to-day, I preferred the more casual look. It felt more me. Like the real me. I liked it.

And now I had bigger priorities, like keeping another human alive, the way I looked was even less important. Although I still always made the effort to look presentable, I'd rather get some extra sleep or enjoy a longer breakfast with Leo and Lorenzo than spend an hour in front of a mirror every morning contouring and prettying myself like I used to.

But tired or not, I should have got up on time to have a shower and get dressed. If I'd followed my normal routine and hadn't looked like I'd been dragged through a bush backwards, the whole video call boob thing could have been overlooked.

I shouldn't have answered the call just like that either. I should have just put it on silent. If I was more in control of the situation and just called back ten minutes later once I'd got myself sorted, things would have been different.

Gosh. Was Viktor really that shallow? I couldn't

believe he'd just terminated our contract, thrown away a long, successful working relationship because he saw me looking like crap.

OMG.

OMG.

OMFG.

Purity Skincare accounted for a big chunk of revenue. Without Viktor's business, a massive amount of income will be gone. Wiped out. Just like that.

We were screwed.

How was I going to pay the staff? All the bills?

What was I going to tell the team?

And once the clients got wind of Purity Skincare dumping us, they'd lose confidence and start resigning too. *It'll be like dominos.*

Before I could stop them, the tears started streaming down my cheeks. Hard to believe I used to find it difficult to cry about anything. These days I was like a leaking tap.

But these tears were warranted.

This was a disaster.

I'd just lost the company one of our biggest clients.

I'd put the business and its future in danger. This wasn't just about getting the business back under control like I'd put on my list. This was now about fighting for its survival.

CHAPTER SEVENTEEN

'It is all arranged,' said Lorenzo as he walked into the living room and put his phone in his pocket.

'What is?'

'This weekend. I am taking you to *Firenze*. You have been sad since the client end his contract last week. I do not like to see you like this. You need some rest. And some fun. Time away from thinking about work.'

I sighed, considering how I was going to let him down gently. 'That's really sweet of you darling, but with all the stuff going on with the business, I can't. What kind of message will I be sending the team if I just go swanning off to Florence for the weekend?'

'You may not realise, but you just say very important word: *weekend*. The weekend is when normal people who work in office take time to rest. We go on Friday, so it will just be one day off. You will be back on Sunday and ready to work again on Monday.'

I heard what he was saying, but this *really* wasn't a good time.

Since that nightmare, I'd been trying to reach Viktor on the phone, but he wouldn't take my calls or reply to my emails. Worse still, he was trying to wriggle out of their contract. There was no way he could just up and leave without at least honouring the notice period. We needed the fees for a start.

I'd even offered to meet Viktor in London when he was over. Hell, I'd consider flying to bloody Canada if I had to. Desperate times called for desperate measures. And to top it all off, although she was back at work again now, Robyn had called in sick again last week.

Ugh. It was too much.

'Sounds nice in theory, but weekend or not, I should be working on a plan. Looking for new clients to replace Purity.'

'One weekend away will make you feel better. You will be fresher. It will help you make better decisions, *si*?'

'It just feels irresponsible. Maybe I should go to London instead. Check on things properly. And then when everything with the business is under control again, maybe I can take an hour off or something to see my family or have a catch-up with Bella and Roxy. I miss them.'

'I know you do. Is not easy to be away from them, but one-hour break is not enough, *amore*. You need more time to relax. I cannot tell you how you run your business, but you have video call with all the managers, no? And you speak with the money man and everything is okay, so you can have one weekend for yourself? We are in Italy. Is time to enjoy *la dolce vita, si*? Remember, life is not all about work. Specially not now…'

Those words stopped me in my tracks. They reminded me of Albert's warning about happiness and love being more important. Lorenzo was right. If I wasn't careful, I'd slip back into my old ways. Working weekends, being stressed and focusing on the business rather than enjoying life. I couldn't let that happen. Especially now I had my two boys. Yes, I did have to fix things with the business, but like Lorenzo said, I'd had a long video call with the managers and the entire team after the Viktor incident and I'd stressed the importance of making an extra effort with clients. I'd told Robyn I needed updates every other day instead of just weekly. I'd also gone through our accounts with my financial director. We had a small buffer, so would be okay for a few months. But after that, things would start getting really tight. We couldn't afford any more fuck-ups.

Hmmm.

I supposed I *could* consider taking a couple of days off. If anyone needed to get in touch on Friday, I'd have my phone with me. It wasn't like I'd be going to Timbuktu or somewhere with no reception.

'Well, it would be nice for us to have a weekend away as a family.'

'No, no, no.' Lorenzo waved his finger. 'This is not family weekend. This is time for *you* to relax and enjoy yourself without worry about work or Leo. Mamma will take care of him.'

Oh jeez. I didn't know about *that*. Being away from him for three days? Giving Marta seventy-two hours of access? She'd completely screw up his routine.

'I don't know…'

'Sophia.' He rested his hands on my shoulders. 'You know I like that you are strong, independent woman. That you make your own decisions, *sì*?'

'Yes…' I sensed there was a *but* coming…

'But, this time, I cannot take no for answer. You *need* this. *We* need this. Will be good for you. Good for *us*. So please. Let me take you to *Firenze*.'

When he put it like that, how could I refuse? As much as I thought Marta wouldn't stick to the schedule, Lorenzo was Leo's father, so it couldn't always be about what *I* wanted. Sometimes I had to compromise. It would make Lorenzo happy if Leo spent time with his grandmother. I had to also remember that as well as being a mum, I was also a girlfriend and it *would* be good for us to have some time away as a couple. This would be a chance for us to spend quality time together and be in a different environment. Somewhere more exciting.

'Okay… maybe we could do with a break.'

'*Fantastico!*' Lorenzo picked me up and spun me around. 'You will have an *amazing* time, trust me.'

I couldn't lie. The more I thought about taking time out, the more I started warming to the idea. And it was really kind of him to organise it all. With all the firefighting I was doing right now, it would be something nice to look forward to.

'I'll get Leo ready for bed,' I said as Lorenzo put me back down.

'Is okay. I will do it. I have made you a bath so you can relax tonight.'

'Wow, thanks!' I planted a kiss on his lips. 'I'm so lucky to have you. I love you so much.'

'I love you more. And *we* are lucky to have each other.'

Awww.

I jumped up, gave him a hug, then went to the bathroom. Soft music was playing on the portable speaker. There were candles all around the bath, which was filled with bubbles and a glass of Prosecco on the side. *What an amazing man.* I couldn't wait to slip into the warm water. A relaxing soak was just what I needed.

I locked the door, stepped out of my clothes and climbed underneath the mass of bubbles.

Ahhh. This is heavenly.

For what felt like the first time in ages, I started to get excited. A weekend away did sound like bliss right now. My mind started to wander, imagining all of the things we could do whilst we were there. Maybe I could have a pampering afternoon. Either a massage or facial would be amazing. Luckily running a beauty PR agency meant I had enough products to help maintain my hair and skin whilst I was here, but it'd been ages since I'd stepped foot in a salon. In my old life, I used to go at least once a week. Then again, Lorenzo and I hadn't had a weekend away with just the two of us since before Leo was born, so I didn't want to spend our precious time apart whilst I was getting pampered. It was important for us to be together. I'd ask Geli if she could recommend somewhere local I could go before the weekend, so I could get my colour done and a fresh blow-dry before our trip. I'd picked up a lot of tips from clients over the years, so could do a decent enough job myself, but there was nothing like getting it done by a proper professional.

Lorenzo knocked on the door.

'You okay?' I glanced down to check the bubbles were covering my body just in case he wanted to come in. *All good.*

'I just speak to Mamma,' he said, talking from behind

the door. 'She will come early on Friday morning and we will leave straight away.'

'Great! Thank you again!'

Amazingly, I'd still managed to avoid seeing Marta since the BJ incident, and even though I knew coming face-to-face was inevitable, if it meant I'd be able to have some time away from real life and be with Lorenzo, I would find a way to deal with it...

~

Friday was finally here. Since I'd got my head around the idea of taking a break, I'd been wishing away the days, hours, minutes and seconds. The weekend couldn't come quick enough.

Any minute now Marta would be round to collect Leo. It was bound to be awkward, but I was ready.

I felt *good*. Not just because I was having a mini break, but also because I'd had a fun day yesterday with my new friends.

I'd started off having coffee at Holly's place. It was the third time I'd been (because Holly always had to tidy up after breakfast and prepare lunch for the family, she said it was easier if I could keep going there) and I was enjoying our little catch-ups. Well, when we weren't being disturbed.

We were having a good chinwag about her last steamy date with Umberto. She was explaining how he'd picked her up on Saturday night, had a pizza in his car, then driven to a secluded spot. The story was just getting juicy when Silvestro came home early again (thankfully, about ten minutes *after* I'd been to the loo) and so we'd had to stop.

There was something about Silvestro. Something was niggling me and I couldn't put my finger on it. There was the bathroom incident for a start. I knew he could walk around however he wanted to, but if there was a guest in the house, would you really do that? Especially if you had a dodgy door?

When I told Holly about my encounter with him, she'd cringed and said it'd happened to her too. She explained that even when you tried to close it, the door often crept open by itself. The lock had fallen off and Silvestro hadn't got around to fixing it. His wife was forever complaining about him sorting it out too.

I get it. Lots of people didn't do odd jobs around the house, which they knew they should. But I'd been thinking about it. Confident or not, wouldn't a normal person be at least a little embarrassed about someone walking in on them?

Hmmm.

Secondly, Silvestro was a bit too friendly for my liking. Rather than just say hello, he'd always take it a step further. Throwing his arms around me, planting a sloppy kiss on each cheek, then hugging me for longer than I was comfortable with, like we were long-lost lovers who'd just been reunited after decades apart. It was a bit OTT. Particularly considering he was practically a stranger.

Okay. Maybe that was just me being overly British. We weren't so good with physical contact when greeting people. Handshakes were more our style. Whereas in countries like Italy, France and Spain, cheek kissing and getting up close and personal was the norm. *But even so…*

And he always had to bother us. I knew that sounded crazy, considering it was his house, so he was free to come and go as he pleased. But he just seemed to linger like a bad smell.

I didn't feel comfortable when he was around. Holly kind of clammed up too. Even though he could barely understand English, I didn't feel like we could speak freely. Whenever I was there, he always seemed to make a point of coming into the kitchen. Just for the sake of it. He'd stand right behind Holly. And I mean, so close that his body was almost touching hers, then he'd reach over Holly to get something.

He would open the cupboard in front of her and quickly shut it again. Or take something out, but put it back immediately. So unnecessary.

Last time, I could have sworn he sniffed Holly's hair as he stretched over her head. It was only for a split second and I may have imagined it, but I'm sure he closed his eyes and inhaled as if he was smelling a sweet bouquet of roses. Sent a shiver down my spine. I asked Holly about it once he'd left, but she brushed it off.

Something told me I needed to keep my eye on him...

Anyway, like I said, apart from our interruption, I'd had a fun morning with Holly. She'd said that as well as a friend, she saw me as a mother figure, which did make me feel old. But I knew she meant it as a compliment. It was kind of sweet. Holly also seemed to like asking my advice about men. Ha! Now *that* was funny. I hardly considered myself an expert, but it was nice that she valued my opinion.

After I caught up with Holly, I headed back home to make lunch and then Geli came round to do my hair.

Yep.

At our last lesson, I'd asked Geli if she could recommend a good local hairdressers and decent beauty salon, and she'd laughed in my face.

'I know the perfect salon for you to visit…when you are eighty! There are no modern salons in this town. You must either go to *Firenze* or I can do it for you.'

'*You?*' I'd said, before realising that may have sounded rude. 'I didn't know you were a hairdresser or, um, beauty therapist?'

'*Sì.* I have many careers in my forty-seven years in this world,' she'd said. I was surprised at her age. Geli certainly didn't look it. 'Worked in salons for many years in my twenties. I also worked as counsellor, social worker, in nursery, restaurants, bars and of course as teacher…'

'Oh wow. Okay,' I'd replied. To be honest, initially I was nervous about letting her near my hair or skin. But after working with hairdressers for so many years, I could tell when hair had been coloured professionally and hers always looked great. So did her skin. She seemed like a good person. Trustworthy. Plus, let's be honest. My options were limited. And she offered to come to my house, which was even better as I couldn't very well ask Marta to do more babysitting seeing as she was already having Leo for the whole weekend.

So Geli came round and worked her magic. It was tricky because at first it seemed like Leo wasn't going to stick to his normal afternoon naptime, but he did. And he slept for hours, so she coloured my hair, gave me a little trim and a blow-dry and a mini facial. I felt like a new woman. I looked like one too. The power of a good pampering session once in a while should never be under-estimated. Nor should taking time out with friends.

Until recently, with my besties hundreds of miles away in London, my options on the friendship front had been non-existent. But spending time with Holly and Geli had shown me how much I'd missed face-to-face female conversation. With all the trouble with the business and trying to navigate this being a mum stuff, I needed it more than ever.

So I'd had my adult interaction fix with my new friends and now I had three full days with my lovely Lorenzo to look forward to. I was sure I'd miss Leo massively, but at the same time, I couldn't wait to feel a bit more like Sophia again. To have seventy-two hours without changing nappies, breastfeeding and getting a decent night's sleep for two whole nights sounded like absolute heaven. I was so excited I could burst!

CHAPTER EIGHTEEN

'Ciao, Marta,' I said confidently as I opened the door. I'd told Lorenzo I would greet her. I knew I couldn't hide forever.

'Sophia...'

Marta still looked at me like she'd just drunk a pint of vinegar, so no change there.

I picked Leo up from his chair.

'Look! It's *Nonna*! You're going to stay with her for a few days, won't that be fun?' I said, thinking *rather you than me*. I handed Leo to her, picked up his bag and opened it up.

'*Latte*.' I pointed to the bottles of breast milk I'd included so she could see that this time I hadn't forgotten. There was also a fresh tin of formula, which would be plenty to get him through the weekend.

I'd been introducing Leo to formula since last week and he'd been fine. Good timing too as it meant I didn't have to prepare a load of milk to leave for him. I'd still have to express whilst I was away, though. Otherwise my boobs would get too full and painful.

Lorenzo and I had also decided that from next week, we'd start introducing him to solids. Couldn't believe Leo was six months already.

Marta nodded to confirm she'd seen what was in the bag, then gave Leo a kiss and a cuddle.

'Everything okay?' said Lorenzo.

'Yeah, I was just showing your mum the milk. Everything's there.' This time I was a hundred percent sure. Like Santa, I'd made a list and checked it twice. Well, more like twenty times. There was no way I was going to fuck up again.

I was glad I'd got seeing her over and done with. It was awkward, but hey. It could have been worse.

Lorenzo chatted to Marta in Italian, I think also checking she had what she needed, and then we said our goodbyes to Leo. He cried for a bit, but after she rubbed his back and said some stuff to him, he was fine.

Marta really did have a knack for keeping him calm. Whatever we thought of each other, it was reassuring to know that I could trust her. There was no way I'd feel comfortable being away from Leo for so long otherwise.

We locked up the house, put our things in the boot and set off in the car to Florence.

～

'So…what's the plan, Batman?'

'Batman?' Lorenzo frowned.

'Yeah…don't worry. It's just a saying. What's on the schedule for this weekend?'

'Schedule, schedule, schedule!' Lorenzo rolled his eyes. 'You know I love you, *mi amore*, but you worry too much about routine. Is good. *Sometimes*. And I have make plan of what we will do this weekend, but some things will happen naturally, *sì*? Please relax. Let me take care of things.'

I guessed I was a bit rigid with my routines. It was the only way I knew how to get everything done. At least I was better than I was two years ago before I made big changes to my life. Well, I hoped so anyway…

'Glad you have a plan! Can't you give me a little, tiny clue?'

'*Scusa*. Sorry, no clues. Is a surprise. I will tell you about our first activity later. You must be patient. Perhaps you would like to have a little rest while I drive?' He smirked.

Oh, he's good. Done like a pro. Lorenzo knew that as much as I always preferred to stay awake when he was driving so that I could keep him company, after a tiring week and the extra-early start this morning, I couldn't possibly pass up a golden opportunity to have a nap. Especially if we were going to be doing a lot of walking around. And if I was sleeping, I wouldn't be able to ask him any more questions...

I know it sounded bad, but one of the reasons I wanted to know what we'd be doing is to find out how much time he'd allocated to sightseeing. Part of me would be happy to just lie in bed all day, but I quickly pushed that thought out of my head. Lorenzo had said this weekend would be about having fun and it'd been a while since I'd done that, so I was definitely up for it. *Fun, that is*. Just to clarify, I meant I was up for *fun* in its purest sense. Not fun in the bedroom…

Oh God. That was a good point actually. We were going to be together. Alone. In a hotel. What if Lorenzo wanted to have sex? *Shit.*

Yes. Let me take his advice and get some sleep. Otherwise I knew I'd spend the whole journey overthinking and fretting about that.

Lorenzo has made a big effort to organise this weekend, so it will be fine.

Yep. Everything will be totally, absolutely, completely fine…

~

'Soph, wake up,' said Lorenzo.

It was really dark. I squinted as I took in the surroundings and saw we were in an underground car park.

'Come. Let us go to the hotel. Is too early to check in, so we will leave our bags and go to the first place.'

'Ooh!'

I was intrigued. Especially as it was only 8 a.m. I did wonder why we'd arrived so early when check-in wasn't normally until the afternoon, but just thought that Lorenzo wanted to make the most of the day. I guessed we'd probably do the normal tourist things like visit museums and check out the famous landmarks. Some of the queues for those places were really long, so I supposed it made sense we got there as soon as possible.

To be honest, I wasn't that cultured and whilst the idea of walking around for hours didn't really appeal, I vowed to try and appreciate every second, because unlike my last visit to Florence, at least this time Lorenzo would be here. Right beside me.

Once we were outside, Lorenzo led me along the streets, passing artisan jewellers, shops with handcrafted books and paper. Looked like some Florentine street-food stalls and people selling leather bags were setting up too.

I could see the cathedral, or should I say *Duomo*, with its striking pink, white and green marble exterior, was nearby. I thought we would be heading towards it, but Lorenzo slipped down a cobbled street, then entered a secluded courtyard, which was surrounded by ancient Roman walls.

Wow.

'We are here,' said Lorenzo.

I saw the entrance to the hotel straight ahead. As we stepped through the doors, I could tell the place was dripping with history.

There was a grand reception desk with a tall vase filled with vibrant red flowers, which was opposite what looked like original exposed-stone walls. The reception area was decorated with a mixture of antique and contemporary pieces, as well as a large ornate gilt mirror. By the fireplace, which was against the back wall, there was a glass table, with a selection of coffee table books neatly laid out and cream leather armchairs on either side. I liked it here. Not too old-fashioned and not overly modern. And it smelt so good. It was like the hotel had been perfumed with the most deliciously sweet fragrances.

'This place looks amazing!' I gushed as we approached the receptionist.

'You will see properly later when we check in.'

'Do I need to change my clothes? Bring anything?'

'No. You are perfect just as you are.'

Awww. I gave him a big hug. That was nice to hear. I figured comfortable clothing was in order for some sight-seeing, so I was wearing jeans, a jumper and my Converse. A step up from my usual T-shirt and leggings combo.

'*Andiamo*. We should go,' said Lorenzo after we'd left our bags with the hotel staff. 'Cannot be late.'

We weaved back through the streets. This location was perfect. Just a short walk from the major landmarks, but yet tucked away from the hustle and bustle. Lorenzo had chosen well. I was excited to see where we were going.

'First, *caffè*.'

Of course.

Before I knew it, we were stood outside a tiny coffee shop in a side street.

'Is my favourite place. When I was working in *Firenze*, I come here every day. Is over a hundred years old.'

You could kind of tell from the dated décor. It had old-fashioned tiled floors, a wrought-iron sign and dark wood tables and chairs. What it lacked in style, it seemed to make up for with authenticity. It was filled with people, who all appeared to be speaking Italian. This definitely wasn't a typical tourist spot.

'Must be pretty special, then. Can't wait to try it.'

The strong aroma filled the air. *Delicious.* I'd always liked coffee, but since moving to Italy, I'd found a new appreciation for it. Not least because I needed it to function every morning.

Lorenzo ordered two coffees and croissants and we

squeezed into a spot by the brown-speckled bar area to eat them.

I took a sip. '*Mmmm…*' It tasted divine. A million times better than what we had in London.

'Is good, no?'

'*Sì!*'

'*Bene.*' He looked at his watch. 'Come. We must go.' I wrapped the rest of my croissant in the serviette and pushed it into my handbag.

He was really serious about getting in these queues early, wasn't he? At least the weather was good. The skies were blue and there was only a slight chill in the air. To be expected at this time of the morning. When I'd checked the weather forecast, it said it might get as high as sixteen degrees later, which Lorenzo said was warm for the beginning of March.

We approached the Palazzo Vecchio. With its grand tower and Michelangelo's David statue (aka the naked guy) outside, I recognised it instantly as one of the most famous sights in Florence. We'd probably be going to the museum. Made sense. Couldn't do the whole Florence tourist trail and not see this.

But hold on…

We didn't join the queue. Instead we walked past the entrance and the statue, down the side of the building. Where were we going?

Lorenzo held my hand tightly as he led me down a narrow street with an arched entrance and then stopped outside a building:

Authentic Tours

Huh? I thought Lorenzo would know Florence, or

Firenze as the Italians call it, like the back of his hand, so why did we need a tour guide?

As we entered the building, there was a Vespa in the colours of the Italian flag parked inside to the left and a vintage Fiat car to the right. We approached the lady standing in front of the computer towards the back. Whilst I checked out the souvenirs and T-shirts on the wall, Lorenzo chatted to the woman and handed over what looked like some documents.

'*Pronta?*' he asked me. 'Are you ready?'

'*Sì,*' I replied. I followed Lorenzo and the lady as she led us out the back.

What?

No way!

As we walked out the door at the rear of the building and onto the street, there was a whole row of vintage Vespas lined up. One, two, three, four…there must have been about eight of them.

'So…as you may have guessed,' said Lorenzo, 'we are going on a tour. But not a traditional tour by foot. We will go on a Vespa.'

'That's actually really cool!' I mean, don't get me wrong, I was also a little terrified. The idea of riding a Vespa in Italy did kind of freak me out, but I was sure Lorenzo would be up for driving. Then all I'd have to do was hold on tight. I could think of worse ways to spend the morning…

'Glad you are happy with this idea.'

'I am! I thought we were going to queue up to visit museums and all the landmarks.'

Lorenzo rolled his eyes.

'Of course not! *I know you.* You have been to *Firenze*

twice before already and visit these places. And I also know that you do not really enjoy looking at art or these things. For you is not exciting. I promised this weekend we will have fun, so is exactly what we will do!'

I threw my arms around him.

'You're the best! Thank you!'

'Ah, is nothing.' He kissed me gently on the lips. 'You deserve. I hope you enjoy.'

Lorenzo held me tight as our guide, Viola, briefed us on the safety procedures and how the Vespa worked and gave us our helmets. She would lead the tour and we'd follow behind. We even had a two-way radio to stay in contact.

At 9 a.m. sharp we were ready to go. Lorenzo sat at the front, gripping the handlebars, and I sat behind him. Then we were off!

We left Florence in a swarm of Vespas, heading along the riversides and tree-lined roads, climbing up and up, higher and higher into the Tuscan hills. Then we made our first stop. *Wow*. As we parked, we took in the amazing panoramic views of Florence beneath us, marvelling at the colourful rooftops and the iconic red dome of the cathedral in the distance. I may have been here twice, but I'd never seen the city like this before.

'Want me to take your photo?' asked Viola.

'Yes please!' I handed her my phone. Lorenzo and I posed in front of our Vespa, with the epic views as our backdrop.

The photos looked great.

After hopping back on to our bikes, Viola took us for a quick visit inside what was apparently one of Florence's oldest churches, then we set off again, winding our way through some narrow streets.

The temperature had risen since we'd first arrived in the city earlier this morning. But as Lorenzo picked up speed and the breeze blew through my hair, it felt perfect. I wrapped my arms tighter around his waist and rested my chin on his back.

It wasn't long before we made another pit stop to admire the lush greenery and the fantastic surroundings. By now, the sun was shining brightly. It was so peaceful. You could even hear the birds singing. It was like the scenery from a postcard. I couldn't resist taking a dozen more photos.

Our group weaved down tiny roads, nestled in between castles, passing through the hilly countryside before parking up to visit a vineyard in Chianti. This was amazing.

Then, after we'd driven a bit further, we stopped at a secluded terrace.

'Time for lunch,' Lorenzo said. We sat down at the tables with the other people on the tour and a waiter brought out boards of ham, cheese and baskets of bread. Since living in Italy, I'd slowly learned to enjoy more cold cuts (prosciutto was my favourite) and cheese (well, mainly just mozzarella), so this didn't freak me out as much as it used to.

'*Mmm.*' I bit into the bruschetta.

'Is good, no?'

'Definitely.'

'So, are you enjoying?'

'I'm having the best time—thank you! I've never been one for motorbikes, scooters or whatever the correct name for a Vespa is, but it's been brilliant. Being on the road, surrounded by such wonderful scenery, with the wind blowing through my hair and my arms wrapped around you, I *love* it. It's pretty romantic. Riding on that scooter, I felt so free. So alive. It was just so... I don't know.... *exhilarating*!'

Lorenzo grinned. 'Make me very happy to hear you say that.'

'I thought I'd be scared, but actually, I felt really safe.'

'*Bene*. Is settled.'

'What is?'

'The journey back. You can drive us to Florence.'

'What?' My eyes popped out of my head. 'Me? Drive? *No. No, no, no, nooo!* I couldn't do that!'

'Why not? You just said you felt safe, no?'

'Yes. With *you* driving. With my arms wrapped around *you*.'

'Is simple. Will be fun. I ask Viola to show you again and I am sure we have time to practice quickly before we go.'

'But...but what about the Chianti?' I glared longingly at the bottle on the table that was from the vineyard we'd passed through. 'I was going to have some wine with my lunch.'

'*Tranquilla, mi amore*. We have plenty of time to drink later, when we get back to *Firenze*. But this afternoon, is about fun, *sì*? Will be good for you to ride Vespa. Move from your zone of comfort.'

'Oh what the hell!' I said, my stomach fluttering. 'I'll give it a go.'

After Viola briefed me and I'd had a quick spin on the secluded road, I felt a lot better. Lorenzo was right. It really *was* easy. And it was automatic, so that made driving it a breeze. We all set off, winding down the narrow lanes, back past the stone houses and vineyards getting lower and lower until the centre of Florence was in sight.

Look at me. Driving a Vespa in Italy. *Very cool.* I felt like a real local.

Before we knew it we were back at the Authentic Tours HQ. Naturally, there was a lot more traffic than when we arrived, but it felt so good to be in a vibrant city again. As pretty as Chiorno was, it was too quiet for me. I missed London. My friends, my family, the familiarity. The *buzz.* At the same time, driving a Vespa back home couldn't compare to doing it in Italy, so being here had its advantages.

After I parked the Vespa, we took off our helmets, then said goodbye to Viola and the rest of the group.

'Thanks again.' I kissed Lorenzo on the cheek. 'I've had a brilliant day.'

'*Day?* Is only three in the afternoon. The day is just beginning. We have more activities to do.'

'*More?*' We'd had a fantastic tour of Florence and the Tuscan hills, plus eaten lunch. What more could there be?

'Of course! First, we will go back to the hotel...' He wrapped his arms around me and gave me a long kiss on the lips.

I could have been wrong, but the moment Lorenzo said the words *back to the hotel* and his lips touched mine, I could have sworn I felt a little tingle. You know—of *desire.*

For the first time in months, we were alone and had enjoyed a few magical, carefree, uninterrupted hours together. Marta had messaged Lorenzo earlier to say Leo was fine. Robyn had emailed to say she'd had another chat with the team and all was well. So I was feeling relaxed. No worrying about feed times, the business, cleaning up or *anything*. Just having fun. It felt pretty great. Maybe I'd worried unnecessarily this morning. Perhaps I *was* ready to get back in the game again after all?

We checked into the hotel. Lorenzo led us up to our room, then opened the door.

It was stunning. As soon as you entered, there was a stylish bathroom right next to the door, then in the main room there were beautiful frescoed ceilings (the fancy way of saying ceilings with pretty murals painted on them), large windows with—*wow*—a view of the Duomo itself, parquet flooring and a bed: a very, very big bed. Fit for a queen and a couple of lovers. A bit like the giant hotel bed on that failed trip to Florence.

Was this it? Was today the day? Was this where *it* would finally happen? Where I'd lose my MARGINITY. Again?

After months of not feeling ready to do anything, I was excited that earlier I'd felt a tiny urge. Then we'd entered this grand room, with this grand bed, so all the signs were looking positive. Maybe it would be just like a film. We'd suddenly become overcome with passion, throw our clothes off frantically, then dive onto it. Just like we used to. I'd feel normal again and confident and we'd be at it like rabbits the whole weekend. That would be amazing.

Yeah.

If it wasn't so terrifying…

My stomach plummeted.

Suddenly a wave of fear washed over me.

My head began to swim with thoughts of all the things that could go wrong.

'I, er… I'm just going to the bathroom,' I said.

'Okay. Try not to be long. I have plans for us…' He winked as he whipped off his jeans and top then flopped back onto the bed. 'And, Soph?'

'Yes?'

'You will not need any clothes. Just your underwear, *si*?'

'Right… o-okay,' I replied before shutting the bathroom door and resting my back against it.

Shit, shit, shit.

Lorenzo wanted me to come out in my underwear. In broad daylight. There was no way he could see me like this. With the way my body looked.

I know I said I thought I felt a tingle earlier, but now when I think about it, maybe it was just because I needed the loo. My weak bladder playing tricks on me.

Lorenzo seemed like he was really up for it. He couldn't get his clothes off quick enough, and now he was there: waiting for me. On the bed.

Christ.

I had a wee, washed my hands, then sat on the edge of the bath, trying to calm myself down.

'You coming?' Lorenzo called out.

'Yep…,' I said, trying to sound normal and not like my insides were tied in knots.

I couldn't hide in here forever. I wrapped a large bath towel around me to cover my stomach and thighs.

Here goes nothing…

I know we'd had a nice day out, and normally afternoon sex in a hotel with my hot boyfriend would be a classic fantasy, but not today.

Not yet.

As stupid as it would sound, I'd have to explain to Lorenzo that even though I was feeling much more relaxed and even though it had now been six months, I still wasn't ready.

Fingers crossed he would understand…

CHAPTER NINETEEN

'Lorenzo, I don't think I can…' As I walked out of the bathroom, I saw a big fluffy robe laid out on the bed and some matching white slippers. Lorenzo was sat upright on the crisp bedsheets in his own robe.

Oh.

'You do not think you can?' He frowned. 'Can what?'

'Um… nothing. Forget it. Nice robes!' I stroked the dressing gown enthusiastically, hoping I'd managed to change the subject.

'So for activity two, we will have massage. You have been very stressed. Will be good for you to relax. I know you used to have in London and you like, so I thought was something we can do today. *Together*. What do you think?'

I gave him the biggest hug.

'God, I love you.'

'I am guessing you are happy,' he chuckled.

'More than you could ever know.'

There I was jumping to conclusions. Thinking he wanted to have his wicked way, when really he had planned something to make me feel better. *What a relief.* I really must learn not to freak out so much.

The massage was bliss. Exactly what I needed. Luckily the room was dimly lit and Lorenzo had his eyes closed so he couldn't see my body. And because I was laid on my front, my stretch marks and stomach weren't exposed. Thankfully the towel was always strategically placed around my bottom and thighs so he couldn't see my cellulite either.

I didn't seem to mind the therapist touching my body. There was something nurturing about her, which instantly put me at ease. Plus she must see women of all shapes and sizes every day, so wouldn't judge me.

It did get a bit embarrassing at one point, though. I was so relaxed that I drifted off. But I woke up suddenly because I heard some loud snoring, then I realised that it was me. *Oops...*

After our massages, I returned to our room to sleep for a couple of hours whilst Lorenzo went out to make some arrangements for the rest of our weekend. If what he had planned was anything like today, I was in for a treat.

In the evening, we walked along Ponte Santa Trinita, a beautiful old stone bridge that crossed the River Arno, and watched the sun set over Florence.

'This is stunning,' I said as I took photos on my phone. 'I didn't get to see this last time.'

'I thought so,' sighed Lorenzo. 'I am glad I finally am with you properly in *Firenze* this time...'

'Yeah. My last trip was kind of a disappointment.'

'I know.' He wrapped his arm around me. 'Which is why it was important for me to make this visit special. When you think of this city, I want you to have good memories. Of days like today. Not me having to work and letting you down. Not what happened before.'

I thought about that failed weekend. A few weeks after we'd first met, I'd returned to Italy to see Lorenzo, but he'd stood me up at the last minute and I was left in Florence all alone. Back then I'd thought I'd never speak to him again. Considering all the ups and downs, it was amazing that we'd even come this far. If you'd have told me when I was standing on the freezing cold platform, soaking wet from the rain on that disastrous visit to Cinque Terre, that less than two years later I'd be back in Florence with Lorenzo beside me, or that I'd be living with him in Italy and we'd have a child together, I wouldn't have believed you. *Crazy.*

'It's in the past. We're building our future now as a family. You, me and Leo. We'll have to bring him here and create even more happy memories together.'

'For sure.' He kissed me gently on the lips.

'I'd love to bring my family here too. Well, if Mum and Dad ever decide to get on a plane and come over,' I sighed. 'Roxy and Bella would love it here, though. Especially the food.'

'*Sì.*' Lorenzo smiled. 'You talk about food, so are you ready for dinner?'

'Definitely. I'm starving!'

We took a nice stroll back into the centre and headed to a restaurant that Lorenzo used to work at. The staff gave us the VIP treatment, bringing out enough dishes to feed an army.

Then we stopped off for gelato. I nearly fainted when I saw a little blackboard on the counter saying that today's special was *The Sophia.* Lorenzo had arranged for his friend who owned the gelateria to create a special selection of flavours in one cone, including a scoop of pistachio, chocolate, berries, strawberry and coconut. Each one of them my favourites. I was supposed to be controlling what I ate, but what the hell. I was on holiday. Calories didn't count. It was okay to give myself a break sometimes and have some treats. Even so, I wasn't sure I'd be able to finish all five scoops by myself, so asked Lorenzo to share it with me.

I'd starting tucking into the coconut one first and seconds later, Lorenzo bent over with laughter.

'*What?*' I'd asked.

'Imagine if Mamma could see you now!' he chuckled. I caught my reflection in the shop window. The white ice cream was smeared around my mouth. My face turned to stone. 'Too soon?' Lorenzo smirked. 'Come on, Soph, is funny! Is important to joke about these things!' I couldn't keep my serious face any longer and burst into a fit of giggles.

'If your mamma saw me like this, she'd definitely pass out.'

We belly laughed about it all the way back to the hotel. That encounter with Marta was definitely the gift that kept on giving. I was glad I could smile about it now. I don't think it was something either of us would forget in a hurry…

After brushing our teeth, we climbed into bed. Even though we could have laid there with our arms stretched out wide and still not touched each other, Lorenzo snuggled up behind me. And it wasn't long before I felt him.

I sighed in my head. I wish I'd been able to bottle that flash of desire I had this afternoon and multiply it. I wished that I had a switch I could just turn on to—*you know*, turn me on. That I could simply press a *time to feel sexy* button and like an engine, my libido would roar into action and start firing on all cylinders. I wished that I had the energy to climb on top of him and go for hours. Actually no. I wasn't even greedy. A quickie would be ideal. We could do the deed and then be off to sleep in ten minutes flat.

Gosh. I used to hate it when it was over too quickly. Now I was willing it to finish in less time than it took me to eat a slice of Lorenzo's cake (which, for the record, wasn't very long at all).

When I'd come to Florence during that nightmare bank holiday trip and had to sleep on that big bed, alone, I'd wished that he was there. Dreamt of all the things Lorenzo and I could have done together. Yet here I was, with his hard-on pressed against my bum, and I didn't want it. I'd rather sleep. How terrible was that?

But the weekend was young. It had only just started and with two more days in Florence, there was still time for me to get my mojo back.

Who knows? With any luck, maybe tomorrow would be the day…

CHAPTER TWENTY

'Y ou okay?' I asked Lorenzo as he checked his phone for what seemed like the hundredth time in the last ten minutes.

'*Sì*. I am just waiting for a… an important call.'

We'd already spoken to Marta first thing in the morning to check in on Leo, so it couldn't be that.

'Oh, okay. Is it to do with today?' I cocked my head to the side, hoping he'd give me a clue about where we were going.

'*Sì*…' He grinned.

Hmm. I wracked my brains, trying to think. We'd been on a tour of the city, he knew I didn't really fancy going to museums, so what else could we be doing? It was another sunny day, so maybe we'd go for a walk through Boboli Gardens. *That would be nice.* As it was almost half eleven, lunchtime wasn't too far away, so perhaps he'd arranged a picnic and was waiting for a call from one of the chefs at the restaurant to say the food was ready to collect. The mind boggled.

On second thoughts, did it really matter that I didn't know what we'd be doing? Rather than thinking about what the plan for the day was, I decided it would be nice to just go with the flow for a change. Let Lorenzo take the reins and just allow myself to be surprised. *Yes.*

Whilst I was waiting, I could send a few photos to my family, Roxy and Bella and tell them about our brilliant day yesterday. *What a luxury.* I couldn't even remember the last time I had time to sit down and message them all properly, without having to worry about Leo or work. Sometimes being able to do the simplest things meant so much. This taking time out thing was a good idea.

First I'd reply to Holly's text. She'd messaged yesterday about Umberto, texting me excitedly in the morning as Umberto had said she could finally come round to his house that evening, but then he'd cancelled at the last minute. Holly asked if I thought she should be worried that he hadn't introduced her to any of his friends or family since she'd arrived.

Um, yes.

I was always a bit concerned that whenever they met, all they ever did was eat pizza in the car and then drive somewhere to have sex. At first I'd thought because Holly was young, maybe she didn't want something serious, but seeing as she'd left uni to be with him, that didn't ring true. Alarm bells were definitely going off in my head. Pretty sure Holly wouldn't have moved to another country if she knew she was only going to see Umberto for a bit of back-seat nookie. I quickly typed out a message.

Me

Sorry for the delayed reply. Full on (fun!) itinerary with Lorenzo in Florence.

I say trust your gut. You moving to Italy to be with him was a big deal and showed a lot of commitment. That you were serious about the relationship, so have a think about what Umberto has done/is doing to show he feels the same way…

I know Holly would have split my one text message into fifty short ones, but *hey*. I was old-school. Hopefully that'd give her some food for thought…

Now time to send some pics.

Lorenzo jumped up and went into the bathroom. Just as I'd selected the photos to send, there was a knock at the door.

'Can you get that, please, *amore*?' he shouted.

'Sure.' Probably housekeeping, wanting to know if we were going out so they could clean our room.

I hopped off the bed and opened the door.

'Surprise!'

OMFG.

I blinked.

Then blinked again.

Then I screamed.

'Bella? Roxy? Oh my God!!'

'Soph!'

They both threw their arms around me and we all jumped up and down with excitement.

'How did you? When did you…?'

Lorenzo came from the bathroom grinning like a Cheshire cat.

'I know you miss your friends, so…' He shrugged his shoulders.

'I can't believe it!'

I pulled him into our huddle and gave him a big squeeze.

'We are *so* happy to see you!' said Bella.

'Me too! I have missed you guys so much.'

Both of them looked well. As always, Roxy was the glamour puss with her long fiery red hair, matching bold pillar-box lipstick, a mini skirt and knee-high boots.

At five-eleven, Bella towered over Roxy. She was wearing skinny jeans and a patterned green top with her brown curly hair tumbling past her shoulders. She looked naturally beautiful, with just a flick of black eyeliner, mascara and a slick of clear lip gloss.

'By the sounds of it, you've been having a bit of a crappy time, so we thought an FTA session was in order. An *international FTA session*!'

Lorenzo must have told them I was feeling down… I hadn't wanted to worry them, but boy was I glad they were here and that I'd finally be able to talk to them properly.

'Yes! I could really do with some food, therapy and alcohol. Does that sound bad seeing as it's only eleven-thirty?'

'Hell no! By the time we get to the restaurant, it'll almost be midday. And anyway, it's been ages, so even if it was eight in the morning it'd be fine.'

'I like your thinking!' I turned to Lorenzo. 'So I'm guessing these ladies were your *important call*?'

'You guess right.' He smirked. 'And that means is time for me to go.'

'You don't have to leave! We've got a lot of catching up to do, but I reckon we'll be back by, I dunno, maybe four or five this afternoon?'

'Not likely! More like five a.m. tomorrow!' cackled Roxy. 'We're under strict instructions to show you a good time, so that's *exactly* what we're going to do.'

'Yeah. We didn't fly all the way to Italy to just spend a few hours with you,' said Bella. 'Our flight doesn't leave until tomorrow afternoon, so we're going to make the most of it.'

'Cool! Okay! Thanks, darling!' I kissed Lorenzo on the lips.

'*Prego*. I will drive back soon and go to work. Tomorrow Flavio will come round for lunch, but let me know what time you want to leave and I will come and take you home.'

I was glad Lorenzo would be having time out too. Even though we were a couple, it was important to do things that we enjoyed as individuals, and I knew that as well as working on new recipes, he also liked watching football and having a beer with the boys. Flavio was one of the few childhood friends Lorenzo had left in the town. The rest had gone to live in bigger cities in Italy or around the world.

'Are you sure?' I said. 'I can find my own way back home.'

I was lucky enough to be spending time with my friends, so I didn't want Lorenzo to cut his time short with Flavio just to come and pick me up.

'Of course! You had better go. The table has been booked for twelve-fifteen for lunch. Bella and Roxy have the details. Enjoy. Mamma and me will take good care of Leo, so do not worry. *Ti amo*.'

'I love you too. And thank you so much again!' I grabbed my phone and handbag, then gave him a long hug. It was so lovely for him to arrange all of this for me.

'Come on, Soph.' Roxy gently pulled me away from Lorenzo. 'Now's not the time for PDA. You'll see him again in twenty-four hours. And I'm sure you'll have time to stop off and get up to no good in the car on the way home!' She cackled again.

'Roxy!' said Bella.

'Nothing wrong with a bit of bump and grind on the back seat! *Ciao*, Lorenzo!' Roxy linked arms with me and Bella as we left the hotel room and shut the door behind us. 'So, young lady, how was yesterday? How are things *really* going with Lorenzo, Leo, the business and of course with getting back *down to business* in the bedroom? We've got so much to catch up on. And no holding back this time. I want to hear about *everything*!'

CHAPTER TWENTY-ONE

'That's fucking hilarious!' said Roxy.

'It wasn't. It was bloody mortifying!'

We were about to order lunch and I was filling them in on what Roxy was now calling Spunkgate: when Marta had caught us in the act.

Lorenzo had booked a table at an authentic restaurant that was hidden within an old church. With its white walls, archways, and dark wooden tables and chairs, it felt very Florentine.

'I don't know why you're so embarrassed. It's perfectly natural and good for you. It's definitely *not* healthy for Lorenzo to be backing up his jizz for so long. And I wouldn't worry about getting it on your face. Apparently it's really great for your skin. Has moisturising properties. They call it a *facial* for a reason!' She cackled.

'Roxy!' shouted Bella.

She hadn't changed.

'You'll get over it. Actually, I thought there was a chance we would walk in and interrupt you lovebirds today because we arrived at the hotel a few minutes earlier than planned. Bella said we should wait until eleven-forty, like we'd agreed with Lorenzo, but I was too excited to see you!'

'I couldn't believe it when I opened the door and saw you standing there. It was the *best* surprise! I know I keep saying it but seriously—I've missed you both so much!'

'We've missed you too, Soph,' said Bella.

We knew we had a lot to catch up on, so decided to order. Thankfully, Lorenzo had given Roxy and Bella a list of dishes he recommended and the best wines to pair with them. He really had thought of everything.

It all looked so delicious. I personally couldn't wait to try the *linguine di pasta fresca con gamberetti e asparagi* for my *primi piatti* or first plate, which I managed to translate myself without looking at Lorenzo's notes as meaning fresh linguine with prawns and asparagus. *Go me.* My Italian vocab was growing. Asparagus always made my wee smell, but *whatever*. I was sure it was worth it.

Bella was itching to taste the creamed zucchini soup with octopus and pasta pockets stuffed with pear and Gorgonzola cheese, whereas Roxy wanted to get stuck into the crostini toscani for her *antipasti* (starters) plus Florentine steak for her mains, or *secondi piatti* as the Italians would say.

Now that our drinks and food were sorted, we could get back to chatting.

'So...' Roxy rubbed her hands together excitedly. 'Come on, then: *spill*! Yesterday did you have an *amazing* night of passion? Were you guys swinging from the chandeliers? I saw the size of that bed!' Her eyes widened. 'You probably spent hours rolling around on it. That's why you look so tired. Bet you two were gagging for it after not being alone for so long. Must have been a sex-fest!'

'Well, no…not exactly…'

'What do you mean *not exactly*? That was prime time, Soph. You're a mum now. These opportunities to go at it without a screaming baby or nosey mother-in-law interrupting you are like gold dust. Please don't tell me you had a night alone with your Italian stallion and you didn't do the deed?'

'Nope. And to be honest we haven't *done the deed* as you call it since—since, er, Leo was born.' I guessed it was time to start telling them the truth about how things were going here. Starting with my non-existent sex life…

'WTF!! But Leo is what? Four months old now, isn't he?'

'Six.'

'Six? You haven't had sex for six months?'

'Keep your voice down, Roxy!' I replied.

Jeez.

If Lorenzo knew we were going to be chatting about stuff like this, he probably wouldn't have recommended we dine in a former church. This conversation was far from holy…

'*Bloody Nora!!* No wonder Lorenzo is spraying his spunk like a fully loaded machine gun. Poor guy must have been like a giant firework waiting to explode. *Six months!*'

'It's not unusual for a woman to not want to have sex after having a baby, Roxy.' Bella rolled her eyes.

'Exactly!' I said. 'Childbirth isn't a walk in the park and my hormones are all over the place. I'm always tired. The only thing I want to do in bed is sleep. And if you think I look tired after the first night I've had eight hours of uninterrupted sleep in months, then I hate to think what you'd have thought if you saw me two days ago.'

'Thank God I didn't have children. I mean, I heard your sex life goes down the toilet after having kids, but I didn't think that would happen to you.'

'Well, it has,' I huffed.

'Six months isn't actually that long.' Bella rested her hand on my shoulder reassuringly.

'Er, it's half a year. I thought your MARGIN days were over, Soph, but yet here we are again. Talk about déjà vu!'

Tell me about it.

'I already feel bad enough about my lack of libido, Roxy, I don't need you sex-shaming me.' This was exactly why I never told them the truth about how things were going whenever we messaged.

'Sorry, darling. I'm just a bit shocked, that's all. Mainly because of the way you guys were. When you got together you were always at it like rabbits. Like that time you went AWOL for days and didn't even message us. And although I wasn't a fan of Lorenzo when you first hooked up, he's proved himself to be a pretty good bf and baby daddy. *So far anyway*. Still early days… And he hasn't let himself go like some blokes do. He's still fit, so I just don't get it?'

'That makes two of us.'

'Don't you fancy him anymore?'

'I do. I really do. It's just… I don't know. Everything's stopped working down there.'

'Have you *tried*, Soph?' asked Bella.

'God, no! I'm too scared.'

'Scared of what?' Bella put her hand on mine.

'Of the pain, bleeding... swallowing him whole. I mean Lorenzo's a big boy, but Leo was almost nine pounds. And after pushing him out, my vagina must be the size of a moon crater. If we have sex, Lorenzo might disappear inside me. Never to be seen again!'

Roxy bent over with laughter.

'Come on, Soph!' said Bella. 'You know full well it springs back to shape and size after a few weeks. Well, *more or less*. Either way, there's no danger of that.'

'But how does it feel to you, though?' asked Roxy. 'Does it feel all big and saggy—you know, when you touch yourself?'

'You've *got* to be joking. I haven't done that.' I winced. Just the thought of it made me want to break out into a cold sweat.

'What?!' Roxy shouted again.

God, it really wasn't a good idea to have this conversation in a public place.

'So not only have you not had any nookie, you haven't even taken yourself to pleasure world either? *Good grief.* At least when Rich wasn't giving you any, you were getting some from your Rampant Rabbit. *Oh, Soph*. This isn't sounding good *at all*. Why aren't you doing any DIY?'

'I told you, Rox. I just haven't felt the urge.'

'It's important to make time for sex, though. It's a basic need. A critical part of a decent relationship.'

'When I had Paul, I didn't feel like it for ages either,' said Bella. 'So you're not alone. After going through childbirth and then adjusting to being a mum, sex is the last thing you're thinking about. But once I stopped breastfeeding and we started to try a bit more often, the desire started to come back.'

'Yeah, I've heard breastfeeding affects it. We're starting Leo on solids next week, so hopefully that'll help. He's already been having formula, which was handy for this weekend—I just gave Marta a tub to use. Should make life easier all round.'

'Sounds like a good plan. I put Paul on formula after a couple of months. I found breastfeeding too painful.'

'Tell me about it.'

'I have to say, you guys sound crazy,' said Roxy. 'Both your kids are cute and all that, but honestly, I don't get it. You carry the baby around for nine months, which must be *so* uncomfortable. Then you have to go through the agony of childbirth, when the baby comes and rips your hoo-ha to pieces. After that, you spend your days and nights wiping up their sick and cleaning their arse. You have to force yourself to function with almost zero sleep, and then on top of that, you lose your libido and can't have sex for years. Tell me: why did you want to have kids again?'

When she put it like that, it sounded like a good question. But, no. I was glad I'd had Leo.

'Because it's one of the best and most rewarding things in the world,' said Bella.

'Yeah, it's hard work and exhausting, but when I've got Leo in my arms staring back at me, when he smiles or lets out a little laugh, it melts my heart. And when I see how much joy he brings to Lorenzo too, it just makes everything worthwhile.' I smiled, picturing the two of them together.

'If you say so, ladies,' scoffed Roxy. 'I'll have to take your word for it…'

My phone pinged. I hoped everything was okay with Leo. I reached in my bag and touched the screen. Ah! It was a message from Geli.

Geli

Ciao, Sophia! On my way to Firenze.

Geli

Want to meet up this evening with your friends?

Geli

I can take you to some cool places. Will be fun!

Geli was another one who sent multiple messages when everything could very easily fit into one.

'Ladies, do we have plans for this evening?'

'Yes! To have fun and basically get you drunk,' laughed Roxy. 'Why?'

'My friend Geli is on her way to Florence and wondered if we fancied her taking us out on the town. What do you think?'

'Geli? Is she the Italian teacher you mentioned?' said Bella.

'Yep. That's the one. She's really fun. I reckon you'll like her.'

'Sounds good to me!' said Roxy. 'She can take us to all the best bars and then we can go clubbing!'

'Clubbing?' My eyes widened. 'I haven't been clubbing since, since… I can't even remember. Since my twenties, maybe? I'm too old for that.'

'Bollocks! If you haven't been for twenty years, that's *exactly* why we definitely have to go. And you're not too old. We're in our prime. Forties are the new twenties.'

'That's what all the forty-somethings say!'

'That's settled, then. We're going clubbing. I suggest you go back to the hotel and get a couple hours' sleep, young lady, because tonight we are going out on the town, and if I have my way, you won't be going to bed until tomorrow morning!'

CHAPTER TWENTY-TWO

'Geli, this is Bella and Roxy. Roxy and Bella, this is Geli.' Geli stepped inside my hotel room. She looked colourful as always, dressed in a bright red velvet skater dress with tights and biker boots.

'*Ciao!* Nice to meet you, Bella,' said Geli, kissing her on both cheeks. 'And *Roxy…*' Her eyes widened and she ran her hands through her blue hair, which was bolder than usual. She must have coloured it this morning. '*Hello…piacere.* You are even more beautiful than the photos Sophia showed me.' She took Roxy's hand and kissed it gently.

Looks like someone has an admirer…

'*Grazie!*' said Roxy.

'*Prego.* So,' said Geli, still clearly distracted by Roxy, 'I see you ladies are all dressed up and ready for some fun in *Firenze.*'

'We certainly are!' Roxy winked. Such a flirt.

Luckily I'd packed a little black dress and some heels, just in case Lorenzo and I went out for a fancy dinner.

Thought it would be good to make an effort and dress up as we hadn't been out on a date in so long. Thankfully, as it was one of my early maternity dresses, it was able to accommodate the extra weight I'd gained and was nice and comfortable. Not sure I could say the same about these heels. It had been ages since I'd worn any.

Roxy of course was in her signature leather skirt and knee-high boots, and Bella had on some smart black trousers and a sparkly silver top. I couldn't remember the last time we'd had a proper night out together.

As much as I missed Leo, I had to admit that it felt good to spend some time away from being a mum. Lorenzo said Leo was absolutely fine when he'd stopped by Marta's to see him, so that helped me to relax even more. I had to admit that there were benefits to having her around to babysit. Without Marta, I wouldn't get the chance to do my Italian lessons, I wouldn't have met Geli and I wouldn't have come away on this weekend. So although I knew we weren't going to become best buddies anytime this century, I was grateful for her help. I'd had an amazing day with Lorenzo and was having such a fun time with the girls today. And now that Geli was taking us out for a night on the town, something told me more excitement was on the cards…

'*Bene*. Let us go.'

We set off down the street, heading towards the centre.

'So, where are we off to tonight, then, Geli?' said Bella.

'First, we will go for *aperitivo*. It is a very important ritual.'

'Isn't that just like happy hour?'

'Pff!' said Geli. 'It is better. In Italy we like to have

THE MIDDLE-AGED VIRGIN IN ITALY   175

drinks and snacks to open the stomach and prepare it for dinner. We will start by going to a few bars, then have dinner and after that—well, we will see.'

'We were thinking it would be fun to go clubbing,' said Roxy. 'I fancy a good boogie, and Soph here needs to let her hair down and get a little release, seeing as she's not getting it in other ways.' There went her famous cackle.

'Christ, Roxy!' I slapped my forehead. 'You're obsessed!'

'What! *Just saying.* Dancing will be good for you.'

As much as I liked Geli, I wasn't sure if I was comfortable with her knowing about my sex life, or lack of it.

'*Perfetto!* I know a great club that we can go to. Tonight will be fun!'

Three bars and two restaurants later, we were on our way to the club. I was surprised I was even able to stand upright.

At the first bar, Geli had ordered multiple rounds of Negroni. She joked that it was 'illegal' to come to Florence and not have one. Thank God we'd had a load of crisps, olives and chips to try and soak up the alcohol. Good thing I wouldn't have to breastfeed tomorrow either.

Around eight, we went to another bar and then another... After that we went out for dinner, followed by a pit stop at her friend's restaurant for dessert, by which point I was ready to burst. And topple over. These heels weren't made for bar and restaurant crawls. Or for holding up a very tipsy woman.

We'd arrived. The club was so hidden that if Geli hadn't taken us here, I doubt we would have been able to find it. Once we got inside, we walked down the winding staircase to the main floor. It was in an ancient crypt, with stone walls and arches, so had a lot more character than most clubs I'd been to in London.

The music was pumping from the speakers. I think it was a seventies or eighties song. The dance floor was just as retro. It had illuminated red, yellow, blue and green flashing squares, like something from *Saturday Night Fever*. Everyone seemed to be having fun, though. It didn't seem like one of those places where people just came to stand and look cool, which was good. The DJ switched to 'I Gotta Feeling' by the Black Eyed Peas and the crowd whooped. Now I was here, I was actually looking forward to shaking a leg.

~

'Look at those two!' Bella laughed as she watched Geli and Roxy on the dance floor. It was one o'clock in the morning. We'd all been dancing non-stop since we'd arrived around eleven-thirty, but now my feet were killing me, so Bella and I had come to sit down for a bit and left them to it.

Geli and Roxy were both singing at the top of their voices to Beyoncé's 'Single Ladies' and giggling as they tried to remember the next move in the routine. Queen B. would be proud. Or, more likely, smiling at how funny they were. But that's what made it great. It was so bad, it was good.

Whilst Geli was attempting the pump walk, with her left hand out in front of her like a teapot spout, Roxy was shaking her hips, dipping and bending and waving her arms in the air like a lunatic. She then started strutting around haphazardly, her face full of sexy attitude and doing the iconic side-wave hand gesture every time the song reached the chorus, pointing enthusiastically to her ring finger.

After her messy divorce, I very much doubted that Roxy wanted to be within five thousand feet of a wedding ring again, but that didn't stop her from getting well and truly into character whilst she was dancing.

It wasn't that long ago that I was single, having a nightmare getting to grips with dating apps, wondering if I'd ever find a decent guy. And now here I was, loved up with a baby. *How times change.*

I'd never really been that bothered about getting married before. Lorenzo often referred to me as his wife and I already felt like we were fully committed to each other, so we didn't really need a ceremony or a piece of paper to confirm that. But, I'll admit, if he *did* ask me, to quote a Holly-ism, I would *totally* say yes. I'd never loved a man so much in my life.

Roxy and Geli kicked their legs up in the air and let out a loud cackle.

'So funny!' said Bella. 'They're from two different countries, they only met for the first time a few hours ago, but they're getting on like a house on fire!'

'Yeah! And they both have the same dirty laugh!'

Just watching them made me smile. Beyoncé she was not, but Roxy was enjoying herself. No wonder *Strictly Come Dancing* was her favourite TV show. She was really going for it, like she was actually auditioning to be a backup dancer. Even Geli was struggling to keep up with Roxy's enthusiastic hip swinging and hand swaying. Everyone else on the dance floor seemed to find her particular version of the routine entertaining too.

A crowd started to gather around Roxy, eager to see what dazzling moves she'd do next. The DJ switched to 'Kiss' and Roxy went wild. She snatched a drink from one of the guys standing beside her, downed it in one and then started slipping and sliding around the dance floor like she was doing the moonwalk. Maybe she thought she was listening to Michael Jackson rather than Prince.

As the song reached the chorus, Roxy grew more excited.

'*Woo-hoo*! Here we go, Italian people!' she shouted. 'How's *this* for a party trick?'

Suddenly Roxy dropped down on the floor into the splits.

Whoa.

Impressive.

How an earth did she manage that? Rather her than me. After having Leo and with everything that had gone on *down there*, I'd be too worried about splitting more than my legs if I even attempted it.

Lucky Roxy's skirt was flared rather than fitted, otherwise it would have ripped. It was currently bunched up around her waist. Thank goodness she was wearing tights and dark-coloured knickers to preserve her modesty. Although I doubt she'd even given that a second thought. She was having too much fun.

Roxy threw her hands up in the air triumphantly like she'd just been given a gold medal at the Olympics.

The crowd clapped and cheered and she lapped up the adoration. It clearly was an achievement. I hadn't been that flexible since I did gymnastics at primary school. I'm sure her trips to the gym, not to mention her frequent bedroom antics, had helped… *Good for her.*

Even if I *could* stretch my legs out enough to do the splits, I'd probably have to stay rooted to the floor indefinitely. Getting down was one thing, but getting up again was another.

Uh-oh…

Houston, we have a problem.

Seemed like Roxy wasn't as flexible as I'd hoped.

She put her hands on the floor, tried to steady her body, then launch herself up again, but she couldn't move. She was stuck…

Roxy tried again, but toppled over onto her side, legs still akimbo.

Geli grabbed one of her arms and Bella and I rushed over to take the other.

'Come on, Rox,' said Bella. 'After three, let's lift her up. One, two, three…'

We hoisted Roxy up in the air.

'*Wheeeee*!' she cheered happily.

'You are *so* drunk!' laughed Bella as we carried her over to one of the chairs and sat her down.

'*Wheeee*!' she said again.

'Yeah, Rox. *Whee*! Glad to see you having fun!'

'I need to *wee*!' she said.

'*Oh!*' said Bella. 'Come on, then. Let's get you to the loo.'

I needed to go too. *As usual.* We all followed her into the ladies.

Roxy's legs seemed to have recovered, so she was almost able to walk in a straight line. *Almost…*

'Hello!' said Roxy as she walked into the toilet and past the large mirror on the wall. 'I mean *ciao*! Sorry, I'm English. Are you in the queue?'

'I don't think she's in the queue,' said Bella, trying not to laugh. You can go on ahead.' Neither of us had the heart to tell Roxy that she was talking to her own reflection... *Bless.*

Roxy stumbled off into the cubicle, pulled down her tights and knickers and plonked herself down on the loo. With the door still wide open...

'How much has she had to drink?' said Bella.

'A *lot.*'

'And God knows what she just drunk from that guy. Roxy, didn't your mum teach you to not take drinks from strangers? You don't know what was in his glass.'

'Yes, Mum,' Roxy called out.

'*Yep.* She's definitely pissed. I mean, we all are, but Roxy's also been doing shots with Geli.'

'Good thing we passed on that fourth round or we might be in here talking to our reflections too!' Bella giggled.

I may have passed, but my legs and my head didn't feel like it. I'd drunk more tonight than I probably did in a month before I was pregnant with Leo. Maybe even two. We might be laughing about Roxy, but like Bella had said, I probably wasn't that far behind her. Pretty sure the ceiling was already moving...

What was I even doing standing here? I needed to go too.

I quickly dashed into the cubicle next to Roxy's, shutting the door behind me.

'Oooh! That feels *sooo* good,' Roxy shouted. Thank God we were the only ones in here.

'I know, right? Since having Leo, I feel like I always need to go to the loo and I was just saying to myself the other day that the feeling of relief after having a wee is better than sex.'

'*What?*' Roxy shouted again. 'Soph, if that's what you think, then you need to get laid much more than I thought!'

She probably wasn't wrong. I flushed the toilet and stepped outside to wash my hands.

'*Oh! Scusa!*' gasped a woman who just walked in, passed Roxy's cubicle and got a full view of her yanking up her knickers.

Only Roxy.

'Sorry, don't mind her,' I said as Roxy finally stepped out. Bella, who was definitely the soberest out of us all, quickly pulled down Roxy's skirt, which was tucked into the back of her tights.

What was she like?

When we got back outside to the dance floor, Geli was at the table with another round of drinks.

Oh God. No way...

'Honestly, Geli, more drinks? I don't think I can.'

'Is not strong. Is almost like water…'

'It doesn't look like water!' I glanced at the yellow liquid.

'Okay, is like lemon juice. Is good for you.'

Roxy and Geli picked up their glasses and drank them swiftly. And despite just saying minutes ago that we were wise to pass on the fourth round of shots, surprisingly even Bella downed hers too. I lifted mine up cautiously and took a little sip.

Mmm. Limoncello.

My memory flashed back to that night in Tuscany when I'd propositioned Lorenzo about giving me *lessons…*

That night was *very* memorable. It was the first time I'd kissed someone after leaving my sexless relationship with Rich. And even though Lorenzo and I hadn't gone all the way, boy oh boy was it enjoyable... Lorenzo had used his magical hands and made me explode like a firework.

I did love a bit of limoncello. I supposed one tiny shot wouldn't hurt. For old times' sake...

The sweet liquid slid easily down my throat.

'*Sooo* good!' I jumped up to my feet and dived into my handbag to get my purse. 'Who wants another?'

'Yes, please!' They said in unison.

What happened to not being that far behind Roxy in the drunken stakes? Don't you think you've had quite enough to drink, Sophia?

Button it, Reasanna. How often did I get to go out, let my hair down and have a fun girls' night?

You don't need to drink excessive amounts of alcohol to have a good time, Sophia. You're going to regret this in the morning...

She was probably right, but I'd worry about that later. Right now I was going to have another shot or two of limoncello and enjoy every last sip.

~

'That's me done.' I fanned myself. It was really hot in here. 'I'm heading back to the hotel.'

'Already?' said Roxy. 'The night's still young. It's only two a.m.!'

'Exactly! And it's a miracle that I've managed to last this long.'

These days, the only time I'd be up at this hour would be to give Leo a feed.

'I guess you've done pretty well.' She shrugged her shoulders. Whilst she was a bit more coherent than she was an hour ago, I couldn't say the same about myself. As well as the ceiling moving, now the floor seemed to be shaking too... 'You okay getting back?'

'Lovely Bella is coming with me.'

'*Oo-er!*' Roxy cackled. *Honestly.* Her mind was always in the gutter. 'Okay, honey.' She gave us both a hug. 'Well, me and Geli are going to stay, so we'll see you at breakfast.'

Geli wrapped her arm tightly around Roxy's waist and stared at her all doe-eyed like a chocoholic who'd just been given a crate of Easter eggs to devour after Lent.

'Yep! Have fun, you guys.' I smirked.

Geli clearly fancied Roxy. As far as I knew, Roxy preferred men, but I wouldn't put it past her to experiment. I was sure she'd fill me in on the details later this morning…

CHAPTER TWENTY-THREE

I looked at the clock on the bedside table. It was either 4.17 a.m. or 4.27–I couldn't quite make out the numbers. Everything looked blurry. I was dying for the loo, but I felt awful. After not drinking properly for over a year, just like Reasanna had warned me, I was crazy to have so much. But I was back safe and I'd had fun, so that was the important thing. Although I didn't quite remember doing it, somehow I also managed to walk to my room, take my clothes off and get into bed.

It felt good to sleep half-naked for a change. Before, I didn't think twice about being completely in the buff, but these days I always wore a nightdress to bed to cover my lumps and bumps.

Dammit. I couldn't hold it any longer. I had to go. I threw off the duvet and got up.

Whoa. The room was spinning. *Definitely* overdid it. I blame the limoncello. The quicker I went to the toilet the quicker I could lie back down.

Steady…

I stumbled across the room. I could barely see. I rubbed my eyes. Maybe I should have put on the light. Couldn't be bothered to walk back to do that now. I'd be fine.

I stretched my hands out in front of me so that I could feel when I'd reached the door. Or at this rate, walked into a wall…

There it is. I opened the door and stepped inside.

Wow. It's bright in here!

Must be some sort of sensor as the lights weren't on a minute ago. But I could have sworn they didn't come on automatically before. I usually switched them on manually didn't I?

I rubbed my eyes again.

In fact, what's happened to my bathroom? It looked completely different. And wait. The bath and the sink had disappeared? And where was the toilet?

Oh dear.

This wasn't the bathroom…

This was the corridor.

I'd opened the wrong bloody door.

The bathroom and the room door were right next to each other. I'd mixed them up.

I was now standing in the very public corridor in just my knickers.

Shit. Shit. Shit.

I quickly wrapped my arms across my chest to shield my boobs.

Someone could come out of their room at any minute.

Oh God.

I looked down. My stomach hung over my knickers. My stretch marks were there for all to see and my thighs were dimpled with cellulite. The thought of Lorenzo seeing me was bad enough, but strangers? That would be even worse.

I tried opening the room door again, but of course it was locked. The only way to get back in would be to go to reception and ask for a key. But I couldn't do that. Then the hotel staff would see me too.

I scanned the walls. I hoped they didn't have CCTV, otherwise there was probably some security guy sat in a basement laughing at me right now.

Roxy and Bella.

I scanned my brain trying to remember their room numbers. I knew they'd got separate rooms as Bella reckoned Roxy might hook up with a guy and didn't want their bedroom acrobatics to keep her up all night. I thought Bella had said her room was on the floor below, but I was pretty sure Roxy was on the same floor as me. Room 204 or 214? Or maybe it was 240…

Think, think, think.

The only way to know was to try…

'Roxy…?' I called out as I cautiously knocked on the first door. 'Roxy?'

I was just about to leave when a bleary-eyed woman opened it. A woman who wasn't Roxy. She looked me up and down with disgust.

'Who are you?' At least she spoke English. 'Bob, why is there a naked woman at our door at four in the morning? I thought we talked about this…' She scowled.

'Sorry…I'm so sorry. I've got the wrong room number.' I rushed off but could hear the woman arguing with him. *Oops.* I felt bad about waking them up and also being the cause of a domestic, but I needed to find Roxy.

Time to try 214…

Please let this be her room, I said, crossing my legs. It was bad enough being almost naked. I didn't want to make the situation worse by wetting myself.

'Well, *hello there…*' said a creepy-looking man dressed only in Y-fronts. He licked his lips. *Gross.*

'Sorry…' I ran off again. This was mortifying.

Suddenly I spotted a silver tray on the floor outside of a room. If there was a napkin on there, I could use it to try and cover my top half and then I could hide my stomach with my arms.

Yes! I was in luck.

I bent down to pick it up.

'Is that you, Soph?' I spun around to see Roxy and Geli stumbling down the hallway arm in arm. 'Thought I recognised that arse,' she cackled.

'God, am I glad to see you!' I jumped up and ran towards her.

'*Steady!* Crikey, there must be something in the air tonight as I seem to be attracting a *lot* of love from the ladies.' She laughed again.

'What happened?' said Geli. She was also wasted, but was slightly more upright than Roxy.

'Locked myself out by mistake. Can I come to your room, Roxy, and borrow some clothes so I can go to reception and get a key? I can't let anyone see my horrible body.'

'*Horrible?*' said Geli. 'Why do you say it is horrible? You are beautiful. If I had body like yours I would not wear any clothes.'

'Yeah, Soph,' slurred Roxy. 'What's wrong?'

'Look at this…and this,' I said, pointing to my stretch

marks, my saggy stomach and wobbly thighs. 'It's a mess. I've let myself go and I need to sort it out. But anyway, can we go to your room now, please? Before anyone else sees me? And before I wet myself?'

'Sure.' Roxy fumbled in her bag and then pulled out the keycard. 'It's room 241. Here.' She whipped off her red vest top and handed it to me. She was now just in her bra. 'I'm not bothered about showing my body. You shouldn't be either, but if you feel better covering up, then take it and go on ahead to my room. When you get to the end of the corridor, turn left.'

'Thanks!' I said, grabbing the vest from her hands, turning my back to Roxy and Geli, facing the wall so they couldn't see my breasts, then slipping it over my head.

I knew Roxy was right. I shouldn't be ashamed, but I couldn't help it. I'd lost my body confidence. Maybe one day I'd get it back, but for now, it was best all round if I kept myself covered up.

CHAPTER TWENTY-FOUR

M*y head.*
It felt like someone had run a steamroller over it and my mouth was drier than the Sahara Desert.

There was a reason I didn't ever drink this much. As well as being a lightweight, I couldn't handle the hangover afterwards.

Back in the day, I used to be sensible and guzzle a load of water before I went to sleep and then I'd be okay-ish in the morning. But I'd been in no fit state to do that last night, so I'd have to suffer the consequences.

Still, it could have been worse. If Roxy and Geli hadn't spotted me, I could be sleeping half-naked outside my room door right now. Or be recovering from the embarrassment of going to reception with just a serviette covering my boobs. In the grand scheme of things, I was lucky.

There was a knock at the door. Must be Bella. I think I remember her saying she'd call for me to go for breakfast together. Might be better for her to head down alone, as I needed to at least wash my face first, express some milk because my boobs were feeling full and, seeing as I still only had my knickers on, get dressed.

I reached for my dressing gown, wrapped it tightly around me, then opened the door.

'Surprise!' said Roxy and Bella.

'What the…?' They barged through the door, whipped off their dressing gowns and stood next to each other with their hands on their hips, wearing just their underwear. 'What are you doing here and why are you both standing there in your undies?'

'Well!' Roxy folded her arms. 'I really didn't like the way you were talking about your body earlier. Seems like working in beauty PR has given you some sort of warped perception of what *real* women look like. So we thought you needed a little reminder…'

'Definitely,' said Bella. 'I was surprised when Roxy told me what happened. I thought because you work behind the scenes and you know all about the airbrushing that goes on, you'd be the last person to buy into that nonsense.'

'Of course I know it's all fake. It's just…' I plonked myself down on the bed. 'I always thought that I could be some sort of super mum who'd be able to get back into shape. Not straight away, of course, and I didn't think I'd be able to look *exactly* how I did before I was pregnant, but I thought I'd at least be making *some* progress. I don't get it. I've been exercising every day, trying to control my portion sizes and cut back on sweet treats—well, not this weekend obviously—but the weight just isn't shifting. And I own a bloody beauty PR agency which gives me access to all the best lotions and potions, so I've been slathering on oils and creams religiously since I was pregnant to avoid getting stretch marks and I'm *still* covered in them.'

'But that's normal! And you're still gorgeous,' said Bella. 'Look at us. We've both got stretch marks either from losing weight or having a baby. And name me one woman you know who doesn't have cellulite.'

'Or flabby bits!' said Roxy, wobbling her thighs. 'But do our bodies look horrible to you?'

'No, of course not!' I scoffed.

'Well, then! And yours doesn't either.'

'Look, I know I shouldn't feel like I have to look perfect and I know I'm supposed to believe in the whole *I'm beautiful no matter what* mantra, but in reality it's hard. My body has completely changed, and the truth is, I don't like it.'

'Take off your dressing gown,' snapped Roxy.

'No!'

'Why?'

'Because I don't want to!'

'Bella, please help me. This robe is coming off!'

'Roxy!' I said as they came closer. 'You can't…'

'Soph, we're not here to force you or make you feel uncomfortable.' Bella touched my shoulder gently. 'We just want to help you. For you to see what we see. Do you think you could take it off? *Please?*'

I saw the fire in Roxy's eyes. She wasn't going to let up.

Oh, what the hell.

They'd seen me naked before, so at least once they saw how different I looked now, they'd understand and get off my back.

'Okay…' I peeled it off cautiously and winced as it dropped to the floor.

'There you go!' said Bella. 'I think you look *amazing*!'

'Holy macaroni!' shouted Roxy. 'Like I said in the corridor this morning, your body is *banging*, Soph! I mean, look at those boobs! Women pay thousands to get knockers like those and yours are *au naturel*.'

Oh? That wasn't the reaction I was expecting.

'Only temporarily, though… it's the milk that's made them bigger.'

'*Whatever*—embrace and enjoy it for however long it lasts. I would. And, yeah, you've got a few stretch marks, but so what? You carried a baby for God's sake.'

'I still have them, just like *millions* of women over the world. That sounds pretty normal to me!' said Bella. 'They're like badges of honour for the life you created. Is that one of the reasons you're afraid to sleep with Lorenzo again, because you're worried about how you look?'

'Yeah.' I hung my head. 'It's not a vanity thing. I've lost my confidence. It's not because I'm comparing myself to others or those glossy celeb mums that miraculously *bounce back* into shape days after giving birth. I know that's not real. I just think about how I used to look and how I look now and feel like I'm falling short. Until I got pregnant, I had a decent figure. I used to be happy with what I saw in the mirror. Well, more or less. But not anymore. I feel like I should be doing better. And I know you're going to condemn me for saying this Roxy because it sounds weak and isn't very feminist, but I also worry that Lorenzo won't fancy me anymore...'

'Too right! But not because it sounds weak, but because it's a load of bull! Like I said before, in the beginning I was sceptical about Lorenzo. I thought he was a player who would screw any woman with a pulse. But even *I* can see he's crazy about you. I mean, you haven't had any nookie for half a century and he *still* looks at you like you're the most amazing woman to have walked the earth.'

'He really does,' said Bella.

'Lorenzo doesn't care how you look. You wear leggings and a T-shirt which is probably covered in Leo's puke all day, but he *still* gets a boner when he snuggles up to you in bed. Now *that's* love. And he watched you give birth. I heard a bloke say that seeing his kid come out of his wife's vag was like watching his favourite pub burn down. But Lorenzo's not like that. I reckon he wouldn't care if you put on ten stone and had the gut the size of a grizzly bear. So stop worrying, darling, and start loving yourself again so you can jump the poor guy's bones before he implodes!'

Classic Roxy. Her heart was in the right place even if she had an *interesting* way of expressing herself.

I guess if I thought about it, even though Lorenzo hadn't actually *seen* me naked in a while, when he wrapped his arms around me every night, he would have *felt* the new flabby bits and changes in my body shape. And yet he never flinched or showed any signs of disgust, so I should give him more credit.

I walked over to the mirror and put my hands on my hips. My boobs *were* pretty impressive. Very full and— what's the word? *Voluptuous.* Lorenzo used to have the time of his life playing with these when I was pregnant and I'm sure he'd love to get his hands on them again. And they looked pretty great in my dress last night…

My stomach and thighs were bigger, but still in proportion I supposed. There was no getting around the stretch marks and I'd be lying if I said I liked them, but what would I rather? Keeping my old, smooth stomach, or having Leo? There was no question. He was worth every line on my belly and more. I wouldn't trade him for the world.

As for my cellulite, it wasn't like I didn't have any before Leo. I'd had it since my twenties, it was just more noticeable now. I remember being shocked the first time I ever saw it, but then I just got used to it. Those dimples on my bum and thighs became normal. Maybe that was the point.

I was feeling bad about myself because I was trying to look the way I *used to*. But I wasn't that person anymore. So instead of trying to be the old Sophia, killing myself with exercising every day and cutting out things I loved, like cake and pasta, completely, I just had to try a more balanced approach. Stay healthy and fit, yes, but at the same time accept that the body I had now wasn't bad, wrong or ugly. It was just a new version of myself. My new normal.

'Thank you.' I hugged them both. 'I know everything you said is true, but maybe I just needed to hear it out loud. From someone else.'

'Yeah. Sometimes it helps,' said Bella. 'I mean, don't get me wrong. We *all* have our insecurities and our down days, but we were worried that you were on the verge of self-loathing, which isn't okay.'

'No, it's not. I'm going to try. To get back my old confidence. Start loving my body again.'

THE MIDDLE-AGED VIRGIN IN ITALY   195

'Oh yeah!' Roxy's eyes widened. 'Speaking of which, I've bought you a present to help you do exactly that.'

'A present?' I frowned. 'It's not my birthday. First you guys surprise me by turning up yesterday, then you surprise me again this morning by coming to my door practically naked, and now you've got me a gift? I'm feeling very blessed right now.' I was excited to find out what it was.

Roxy reached down on the floor and put her hand in her dressing gown pocket, then pulled out a little pink box.

'Here you go…' She grinned. I untied the ribbon and lifted off the lid.

'Oh… a travel-sized vibrator. Just what I've always wanted… Erm, *thank you*, Roxy!' Whilst I was grateful, that wasn't what I was expecting. Then again, this was Roxy. I gave her a hug. 'Honestly, you do make me laugh. You've been in Italy for twenty-four hours and spent most of that time with us. How did you manage to find a sex shop?'

'*Duh!* Google. I went yesterday after we finished lunch. It was an emergency shopping trip. God knows when I'll see you again, and I couldn't trust you to buy one. They probably don't even sell them in that poxy little village of yours. You need to learn to appreciate yourself again, my friend. That includes rediscovering your body and giving it lots of *self-love*. I picked this one out especially. It's nice and compact. Small enough to carry around in your pocket or your purse.'

'Yes, I can see…' I took it out of the box and held the bright pink toy in my hand.

'It'll be good for you, Soph. Help you release some stress. It's ideal for the busy mum. Extra powerful, so it can get you off in seconds, which means even *you* will be able to find the time to use it every day.'

Every day? Chance would be a fine thing.

'I don't know about that…'

'Of course you can! You've got to brush your teeth, right? So whilst you're doing that in the morning, you can use your other hand to give yourself a quick thrill. Start your day with a bang! Or, if you're waiting for the pasta to boil at lunchtime and are feeling saucy, you can do it in the kitchen. Just make sure you wash your hands afterwards!' Roxy cackled.

'Oh my God. Only you, Rox. *Only you*. Great sales pitch, though. I can see why you're good at your job… anyway, enough about me and *my* sex life. Let's talk about *yours*. What happened with you and Geli last night?'

'Ooh, is that the door?' Roxy jumped up and rushed over to open it. No one was there. 'Just going to the loo,' she said, going in the bathroom and shutting the door behind her.

Bloody cheek. There she was always asking me about my bedroom activities and yet she was suddenly all shy about discussing her own. I wasn't going to let her off the hook that easily…

A few seconds later there really *was* a knock at the door. I reached for my bra. Getting my boobs out for my best friends was one thing, but showing them to strangers was another.

Bella got up and looked through the peephole.

'It's Geli.'

'*Buongiorno*!' she stepped inside.

'Hi, Geli, did you sleep well?' I said slyly, trying to gauge her reaction.

'*Very well*, *grazie*.' She untied her robe and tossed it on the chair, leaving her standing in just her underwear. 'So, you have had a good chat with Roxy and Bella, *sì*?'

'Yes, I did.'

'Good.'

I guessed that Roxy and Bella had asked Geli to wait in the room until they'd finished as they probably knew that I was more likely to open up if it was just the two of them. Strictly speaking, I should put my dressing gown on again now too, but somehow I was okay. Even though I hadn't known Geli that long, I felt at ease and that she wouldn't judge me. In fact, maybe this was all part of the process: like a training exercise or a self-fulfilling prophecy. Maybe the more I told myself it was fine to show my body or sit around in just my undies, the more comfortable I would become doing it.

Roxy came out of the bathroom.

'Hey, Geli,' she said breezily. Geli looked like she was going to melt in a puddle on the floor. Now it was *her* looking at Roxy like she was the most amazing woman on earth. I really wanted to know what had happened… 'Breakfast is on its way up. I thought we could have it in here, so we can be more relaxed and enjoy our last few hours together.'

'Sounds great. I didn't fancy having to haul myself downstairs.'

The door knocked again.

'Right on cue.' Roxy jumped up from the bed, gathered the other dressing gowns, threw them on the chair with Geli's so they were out of reach, then opened the door. 'Come in!' she said to two room service guys.

As they wheeled in the two trolleys, which were

packed with plates of food, with silver metal covers and buckets of what looked like Prosecco, their eyes popped out of their heads. Geli and Bella were standing proudly in their undies and Roxy strutted over to the bed like it was all perfectly normal.

'Jump up, please, Soph,' she said. I climbed off and stood next to Bella. 'If you could set the plates and the cutlery out on the bed, please. We're all going to eat on here.'

'*Sì, signora*,' said one of the guys, trying desperately to look anywhere but at her body.

Four half-naked women in a hotel room. They both probably thought we were having one big orgy. Especially with the size of this bed.

'*Grazie*,' she said as they hurried out of the room.

'This looks great! I definitely need this. I felt awful before, but now I'm feeling a bit better. Actually, I'm starving.'

'Good, good,' said Roxy. 'We can all get stuck in a mo', but first, let's have a toast.'

Crikey. More alcohol? I know I said I was feeling better, but…*oh well*. Would be rude not to.

Roxy poured some orange juice into the glasses, then topped them up with Prosecco to make a Buck's Fizz. She passed me a flute.

'Bella, do you remember when Soph used to have her glass OCD thing?'

'I do!' said Bella.

'Yep,' I laughed, thinking back to when I couldn't drink out of them unless there were zero smears or marks. 'I've been over that for *ages*.' I'd learnt to rotate the glass to avoid the 'dirty' bits. Although I couldn't lie. Given the chance, I'd still swap it for one that was clean and streak-free…

'Glad to hear it! Anyway, back to making a toast,' said Roxy. 'Here's to friends, old and new.' She looked at me and Bella, then smiled at Geli.

'To friends, old and new,' we all repeated.

'And here's to Soph. We hope you continue to do well with your new life in Italy, that you learn to love your body and of course that you go home later and shag Lorenzo senseless. Cheers, everyone!'

Dear God. What was she like?

CHAPTER TWENTY-FIVE

'I thought she would not get back up again!' Geli cackled.

We were in the car about fifteen minutes away from Chiorno and couldn't stop laughing about when Roxy had dropped down to do the splits in the club. *Hilarious.*

When I asked Geli if I could get a lift home with her so Lorenzo wouldn't have to drive all the way back to pick me up, she agreed straight away. She even offered to drop Bella and Roxy to the airport too.

I pictured Roxy on the floor again and smiled. I'd had *such* a great weekend. Seeing Bella and Roxy was a real tonic. It was great having video calls and technology to help us stay in touch, but nothing beat seeing your friends in the flesh. I'd laughed so much that my cheeks hurt, but it wasn't just the fun that I'd had that made me feel better. Some time away had helped me to see a few things differently too.

It felt good to be a bit more relaxed and just go with the flow, so I wanted to ease up on the rigid regime I followed. Starting with cutting back on my daily workouts. Instead of pushing myself to get back into shape like I'd put on my list, my goal now was to just try and be healthy, which was something I could do by exercising two or three times a week or whenever I could. I didn't need to pile on all that extra pressure.

And maybe when I'd written the list, I'd been looking at the Marta situation all wrong. These past few days, I'd realised that giving up some control over who looked after Leo and being more flexible about his routine had its benefits. It made Lorenzo happier as Marta got to spend time with her grandson and it had also given me the chance to have an amazing weekend away.

Instead of seeing Marta as a hindrance, I'd try and see her more as someone helpful. I was lucky to have a babysitter on tap, so maybe I should make more use of that. I mean, she might still be a pain in the arse at times, but she did a good job of raising Lorenzo, so it wasn't like she didn't know how to be a good mum. She just had different methods. I didn't have to like her. I just had to tolerate her and be civil. Plus, it would be good for Leo to be bilingual, so that he would never have to struggle with Italian like me. So being around Marta would be good for his language skills.

After taking time out, I also felt less stressed about the business. I was ready to tackle work stuff tomorrow, and when I did, my mind would be much clearer. It would be easier to make decisions. Yep. This trip was a game-changer.

'So I understand that you are worried about having sex again. After having Leo?'

Whoa.

My eyes popped out of my head. *Where did that come from?*

One minute we were talking about our night out in Florence, the next, Geli looked at her watch then suddenly switched to that statement.

'Um…'

'No need to be shy. We are both adults. I have a son. He is twenty-five now, but I remember what it was like with my husband.'

Geli had a son and a husband. *Huh?* There was so much I wanted to ask about her right now…

'I didn't realise you were married.'

'*Sì.* Long story. Anyway, people can overthink. Sometimes you must just do it, *no*? Just try. Not worry about what will happen if you do this or that. Just jump. But of course, a woman should not feel pressured to do anything. I know what men, especially Italian men, can be like.'

That was a bit stereotypical…

'Lorenzo isn't like that…'

'Well, I will admit, it has been a while since I have been in this town, I try to avoid coming back as much as possible, but I remember when I lived here before how popular Lorenzo was with the women.'

That didn't really surprise me. I knew he had a past. Didn't we all? Okay, maybe *I* didn't have much of a history with men as I was in a long-term relationship and always working, but you know, normal people did.

'I'm aware of his past.'

'*Sì. Every* woman here wanted to have sex with him and he certainly take advantage.'

What was the point of this conversation? Was she shit-stirring? I thought Geli was nice.

'Well, he was young. He's a man now. A father. He's totally committed to me.'

'Yes, I am sure he is. He is still a *very* sexy man. Even *I* can see that. And he is still popular with the ladies. My mother asks about him and she is in her seventies.' She let out a raucous laugh.

Of course I knew he was sexy. I thought that every time I saw him.

'I'm sure he'd be very flattered to hear that.'

'I mean, he has a very good body, no? I imagine, a *very* muscular chest and very firm thighs and, well… I have also heard that he is a *very* big man…' She smirked.

I wasn't quite sure that I liked her perving over my boyfriend's body and discussing the size of his manhood. Although of course she was right. He was very muscular and well hung.

'Well, I… he does have an amazing body, yes.'

'With all of the women that he has had in his bed, I am sure he is very experienced. I imagine he is *very* generous lover. The kind of man who pick you up and throw you onto the bed and make every part of your body happy, no? He start with your lips, kiss your neck, then your shoulders, his tongue move down and circle your nipples. His hands grab your breasts and then he touch you, stroke you. *Slowly*…' She purred, then licked her lips.

Was it me, or was it getting hot in here? I started to fan myself.

God, I used to *love* it when Lorenzo kissed my neck and when he used to stroke me…

And his tongue… when it used to travel down past my belly button, I was always so overcome with anticipation I thought I was about to burst.

When he touched my clit, it was like lightning had struck.

Oh, I remember… I remember that feeling so well…

My heart started beating faster.

I felt a tingle.

And then another one.

I pictured Lorenzo's body. He always looked so hot—especially when he'd just come out of the shower. All clean and smelling of that shower gel I loved, with just a towel wrapped around his firm waist, flashing his washboard stomach. The drops of water running down his chest…the way his muscles flexed when he ran his fingers through his wet hair.

And when the towel dropped to the floor, seeing his solid thighs and his crown jewels…

I remember so many times how he'd walk into the bedroom after his shower and I'd pull him on top of me because I couldn't resist. We'd work up such a sweat that he'd have to shower again, then rush to work because he was late. In the end, he started waking up half an hour earlier to give us enough time for our morning sex sessions.

God, I used to love those.

And our Sunday afternoon sex sessions were pretty epic too…

I'd love to have one of those today… I'd love for Lorenzo to climb on top of me and ravish me…

Oh my God.

It's back.

I think it's back.

My mojo.

Desire.

I want Lorenzo.

I want Lorenzo. *Right now.*

I looked out of the window. We were close to home. Probably only a few minutes away.

Suddenly I just wanted to be at home, laid out on the bed or on the sofa or *anywhere* with him. On top of me.

I was ready. Ready to do the deed.

Finally.

'You okay, Soph?'

'Mmm?' I snapped out of my thoughts.

'I imagine you are thinking about your big, sexy husband. The most popular man in the town, that *every* woman desires, but he is yours. He wants you. *Only you.* He thinks you are beautiful. He wants to make love to you. He is excited for you to come home. You are excited to go home now, no?'

'Yes, I am.'

'And when you arrive, you will not think too much. You will just let your mind relax and be free. Like you have felt this weekend. You will go to the bedroom with Lorenzo, take charge and show him *exactly* what you want.'

'I will.'

'That is good. We are here now.' She pulled up outside of our house, unfastened her seat belt, stretched across me and opened the passenger door. 'Go. Go now, Sophia, and *enjoy…*'

CHAPTER TWENTY-SIX

I burst into the house, locked the door, then put my suitcase and the hallway table in front of it. This time, we would *not* be disturbed.

'*Ciao, amore*!' Lorenzo walked towards me. 'Welcome back! Did you have a good ti—'

'What time is your mum bringing Leo home?' I snapped.

'In about an hour, maybe hour and a half…?'

'Good.' I pushed him against the wall, grabbed his belt and started unbuckling it. 'Because we've got some business to take care of in the bedroom before she gets here…'

Lorenzo's eyes widened. 'You mean…?'

'Yes…' I pulled his jeans and his boxer shorts down. 'I want you. *Right now.*'

'Are you sure you are ready?'

'Yes! Stop talking and go to the bedroom!'

'O-okay!' He stepped out of his jeans and walked quickly towards the room, giving me a delicious view of his firm arse.

I pushed him down on the bed and took a deep breath.

No more overthinking. No more fear. It was time to stop hiding.

I peeled off my leggings, jumper and underwear and stood at the end of the bed.

I'd done it.

I was naked in front of Lorenzo. And he was still there. He hadn't run out of the room screaming. Instead, his eyes were filled with desire and his dick was standing firmly to attention.

Thank God.

Okay. Time to take control.

I climbed on top of him.

'Sophia…,' he said, running his hands over my shoulders, my breasts across my stomach, as if he was so overwhelmed and excited, he didn't know which part of me to touch first. 'You are so beautiful.'

What I'd known deep down and what the girls had said was true. Lorenzo loved me. Even though it looked different, he didn't care. Lorenzo loved my body. I had nothing to fear.

As I felt him grind beneath me, his rod rubbed against my clit, and for the first time in months I wanted him. *So badly.*

The combination of having three fun days with Lorenzo and my friends, being away from the monotony and the stress of daily life and getting a proper night's sleep (well, on Friday at least) made me feel more relaxed. More open to going with the flow.

Geli performing her kind of strange, hypnotic and erotic magic, getting me all worked up about how sexy and desirable Lorenzo was, played a part too. My libido and the lioness inside of me had finally awoken. And just like those early days when Lorenzo and I had hooked up, she was ready to roar…

I started pushing my body into him. Lorenzo reached up and began fondling my breasts. It felt weird at first because I'd become so used to seeing them as a milk machine. But not today. This moment, right here, right now, wasn't about me being a mum. For the next hour at least I was just Sophia again. The new version. Sophia 2.0 with big, sexy boobs that I wanted my hot boyfriend to enjoy. I was going to make the most of them whilst they lasted.

'*Mmmm…*'

Lorenzo started stroking my clit and it actually felt incredible. Any minute now, I'd be ready for him to be inside of me.

Yes. It is on.

Suddenly, as I leant forward to kiss him, a burst of watery liquid sprayed all over his face.

OMG.

I looked down at my breasts.

Milk was spurting from my nipples all over him.

'Shit, shit, shit!' I jumped up, grabbing my T-shirt off the floor and covering my boobs. 'It's because I haven't been breastfeeding, so they're full.' *So much for being sexy.* I was supposed to express earlier but got sidetracked when Bella and Roxy showed up. I grabbed some tissues from the bedside table and started wiping his face. 'I'm sorry.'

'No worries—is natural. *Come…*' He gently pulled me back on the bed. 'You want to carry on?'

I mopped up the milk from my nipples and my stomach, then threw my T-shirt back on the floor.

'Yes, yes… *of course…*'

This time, Lorenzo climbed on top of me and started kissing my neck.

That felt good.

Actually, maybe I should put my bra back on my and get some fresh nursing pads? That way I wouldn't squirt him again.

He started stroking in between my legs.

Ohhhh…

I just needed to enjoy this. To relax. I didn't want to start overthinking because then I'd get scared and it wouldn't happen. Like Geli said, sometimes you have to just jump. I needed to do it.

It was now or never.

'I want you inside me.'

'You sure? You are definitely ready?'

I know he was being considerate, but the more Lorenzo asked me, the more I'd think and the less likely I would be to see it through.

'Yes. I'm ready.'

As I felt his tip push against me, I froze.

This was really happening.

It would be fine…

Just like ripping off a plaster, I had to do it quickly. The longer it took for him to enter, the tenser I would become. He just had to go for it.

I wrapped my hand around him, took a deep breath and pushed him inside.

'Ouch!' I screamed so loudly my ears hurt.

Jesus Christ.

I knew it would be painful, but *whoa*.

'Sorry. You want me to stop?'

'No, no,' I gasped. 'Just…maybe try going slow.'

I closed my eyes as we gently rocked back and forth. There was a *lot* of friction. It felt really raw. Like rubbing sandpaper against an open wound. I thought I was ready. That I would at least enjoy it a little bit. But so far…

'Ow!'

'Sorry. Are you okay?'

'Yes…no…*sort of.* It's just a bit sore…'

It wasn't *a bit* sore. It was *really* sore. *Very, very painful*. Even more painful than losing my virginity. But it was to be expected, right? That was how the mums in those forums and the articles had said it would be. Like giving birth, I just needed to push through the pain barrier.

'Maybe we can use something? Some, how you say? Jelly?'

'KY Jelly. Um, yeah. That might help.' I winced. 'But I don't have any…'

I hadn't ever needed it before with Lorenzo.

'The pharmacy is not open here on Sunday. But I can drive to the city.'

All the way to Florence? I couldn't ask him to do that. And anyway, by the time he got back, I probably would have lost my momentum and wouldn't want to do it anymore.

No. We had to continue.

Oh God.

Never before had I wished a guy was small as much as I did right now. I mean, because Lorenzo was big, the initial entry was always a bit of a shock to the system. But right now he felt *huge*. It was like there were two of him in there.

I didn't know how much of this I could take. I know I was supposed to persevere, but honestly, this was awful.

But no pain, no gain, Sophia.

Reasanna piped up.

Childbirth was no walk in the park, but at the end of it you got Leo. A beautiful baby boy.

Baby.

I hadn't even thought about the whole baby thing.

We were having sex and I wasn't on the pill. What if I got pregnant again?

No, no, no!

One child was hard enough. Although annoyingly, people had already started asking when we were having another, I wasn't ready to even think about that right now.

My whole body tensed.

I flashed back to being on the hospital bed, giving birth. The pain. What I'd been through down there. And now I was voluntarily putting myself through this?

Lorenzo thrust again.

'Stop! Please stop! I'm sorry. I can't!' Lorenzo pulled out and rolled over beside me.

I didn't want to give up, but I couldn't take it anymore. I looked down at the sheets. Oh God. There was blood. I was bleeding.

I jumped up and ran into the bathroom and slammed the door.

'Sophia,' Lorenzo said softly as he followed me. 'Are you okay? Please do not worry. Soph?'

'I'm sorry. I just need to be alone.'

I heard Lorenzo return to the bedroom.

I sat down on the toilet with my head in my hands. I'd been so sure that I was ready. I'd finally got my libido back, I'd been relaxed, I hadn't overthought, I'd just gone with the flow and I'd still failed.

Shit.

I know the mums said it would get better the more we practised, but after experiencing that level of pain, right now I couldn't see how I would be able to bring myself to even want to try again. *Ever.*

CHAPTER TWENTY-SEVEN

It was only 9.20 a.m. on Monday morning and my relaxing weekend—well, the part up until the cringey attempt to relight the fire in the bedroom—already felt like a lifetime ago.

Yesterday, after I'd fled to the bathroom, at first, I'd sat there feeling sorry for myself. I was so disappointed. I was gutted that I couldn't even manage to have sex. Something I'd been doing since I was a teenager. But then Reasanna piped up and helped me to see sense.

Come on, Soph, she'd said. *Stop being so hard on yourself. It was your first time after having Leo. Your body has been through a lot. After pushing another human out, sex is bound to be painful. Even after six months. Especially considering you jumped into it literally minutes after being on the bed. Maybe take things slower next time, get your body properly ready. And if you don't have KY Jelly, use coconut oil or something. You had plenty of that. And look on the bright side: you had sex and Lorenzo is still alive. You didn't swallow him whole. He didn't disappear inside you like you feared. Don't give up.*

She was right. It was a setback, yes, but I'd overcome it. I'd unlocked the door and gone to the bedroom, and Lorenzo and I had laid on the bed in silence. He'd just held me and stroked my face. I was glad, because I hadn't felt like talking or analysing what had happened anymore. Even though I'd decided we would try again at some point, at that moment it was too painful. Not just mentally, but physically too. I was still sore today.

When Marta turned up, I decided to go and open the door. I meant what I'd said before. I wanted to make an effort and say thank you. I didn't get much of an acknowledgement back, but *whatever*. I'd tried.

It was great to see Leo again. But he'd been a bit fussy with his milk. I'd made up a bottle for him, but he didn't seem to want it. I figured maybe he was full, as Marta said she'd fed him not long before she dropped him off. But then he was funny again this morning. I planned to start him on solids today, so we'd see how that went.

Right now he was having a nap. I'd missed his lovely face. He looked so adorable when he was sleeping. His chest rising and falling, his chubby cheeks and long dark eyelashes. He'd only been on the planet a few months and they were already longer than mine. *So not fair.* Leo was wearing a cute 'I'm not crying, I'm just ordering dinner' sleep suit that Lorenzo had found online. I quickly snapped a few photos to send to him. I knew that would brighten up his day.

Anyway, now he was resting, it was time to check my emails. I'd been good. I hadn't looked at them since last Thursday, so four whole days. I felt better for it too.

I fired up my computer.

Only sixty-seven. *Not too bad.* When I was running the agency full-time, I could easily get double that in a day. I started scrolling through. Some were just messages I'd been cc'd into from the team to keep me in the loop.

One popped up from *PR Update*, a top industry magazine. *She's doing well.* I opened it up to see a large photo of Rhonda Jones. I clicked on the link to read the interview on their website.

I'd known Rhonda for over a decade. She'd interned with me for a few months one summer when she was just starting her career, and even then I could tell she'd become a big player in the industry someday. Not long after she'd finished working with me, Rhonda had decided to move to New York, and after several years climbing the ladder and building her contacts, she'd opened her own agency. I bumped into her at big events or conferences every now and then and we'd always got on.

I skimmed the feature quickly. Rhonda was talking about her plans to open an office in London or Paris. Didn't surprise me. She'd always been ambitious. I supposed that meant more competition for us, especially as she had a good reputation, but so did we. Plus, I had a lot more experience and even though Purity had dumped us, our client list was still strong. We'd be fine. *Yep. Nothing to worry about…*

Anyway, mustn't get distracted. I'd read the article properly another time. I still had a lot to get through before Leo's next feed.

I clicked back to my inbox and continued scrolling.

More client emails. I hope Robyn hadn't cancelled more meetings.

What the…?

My heart sank.

Not another one.

And another?

'No, no, no!' I jumped up.

This *couldn't* be happening.

If only these emails were just about meetings being cancelled. *I should be so lucky.*

Not one but *two* clients had emailed to terminate their contracts.

Not small ones, either. Two more of the biggest.

Oh God.

Losing Purity was already terrible. But *three* large clients in a couple of weeks? That was catastrophic.

I put my hands on my head.

How the hell could the business survive this?

And—oh no…

Gail was resigning too?

She couldn't. She was one of the main points of contacts and was really popular.

I might as well throw in the towel now.

Especially with young, hungry and ambitious agencies like Rhonda's circling, fishing for new clients and probably gearing up to poach staff too.

There was only one thing for it. If the agency was to have any chance of survival, I'd have to go to London to sort this out. And it couldn't wait. I had to go.

Immediately.

∾

I'd landed safely and was in a taxi en route to my house. Mum was going to meet me there and take Leo. Thankfully he'd been good during the flight and was now sleeping.

It was a mad rush to get everything together. I'd called Lorenzo straight away, told him what had happened and that I needed to go, and even though I knew it would be full-on, I thought it was best to take Leo with me. He understood and luckily, was able to leave work to drive us to Pisa airport.

There wasn't much I needed to take, so I just flung a load of stuff in a suitcase, mainly for Leo. I thought we'd have to get some formula on the way so I could make up some bottles, but then I remembered the tin I'd bought Marta was still in Leo's overnight bag. There was loads left, so not sure how she managed to make that amount stretch three days, but anyway, that saved me some time.

It was strange to be back. To hear the familiar sound of people speaking English. To be surrounded by hustle and bustle, the buzz of being in a busy city. But as much as I wanted to stare out of the window, I needed to focus. Think of a plan of action.

Apart from Lorenzo and Mum, I hadn't told anyone that I was coming back. Not even Harrison, as I didn't want to risk him letting it slip to the team. I needed to have a true picture of how everything was running. See what was *really* going on at the office for myself.

After Mum collected Leo, I showered, did my hair and make-up and slipped into a bold yellow structured dress. Today wasn't a day for casual clothes. Today I was fighting for survival. I needed my armour. I had to look the part. I had to take charge and be Sophia, the strong, in-control boss.

As I strutted through the open-plan office with my heels clinking against the solid oak floor and past the rows of glass-and-chrome desks, the gasps were audible.

'Hello, everyone,' I said as I walked up the floating glass staircase that led to the mezzanine directors' floor and my old office.

Robyn had her head on the desk. Was she sleeping? No wonder things were going down the toilet if she was having afternoon naps. I opened the door.

'What the hell's going on?'

She jumped out of her seat and stood up. God. I hated to say it, but she looked *awful*. All the colour had drained from her face, her eyes were bloodshot and it was like she'd stepped out of bed, then dragged herself to the office without showering or putting a brush through her hair.

That was not like Robyn at all. Clearly she still wasn't well. I felt a twinge of sympathy and guilt for shouting at her, but this was serious. I had to get to the bottom of things.

'Sophia! What are you doing here? I was… I was just going to call you…about the emails this morning—I…'

'Enough!' There was so much steam coming out of my ears, I could power a hundred trains. 'Enough of the excuses! Three major clients, Robyn. We've lost *three* of our biggest clients in less than a month and Gail has resigned…'

'She's what? Oh no!'

'You didn't know? *Jesus*. What is up with you? You used to be so reliable. I trusted you to take care of things. I even took on more work because I suspected you were getting overwhelmed. I've asked you so many times if you could handle things. And you assured me you could.'

'I know, I know. I…'

She broke down, crashing back on to her seat.

Not the waterworks. I hope she didn't think a bit of crying was going to make me forgive her. This was serious. Without those clients, I would almost certainly have to lay off several members of staff. And it wasn't just the jobs that were at stake. It was the entire company. If I had to close, it would affect *everyone*.

'I've let you down, I know that,' she sobbed loudly. 'It wasn't planned. I was careful, I was sure I was, but then *bang*, it happened. And since then, I've been so ill I haven't been able to function and…'

'What are you talking about? What wasn't planned?'

'The baby. I'm pregnant.'

WTF.

'Pregnant?' My eyes widened. 'I didn't even know you were seeing anyone.'

'I wasn't… I'm not. It's complicated. I never had time for a relationship because I was always working… It was just something casual. He doesn't want anything serious and *definitely* doesn't want me to keep the baby, so there's been lots of arguments with him and stress. And then I've had HG…'

'HG?'

'Hyperemesis gravidarum. It's completely wiped me out.'

I'd heard about the HG thing. That was the pregnancy sickness that Kate Middleton had where you suffered from extreme nausea and vomiting.

'How far along are you?'

'Fourteen weeks…'

Jesus.

'Robyn, you should have told me.'

'I didn't know how to. I thought I could handle it. I tried to hold it together but I've been literally vomiting four or five times a day and I found it difficult to focus. That time I cancelled the Purity meeting, it was so awful I had to go to hospital.'

'Shit!' Morning sickness was bad enough. I couldn't even begin to imagine what she'd been going through.

'I didn't want to let you down, Soph. You had a lot on your plate with moving to a new country and having a new baby, so I wanted to take care of things so you didn't have to worry. I knew how important the business was and still is to you—to all of us. And I've wanted this kind of responsibility for years. Then just as I finally got it, *this* happens.' She put her hand on her stomach and started sobbing again.

As upset as I was about the business, I really felt for Robyn. I knew first-hand what it was like dealing with a surprise pregnancy and worrying that you'd have to do it alone. At least in my case, once Lorenzo had come back to London and explained what had happened, I'd realised that he *did* want to be a part of our lives. But the father of Robyn's baby seemed pretty adamant about not being involved at all. Then on top of that she had the pressure of running a company for the first time and her illness… couldn't have been easy.

'Oh, Robyn.' I went over and gave her a hug.

'How did you do it, Soph?' she took a tissue and blew her nose. 'I mean, I knew it would be difficult, but it's so much to handle. Dealing with all the staff and their issues, keeping the clients happy, overseeing the campaigns. I work late almost every night if my body allows me to and weekends and I'm *still* not keeping on top of things.'

By having no life, Robyn. That's how.

I wouldn't wish that on anyone I cared about. It made me sad to hear that Robyn was spending so much time at work that she had no room left in her life for a boyfriend or proper relationship.

It reminded me of me. How my life used to be. Before I'd realised that wasn't a good way to live. Before I'd seen the light.

I could say with absolute certainty that doing all those long hours wouldn't be good for Robyn and they definitely couldn't be good for the baby. I didn't want that on my conscience.

I was torn. On the one hand I felt for Robyn. Years ago the decision would've been a simple one: *do whatever it takes to save the business*. That would have been the most important thing. But after my dear friend Albert's passing, my change in perspective, meeting Lorenzo and becoming a mum, I saw that Albert was right. There *was* more to life than work. Yet at the same time, I couldn't avoid the fact that, like it or not, the business was still my responsibility and the livelihoods of dozens of staff were at stake. If the company closed or we lost any more clients, how would my team pay their rent? How would they put food on the table?

'Listen, don't worry. I'm going to find a way through this, but I need you to go home and get some rest. We can talk on the phone tomorrow.'

'Are you firing me? Please, Soph, I really need this job, especially now with the baby coming and—'

'Of course I'm not firing you! There's no way I'd do that. I know *exactly* what you're going through and right now I want you to focus on taking care of yourself and the baby.'

'But, what about the clients and work…?'

'I'll handle it.'

'Thank you.' As she threw her arms around me, I could feel the desperation and relief melting away. Carrying this secret must have been eating away at her for months. 'I'm so sorry to let you down.' She picked up her coat and bag.

'Just get home safely.' I picked up my phone. 'You're still living at the same place, aren't you?'

'Yeah.'

'I've called you an Uber. It should be here in a minute, so just wait in reception. We'll speak tomorrow, okay?'

'Okay.'

I closed the blinds, plonked myself down on the yellow sofa beside the desk and sighed. I'd known when I'd jumped on the plane back to London that I was walking into a shitstorm, but I hadn't anticipated Robyn's news on top of all of this.

I didn't blame her. Even though we all know how babies are made, I could understand how simple it was to find yourself in that situation. I'd also got pregnant 'by accident,' so I knew all about getting swept away in the moment. Especially if you'd been working as hard as Robyn had and then were offered the chance to finally let your hair down and have some fun.

No. Although she clearly thought it was, in my eyes, getting pregnant wasn't Robyn's mistake. And even though her not telling me had caused huge problems for the business, I also understood why she hadn't fessed up sooner. In truth, the mistake that Robyn had made was not being honest with herself.

Her failing was taking on more than she could handle. Believing, despite the evidence suggesting otherwise, that she could manage the business, the baby and all the other new challenges happening in her life and keep up the façade of convincing everyone that everything was fine. But now that everything had come crashing down around her, she realised it wasn't.

The penny had finally dropped.

Although the thoughts racing through my head were initially about Robyn, the *she* I was now referring to wasn't her.

It was *me*.

I suddenly realised that, like Robyn, *I* was living a lie. Thinking *I* could have it all.

Thinking that all I had to do was follow the plan. Stick to the schedule, follow some rigid routine, and I could be the perfect mum, the perfect girlfriend, have the perfect life and still run a business successfully.

Thinking that just by making a little list, I could solve all my problems.

Thinking I had everything under control, when the reality was I didn't. I was running myself into the ground trying to keep on top of things and pushing myself to do everything perfectly. I couldn't continue like this. I needed a different approach. Otherwise I'd end up unhappy, just like I was before. I had to tackle this seriously. Permanently. Something had to give.

Having it all wasn't about having an amazing career, husband and family like society tells us. Having it all was about having everything *you* wanted.

I'd said this before to Roxy, that night at my fortieth birthday party when Lorenzo had first invited me to Italy. I'd told her that success wasn't about having the biggest agency. It was about having the courage to step away from convention and make the choices that were right for *me*. But since then, I'd chickened out, got caught up in following my list and lost my way.

But no more.

Just like that, I decided.

It was time.

Time to let go.

Time to prioritise. *Properly.*

I knew what I wanted. What *having it all* meant to me.

Just like Albert had said before he died, it was happiness and love that was important. And that meant focusing on my new life with Leo and Lorenzo.

It was time to sell the business.

I was finally ready to hand over the reins.

Once and for all.

CHAPTER TWENTY-EIGHT

I certainly didn't miss this.

As much as I hated being away from my friends and family and enjoyed the buzz of being in London, I definitely wasn't loving running a business again full-time.

I'd been here four days now and had worked late every night. If I did this much longer, Leo would forget who I was.

Each night I'd tried to get back in time to give him his bath and put him to bed and each night I'd failed. I'd either been stuck in meetings or on phone calls. Trying to do everything I could to salvage this business so there was something left to sell.

Thankfully, I'd managed to persuade both clients to stay. But only for another six months, at which point they'd evaluate the results achieved. And I'd also had to agree to a reduction of their fees.

Speaking to them in person definitely helped. Seeing them face-to-face did, however, mean getting back into the whole full-on grooming routine. Having my hair done, facial, manicure, make-up and diving back into the designer clothes. What had happened with Purity Skincare (Viktor was still refusing to even talk to me to discuss their contract) had reinforced how shallow clients could be and how important appearances were to them, so I had to go all out. I couldn't leave anything to chance.

After being away for so long, you'd think I'd be thrilled at the prospect of a marathon all-singing, all-dancing salon pampering session. Having freshly blow-dried, bouncy hair, immaculate nails and a full face of make-up. But actually, I didn't enjoy it half as much as I used to.

I'd loved my massage in Florence and my beauty session with Geli, but that was different somehow. It was more for pleasure. For fun. But the old *getting dolled up for clients* regime didn't feel like me anymore. It felt fake. Forced. Staged. Like I was an actress playing a role.

And I also found the conversation really shallow. I mean, I know I probably yabbered on about Leo to most people I met, so my topic of choice was no better at times, but theirs was always all about what people were wearing and how they looked. Which of course, *duh*, was to be expected. Because that was what we were promoting: image. Beauty. But the truth was, I didn't really care whether the coral, peach or apricot eyeshadow would look best on the model for the new ad campaign (can you believe I wasted half an hour of my life in a meeting whilst the client discussed this? *Jesus*). They all looked the same. I just couldn't give a toss about that stuff anymore. I had different priorities.

Don't get me wrong. I knew the power of a great haircut or how a lipstick could lift your mood. I still believed that talented hairdressers, beauty therapists and make-up artists were like magicians. They could make people feel so much better about themselves. But I just didn't want that to be the focus of my life anymore. That conversation with Robyn had really brought it home to me. I saw everything more clearly now. That was it. I was done. Ready to move on.

And I wasn't the only one. As much as he'd been trying to put on a brave face during our phone conversations, I'd thought Harrison didn't seem like his normal self. After having a chat and probing him repeatedly, he finally admitted that he'd wanted to try a different career path for ages, but didn't want to let me down. He knew how much I'd relied on him being here. Apparently, he was going to speak to me about it last year, but when I'd announced I was pregnant, he felt like he needed to stay.

He was still young—barely thirty-one—and I didn't want to hold him back. It made me sad to think about all of the people who were staying in the business, making their lives unhappy, doing things they didn't like, just because they didn't want to let me down. I hated it. So this time, I was sticking to my decision. I was definitely going to sell the company.

Because I wanted to sell and leave the business quickly, I knew I wouldn't get as much for it as I would have hoped, but I didn't care. Sometimes you had to take a step back to take a step forward. My freedom, happiness and my conscience were worth a lot more.

I gave Leo a kiss goodnight, quickly sent a few cute photos Mum had taken of him today to Lorenzo and headed back to my house. I had an important breakfast meeting, so it would be easier to go from there. If Leo saw me when he woke up, he might not settle.

Time to relax and unwind. I poured myself a large G&T and took it up to my bedroom. My phone pinged.

It was Bella in the group chat. So ironic that they'd flown all the way to Italy to see me last week and now I was back in London. As it turned out, it was a good thing that they had, as Roxy was away at an exhibition in Birmingham this week with the beauty tools company she worked for, Bella was back teaching English full-time to foreign professionals working in the city and I was snowed under, so meeting up for a leisurely FTA session wouldn't have been possible.

Bella

Hey, Soph. Just checking you're okay?

Me

Hey! Sorry I've been a stranger. Have had zero time to message with all this work drama, but things are looking up. I've got something in the pipeline... will keep you posted. Anyway, just got home and now I'm chilling.

Bella

Brilliant! Glad to hear it.

Roxy

Evening, ladies!

. . .

Me

Hey, Rox—how's the exhibition?

Roxy

Fab! Sales are going great

Roxy

And I've made a new friend…

Me

Let me guess… A man?

Roxy

Haha! You know me so well!

Roxy

He's FAF!

Oh, here we go. Roxy and her bloody acronyms.

Me

FAF???

. . .

Roxy

Duh! Fit As Fuck!

Roxy

Talking of men, you didn't tell us how it went with you and lover boy Lorenzo when you got back home. Did you do the deed?

She was right. I hadn't told them. That was something I'd really rather forget.

I paused.

Roxy

I'm guessing from your silence that you either didn't or it didn't go as planned…?

I couldn't hide anything from her. It was like she could see inside my bloody brain.

Me

Sadly we did try and, well, it wasn't good…

I filled them in on everything that happened. Typical Roxy joked that me spraying him in the face with my milk was my body's way of paying him back for covering me with his spunk. *Honestly.*

.   .   .

Bella

Like you said, Soph, it was your first time. It wasn't great for me the first time either. But if you keep trying, regularly, eventually it will get better.

Roxy

What did you use to ease him in, Soph?

Me

Huh?

Roxy

Whilst you were talking, I Googled painful sex after birth and one of the articles I'm skimming now says you need a lot of lube. Like bucketloads. Enough to sink two ships. Or rather one giant dick!

She added a row of aubergines, hot dogs and baguettes.

Roxy

Did you lube up before Lorenzo made his big entrance?

.   .   .

As delicate as a sledgehammer. Roxy always had a way with words.

Me

No. I know I should've done. I will next time.

Roxy

FFS! You MUST!!! And have you used my gift yet? It'll help if you get to know your new body better first too.

Roxy

You've been under extra stress lately, so now is the perfect time to get your rocks off.

Roxy

I'm telling you! You'll feel so much better afterwards!

Me

I've been in the middle of a monumental shitstorm. Trying to save the business. Making massive decisions that will affect people's jobs. Their LIVES. The last thing I've been thinking about is sex.

I added the eye-roll emoji. *Honestly. Talk about priorities.*

. . .

Roxy

Don't think of it as sex. Think of it as stress relief. Relaxing your mind so that you can make BETTER decisions.

Roxy

And didn't you just say to Bella that things were looking up now? That you were at home relaxing on your bed? Alone? So what are you waiting for?

She didn't miss a trick…

Me

Yes…true… But anyway, your gift is in Italy. It was a race against time to catch my flight, so surprisingly, a mini vibrator wasn't at the top of my packing list.

Roxy

Well, that's why you have forward-thinking friends like me…

She added a winking face.

Bella

What did you do, Rox…?

.   .   .

I was just thinking exactly the same thing…

Roxy

If you check the little make-up bag you keep in your handbag, I think you'll find something in there…

She didn't…

Roxy

Now that you're all down-to-earth and a busy mum, I know you don't wear much make-up anymore…

Roxy

But I also know you don't go anywhere without the travel toothbrush and other bits and bobs you keep in there. So I knew it would be safe.

Unbelievable. I rushed downstairs, looked in the bag and sure enough, there it was. Discreetly wrapped in a velvet pouch. I picked it up and returned to my room.

Me

I cannot believe you!

Roxy

You're welcome.

Me

What if I'd been stopped at the airport?

Roxy

Obvs I planned to tell you… Just didn't realise you'd be flying to London so soon.

Roxy

Anyway, no harm done! I'm sure they're used to seeing vibrators on airport scanners all the time. I always travel with at least one!

Bella

You're hilarious!

Roxy

Thanks! Anyway, Bella, I think we better go. Now that Soph has found her second gift, we should leave her to take care of business… and I'm not talking about her PR agency…

Me

Bye, ladies. Let's try and speak tomorrow. Xxx

. . .

We all said our goodbyes and I flopped back on the bed. I laughed. I couldn't believe Roxy had bought me *two* bloody vibrators. I also had my own one here. *Somewhere…* I'd put it into retirement when Lorenzo had come back on the scene and hadn't needed it since.

I took a glug of gin and then slid the vibrator out of its pouch. This one was purple and glossy.

Hmmm…

I still had at least another half an hour before Lorenzo got back from work and we did a video call. We'd been doing them every night since I'd got here. It was nice to see his face and chat for a while. I missed him so much.

It was silly little things, like the heat from his body. I missed having him beside me. The feeling of his heart beating, him holding me until I fell asleep. The way the same cute tuft of hair always stuck up on his head when he woke up. I missed his laugh. *Everything.*

I pictured Lorenzo in my head. His gorgeous smile. His beautiful body…

I took another drink.

I supposed I *could* try it out…

I mean, I wasn't going to do any more work tonight and maybe Roxy was right. Maybe releasing some stress could be good for me…

I lifted up my hips, slipped off my knickers, picked up the shiny new toy, pressed down on the button, then held it between my legs.

Okay. Let's do this.

First I needed to clear my mind.

Stop thinking.

Come on. Come on.

Relax. Just relax.

Yeah…that's it…

Now think of something sexy…

Lorenzo naked.

Lorenzo after he's just stepped out of the shower.

Mmmm…

I pressed down on the button again, increasing the speed.

Oooh!

It was certainly powerful.

Hold on... I think something's happening.

I feel something.

Something *wonderful…*

OMG.

Yes...

Woo!

Aaaarghhhh…

Oooh...

I did it.

Finally.

I closed my eyes. My mind was racing and my body was tingling all over. I exhaled loudly.

That felt good. *Soooo good.* I grinned. Now I remembered. I used to love that feeling. The high after sex. I wanted that back. With Lorenzo.

I was going to take Roxy's advice and start investing in myself. Practising some more *self-care*.

As well as sorting out the business, whilst I was here I wanted to dedicate at least a few minutes a day to rediscovering my body so that when I returned to Italy I was ready. Ready for Lorenzo to rediscover it and ready to lose my MARGINITY again.

And this time, for good.

CHAPTER TWENTY-NINE

Right on time.

R _ight on time._ I glanced at my watch. In fact, eleven minutes early. That was a good sign. It showed that not only was she professional but she was also interested.

I'd secured prime window seats at Darwin. Overlooking the Thames on Level 36 of the Sky Garden, it was London's highest rooftop brasserie. The fantastic views of The Shard and countless famous landmarks were the perfect backdrop for what I had planned for this morning.

I stood up to greet her.

'Rhonda, hi.' I gave her a kiss on each cheek. 'How are you?'

'Good, Soph. Great to see you!' she sat down.

'Likewise. Can I get you something to drink?'

'The kale juice would be good, thanks.'

She looked sharp as always. Striking jet-black blunt bob, structured royal-blue dress with shiny skyscraper heels and the kind of 'natural'-looking make-up that took much longer to do than it would appear (I knew this because I used to do that every day, today included). Yep. Rhonda was polished and ready to do business.

I called the waiter over and ordered the drinks and some breakfast. I was feeling good. Calm. Even though this could potentially be one of the most important meetings in my life, I had to keep my cool.

We did the whole small talk thing. Spoke about how things were going with her, showed her photos of Leo and Lorenzo, but I knew she had to catch a flight back to New York soon, so it was time to get down to business.

'So: I mentioned on the phone that I had a proposition for you.'

'Yes, and I'm very intrigued. Tell me more.'

'Well, I was reading in *PR Update*—nice interview by the way—that you had plans to expand and open an office in either London or Paris and I wondered what stage you're at with that?'

When I was scrolling through Instagram a few days ago, I saw that Rhonda had posted about how great it was to be back in her home city. And after I'd read about her expansion goals in that article before, a lightbulb had gone off. I *knew* I had to get in touch with her. Surely it was fate that we were both in London at the same time. She was looking to open a business here and I wanted to sell one—I was convinced it was a sign.

'It's at the very early stages at the moment. Takes time to find the right premises, set up, put a team in place. *You know the drill.* But I'm going to make it happen.'

'I know you will. Which is why I called. How would you like to make it happen right now? How would you like to open the London branch of your agency immediately?'

'What?' She frowned. 'I mean, of course, I'd love that

but how…?' Then the penny dropped. 'BeCome? You're selling up? But, that business is in your blood. It's part of you. That's your baby! How would you even…? I remember how hard you worked. I mean, I heard rumours that you were thinking of selling last year, but I knew it would never happen. And I know you wouldn't let some-thing like having a kid get in the way of that. You'd just hire a nanny or au pair if it got too much, so I don't get it.'

'You're right. I don't *have* to sell it, but I'm ready for a new start. Look, I know so many agencies would kill to have what we have and it could all be yours. If you want it.' I put my hands together and leant in closer. 'Just think, if you took over, you'd have an instant London office in a prime location, a ready-made roster of the most prestigious clients in the industry, a talented team. You'd become a truly global player in the PR world.' Her eyes widened. I could tell Rhonda could see it. She could picture the dream. 'The media would *love* the story. I could see you splashed across the front pages of the Sunday *Times* busi-ness section. *Everyone* would want to cover the story. With your clients and mine, you could dominate the industry. Even more clients and staff would come flocking. You'd be untouchable. Just think: you could own it all. For the right price…'

'I'm in!' she said. I'd barely managed to get the words out before she'd agreed. Her saying yes wasn't enough, though.

'We'd need to discuss figures and terms, of course. I have other parties who've been hounding me to sell to them for months'—I dialled up the sales pitch—'and I've said no, but now I'm ready, I thought I'd come to you first—'

'Forget about them,' she snapped. 'I want in. I'll buy your business. I told you, I want a London office. I have the money. I can make this happen quickly.'

That would be ideal. If I could get this business off my hands tomorrow, I would, but I couldn't show my desperation. And it had to be right. Even though I wanted to move on sooner rather than later, it wasn't just about offloading it to the quickest or highest bidder. BeCome was and in some ways always would be my first baby, so it was important to hand over the reins to the right person.

I respected Rhonda. I liked the way she ran her agency. She had a strong management team supporting her. Her clients and her staff respected her too. That was crucial. I needed to know that my company would be in good hands. That my team would be looked after. She had smart investors backing her. Like Rhonda, they would know a good opportunity when they saw it.

'How quickly did you have in mind?'

'I can get on the phone to my lawyers this morning and get the ball rolling immediately. Naturally they'll need your financials and want a ton of information, and like you said, we'd have to talk figures, but provided we all give each other what we need, there's no reason we can't get this done in a matter of weeks.'

Weeks? I was sure it would take longer than that. Then again, weeks could mean anything. Anything from five to fifty-five. I didn't want to be waiting around for over a year, though…

'I could work with that. My financial director already has everything in order and ready to send over. I do have other opportunities on the table, though, and don't want to drag this out, so once you've spoken to your people, if there's a chance you can't go ahead quickly, I'll need to move on to the next buyer.'

'No! Trust me. I want this. I'll get this done. *Fast*. I assure you. And your plans? Will they involve staying in the industry?'

I knew what she was asking. She wanted to know if I'd stick around not just in the industry, where I could potentially be some kind of alternative competition, but also if I'd want to remain in the business.

She didn't need to know that I had absolutely no idea what I'd do after this. But I was sure it wouldn't involve beauty PR and that was all that was important to her.

'No. I want this to be a clean sale. Pardon the pun, but this will *become* your business. It will be *your* vision, *your* direction, *your* team. *Your* dream. I'll be happy to provide some level of consultancy, if you need it, for say the first couple of months, but after that, I want to put all of my efforts into projects completely outside of the industry.'

Rhonda was beaming. I knew she was as much of a control freak as I was. She would like to take the business and make it her own from the get-go. The last thing she'd want was me sticking my oar in. I didn't want to be involved and she wouldn't want my involvement. It was the perfect scenario. Win-win.

'You've got yourself a deal.'

And those were the magical words I wanted to hear.

As we shook hands, I felt a flood of relief rush through me.

It was still early days and there were so many more things to discuss. Not just money. I also wanted to make sure that people like Robyn were looked after, but right now, the signs were looking good. There was hope.

I was one step closer to freedom.

CHAPTER THIRTY

'Okay, Mum, we're off.' I picked up Leo and walked towards the door. 'Thanks so much again for everything.'

'My pleasure, darling. You know your dad and I love spending time with our gorgeous grandson.'

'Yeah, Dad said the same before he left for the dentist earlier.'

'Poor thing is in agony with his tooth.'

'I know. He was going to cancel his appointment so he could be here to see us off, but I said no way. He needs to get it sorted.'

'Exactly. Are you sure you can't stay longer?'

'We should get back. We've been here ten days already and we really miss Lorenzo.'

'Yes, of course. Will you come again soon?'

'I'll let you know. You could always come over and see us, though?' I raised my eyebrow.

'*Oh, darling.* You know I'm not very good with planes. We'll see. Now,' she said, changing the subject, 'you've got the list of all the meals Leo's been enjoying, haven't you? He loves the potato and broccoli in particular.'

Mum had been a superstar. Making fresh homemade dishes for lunch and dinner to get him started on solids.

'Yep. Got them. Thanks.'

'And remember to buy some more formula as the tin has almost finished.'

'Will do.' I glanced down at my phone. 'We'd better run—the Uber's outside.'

Mum gave us both a big hug and we were on our way.

I couldn't *wait* to get back to Italy. Not so much to Chiorno, but to see Lorenzo. It felt like ten weeks rather than ten days since I'd last seen him. Whilst it was great to be able to video call, it wasn't the same. I missed being in his arms. His smile. His body...

Yes. I could safely say that this trip had helped to relight my fire—down there. I was definitely feeling desire again. Since that evening where I first tried out Roxy's 'gift', I'd been making time for self-care every night. Straight after speaking to Lorenzo. Seeing him sat up in bed with his top off, his bronzed, sculpted chest in full view, was enough to get me going. As soon as I'd put the phone down, I'd reach for the toy and would come in seconds.

I had also taken time to explore my body. It wasn't that different to how it was before. I'd been worrying unnecessarily. After a couple of nights, I managed to hunt down my old vibrator and started practising with penetration. It was really painful at first, but through some experimentation, I started to get used to having an alien object in my body again and the pain had become a lot more bearable. Naturally, the real thing would be different, but I was more prepared than I had been the first time we tried. And lube definitely helped. I'd been to the chemist and bought several tubes. Meant I'd need to put my case in the hold, though, as that would exceed my hand luggage liquids allowance. Would also avoid the embarrassment of the airport scanner people seeing it and raising their eyebrows…

So, yes. I was definitely *ready to rumble*. I'd even exfoliated my body and pruned the lady garden this morning, so everything was looking extra tidy downstairs. I was a woman on a mission. As soon as I put Leo to bed tonight, I intended to jump Lorenzo. We had a *lot* of time to make up for.

∽

'Welcome home!' Lorenzo opened the door and wheeled in my suitcase.

'Awww, you didn't have to do all of this!' There was a *Benvenuta a Casa* banner that Lorenzo had made himself hanging on the living room wall, which thanks to my growing Italian repertoire I knew meant *welcome home*, and a big bouquet of flowers in a vase on the coffee table.

'I wanted to. I have missed you so much.' He leant forward and gave me a long kiss.

Yep. Desire was definitely back in the house…

'I have made your favourite mushroom risotto and Florentine orange cake for dessert.'

I looked down at Leo. He was still fast asleep in the car seat. All the travelling had tired him out. He seemed comfortable. Like he could probably sleep through a rock concert. I moved him over to the rug. I reckoned we had some time…

'Thanks! I was thinking, how about we eat *later*…?' I wrapped my hands around Lorenzo's waist. 'Leo is sleeping and I haven't seen you for ten whole days, so maybe there's something else we can try first…' I glanced over at the bedroom and winked.

Lorenzo's eyes widened. 'Sure?'

'Sì!'

Lorenzo licked his lips, scooped me up in his muscular arms and carried me to the room. I inhaled his woody, masculine scent. God, he always smelt so good. He laid me down gently on the bed.

'We take it slow, okay?'

'Sounds good.'

He reached into his drawer and pulled out a tube of KY Jelly.

'You got some too!' I laughed. 'I picked up about half a dozen tubes in London.'

'How you say? Great minds?'

'Yes, great minds think alike.'

Lorenzo climbed on top and started kissing me. Slowly. Then his kisses became more urgent. He slipped his tongue in my mouth and flicked it against mine. Within seconds I could feel Lorenzo's hard-on pressing in between my legs. I was tempted to tell him to take me now, but this time, it was important we didn't rush things.

I ran my hands over his bum, slipped my hands under his T-shirt and lifted it over his head. He looked glorious.

After all of these months of sexual starvation and getting myself worked up in London, I was ready to take control. I pushed him on his back, whipped off my jumper and leggings, tossed them on the floor and climbed on top of him. First, I ran my hands all over his solid bronze chest. I'd fantasised about it enough whilst I was away. It felt so good to touch it properly.

I could feel Lorenzo's heart beating fast. I pulled off his jeans and boxer shorts, freeing his thick rod, and then started rubbing myself up against it.

Oh my God.

Lorenzo reached out to grab my breasts. As his hands touched my back to start unfastening my bra, I paused. Maybe it was better to leave it on so I didn't risk spraying him again with milk. Even though I'd stopped breastfeeding, they still tended to leak.

Fuck it.

If they did, who cared? Certainly not Lorenzo. It was only a bit of milk. All natural. It wouldn't kill him.

I let him continue. He threw my bra on the bed, pulled me down towards his face and then started sucking on my nipples. *Mmm.* I rubbed my hands up and down him, I was so ready, but I needed to be patient. I wanted to enjoy this. Savour every moment.

He rolled me over on my back and started kissing my neck, my shoulders, circling my breasts, kissing my belly button, then trailing down my stomach until he reached in between my legs.

Holy shit.

As his tongue gently flicked against my clit I thought I was ready to explode. I groaned loudly before remembering that if I wanted to continue, we needed to stay as quiet as possible. The last thing I wanted now was for Leo to wake up and interrupt us.

I'd always loved Lorenzo going down on me, but *this*

—*this* was insane. How on earth had I survived so long without feeling *this*? Thank God my desire had returned.

It was like every nerve-ending in my body was sparking all at once. Lorenzo always knew exactly where to put his mouth. The pressure and rhythm were perfect. I didn't want him to stop, but if he carried on like this I was going to come.

'I'm ready, Lorenzo. *So ready.*'

He looked up from between my legs and smiled. Lorenzo reached for the jelly. He'd made me so wet I didn't even feel like I needed it, but after last time, it was better to lube up, just in case.

He rubbed it between my legs and then looked at me again, just to check I was sure.

'*Take me,*' I gasped like a horny woman in a romance novel.

Lorenzo thrust inside me.

I gasped. It hurt, but nowhere near as much as before. And this time, I didn't care. I knew any initial discomfort was going to be worth it. The adrenaline was rushing through my veins like a Formula One driver speeding around a racetrack and it was feeling *good*. And I knew that when I came, it was going to be even better.

'You okay?' said Lorenzo.

'Yes.' I wrapped my legs around his waist. 'Keep going.'

We rocked back and forth and the more he was inside me, the more natural it felt. Like breathing. I could tell Lorenzo was enjoying it too. After last time, I bet he thought I'd never want to have him again.

He slid in and out of me and I groaned with every

thrust. Then he started rubbing my clit with his hand and I lost my mind. This was it.

Game over.

I felt the wave building and building. Lorenzo recognised the signs and picked up the pace. I tried to hold on, but I couldn't. As he tipped me over the edge, I screamed like a wild animal. Never mind waking up Leo. I think everyone in the town would have heard me, but I didn't care. It could be because I hadn't had sex in almost seven months, but that was one of the most intense orgasms I'd had. *Ever.*

Lorenzo exploded inside me and then collapsed on my chest. My head was spinning and my whole body trembled. I wanted to tell him how mind-blowing it was but I couldn't speak. I just needed to lie here in silence. Get my thoughts together.

Lorenzo clearly felt the same. He rolled over onto the bed, his chest heaving.

After several minutes, we managed to regain our composure.

'You okay?' he said.

'Okay? I'm *more* than okay. That was…that was… *epic.*'

I turned on my side to face him and a massive grin spread across his face.

'For me it felt amazing, but I wanted to make sure I did not hurt you.'

'Will I be able to walk properly tomorrow? Probably not. But it was more than worth it.' I kissed him on the lips. 'Thank you for being so patient.'

'But *of course*. I knew that we would be great again. You just need time. I was not worried.'

'Well, I was, but I'm so glad my mojo returned. Maybe I should have gone to London sooner.'

'Maybe,' Lorenzo chuckled. 'But I am glad that you are back.'

'Yep!' I smiled, feeling like the cat that had all the cream and then some. 'Back in Italy and *finally* back on track in the bedroom.'

CHAPTER THIRTY-ONE

Nice place.

We'd just arrived at Geli's house for our Italian lesson. Whilst the décor itself was very traditional, she'd just taken us into the living room, where there were lots of colourful paintings and trinkets on display. Some looked like they were from Africa, others from India and maybe South America? I guessed Geli had picked them up from her travels.

'You may wonder why today I have invited you to the home of my mother, *si*? Well, I told you at the beginning of our lessons that we were going to learn about practical things that will help you every day. So today I will teach you about things you may use *a casa*—at home. Okay? Let us start here, in the living room. What types of things might you want to say in this room? Daphne?'

'I have absolutely no idea.'

'That is helpful.' Geli rolled her eyes. 'Holly?'

'How about: please can you pass me the remote control?'

'*Bene*. To ask that, you say *per favore mi passi il tele-comando*.'

'Cool, thanks.'

'*Prego*. What else? Sophia?'

'Shall we watch Netflix?'

'Good. You say: *guardiamo Netflix?* Or even better, you could say *ti va di va di guardare Netflix e rilassarci un po?* which means, *would you like to Netflix and chill?*' She winked.

I swear Geli was some kind of psychic. Although the massive grin plastered across my face was probably a dead giveaway. Lorenzo and I had been *Netflixing and chilling* almost every night this week. I couldn't get enough of him. I felt like a completely different person. Crazy that less than a month ago, I'd been terrified of having sex again. I'd had *zero* desire. But *now*, I was thinking about it constantly. I was like a dog in heat.

As soon as Leo was asleep, we would literally jump on each other. Back then, in my dark no-libido days, I thought I'd never do it again and definitely not with Leo in the room, but that time away in Florence and London, my conversations with Roxy, Bella and Geli and making a point of exploring and familiarising myself with my new body had gradually made me more relaxed. Not breast-feeding probably played a part too.

Everything I'd experienced over the last few weeks had also helped me put a lot of things in perspective. I knew now what was important in my life, which was really liberating and helped my mind and body feel free.

As for Leo, he was a baby. He didn't know what was going on. At this age it was fine. There was no risk of him being mentally scarred if he happened to wake up and see daddy on top of mummy. Although lately it had been more like *mummy on top of daddy*…

After my bedroom gymnastics with Lorenzo, every step I took was still an effort. But this time, a little bit of post-sex pain was worth the gain. I reckoned I was getting a lot fitter in the process too. Much more fun than forcing myself to do those exercise classes online.

It wasn't just on the bedroom front that things were looking up. I was *this close* to confirming a deal to sell the business to Rhonda, which had been a *massive* weight off my shoulders, and since my visit, Harrison said the team seemed more motivated too.

And now here I was, back at my lessons with Geli, which had become another source of—dare I say it?—enjoyment. Life in this town was finally starting to become more bearable.

Geli took us through various rooms in the house. She taught us how to ask for different ingredients in the kitchen. After that, we helped to lay the table in the dining room, learning the names of cutlery and crockery. Then we all sat down and ate a meal she'd cooked us, which she used to teach us how to ask someone to pass things like water or wine, how to say we liked the food, wanted more, were full or hungry etc. All essential vocab for living in Italy.

Next we went to the bathroom, where we learnt how to say *muoviti, mi serve il bagno*, which meant *hurry up, I'm bursting for the toilet*, and *puoi abbassare la tavoletta per favore!—can you please put the toilet seat down!* Again, really useful stuff.

Then it was on to the bedroom. She introduced

everyone to her mum, who was recuperating in bed, then took us to the spare room.

'So, the bedroom. Important phrases you may want to know: *non stasera amore, ho mal di testa*: means *not tonight, darling, I have a headache.*'

'Sorry, I didn't catch that.' Daphne perked up. 'Can you repeat that, please?' She quickly wrote it down in her notepad. *Bet she's glad the lessons are practical now.*

'Or…' Geli looked straight at me. 'You may wish to say: *amore, prendimi adesso*, which means *darling, take me now.*' She winked. I tapped away on my phone and showed it to Geli to check the spelling.

'Correct. You do not always need to take notes. I will send the important phrases in my WhatsApp message and voice note.'

I really liked when she did that every week because sometimes I didn't remember how to pronounce things, so having the voice note was handy to help me check I was saying things right. Now I wasn't exercising every day, I had more time to listen to them and practise. I was defi-nitely feeling a lot more confident about my Italian.

'Geli,' said Holly cautiously, 'how do you say, "No, please don't come in. I'm not interested"?' Geli's eyes widened. I also frowned. I assumed that she was talking about someone not coming in her bedroom? That was an odd thing to ask.

'Er, you say: *no per favore non entrare, non mi interessa.*'

Holly wrote it down and repeated it twice out loud. *Hmmm…*

Before I knew it, the lesson was over. As usual, Daphne

was the first to leave. *Honestly*. I didn't know why she kept coming if she hated it so much. I was definitely finding the classes helpful. I was glad I'd continued and hadn't just dismissed them because they didn't follow the structured way I'd learnt a language before. I still had a *long* way to go with my Italian, but at least I was making progress. Geli made learning fun. I was a bit worried about Holly, though.

'Is everything okay?'

'Yeah,' Holly stuttered. 'Fine, thanks.'

'And with work? The parents, or rather, Silvestro, isn't giving you any trouble, is he? Pressuring you to do things you don't want to?'

Her face fell.

'No, no. It's cool. Anyway, I better get back.' She rushed towards the front door. 'Thanks for the lesson, Geli.'

I wasn't convinced.

'Hmmm.' I turned to face Geli. 'I'm not sure if she's really okay. What do you know about the people she works for? Particularly the dad, Silvestro?'

'I do not know how he is recently, but I know when I last lived here, Silvestro was a dog. Had many affairs. He is very sleazy man. If I was a young woman, I would not like to work with him in the house.'

I'd always sensed something wasn't right about him. Maybe that was why Holly wanted to learn phrases about being left alone? I didn't like the sound of this at all.

'I'm going to message Holly. See if she wants to meet up away from that house and have a proper talk.' I couldn't shake the feeling that something had happened and I wanted to get to the bottom of it.

'Good idea.' Geli cleared the plates away from the dining room table. 'Would you like to stay for a drink?'

'Yeah, why not? Lorenzo will be home soon to take over from Marta, so I don't have to rush back.' That said, I was hoping for some sexy time tonight, so I'd better not get back late or we'd both be too tired.

'I saw Marta again today,' said Geli. 'I did not know she was friends with Claudia.'

'Who's Claudia?

'She is another mum in the town who has baby too – probably the same age Leo. *No*—perhaps older. She lives on this street. I saw Marta coming out of her house this afternoon and a few weeks ago. The Friday you went to *Firenze*. She had Leo with her.

'No idea. Maybe she brought Leo there to play with her baby?'

'Perhaps. But Leo was not with her this afternoon…'

'I don't know. Maybe she helps her out with babysitting or something.'

'Maybe…' She shrugged her shoulders. 'So I am guessing from your glow that you are having fun again in the bedroom with Lorenzo?'

I blushed. Not sure why. Geli clearly knew the situation and she'd played a part in helping. *What the hell.* I didn't mind talking to her about it. Especially now things were going so well.

'Yes. Yes, I am! The first attempt didn't go to plan, but all good now. And thank you for your erm… your *encouragement* in the car when you dropped me off from Florence.'

Geli let out one of her loud laughs.

'*Prego*! I thought you needed a little push… I wanted to help you think about what it could be like…'

'You certainly had a way with words,' I chuckled.

'I have lots of practice. I used to be phone sex operator.' She winked.

'Really?'

'*Sì!* Remember I told you: I have many, many jobs.'

I could see her doing that and being very good. She had the voice for it and I'd imagine a lot of people would find her accent sexy.

'How come you've had so many jobs?'

'Long story,' she sighed. 'When my son was one year, I left my husband and this town and decided to travel. Sounds crazy, but my marriage was like prison and I wanted to be free. I was single mother. I had very little money. Wherever we went I had to take whatever job I can. Sometimes cleaner, sometimes work in bar or salon or restaurant or at home, talking to dirty men on the phone…'

'Sounds like you did what you had to survive.'

'*Sì*. It was not easy. But I was lucky. Most places we lived had good community. Women who were happy to give support. That is why I try to help good people, because without those women who take care of my son when I had to work, I would not have survived.'

That explained why Geli was always so selfless. Always looking out for others. Her mum, me, Holly.

I was intrigued to hear about her husband. She'd mentioned him briefly in the car on our way back from Florence and I'd been wondering about him ever since.

'Didn't your husband give you any support?'

'Ha!' she laughed. 'He would not speak to me. He think I humiliated him. I cannot blame him completely.

Our marriage: it was fake. I did not love him. I knew it was wrong.'

'In what way?'

'Ever since I was young, I knew I was different. Felt like I did not belong. I had not many friends. I think there was something wrong with me. It was lonely. When I was nineteen, all my friends start to get married and have babies. For woman here, the goal is to have family. In this town there is not much to do, so they start early. I begin to feel more alone. I think my life would be better if I did the same as them. So I said yes to the first man who ask me out. It did not feel right. I did not really like him and I definitely did not enjoy the sex. But…' She shrugged her shoulders. 'And then I become pregnant, so we had to marry quickly. I was very unhappy.'

'What changed? What gave you the courage to leave?'

'A tourist.'

'Huh?'

'One day I was alone in *Firenze*. An English woman, she ask me for directions. We started talking. She was single mother. Her daughter had gone to university and now her life felt empty, so she decide to do something for herself. To travel the world. I said she was an inspiration. We went for coffee and she told me about her experiences. We talked for many hours. I thought she was amazing. In every way…' Her voice trailed off and a big grin spread across her face.

'You mean romantically too?'

'*Everything*. Spiritually. Intellectually. Sexually. We had only known each other for hours, but I feel like she understood me better than people I know my whole life. She was strong woman. Woman with goals and dreams. I did not meet many people like that in this town. But she had waited until her daughter was eighteen to live her life. After speaking to her, I was inspired. I did not want to wait. I could not wait seventeen more years. I could not imagine stay with my husband for that long. I wanted to live now. So two weeks later, I left him.'

'Wow! That must have been scary?'

'Not really. I was more scared of how my life would be if I stay.'

I understood what she meant. After Albert died and I realised my life was a mess, I knew I had to take the leap and leave my fifteen-year relationship with Rich too.

'And what happened to the woman?'

Geli smiled slyly. 'We stay in touch…'

I read between the lines…

'That must have been a big change on so many levels, I mean, leaving your husband, leaving your home and also discovering your sexuality.'

'*Sì*, in some ways, but I do not really give much thought to these things. I just know that I could not stay in this town. It was too closed. I could not be free. In this town people are used to follow tradition. They think they must be like everyone else. But that is too rigid for me. I do not like labels. Especially for relationships. It is not about liking man or woman. It is the person. Their spirit. *That* is what I am attracted to. I want to be free to fall in love with anyone. To be open to all experiences. Labels and boxes are for products, not people.'

So true. People should be who they wanted to be and love whoever they pleased. And that was definitely something that would be difficult to do here. It was a very traditional town.

'You thought that tourist woman was an inspiration—well, you are too Geli. Having the courage to get up and start a new life isn't easy. And making friends in different places and finding jobs to make ends meet must have been tough too. I've definitely found it hard and I have Lorenzo's support.'

'Was not easy. But was worth it. I am proud of my son, Ravi.' Interesting name. I was sure that meant something like *sun* and was an Indian rather than Italian name. That would be just like Geli, though. Not wanting to follow convention. 'He is one of the most educated men I know. Not because he went to fancy school. Sometimes I had to teach him at home myself. He is smart because of his experiences. Travelling, meeting many different people, seeing many cultures. That help to make him the man he is. That is why I do the lessons in this way. Learning is not always about textbooks and rules. It is experiencing life that teaches us the best lessons.'

That was a good point. I think in many ways I've always believed that most problems could be solved with hard work and a good plan. Of course, I'd known that moving to Italy would be a challenge, but I'd just assumed that if I did all the right things and ticked off tasks on my list and approached life in a structured way, everything would fall into place. But now I was seeing that wasn't always true. Especially when it came to studying Italian.

By being open to trying a different approach and letting go of my need for everything to be so controlled, I was much better off. I'd learnt more from Geli's lessons than I would from just using my textbooks. She reminded me of Mr Miyagi in *The Karate Kid*. Just like Daniel, who worried at the beginning that he wasn't being taught any karate skills, the more I studied with Geli, the more I realised that not only was she helping to improve my Italian, but she was also giving me deeper life lessons too.

'You've obviously experienced a lot. With your travelling and all those different jobs. You're clearly a woman of many talents…' We both burst out laughing as we realised how that sounded. 'I didn't mean…'

'It is okay, I understood what you mean. But it is true. I do have *many* talents.' She smiled again as if she was reliving some happy moments. 'How is Roxy?'

Whoa. That seemed to come from nowhere. *Or did it?* Perhaps Roxy had experienced some of Geli's skills…

'She's fine. I didn't get to see her whilst I was in London. She was really busy.' The fact that Geli was asking how Roxy was meant she hadn't spoken to her. And if something *had* happened between them and Roxy was avoiding her for whatever reason, I didn't want to drop her in it.

'*Sì.* She must be because she has not replied to my messages…'

Uh-oh.

'If you don't mind me asking, what went on in Florence?'

'Hmmm…' She paused. 'A lady never tells. What happened in *Firenze,* stays in *Firenze…*'

What was it with those two? They were both always ready to discuss *my* sex life but miraculously lost the ability to speak whenever I asked about theirs. Actually, that wasn't strictly true. Roxy was normally very quick to share every detail of her escapades with her latest fuck-buddy, but this time, with Geli, she was uncharacteristically coy. I should get my friend Fran on the case. When we'd met on the Italian cookery holiday, she'd been an expert at extracting information about Lorenzo, so she would definitely be able to find out what went down that night. Speaking of Fran, that reminded me. I should message her to find out how she was.

'Fair enough.' I said, thinking that I would let it go. *For now*.

Call me nosey, but I wanted to find out. I had to live in this town and saw Geli often, so if Roxy really was avoiding her messages, it could get awkward.

Yep. Next time I spoke to Roxy, I'd ask her again to spill the beans. After she'd constantly probed me about my love life, it was only right that she reciprocated. I wasn't letting her off the hook that easily…

CHAPTER THIRTY-TWO

I was glad that was all arranged.

I'd just finished messaging Holly and invited her over for a coffee tomorrow afternoon. Her questions to Geli had been going round and round in my head all day. Something was off. My guess was that sleazy Silvestro had been trying it on and that worried me.

Holly was such a trusting person who liked to see the positives in every situation and the good in everyone. So if he was overstepping the professional boundaries, I wasn't sure if she'd stand up to him. She'd probably make excuses for his behaviour or just brush it off and carry on as if it didn't affect her. But if I was right, Holly was living in a toxic environment. It was a ticking time bomb, waiting to explode. Like me, she probably didn't have many friends in this town, so it was important I looked out for her.

Talking of friends, tonight I was having a video call with Bella and Roxy. After our trip to Florence, we'd vowed to try and speak once a week. And rather than texting, we thought it'd be nice to actually see each other.

The phone rang.

'Hey, Soph,' said Roxy. 'One sec. I'm just going to add Bella.'

Bella appeared on the screen. She was sitting up on the bed, like me and Roxy.

'Hi, ladies!' said Bella. 'Nice to see you.'

'It *is*!' I took a sip of my G&T. 'So glad we're doing this. Let's hope we can keep it up.'

'That's what I say to all the guys over thirty-five that I sleep with,' Roxy cackled.

'*Gosh!* We've barely spoken for twenty seconds and you've already taken the conversation to the gutter,' Bella sighed.

'Exactly! Anyway, who are you kidding, Rox?' I said. 'We all know you don't sleep with any men over thirty!'

'You know me, darling.' Roxy winked. 'Well, there was this one time…'

I vaguely remembered the guy in his fifties that Roxy slept with after her divorce had come through, but that was definitely a one-off. Twenty-five to thirty tended to be her preferred age range.

'Actually… you say we know you, but do we? *Really?*' I raised my eyebrows.

'Of course you do!' said Roxy. 'I'm always wide open!'

Bella cringed.

'I didn't mean *that*! Now whose mind is in the gutter?' she cackled again. 'I meant I'm always open with you guys.'

'If that's true, then what's the deal with you and Geli? What happened between you two?'

'*Hello...hello...are you there*?' Roxy started making a cracking noise. 'You're breaking up… I think I'm losing signal...'

'Roxy!' I shouted. 'Your signal is perfectly fine! What's up with you? Why are you avoiding talking about Geli?'

'Yeah,' said Bella. 'If you like women too, it's okay. We're not going to judge you. It's fine to be bi or pansexual.'

'I'm *not*!'

'Well, then, I don't understand…' I frowned.

'Look, I was drunk, okay? And she was coming onto me and I was curious, so we dabbled, but it wasn't for me. I prefer guys.'

'So what's the big deal? Why are you avoiding her? She says you're not replying to her messages.'

'Yeah… I've been busy. I will, though... I can tell she's really into me and she's cool, but it's awkward.'

This wasn't sounding like Roxy at all. She was squirming and even seemed a bit embarrassed. Never had I thought I'd see the day that Roxy would act shy about anything sex-related.

'I don't get it. You don't normally have a problem telling people you're not interested.'

'I know. It's just, she kind of got in my head. She was saying I enjoyed it and that I should try to accept it instead of fighting my feelings.'

'And *did* you enjoy it?' asked Bella.

'*Maybe*. But it doesn't mean I'm gay. I like *guys*.'

'So you keep saying,' I said. 'I mean, to be honest, I

don't even know why you're getting so caught up in it. Aren't you the one who's normally all *go with the flow*? I'm surprised it took you this long to experiment!'

'I'm confused. I thought I knew who I was and what I liked. I've always loved men, fit hunky young guys who are hung like a donkey. *That's* always what got me going, but then *boom*! One night out with Geli and it's thrown my world out of sync. Now I feel like I don't know who I am.'

'I've only ever been with men, so I'm no expert, but maybe it doesn't have to mean anything more than the fact that you connected with a person who just happens to be a woman?' I added, thinking of what Geli had said about not putting labels on who we're attracted to.

'Just tell her how you feel, that it scared you and you're still trying to process it. I don't think she's expecting a relationship. You two get on well, so just a friendship could be good enough. I'm sure she'd be happy with that. Especially as she's always travelling. Just don't ghost her.'

Ghosting was the worst. When I was dating, I never understood why some of the men I was messaging on apps couldn't just grow some balls, be honest and say they didn't feel that connection, instead of just disappearing off the face of the earth, leaving me hanging and wondering what I'd said or done wrong. Someone kind like Geli deserved more.

'Okay, I'll message her. Who knows, maybe one day I'll be up for some GOG—sorry, girl-on-girl action—but right now, I've got my hands full with plenty of cocks, so I don't have time to start adding any vag to the mix!' She let out her trademark cackle.

'Put so delicately as always.' I rolled my eyes. 'Once

you've spoken to her, just add it to your many experiences and move on. And like you said, see what happens in the future. Never say never and all that.'

'But seriously, Rox,' added Bella, 'if one day you do feel a connection with someone, know that it's okay. It happens. Society is becoming more open. Maybe look up some interviews with celebs like Miley Cyrus or Janelle Monae. They've been very vocal about their sexuality.'

'Be whoever you want to be and do whoever you want. It's nobody else's business who you have in your bed,' I said. 'Well, except for me! Now I've settled down, I want to hear all about your sexual antics so I can live vicariously through you!' Now it was my turn to laugh loudly.

'Me too!' said Bella.

'Okay, darlings! I'll keep you posted on my sexcapades. Thanks for being so cool about it. And, yeah, I'll message Geli later.'

'Of course! Sounds good, and when you do, don't overthink it. Whatever happened, happened. Just tell Geli it was fun, but you'd prefer not to take it further.'

'Bloody Nora! Can't believe *you*, Sophia Huntingdon, overthinking gold medallist, are telling *me* not to overthink.'

'I know! Always easier to give advice than to take it. And I *am* better than I used to be…'

I thought back to when I'd first met Lorenzo and my dating days. *Jeez*. So embarrassing. Fish out of water didn't even cover it. I'd overanalysed *everything* a guy did or said. I was definitely glad that I was all settled and happy now.

I saw what Holly was going through with Umberto. She was in a constant state of questioning and I was so glad I didn't have to go through that crap anymore. Although to be fair, Holly was right to overthink. She might be in awe of his good looks, but to me, that guy had more red flags than a football tournament.

'You are better,' said Bella. 'But anyway, it's nothing to be ashamed of. Dating again after coming out of a long-term relationship isn't easy. It can make any normally sane woman develop overthinkingitis.'

'Yep! And man did you have it bad with lover boy Lorenzo!' said Roxy. 'Speaking of which, how are things back in the sack?'

A massive grin spread across my face.

'That looks like a good sign!' said Bella.

'*Oh yes!*' Roxy's eyes widened. 'Looks like *someone* is back on the pitch and scoring big time!'

'I am indeed!'

'Details, Soph. We need deets!'

I gave them an ABC version of our bedroom antics (they didn't need to know *everything)* and they were really happy for me.

Then we chatted about work stuff. Bella's teaching was going well. Roxy was under a lot of pressure as she was now pretty much running the company she worked at since her boss Colette had taken a big step back. After my experiences with the business, I didn't envy Roxy having that level of responsibility, but she was enjoying the challenge, so that was the important thing. I also updated them on my deal, which, if all went to plan, should go through in a couple of weeks.

'Sounds like things are really starting to look up for you over there,' said Bella.

'Yeah. *Finally!* The company stuff's getting sorted,

I've got a couple of friends. I'm even kind of getting on with the mother-in-law. Actually, *tolerating* is a better word. I must admit. It's been handy having her look after Leo.'

Saying that out loud made me think about my conversation with Geli. Listening to her speak about the importance of community when she was raising her son, I realised how much easier things were and how much happier I was when I allowed reliable people to help me.

When I'd written my list, I'd thought learning the language and being more independent was the key to solving my problems, but now I saw there was no shame in having support. Just like with my business, I didn't have to do everything alone. Whether it was my parents looking after Leo whilst I was working in London, Marta babysitting when I went to lessons, or asking my friends for advice, having a community was essential. I could be strong and independent and still ask others to lend a hand.

'I'm so happy you're making the most of her offer to babysit. It's important to give yourself a break,' said Bella.

'Yeah, things are good on that front, and thanks to Lorenzo and our almost daily *workouts*, I'm feeling much more relaxed too. No need for those gifts you bought me, Rox!' I laughed.

'Glad to hear it! But don't get complacent. You've got to keep the excitement going. Have you tried dressing up for him or role play?'

'Er, *no*! I'm just relieved to even be having sex again. A month ago I thought I was destined for a life of chastity.'

'The transformation has been amazing, Soph! Told you

things would get better once you stopped breastfeeding and practised more often.'

'And started exploring your body again...'

'Yes, *thank you*. You both gave good advice. It's still early days, though. Don't want to run before I can walk. And we're a bit limited on fancy dress here. Not as if I can just nip out and buy a nurse's outfit!'

'You don't have to dress up like a French maid or nurse. It could just be something simple, like sexy secretary. Do you have a mac?'

'Yes...'

'So when Lorenzo comes home, just, *you know*, greet him in your heels, coat and nothing underneath. Then when he opens the door you can appear, drop the mac to the floor and *ta-da*! That'll *definitely* get him going.'

'Sounds like you're an expert.'

'Might have done it a few times...' She winked.

Maybe I'd consider it. Would be good to keep the excitement going.

'Guys, I hate to be a party pooper,' said Bella, 'but I've got a lesson to prepare for tomorrow, so I'm going to have to love you and leave you.'

'No worries, I better get going too,' said Roxy.

'Getting ready for a booty call?'

'No! I'm not all about sex, you know.'

Bella and I burst out laughing. 'Could have fooled us!'

'*Bloody cheek!* I'm a *businesswoman* with responsibilities. No nookie for me tonight. I need to get my rest so I can be fresh for my eight a.m. meeting.'

'Good for you!' I nodded. 'And now Leo's fast asleep, I'm going to clean up the kitchen and then get ready for Lorenzo to come home...'

'Go get it, girl!' said Roxy. 'And remember. *Sexy secretary…*'

I rolled my eyes. 'Goodnight, lovelies.'

'Night, night,' they said.

Ah, I loved those ladies. I really did hope we could keep up our phone calls and messages. Speaking to them really lifted my mood. And it seemed almost criminal to have all this technology that allowed us to communicate so easily and not use it.

I remembered living in France for a year when I was at uni. I had to wait days to get Bella's handwritten letters in the post. There was no WhatsApp, FaceTime or Zoom. *Jeez.* Sounded like I was born in the Dark Ages. I was so used to my smartphone and apps, it was hard to imagine a time without them.

Anyway, enough reminiscing. It was almost ten. Lorenzo would be home in half an hour, so no time to tidy the kitchen. I'd do it in the morning.

Maybe I'd take Roxy's advice and put on some heels and a mac. Give Lorenzo a nice welcome home after a hard day at work. *Yep.* I was becoming more comfortable about getting naked. Wearing a nightdress to bed was now a distant memory.

I'd barely got my T-shirt and leggings off before the door slammed. Lorenzo was home early? I heard him talking Italian. Probably on the phone. He'd want to end his conversation once he saw what I had in store for him…

I quickly took off my underwear, slipped on my coat and some heels, then stuck my leg out of the bedroom door so he could see me as soon as he walked into the hallway.

'I'm in here, loverboy,' I purred, sliding my leg up and down the doorway as seductively as I could.

'Soph, can you come out here, please?' Lorenzo called out. Thank goodness Leo was in a deep sleep. From the sound of his voice, Lorenzo had only just reached the hallway so must have missed me sticking my leg out the first time.

'So you want to shake things up again? Fancy doing it on the sofa?'

It was always fun to experiment outside of the bedroom. *Exciting.*

I slid my leg out again and just as I was about to step outside the room and drop my mac completely, Lorenzo cried out.

'Sophia! Mamma is here! With me.'

WTF.

What was Marta doing here at this time of night?

And Jesus. I hoped she hadn't seen my leg. For once I was glad she didn't speak English; otherwise she would have understood what I was saying. Thank goodness I hadn't gone ahead with flashing Lorenzo either. I didn't need to add another *caught in the act by the mother-in-law* encounter to my list.

I tightened the belt around my mac, slipped off my heels and stepped outside.

Huh?

'What's going on?' I frowned, staring at the large suit-cases beside him. 'What's with the cases? Is Marta going on holiday?'

Although I'd miss the babysitting, I definitely wouldn't miss her judgemental looks. I wondered how long she'd be gone for.

'No… there was an accident, that is why I am home early.'

'Accident?'

'There was a fire. At Mamma's house.'

'Oh God! Is she okay? Was anyone else there? Did anyone get hurt?' Whilst she wasn't my favourite person in the world, I didn't dislike her enough to want any harm to come to her. I glanced at Marta, looking for signs of injury. She seemed a little paler than usual, but generally okay. Like always, she looked at me like she was sucking a bitter lemon. Yep. Marta was fine. Lorenzo still hadn't explained the suitcases, though...

'There was no one else there. Mamma is a bit shaken. Thank God is nothing very serious.' He wrapped his arm around her and gave her a gentle squeeze. 'But the kitchen is badly damaged and she needs to cook. An Italian home is nothing without a kitchen!' He smiled. 'And we will need to get experts to check the house. To make sure it is safe. So Mamma cannot stay there.'

Oh no.

No, no, no...

Please don't tell me he's going to say what I think he's going to say...

'So of course, I said that Mamma can stay here. With us.'

My eyes popped out of my head and my stomach plummeted so far I was surprised it didn't fall through the floor.

Marta? Living here? In the same house? Under the same roof? Scrutinising me and our lives twenty-four hours a day?

You have *got* to be joking.

CHAPTER THIRTY-THREE

'Lorenzo, can we talk in the bedroom, please? *Now.*'

He told his mum he'd be back in a minute, followed me into the room, then closed the door.

'Don't you think we should have discussed this first?'

'It was not planned…'

'I know what happened wasn't intentional and I'm glad Marta's okay and everything because it could have been a *lot* worse, but you could have called to let me know or something instead of just springing this on me.'

'There was no time. When I heard it had happened, I left work straight away and I try to calm Mamma down, then speak to firemen about the damage. And when they said it was safe to get some things from her bedroom, I help her pack. After that, we came straight here.'

Fair point. I could imagine it was full-on. Must have been a big shock for both of them, but did she really have to come here?

'Can't she stay with a friend? She must know a lot of people in this town.'

'Sophia. She is my *mother*. If the same thing happened to your mum, would you think it is right for me to ask her to stay with friends? Mamma can sleep in Leo's room. It will only be for a few days.'

I know I'd said to Bella and Roxy that I was learning to tolerate Marta more, but this was different. It was hard enough when she came to visit for a few hours. A few days living with Marta would feel like a life sentence.

Lorenzo was right, though. If the shoe was on the other foot, there was no way I would let my mum stay with friends. As irritating as she could be, I'd have to put my feelings to one side and suck it up.

'Okay,' I huffed. 'I suppose it's fine if it's only for a few days.'

'*Grazie!*' He hugged me. 'And she can help with Leo and with the cooking. It will be good for you, no? With the deal.'

That was true. As the deal got closer, there was probably going to be even more to-ing and fro-ing with the lawyer and Rhonda. It would be easier to manage everything with an extra pair of hands. But one thing was for sure: if Marta was going to be living here, I wasn't going to pander and tiptoe around her like I did before. Although I was grateful for Marta's help and recognised the benefits of that support, I would no longer allow her to keep walking all over me. My perspective had changed on a lot of things lately, and just because she was Lorenzo's mum and would be helping out with Leo didn't mean I was going to put up with any more shit.

When I thought about all the sucking up I'd done in the beginning, trying to impress Marta with cooking that she never appreciated and biting my tongue whenever she was rude, it made me sick. *Yes, Marta, no, Marta, three bags full, Marta. No.* Those days were gone. I had never been a people pleaser before. I knew that I couldn't be everyone's cup of tea. But when I'd come here, somehow I'd been so desperate to make her like me and think I was a good mum and good for Lorenzo that I'd lost my backbone. It had returned now, thank God, so although I'd be civil and polite, I was done kissing her feet. Whilst Marta was staying under our roof, she'd have to live by *our* rules.

Lorenzo and I walked back out to the living room, where Marta was still standing.

'I will go and prepare the bed in Leo's room,' he said before translating it for his mum and leaving. Now I was regretting having a bed in there. We'd added one so that I could sit on it to breastfeed Leo in the middle of the night, or so that if he wasn't well, I could try and soothe him without having to wake up Lorenzo.

It was just me and Marta here. In silence.

Although she wasn't my favourite person in the world, I still had a heart. It must have been scary to see her kitchen on fire, so she must be pretty shaken up.

'*Siediti,*' I said, remembering the Italian and gesturing towards the sofa for her to sit down.

Marta snarled and shook her head violently. Pretty sure I heard her mumble *sporca*, which I think meant *dirty*.

Oh, I see. It seemed like Spunkgate was still at the front of her mind. She obviously thought it was soiled from my sexcapades with Lorenzo…

There I was trying to be nice and she had to get all uppity.

Fuck it. I was tired of her looking down on me.

'Yeah, you're right.' I smirked. 'Maybe it's best you

don't sit there. That's where me and Lorenzo had *wild* sex last night, so maybe this armchair would be better...' I know it was bad and a little childish, but I couldn't resist, especially knowing that Marta didn't have a clue what I was saying. This was *our* house. Why shouldn't we have sex on the sofa if we wanted to? And so what if I gave my boyfriend a BJ and he came all over me? There was nothing wrong with me giving him pleasure. I'd spent too long feeling embarrassed about her catching us in the act, but not anymore. Now I found it funny. Maybe Marta should get a sense of humour about it too. Shit happens, for Christ's sake. Move on.

Marta huffed, picked up a bag which looked like it was filled with pots and pans and walked into the kitchen. *How did she rescue those from the fire?*

Suddenly she started shouting in Italian, and as I went to see what was wrong, I saw her throwing her hands up in the air. She was saying it was a mess. Good thing Geli taught us the useful phrases in the home as I wouldn't have understood otherwise. She continued moaning about the dishes. *Hold on.* Did she say this house was a disaster and we needed her?

See? This was exactly what I was talking about. She'd barely been here five minutes and already she'd called the sofas dirty and started criticising the state of the kitchen. I was going to wash up tonight but ran out of time, so had planned to do it in the morning. How was I to know that she was going to come round at ten at night to do a bloody hygiene inspection?

Grrr.

If you want to wash up, Marta, be my guest. One less job for me to do. But I will no longer allow you to make me

feel bad about the fact that I haven't done something that
you expect me to. You are not my keeper.

I turned around calmly and walked into the bedroom. I
was going to shut the door and go to sleep. I wasn't going
to let her wind me up.

Yes. Staying calm and ignoring Marta was the best
option.

Something told me this was going to be a long few
days...

∼

I was in Casini's with Holly. After Marta had arrived last
night, I wouldn't feel comfortable inviting Holly here
and asking her about what was going on with the host
family, and I definitely wasn't going to hers, where
Silvestro was guaranteed to interrupt us, so I'd suggested
we go to the bar we usually met at for our Italian
lessons. Geli seemed to know the owner and it was nice
and quiet. It felt like a safe environment to have a
private conversation.

We'd spent the last twenty minutes on small talk and
Umberto. She still hadn't met his family or friends. It was
just another account of them meeting up, going for a drive
and how hot he looked. I knew I was going to sound like a
grandma saying this, but I just couldn't stand to see her
wasting her life.

'I know you think he's the bee's knees, drop-dead
gorgeous and good in the sack, or rather on the back seat,
but a guy being into you isn't just about sex. It's about
wanting to spend quality time with you. Making plans for
the future. Introducing you to the important people in his

live, like his friends and family. It's about showing *real* commitment.'

I thought about when I'd fallen for Lorenzo. At first it *had* been about the attraction and his good looks, but there was no way we could have got this far if that was all there was to it. Especially when Leo was born and sex was well and truly off the menu. We had a deeper connection, a lot in common, and Lorenzo constantly did things to show that he was in this with me for the long haul. But we were at a different stage of life to Holly and Umberto. Maybe neither of them was ready for that level of commitment at their age.

'Are you sure Umberto's looking for a relationship right now? That he's really the one?'

'*Totally!*'

Oh dear.

'And when you first told him you were thinking about coming to live here, how did he react?'

'Umberto said it would be cool and he'd love to spend more time with me, but maybe it wasn't possible because there were no jobs in the town or places to stay.'

So she'd given up uni to come and live with a guy who thought it would be *cool* to spend more time with her? *Shit.* This was worse than I'd thought. I bet he'd got the shock of his life when she *had* found a job and moved here.

I couldn't judge Holly, though. When we're in love, sometimes we just can't see sense. Hopefully soon she'd realise he wasn't right for her. Until then, I'd just have to be there for her. Anyway, right now, as much as I didn't like the sound of the guy, it wasn't Umberto I was most worried about…

'Right. I see… So,' I said, swiftly changing the subject, 'tell me about Silvestro?'

'Well…' Holly frowned. I was sure she wanted to talk more about Umberto, but I was determined to get to the bottom of what was going on. 'You've met him. He's… full-on. In your face. A bit too familiar. *Creepy*…'

'Definitely. Way too *familiar*. I have to ask, has he ever tried it on with you?' Holly's eyes darted down at the table. 'It's okay. You can tell me.'

'No…' She took a deep breath, 'I mean…yes…sort of… *maybe*. He hasn't kissed me or forced himself on me. Just—*y'know*—patted my bum a couple of times. And stood so close behind me I could feel his, you know… his boner.'

'Fuck!' I thought of all the times he'd stood behind her to get something out of the cupboard. *Did he have a hard-on then? What a pervert.*

'It's not a big deal. I mean, it's not like he properly forced himself on me or anything, so—'

'Holly, that is *not* okay. That is sexual assault.'

'But he didn't hit me, pin me down or try to, y'know, rape me.'

'Sexual assault doesn't have to involve violence or leave visible marks. It can affect you emotionally or psychologically—in ways that *can't* be seen. No one should touch you in a way that you don't want or bloody rub themselves against you. That's disgusting. He should be reported!'

'No… I don't want any trouble. I can't lose my job. I need to be close to Umberto. It was hard enough to find a family in this town. And I don't want the agency to black-list me.'

'Blacklist *you*? For outing a pervert? It's *him* that should be blacklisted. You're probably not the first person he's done this to, and unless you speak up, you won't be the last.'

'I don't want to, okay?' she snapped. I could tell she was getting irritable. That wasn't like her at all. Holly was always so cheery, but she was obviously scared. I needed to tread carefully.

'Look, I can't force you. It's your decision, but just think about it. *Please.*' I could tell Silvestro was a real sleazebag. And I bet he'd done more than she was letting on. I mean, she'd asked Geli how to say not to come in her room in Italian, which definitely wasn't a good sign. 'Does he try and come in your bedroom?'

She paused.

'A couple of times, but I just put the chair behind the door now.'

'Oh, *Holly*! That's no way to live. You can't spend every day in fear. I just worry that if you don't say something and report him, it will escalate.'

If he'd tried to come into her bedroom, I bet he'd probably walked in on her in the bathroom too. I was beginning to think that lock was broken for a reason…

'Look…' She hurriedly put her arms in the sleeve of her jacket and picked up her bag. 'I better go. Can we not talk about this again? It's nothing. I just want to forget about it and get on with my job.'

'Okay,' I said, knowing full well it definitely was not. 'You've got my number. Call or text me anytime if you need me. *Promise*?'

'See you later, Soph.'

Then she was out the door.

I slumped back in my chair. It made me *so* angry that creeps like him thought it was their right to touch women and do whatever they wanted. To make Holly feel so uncomfortable that she was afraid to speak up. I wish I could do something. Tell his wife or the police. *Someone*. But I had to respect Holly's wishes. At least at the moment, she was talking to me. I didn't want to push her so much that she closed up completely and suffered in silence. I wondered if she'd even told Umberto.

I'd give Holly space. *For now*. But I would have to follow up at some point soon because who knew how far it could go? Holly might have been able to fight off his unwanted advances by putting a chair behind her door, but for how long? And what if the next au pair wasn't so 'lucky'?

CHAPTER THIRTY-FOUR

'I can't stop thinking about that tiramisu…' I licked my lips.

'I am glad you liked it.' Lorenzo smiled.

'I didn't like it, I *loved* it!'

'*Grazie*. Is better when it stay in the fridge overnight. More flavour.'

'Well, to me, it was amazing!'

This morning, Lorenzo had got up at the crack of dawn to try out some new recipes, including a limoncello tiramisu with shavings of white chocolate sprinkled on top, and the word *delicious* didn't even begin to do it justice. It was rich and creamy, without being too heavy, with just the right amount of lemon liqueur. *Pure perfection*.

Now we were taking a stroll in the sunshine with Leo before Lorenzo's friends came round for lunch. The views were spectacular. So far we'd passed beautiful evergreen cypress trees lining the roads, walked through local vine-yards, and in the distance I could see rows and rows of olive trees starting to flower with tiny clusters.

The sky was blue and the air was so fresh I could literally feel my lungs expanding with every step. This really was something. I could see why I'd fallen in love with this place when I'd first visited.

'So,' I said, glancing down at Leo in his pushchair to see if he was still awake. He was and must have been enjoying the views just as much as we were, as he was nice and calm. 'Do you think you'll add it to the menu?'

'Hmmm…' Lorenzo sighed. 'We will see. The people here prefer traditional tiramisu. Perhaps is better for summer, but I can try and see what happen…'

It broke my heart to know Lorenzo literally cooked the same traditional dishes day after day, over and over, when he was capable of so much more. Although Leo and I visited him sometimes at the restaurant during our daily walks and it cheered him up, I knew working there made him sad. I could see it in his eyes. That place stifled his creativity.

'It must be so hard for you. I wish they would just take a chance, listen to your suggestions and shake things up a bit.'

'The managers say we give customers what they want.' He shrugged his shoulders. '*Sì*. Is difficult, for me, but we must make sacrifice sometimes. You make sacrifice to come here too, so is the same. I have been lucky to work in different places before and create many different dishes. At the moment is not possible, but working there means I can spend more time with you and Leo and that is the most important.'

My heart just melted. 'Well, Leo and I appreciate you,' I kissed him on the lips. 'And like you said, we all have to make sacrifices, so as painful as it'll be, if it helps you out,

I *suppose* I can force myself to eat any new dishes you want me to try. It'll be a tough job, but I'm willing to do it, *just for you…*' I chuckled.

'You are *so* kind!' He laughed, wrapping his arm around me.

'This has been lovely. I do enjoy our Sunday walks. Especially now it's getting a bit warmer.'

'*Sì.* Is very beautiful here.' He stopped, took Leo out of his pushchair and carried him over his shoulder as if to give him a better view. I loved seeing them together like that. I couldn't resist taking my phone out and snapping a few photos.

Lorenzo was right. It *was* breathtaking here. An environment like this would be ideal to raise Leo. *In theory.* But as the saying goes, not all that glitters is gold. It wasn't just about how a place *looked*. It also needed to *feel* like home. And as gorgeous as the views were, this didn't feel like where we were meant to be.

We needed to live somewhere that allowed us to be fulfilled both personally as a family and professionally. Lorenzo's talents were too big for this town, and as much as I was trying, I just didn't see myself fitting here long-term either.

'What time are the boys coming over?'

'In forty minutes. Maybe we should start walking back.'

'Okay. I'm going to have a little look at the antiques market in town that I've been meaning to check out for ages, then pop round to Geli's for a coffee. Give you guys time to catch up together.'

Lorenzo didn't get to see his friends that often, so I

thought it would be nice to give him some space and time for man talk. And of course, it was good to keep my distance from Marta. Yes, she was still there. It wasn't ideal, but now I'd decided not to put up with her shit, I was feeling better about things. If she did something I didn't like, I made a point of letting her know.

With any luck she'd still be at church by the time we got back, but *whatever*. If she was at home, I'd just stay out of her way.

'You will join us for lunch?'

'*Lunch?* After all that food you *forced* me to eat this morning, I don't think I need to eat for another week!' I laughed. 'Thanks, but I'm good and I packed some stuff for Leo too, so I'll probably just feed him at Geli's. You guys enjoy. I'm sure they're going to love the limoncello tiramisu just as much as I did!'

∾

'We're home!' I said, stepping inside. The antiques market was actually better than I'd thought. I hadn't bought anything, but there were some cool things there. I was glad I went. We'd had a nice time at Geli's too.

I could see Lorenzo, Flavio and Amadeo sitting in the garden laughing and enjoying a beer. I gave them a quick wave and took Leo out of his pushchair. Lorenzo wasted no time in jumping up to come and give us both a kiss before scooping up Leo and taking him out to see his friends. I'd go out and say hello properly in a minute. I was on my way to the toilet when I spotted Marta in our bedroom.

What the hell.

Marta was standing with her back to the door, holding my lacy red thong in the air.

'*Cosa stai facendo?*' I snapped, asking her what she was doing.

She pointed to a pile of clothes on the bed. I think she said something about washing. No. Folding. She was folding the laundry.

I could see she'd already done some T-shirts, leggings, Lorenzo's jeans and some of Leo's clothes. I hadn't got round to it, so yes, it was helpful, but *boundaries, woman.* She couldn't go around touching my knickers. That was personal. For all I knew, she could be planting ant powder in them to make me itch or something. Okay. Maybe I was taking my paranoia too far. But I didn't like the idea of Marta doing that. If she started touching my lingerie, then she'd have an excuse to start rifling through my underwear drawers, saying she was 'just putting them away.'

No. It was too much.

'*Grazie*'—I plucked my thong from her hands—'*ma lo farò.*' I told her I would do it.

I was surprised Marta even wanted to touch my undies after being so prudish about catching Lorenzo and me in the act. Maybe she was wondering if they could fit her.

Ha! Imagine uptight Marta getting frisky.

Actually, I'd rather not…

I wondered if she'd ever thought about dating again. There must be other single pensioners in this town. I reckoned it'd be good for her. As far as I could see, her life revolved around Lorenzo and Leo. They were her purpose. Being here and doing housework was probably her way of feeling useful and keeping herself occupied.

Take ironing for example. That was one chore I only did if I absolutely *had* to. The clothes I wore these days didn't need it, and neither did most of Lorenzo's. I sometimes ironed his chef's jacket or jeans if he didn't have time to do it himself. But unlike me (and probably a lot of people), Marta seemed to get a massive kick from ironing. She'd dedicate *hours* to it. She would do it all. And when I say *all*, I mean she ironed *everything.* Not just clothes. Bed sheets, duvet covers, pillowcases, Leo's bibs, romper suits, cushion covers and blankets too. Even Lorenzo's underpants and socks for goodness' sake. The other day I saw her ironing the tea towels. *Each to their own, I suppose.*

Actually, now that I thought about it, what Marta was doing was pretty harmless. I mean, climbing onto those freshly washed and ironed bedsheets the other day had felt lovely. And did I really want to spend what was left of this afternoon folding laundry? If that was the kind of thing that floated Marta's boat, I'd just let her get on with it and have her fun. But definitely not with my underwear. Some things were sacred.

I scooped my bras and knickers off the bed and put them away in my underwear drawer.

'*Grazie. Per favore continua.*' I smiled, asking her to carry on, then went to the loo.

I headed out to the garden. It was still sunny and warm and the views of the rolling hills in the distance looked so green and perfect, it was like they'd been painted straight onto a backdrop.

'*Ciao!*' I greeted Flavio and Amadeo with two cheek kisses.

'*Ciao, Sophia, come stai*?' said Amadeo, running his fingers through his dark hair, which was all slicked back.

'*Bene, grazie, e tu?*'

'*Bene, bene.*'

'*Come sta la tua famiglia?*' I added, asking Flavio how his family was. He had four kids, aged five to fourteen, so his household was hectic. According to Lorenzo, Flavio joked that was why he'd gone bald in his thirties. Whenever I saw him his head was always freshly shaved. It suited him.

Flavio said everyone was well and he was enjoying having some peace and quiet by coming here. I replied saying I hoped that Leo behaved himself this afternoon. Then I asked them if they'd enjoyed Lorenzo's tiramisu, which of course they had. His cooking really was amazing.

Neither of them spoke English that well, so it felt good to be able to have a little conversation with them. Don't get me wrong. It'd be a while before I'd be able to have a deep discussion on the state of the world or politics (probably good subjects to avoid anyway), but at least I'd been able to communicate, which was a lot more than I could do before.

'*Vuoi un'altra birra?*' I could see they'd almost finished their beers so asked if I could get them another one.

'*Sì, grazie.*' Flavio flashed an enthusiastic smile.

I went to the kitchen and took some beers out of the fridge. It'd been a couple of hours since they'd eaten lunch, and although Lorenzo had probably given them enough food to feed an army, I'd take out a little bowl of crisps too, just in case they wanted something to snack on.

I opened the cupboards.

FFS.

She'd done it again.

Marta had rearranged everything. When she'd first done it the morning after she'd moved in, it had taken me almost ten minutes to find where she'd buried my herbal tea. And she'd thrown a perfectly fine, almost full bottle of tomato ketchup in the bin. *Bloody cheek.* Yeah, I know she'd probably done it because she didn't approve, but I liked ketchup. Sometimes if I felt like some chips or potato wedges, I liked to squeeze a big dollop all over it. Who didn't? Well, clearly Marta, but I shouldn't feel judged in my own home for what I ate. I'd told her not to move things around and I'd thought she'd listened, but clearly that didn't last long.

Folding and ironing the laundry was one thing. *That* was helpful. But rearranging stuff after I'd asked her not to was *not* okay.

I walked into the bedroom calmly. *I mustn't let her get to me.*

'*Marta, gli armadi… lascia per favore.*'

'*Non capisco,*' said Marta.

Oh, here we go again. The old *I don't understand* routine. I know that I definitely said *cupboards* and to *please leave them alone.*

Let's try again. This time I'll ask her to come into the kitchen.

'*Per favore, la cucina.*' I gestured towards the kitchen because, annoyingly, I couldn't remember how to say the word for *come.* She followed me reluctantly.

'Please do not touch,' I said, opening the cupboards and waving my finger.

'You need help with the beers?' Lorenzo walked into the kitchen.

'Sorry! I haven't forgotten. I was just trying to explain

to Marta that I'd prefer it if she didn't rearrange the cupboards. It makes it *really* difficult to find things. I wanted to bring you guys some crisps to go with your beers, but everything has been moved.'

Lorenzo nodded and then started speaking to Marta in Italian. Sure enough, I heard him use the same words I had for cupboards and to not touch them. He rested his hand gently on Marta's shoulder and gave her a kiss on the forehead. She nodded, squeezed his cheeks and then left the kitchen.

'Is all fine. Mamma understands. You want me to help you find them?'

'It's okay. I'll do it. You go back to your friends.'

'*Grazie*. You are doing *very* well with your Italian, Soph. I am proud of you.' He wrapped his arm around me and gave me an encouraging squeeze. 'Is good to see you have conversation with Flavio and Amadeo. The lessons and your studying is helping, *sì*?'

'Awww, thanks!' I kissed him firmly on the lips. It was nice to hear that he thought I was making progress too. 'Yes, they are. Still a long way to go, but I'm feeling more confident.'

'*Bene*. I go back to the garden. Flavio is with Leo.'

'Cool, I'll be out in a sec.'

Once I'd found the crisps and taken them out to the boys, I'd come and put the cupboards back how they should be. I didn't mind Marta helping out, but I wasn't going to allow her to take over. Yes, she was his mother. But ultimately, she was a guest. This was still our home. Lorenzo and I made the rules. If I wanted to eat ketchup, I would. If I wanted to keep my herbal tea in a certain place, that was where it would go. There would be no more sucking up or biting my tongue to please her.

Yep. If Marta didn't like the way the cupboards were arranged or anything else in this house, she had two choices: get over it or leave.

CHAPTER THIRTY-FIVE

'Sophia, *come si dice…* how do you say *where can I find the fish?*'

'Do-vey peskay?'

'Almost: you say *dov'è il pesce*,' said Geli. 'And you pronounce fish *PEH-sheh*.'

I repeated it a few more times until I got it right.

We were at Casini's having another Italian lesson. I was so relieved when Holly turned up. I was worried that after our conversation last week, I'd scared her away. She seemed quieter than normal. I hoped that was just because she'd had a long day and not because her pervy boss had been trying it on again. Hopefully we'd have time to speak at the end of the lesson so that I could check she was okay.

Today we were learning about how to ask for things in the supermarket. That would have come in handy a couple of months ago. I hadn't stepped foot in that place since they'd run me out of the store. Lorenzo and I had been driving to a big supermarket out of town and he often brought stuff home that he'd picked up whilst shopping for the restaurant.

After we'd spent another hour running through vocab and phrases, Geli announced we were going on a little field trip. As we were leaving, she asked if I remembered how to say arsehole. Strange question, but I told her I did: *stronzo* for a man, *stronzi* for men, *stronza* for a woman and *stronze* for women. Funny how I remembered the swear words so easily…

We put on our jackets and stepped out of the bar, following Geli, who was leading the way. I walked beside Holly.

'How are you?' I said.

'Fine, thanks, you?' she said, avoiding eye contact. Nope. Holly definitely wasn't her normal bubbly self. Her shoulders were slouching like she had the weight of the world on them. I wanted to ask her about things at home again, but I needed to tread carefully.

'Yeah. *So-so*. Still got the mother-in-law staying… not ideal, but hey, ho.'

Marta had been there for a week and there were still no signs of her leaving. First it was a problem with the builder *apparently* and now there was a delay with her new oven arriving, and of course, there would be no way she could go back home without a fully functioning kitchen…

Whilst I seemed to have stopped her messing with my stuff in the kitchen, the same couldn't be said for things in the bedroom. No, she wasn't sleeping in our room or anything (though she was so attached to Lorenzo I wouldn't have put it past her to try). Instead, she had killed our newly revitalised sex life. *Dead*. Lorenzo said it wouldn't be right for us to do anything whilst his mum was there. Because she was in Leo's room next door, he thought it would be disrespectful. So that was that.

I was climbing the walls. I wanted Lorenzo so badly. But what could I do? He'd been patient for months when I wasn't ready, so I had to do the same and respect his wishes. Talk about sod's law. If this had happened when I'd lost my libido, it wouldn't have been so bad. But, *oh no*. That would have been far too convenient. *Typical*. We'd finally got things back on track, got the flames of passion burning again, and Marta had come and poured cold water all over them. *Great.*

One silver lining of the massive Marta cloud was that as well as doing lots of housework, she'd been helping out a lot with Leo. She particularly seemed to enjoy feeding him. She'd cook homemade food for him every day and always insisted on giving him his bottle. If he cried, she'd be there in a second to soothe him. To be honest, I didn't believe in picking him up every time, but I was trying to be less rigid.

I also enjoyed feeding Leo. I loved the way he'd stare up at me with his big brown eyes as he sucked on the bottle. But Marta was completely dominating his feed times. If I hadn't had so much to do with this deal, I would have put my foot down, but going through these contracts was so time-consuming. If all went well at my meeting tomorrow, the deal should go through next week, which would be a huge weight off my shoulders.

'Must be a right pain in the arse having her hanging around,' said Holly. 'I prefer it when the 'rents are out of the house too, so I can just get on with teaching the kids without them sticking their noses in.'

'Rents must mean the host parents. *Got it.* Sometimes

keeping up with Holly's slang was like understanding another language.

'Yeah, sometimes it's good to have your own space. Hopefully my mother-in-law won't be staying for too much longer. So…' I paused, hoping she was relaxed enough to open up. 'How are things at the house? With Silvestro? Has he—'

'We are here!' said Geli.

Dammit. I wanted to hear how things were with Holly. I looked up to see where we were. The supermarket? *Oh gosh.* Did we really have to go here? I supposed I couldn't avoid it forever. Actually, *no.* Why should I? I'd done nothing wrong.

We walked in and I spotted the horrible women straight away. They were in the corner talking loudly. They looked at us and then went back to their conversation.

'*Allora,*' said Geli. 'I would like each of you to go up to the women and ask for something. Daphne, I want you to ask where the cheese is, Holly, I would like you to ask for rice and, Sophia, ask for some dried fruit.'

We each took it in turns to approach them. I repeated the phrase I remembered in my head and asked for *la frutta secca* just as Geli had asked me to. One of the ladies grunted, then pointed, telling me it was in aisle two on the right. I was pleased that I understood what she'd said.

Next we did role play with Geli, asking for various things in Italian. I definitely felt more confident about shopping by myself in the future. Just as we were about to leave, Geli called us over to where the women were still standing and chatting away.

She pulled me to the front and I think she told the women to be quiet a moment and they suddenly fell silent.

I understood her say that I was her British friend. The next few words I didn't follow... I picked up on some of the others, though. *Baby. Crying. Leave. Rude.* Geli became more animated. Waving her hands, glaring at them angrily. The women folded their arms and started getting agitated.

Hold on. I think she's having a go at them. About how they treated me when I came in with Leo.

Yes. She was!

Now she was telling them to say sorry.

They started shouting and saying no.

Geli then called them ignorant and stupid.

'Sophia, these idiots are refusing to apologise for their behaviour. What do we call people who do that? *Arseholes.* How do you say arseholes in Italian?'

I paused. Geli was asking me to insult them to their faces. This was a small town, so if I did I'd probably make some enemies.

Fuck it.

After the way they'd treated me, they bloody deserved it. And I had no plans to come in this shop again anyway. I refused to give them my money.

'*Stronze!*' I said, looking them all straight in the eye. The women gasped, putting their hands to their mouths.

'Time to go, ladies!' giggled Geli. We walked out laughing. Well, everyone except Daphne.

'Was that *really* necessary?' Daphne snarled.

'*Absolutely!*' Geli lifted up her hand for me to high-five.

'I do my shopping there regularly, so insulting them is going to make my life very difficult.'

'What you do not understand, Daphne,' Geli raised an

eyebrow, 'is that just like they have insulted Sophia, they have also insulted you too.'

'*Me?*' Daphne frowned.

'*Sì.* Said that you are a stuck-up lady who thinks she is better than everyone else in the town and that your husband should leave you and marry the woman he used to date who lives here. I forgotten her name…maybe Guilia?'

'No!' Daphne's mouth dropped open. 'They said *that*?'

Geli nodded.

'Those gossiping little…' Daphne stormed back into the shop with a face like thunder. We quickly followed behind to see what she was going to do. '*Vaffanculo!*' she screamed, sticking her middle finger up at them. Daphne then walked out of the shop calmly.

Geli, Holly and I all stared at each other, our eyes wide. I couldn't believe she'd just told them all to fuck off.

'Wow…Daphne…I am surprised…' Geli was still trying to get her head around it too.

'That felt good,' Daphne exhaled.

'But I thought you didn't like swear words?' God bless Holly for asking what the rest of us were already thinking.

'There is a time and a place for such language and that was it. I thought my husband was at least being discreet about his illicit affair with that woman, but now the whole town is gossiping about me, it's time to put on the boxing gloves. She's welcome to the cheating *testa di cazzo*. I'm getting a divorce. Goodnight.'

And just like that, Daphne was gone. Walking with her head held high.

We were all still rooted to the spot in shock.

'Did that really just happen?' said Holly.

'I believe it did,' I replied.

'And there I was thinking she was all bougie with the perfect life.' Holly shook her head.

'*Nobody* has a perfect life.' I turned to Geli. 'Did you really hear them say all of that?'

'More or less… that was the polite version. I do not like those women in there. They are bad. And I also do not like the way the husband make a fool out of Daphne. Yes, she is snooty, but she does not deserve to be humiliated.'

'Humiliated?' said Holly.

'Yes. He kissed this Guilia woman in public. He has not even been married to Daphne for very long. He takes money from her and leaves Daphne at home with his parents, who do not speak English, then he go to stay with other woman. Is wrong.'

'Married men,' huffed Holly. I looked at her, wondering if she was referring specifically to creepy Silvestro. 'Anyway'—her eyes darted down to the floor—'I better run. See you next week.' She must have sensed that I was about to try and ask her again how things were at her place.

'Bloody hell,' I said as Geli and I started walking home. 'Who knew there could be such drama in a small town? I guess it doesn't matter if it's a big city like London or a place like this, nowhere is immune to dishonesty.'

'That is right. Sadly some people cannot be trusted… I heard you talking about your mother-in-law earlier. I saw her again this afternoon.'

'Yes, I think she went to do food shopping. She came back with some bags. Don't know why. There's enough food in the house to feed a small country.'

'I did not see her at the supermarket. I saw her at the house of Claudia again. I was across the road as she arrived, so this time I hid behind a car to watch. Claudia give her a bag. Then she run back inside and give her what look like a bottle, for a baby, and she put that in the bag, then zipped it up. Do you know why she would do that?'

'Could you see what was inside the bottle?'

'No. Not really.'

'So it could have been empty?'

'Maybe, but…'

'She probably left it round there when she took Leo to play with her kid and the woman was just giving it back to her.'

'Perhaps you are right, Sophia. I do not know. But if I was you, I would investigate. Something feels, how you say? Fish?'

'You mean fishy?'

'*Sì*. This situation smells fishy. Something is not right. Like you say, some people are dishonest. I think you should ask Marta what she was doing there. At her house. Why she gave her baby bottle. Something tells me your mother-in-law cannot be trusted…'

CHAPTER THIRTY-SIX

I'd been worrying about it all night. Thinking about what was going on with Marta and that woman. Why she'd been going there.

Part of me said not to overthink things. That it was completely innocent. That maybe Marta was just helping the woman out. Apparently her husband had left before her youngest daughter was born, so she was a single mum. Marta probably was doing her whole martyr Mother Teresa stuff and helping out with babysitting, as the woman also had two other kids under five to manage. God knows how she did that.

But the other part of me, my gut, sensed that Geli was spot on. Something *wasn't* right. The annoying thing was, I hadn't even had time to try and discuss it with Lorenzo or Marta earlier today because Rhonda had flown over to meet me in Florence.

We'd agreed on a figure and terms. If I'd pushed, I could have got more or looked for other buyers, but it wasn't about that. Rhonda wanted to move quickly and doing this deal would give me my freedom, which was priceless. There would be no long tie-ins. Just a three-month consultancy role, covering my time if Rhonda needed my input to make the transition with clients and the team as smooth as possible.

Over the past few weeks our legal teams had been going through the paperwork, doing the relevant checks and drawing up various drafts of the contracts. This afternoon, Rhonda and I had gone through a few final sticking points, but in essence, the deal was agreed, and all being well, it would go through in a few days.

Surprisingly, we'd even finished early, so because Lorenzo couldn't get away at that time, I'd got a train to the nearest station and was now in a taxi home. I needed to make a quick call.

'Hi, Robyn, how you doing?'

'Fine, thanks, Soph. How did the meeting go?'

'Good. Really well. The deal will be going through any day now and I've spoken to Rhonda again about you and how important you are to the company and it's all fine—you're safe, so please don't worry.' I'd had a chat with Robyn before to let her know my intentions and to reassure her that she and the team would be taken care of. She said she understood, but I sensed that Robyn was still a bit nervous about her future.

'I really appreciate that, Soph. That's a weight off my mind. And congratulations!'

'Thanks! Until it's all signed and sealed, anything can happen, but I just wanted to keep you in the loop. Well done by the way on the great coverage recently. Especially that feature on *Vogue*'s website yesterday.'

The team had been pushing hard to secure more editorial and it was paying off. The clients seemed much happier, which was exactly what I needed. Especially in light of the sale.

'Yeah! We were really chuffed with that.'

'So… have you given any more thought to what you might do after your maternity leave?'

'Not really. To be honest, I'm just trying to get through the pregnancy.'

'Yep. I remember those days. Look, like I said before, your job will be safe, so if you want to come back to it afterwards, then go for it. But just speaking as a friend and not your boss, don't be like me and work yourself into the ground. It's not worth it. You've got to take care of your health now and also when the baby comes. Remember, you're young and smart so whether you stay at BeCome, which I'm sure everyone hopes you will, or you choose to do something else, there's so much you can do with your life. Don't think that having a child has to stop you, okay?'

'Okay. Thanks, Soph.'

'And if ever there's anything you need, personally or professionally, just ask. You're not alone.'

'That really means a lot. I reckon I'm going to need loads of advice, especially on this motherhood stuff. I'm shitting myself.'

'I'm no expert on that, I'm just figuring it out as I go along, but I'm happy to share what I've learnt or just offer an ear when you need someone to listen. Anyway, I better go. Speak soon.'

'Speak soon. And thanks again for being so patient and looking out for me.'

'No worries.'

I exhaled. I was glad we'd had that chat. I knew what

Robyn was like. Apart from these past few months because of her sickness, which couldn't be helped, like me, she was a perfectionist. I could already see her pushing herself to work long hours for Rhonda before she went on maternity leave, then trying to be a super mum and rush back to work once she'd had the baby. So just like Albert had helped me see the light, it was important that I paid it forward. I didn't want Robyn to wake up one day like me and realise she could have been happier if she wasn't so focused on work.

I looked at my watch. *That's good.* It was approaching seven, so I'd be back in time to give Leo his bottle and put him to bed. And have a chat with Marta about this Claudia woman. Hopefully Lorenzo wouldn't be far behind me, so he could always translate if she started saying she didn't understand. I needed to get to the bottom of whatever this mystery was about as it was really bugging me.

As I closed the front door, Marta called out for Lorenzo. I walked down the hallway and saw a glimpse of light coming from Leo's room. I pushed the door open. Marta was giving Leo his bottle. When she saw me, she jumped. Why was she looking so nervous?

'I will feed him.' I walked towards her. '*Gli darò da mangiare.*' I *think* I said that right…

'*No, va bene.*' She smiled.

Hold on. Marta had just smiled at me. Something was *definitely* wrong. She never did that. She quickly wrapped both of her hands tightly around Leo's bottle, so I couldn't see what was inside. I needed to play this smart. Because now I had some worrying thoughts running around in my head and I had to get my facts straight before I jumped to conclusions.

'*Bene.*' I smiled. I left the room and headed straight for the kitchen. I opened up the cupboard. *FFS!* She'd moved everything again. I'd have to speak to Lorenzo about this. She was taking the piss.

I gently opened and closed them until I found the cupboard with the formula, then opened the tin. It had been used, but not enough. This was one I'd bought in London. There was no way there could be this much left if she'd been giving Leo his milk every day. I hunted through the cupboards again just in case there was an open tub I didn't know about. *Nothing.*

Next, I rummaged around the bins. Not my favourite thing to do, but now wasn't the time to worry about getting my hands dirty. No tins in here either.

Hold on.

As I got to the bottom, there was a pile of powder. I scooped some up into my hands and smelt it. It was formula. She'd been throwing it away.

If Marta hadn't been feeding Leo formula, then what the hell had she been giving him?

I washed my hands, opened the fridge, then frantically pulled everything out. Right at the back was an opaque blue container. I opened it to find two full bottles of milk. Milk that didn't look like formula. It was too watery. I tipped one bottle onto the back of my hand. Then the second one onto the other.

I knew it.

The colour, the smell, everything told me it was breast milk. And I hadn't breastfed Leo for weeks. So whose milk was…

That woman.

The woman with the baby that Geli had seen.

Claudia.

I could not *believe* Marta had done this.

I stormed back in the room.

'Give me my son!' I yelled, trying to pull Leo from her arms.

'*No!*' she said defiantly, babbling something in Italian.

As she used her hands to try and stop me from taking Leo, the bottle crashed to the floor. I swiped it up and quickly shook some onto my arm this time. It had the same smell and consistency as the ones in the fridge.

'This isn't formula,' I snapped. 'This is *breast* milk. You've been feeding my baby milk from another woman's breasts!'

'*Non capisco.*' She shook her head.

'Don't give me that bullshit about not understanding. You know *exactly* what I'm talking about. You've put my baby's life at risk!' I shouted. 'Disregarded my wishes. *Our* wishes to give Leo formula. You had no right!'

That's it.

I tried wrestling Leo from her arms, but Marta was holding on tight.

'Give him to me!' I screamed. 'You must have known it isn't safe to give him someone else's milk. That other woman could have diseases you don't know about which she could have passed on to Leo. Give him back!'

As we both tried to hold on to him, Leo started crying.

'What is going on!' Lorenzo's voice boomed as he came running into the room.

'Your witch of a mother has been giving Leo another woman's breast milk!'

'What? *No…*' He shook his head.

Marta finally released Leo and I took him into my arms, stroking his back to try and calm him down.

'*Yes*, Lorenzo. She *has*! Look at this milk.' I pointed to the bottle. Look at the colour! *Smell it.* It isn't formula! And Geli saw her. Getting bottles from Claudia—the other woman's house!'

'*Mamma, è vero?*'

He was asking her if it was true. She started waving her hands in the air, giving me dirty looks. I understood a few snippets including *Breast milk being better for Leo.* Thank God for Geli's lessons.

I'd always known that she didn't approve of me stopping breastfeeding, but I never even imagined she'd take things this far. This was our baby, not hers. Lorenzo and I had decided together that he would be breastfed for six months and that was it. I was surprised I'd even lasted that long as sometimes it was painful. Either way, what Marta had done was dangerous, deceitful and disrespectful. His mother or not, she had to go.

'I want her *out*, Lorenzo! This is the last straw. I've had enough of her interfering.'

He looked at his mum and looked at me. I could tell he was trying to work out what to do or say to keep the peace, but I wasn't backing down on this one.

'Soph, she is my mamma. She has nowhere else to go.'

Marta started smirking. *Bitch*. Bet she understood that he was sticking up for her.

'I am *not* living under the same roof as a woman who has gone behind our backs in the worst possible way and put Leo's health at risk.'

'Mamma would never do anything to hurt Leo. She loves him.'

'Lorenzo! I am not living here with *her*. So either she leaves or Leo and I do. It's up to you!'

'Soph… no, please.' He stroked my shoulders. 'We must talk about this…'

'There's nothing to talk about. If you're not going to ask her to leave, then we'll go,' I grabbed Leo's bag, stuffed some clothes and nappies inside and started putting on his pram suit. 'I can't stay here with that woman. We're leaving.'

'Sophia!'

I put Leo in his pushchair, opened the front door, then slammed it behind me.

I couldn't believe he'd chosen his mother over us.

I thought Lorenzo was different. That he wasn't a *cocco di mamma*—a stereotypical mummy's boy.

Was this how it would always be? Lorenzo taking Marta's side, no matter what?

How could I stay with a man that was always going to put our needs second? A man who didn't take my concerns about our baby's health seriously?

As much as it hurt me to say it, the answer was, I couldn't.

CHAPTER THIRTY-SEVEN

M y head was spinning.

I was at Geli's and had just put Leo to bed. When we'd left, Lorenzo had run after us and said there must have been some kind of mistake. He asked me to come back so we could discuss it, but as far as I was concerned, there was no confusion. I told him that whilst his mother was there, I would not be stepping foot inside that house again. After a few attempts, eventually he left.

Even though it had happened a couple of hours ago, I was still fuming.

'Here you go.' Geli passed me a large G&T.

'Thanks.' I knocked it back, then slammed the glass on the table. 'I still can't believe he defended her. He should have stood up to Marta. Instead he just wants to make excuses for her.'

'You should not be surprised. That is Italian men. Mamma will always come first. If you cannot accept that, then you cannot be with him.'

The thought of being without Lorenzo made me sick to

the stomach, but this was serious. Whilst Geli was in the kitchen, I'd looked it up on the internet again to make sure I wasn't overreacting or being overly paranoid and I was right: what Marta had done really was dangerous.

According to the experts, HIV could be transmitted through breast milk. There was also a small possibility of Leo catching hepatitis and the chance he could get yeast or bacterial infections or viruses like herpes. It was nothing to be sniffed at. Every article I scrolled through stated that unless you had their complete medical history, it would be too risky to let your baby drink another woman's milk. And I was pretty sure Marta hadn't shipped Claudia off to the doctor's to get her checked out first.

'I really don't want it to come to that, because I love him so much and he's a great father, but unless he tells Marta she was wrong and asks her to leave, I can't see a way past this.' My stomach knotted up. 'I know it might seem bad me asking him to choose, but she showed zero remorse. And if we let something like this go, we'll be sending her the wrong message. Telling Marta she can do whatever she wants, go against our wishes on how we want to bring up our son and it'll be okay. That'll be condoning her actions. Giving her complete control. And if she can do something like this, what on earth would she do next?'

'You are right. I knew when I saw her with Claudia that something was wrong. I am just glad that you found out what was happening.'

'Thanks to you.' I gave Geli's shoulder a gentle squeeze. I was so grateful to have her as a friend right now for so many reasons. For telling me about seeing Marta and for taking Leo and I in tonight. There was no way I could have stayed in that house and it wasn't like there was a nearby hotel we could have gone to.

'I wish I'd found out sooner,' I sighed. '*So stupid.* I should never have let Marta take over feeding Leo. But I was trying to be less rigid and more accepting of her. I knew she enjoyed it. And yeah, I admit, as much as I loved feeding him too, selfishly I was glad to have her help out so that I could get work done and get some extra sleep. I shouldn't have done that. I should have been a good mum and looked after him properly myself.'

'Trusting the grandmother to feed your son so you can do other things does not make you a bad mother. You have had many things to manage recently. It is natural that you ask for help whilst you finalise this deal. You are doing it so that you can make a better life for Leo and be more present in his life. And raising a child is tiring. I do not know one mother who would not take the opportunity to have more sleep if it was given to them. You did not know she would do something like this.'

'True, but I just feel so guilty. Anyway, I need to focus. Now I know what she's done, I have to deal with it. My first priority is to get Leo checked out fully.'

'Yes. Would you like me to come with you so I can translate anything you don't understand?'

'That would be great. Thanks, Geli. I hope to God he's okay.'

～

We'd just come back from the doctor's. As I'd suspected, we'd have to wait for the results, which would be agonising. I didn't have much confidence in the doctor, to be honest. It was almost as if he thought I was wasting his time.

I wasn't happy to just leave it like this. I'd prefer it if my own doctor checked him out. That would mean returning to London, so I'd booked the first available flight, which was leaving Pisa airport tomorrow evening.

Lorenzo would hardly be able to complain about me taking Leo away again, seeing as his mother was the reason I had to take this drastic action in the first place. In fact, given the situation, maybe it wasn't a bad idea for us to have time apart. Perhaps some space would give him the chance to think about what had happened properly and reconsider his choice.

It would also give me an opportunity to really consider the future. This was bigger than the whole situation with Marta. Even if Lorenzo did come to his senses and ask her to leave, I had to be honest with myself. I didn't see myself in this town. I'd tried. I genuinely felt like I'd done everything I could to assimilate. I'd been learning the language, which was going well and I'd attempted to fit in, but it just didn't feel right.

I thought about it and I think some of the reasons I'd liked the town when I'd first visited were actually why it didn't float my boat now. Initially I'd thought it was good that it was off the beaten track, peaceful and not too touristy. But whilst the quietness might be okay for a few weeks, it was too much for any longer than that. It might be an okay place to live if I was retired, but I wasn't ready to kick up my feet completely yet. And I knew there were other places in Italy that were more vibrant and had a more diverse range of people who were more *me*.

Saying that, I also had to consider whether Italy was

even where I truly wanted to be. I missed my family and friends. Why put myself through the hardship of starting over again when I didn't have to? I still had my house in London and there was a lot more space there. I'd thought about selling or renting it so many times, but something told me to keep hold of it. Maybe I knew that a day like this would come and I might need it. If I moved back, everything would be familiar. The language, the people. Life would be so much easier.

And then there was my career. Once the deal went through, I'd need to keep myself available for three months, but what then? As well as looking after Leo, I knew I wanted to work, but ideally not full-time, and after burning out with the agency before, nothing with too much pressure or responsibility. So wherever I lived needed to also enable me to have some sort of career.

I had a lot to think about. Lots of decisions to make. Something told me it wasn't going to be easy…

CHAPTER THIRTY-EIGHT

I definitely needed an early night. It had been a busy day. As well as the normal Leo-related stuff, I'd been helping Geli clean the house. It was the least I could do after she'd kindly put us up. And it also helped to take my mind off the situation with Lorenzo.

I'd just been messaging him to let him know that Leo and I would be going to London tomorrow evening and he'd asked if he could see Leo to say goodbye. So we'd arranged to meet.

I wasn't sure how well I'd hold it together. I missed him like crazy, but was still angry. Hopefully I'd be able to stay calm when I saw him. I guess only time would tell how I'd react. *Who knows?* Maybe between now and tomorrow, he'd come to his senses and Marta would have left.

Oh well. Thinking about it won't change anything. The best thing I could do now was to sleep.

Just as I was about to get myself ready for bed, my phone rang. Maybe it was Lorenzo calling to change our meeting time. Better answer quickly before the ringing woke Leo up.

I glanced at the screen. It wasn't Lorenzo.

'Hi, Holly, are you okay?' She didn't answer, but I could hear faint sobbing. 'Holly?'

'C-can I come…can I…you said I could call you, if…' My heart started racing. This wasn't good.

'Where are you?'

'I-I'm outside Geli's house, b-but I didn't want to ring the bell, j-just in case…I wasn't sure if you were, if you were still staying there or if…if you'd gone home…'

Thank God I'd messaged her earlier to let her know I'd fallen out with Lorenzo and I'd be at Geli's if she needed me.

'Yeah, I'm still here. Wait there. I'm coming now.'

I jumped off the bed and knocked on Geli's bedroom door.

'*Sì?*' she called out. 'Come in.'

'I think something's wrong with Holly. She's outside…'

Geli leapt out from under her blanket and we both raced to the front door. When I opened it, Holly was standing there in tears.

'Oh, darling!' I threw my arms around her.

'Come in, come in,' said Geli, ushering her inside.

I released Holly, took her hand and led her into the living room.

She plonked herself down on the sofa.

'What's the matter?' I squeezed her hand. 'What happened?'

Holly buried her head in my shoulder and started sobbing again.

'She needs a drink,' said Geli, rushing to the kitchen. She returned seconds later with a large glass and a bottle of gin. 'Here,' she said, pouring enough liquid to sink a ship and passing the glass to Holly. 'Drink.'

Holly lifted up her head and gulped it down.

'What is it?' I asked gently. I bet it had something to do with her bastard boss.

She took another gulp of gin and took a deep breath.

'Silvestro…'

'I knew it!' I shouted. 'What did that arsehole do to you?'

'He…he put…he…' She paused as if to compose herself. 'He put his hand up my skirt. He touched me.'

'That fucking pervert!' I hissed. I was so angry I wanted to go round there right now and give him a piece of my mind.

'*Testa di cazzo!*' Geli snarled. 'And you kick him in balls, *si*?'

'No! I just froze. I didn't know what to do. I was so shocked. I couldn't believe it was happening. And then he smiled and said he knew I liked it. That I wanted him to touch me. But I *didn't*!'

'Of course not. What a creep!'

'I just couldn't move. I wanted to speak, to say no. But at first, the words wouldn't come out. Then I said it. "*No, no, no! Don't touch me!*" I screamed. "Leave me alone!" Then his son came in and I just ran. I grabbed my bag and ran out of the house. I didn't know what to do. So I called Umberto. He didn't answer. I kept calling. No answer. Eventually he called me back. Said he was out with his mates. I said it was urgent. He asked why. I told him what happened. That Silvestro had put his hand up my skirt.'

'What did he say?' asked Geli.

'He said…' She started crying again. Geli topped up her empty glass. 'He asked…' Holly gulped down more gin. 'He asked how short my skirt was…'

'He didn't?' I shouted. 'What a dick!'

'I told him it wasn't that short. Just a normal one.'

'I would not have answered him,' snapped Geli.

'And do you know what Umberto said? He said that maybe… he said I should wear jeans or something instead so that I don't tempt Silvestro. So that he doesn't get the wrong idea.'

'You've *got* to be joking! What a pig! Sorry, Holly, I know you think the sun shines out of his arse, but that's out of order!'

'It's not that short, is it?' she tugged at it as if she was trying to stretch it. 'I like wearing skirts. Maybe I should have worn a longer one…'

'Listen to me: the problem is *not* with *you*, or what you were wearing. The problem is with Silvestro. Putting his hands where they were not invited or wanted. That's assault. You didn't ask for it and you didn't deserve it. We need to call the police and report him. He can't get away with this! We need to report him to your agency too. And as for Umberto, I'm sorry, Holly, but for him to say that to you, in your time of need…well…'

'I don't want to go to the police. They'll laugh at me. Think I'm just a slut or a dumb blonde. It'll be totally embarrassing.' She winced. 'I just want to forget about it. It's not like anything will happen to him anyway, so it's not worth the hassle.'

I understood why she thought that way. Too often victims were blamed. Women must have done something to *ask for it* or encouraged the man in some way. It was bullshit. But we had to find a way to help change this perception. And one of the ways to do that was by speaking up.

'I'll be honest.' I rested my hand on hers. 'I can't say what will happen or promise that if we report it that Silvestro will definitely be punished. All I'm saying is that if you feel up to it, it will be worth at least *trying*. So that you know that you did all you could. It's your decision, but take time to think about it, okay?'

'I'll try.'

'Of course, you stay here with us tonight,' said Geli. 'In the morning we can decide what to do, *si*?'

'Okay,' said Holly.

'Good,' I said. 'Until then, maybe it's a good idea to put your clothes in a bag. It will have his DNA on it and it might help if you do decide to go ahead and report it.'

Holly nodded. I felt so bad that I would be going to London tomorrow and wouldn't be around to help her through this, but my flight was booked and I had to get Leo checked out.

Talk about a crazy few days. Why did everything always happen at once? At least Geli would be here, though. Something told me that Holly was going to need her.

CHAPTER THIRTY-NINE

'So? Has she gone?'

I was sitting in the car with Lorenzo outside Geli's house.

It had been a busy morning. I'd called the au pair agency first thing to tell them Holly would be leaving with immediate effect due to concerns about her safety and that we'd be in touch once we'd taken legal advice. Then Geli and I had gone to Holly's host family's house to pick up all her stuff. Understandably, she was still upset about what had happened and couldn't face going back there. She was still adamant that she didn't want to go to the police, so we had to respect her wishes.

When we came back to Geli's, Holly said she'd decided to go and stay with her friend in Florence for a few days. Geli tried to persuade her not to leave, but Holly said she needed to get away and clear her head. So Geli was now in the house watching Leo, whilst Holly packed.

Once I'd finished speaking with Lorenzo, Geli would drop Holly off at the train station. She'd offered to take her all the way to Florence after she'd driven me to the airport, but Holly didn't want to wait. She said she needed to get out of town as quickly as possible.

Fair enough. I supposed part of her was also worried about having a long car journey with us trying to persuade her to report Silvestro. We wouldn't have done that, though. As much as I wanted him to be punished, I knew Holly had to do whatever felt right for her, right now.

After he'd come inside and spent some time with Leo, Lorenzo had asked if we could have a quick chat. As Geli's mum was resting at home, I knew things might get heated and I didn't want to argue around Holly because she needed a calm environment, I suggested we sit here instead. So here we were.

'I cannot ask her to leave,' Lorenzo sighed. 'Mamma has told me that she would not do anything to hurt Leo. She said she was looking after the milk for Claudia because her fridge was broken and she must have picked up the wrong bottle to give to Leo by mistake.'

'*Oh, come on!*' I rolled my eyes. 'And you believed her?'

'She is my mother.'

'So that means you believe everything she tells you?' Lorenzo was normally a level-headed, intelligent man. But he had been blinded by Marta. In his eyes, she could do no wrong. 'She's a liar! I don't know how you can't see that!' Lorenzo ground his teeth.

'Sophia, this is a very difficult situation. I love you, very, very much, but I am not happy that you insult my mother. Without my brother here, I am her only family. She needs to be in our lives, so I am asking you to find a way to accept her.'

'Well, I can't,' I snapped.

He sighed again. I could tell he was torn, wrestling with himself about what to do for the best, but I wasn't budging. I knew he loved Marta and that it must be a tough decision for him, and ordinarily, even though she wasn't my favourite person in the world, I wouldn't have dreamt of asking him to choose between us. But these weren't ordinary circumstances. His mother or not, she'd well and truly crossed the line.

After sitting in silence for a few minutes, neither of us knowing what to say, Lorenzo looked at his watch.

'I have to go back to work. We talk about this later?'

'Unless she's leaving, there's nothing to talk about. I've already told you, I'm not staying there with *her*. She's not the sweet innocent lady you think she is.'

'No!' He raised his voice. 'Mamma is a good woman. She has done so much for me.'

I had no doubt that she had. Just like he worshipped her, she absolutely adored him. That was clear. But that didn't mean that she was perfect. Nor did it excuse her actions.

We were going round in circles.

'Look, I need to pick up our passports and get some stuff to pack for Leo to take with me to London, but like I said, I don't want to see your mother. Do you know if she'll be going out this afternoon?'

'*Sì*. She will go to check on her house today after lunch, so should be out between three and four.

'Okay.' I got out of the car. 'I'll make sure I go during those times.'

As I watched him leave, another piece of my heart crumbled. Before Marta moved in, things were fine between me and Lorenzo. We were back on track. Even through our ups and downs, amongst all the challenges of living here, he was always my one certainty. The person I could rely on to have my back. But that stability had gone. Lorenzo and I both believed we were in the right. We'd reached a stalemate. We couldn't seem to find a way through this. His mamma had finally come between us. In a big way.

And now, because of Marta and her meddling, I was on the verge of losing the love of my life.

For good.

CHAPTER FORTY

The door was locked. *Good.* That meant Marta was definitely out.

I crept inside. What was I doing? This was supposed to be my home. I shouldn't have to feel like I was an intruder invading Marta's sacred space.

The place felt different. Of course it was immaculately clean and tidy. There were new throws over the sofa and all of the chairs. She was still obviously obsessed with thinking they were dirty. There were some new photographs in frames too. One of her by herself and another with Lorenzo. *Jeez.* I'd only been gone a few days and she'd already started making her mark.

I went into the kitchen, which of course was like a show home. No dishes in the sink, worktops completely clear and sparkling. Shiny floor which looked like it had been freshly mopped today. I got it. She was the model mum. But she also had nothing to do in her life. If I had hours and hours of free time, I could make this place look spotless too. Truth be told, I probably wouldn't. I'd find something more interesting to do.

Anyway, I wasn't here to do a hygiene inspection. I had to pack. I'd leave that kind of snooping to Marta.

I went into Leo's room and picked up the packet of nappies. Marta probably didn't approve of using disposable nappies either. Bet she was so perfect that she used cloth ones for her kids and washed and ironed them every day.

Just as I stepped over to the wooden chest of drawers to get some more clothes for Leo, my phone beeped. I hoped everything was okay.

I'd left Leo sleeping at Geli's as I didn't want to disturb his afternoon nap, particularly as we'd be travelling later and Geli said she'd keep an eye on him. She'd been such a gem. Putting us up, watching Leo when I spoke to Lorenzo and whilst I came here, dropping off Holly. Plus she'd be driving us to the airport later and still had to help look after her mum too. If you asked me, Angelica *was* a fitting name. Geli really was an angel.

I rested my phone on the top of the drawers and clicked on the message.

Geli

Leo is awake. You prefer I put him back to sleep or let him stay up?

Geli

I know you have a routine so do not want to change it.

That was nice of her to ask. At least there was *someone* who respected how I wanted to raise my son. I clicked the record button. It would be much easier to send a voice note than to stand here and type. I wanted to be in and out as quickly as possible, so that I could get back to feed Leo before Geli drove us to the airport.

'Hi! Can't believe he's awake already! Yes, please try and put him back to sleep if you can. It's only three-thirty, so it would be good if he could sleep until around four-thirty.' I took a pile of clothes out of the drawer, walked to the opposite side of the room and put them down on the bed. She should still be able to hear me from here. 'I should be back by then anyway, so no worries. But if he doesn't settle, it's okay, just keep him awake and...' Just as I started to put some clothes into a bag, the door flew open and Marta stepped inside. I thought Lorenzo said she wasn't going to be back until around four?

Tough.

I was here now and I wasn't going to let her intimidate me.

'Well, well, well. If it isn't the evil grandmother.' I put my hands on my hips. Maybe that was harsh, but it was true. What she did was out of order. Not like she under-stood me anyway.

She laughed.

'You call me evil? It is *you* that is evil...'

WTF.

Am I dreaming, or did Marta just speak to me in English?

All this time! All this bloody time she'd played dumb and insisted she didn't understand me and all along she had. What a devious little...

'*You* are the evil mamma,' she snapped. 'You give Leo chemicals. Fake milk. I save Leo. What I give him is natural. Milk from mamma. *Good* mamma. Because you lazy English woman. You should feed him breast until he walk. At least for one year, but you are selfish. You care more about work and give sex than your son. You forget milk because you like give *pompino*!' She scowled, shaking her head with disgust. '*Puttana!* My Lorenzo will never stay with you. My son, he need real woman. *Italian* woman he can marry. *Young* woman who can give him more child. You too old. Lorenzo is good son. Italian man always need his mamma. He will stay here with me in this town until I die.'

She folded her arms and smirked.

OMFG.

I was rooted to the spot. I couldn't believe what I had just heard. I'd known she didn't like me, but this? *This?* The venom that was shooting from Marta's mouth was some next-level hatred. Judging me because I'd had Leo later in life and reminding me what I already knew: that it was going to be harder to have another child at my age. I hadn't even decided if that was something I wanted, but it was a low blow.

'Are you for real? I've never heard someone talk so much complete and utter bollocks!' I felt my blood boiling. Marta said so many things to piss me off that I could respond to at length, point by point, but I wasn't going to waste my breath. I knew I wasn't a whore. I knew Leo was more important to me than work and giving blowjobs for God's sake. I mean, *WTF*? And despite what had happened, I knew that if things didn't work out with me and Lorenzo, it wouldn't be because he wanted to trade me in for a younger Italian model. That wasn't him. Marta was wrong, so I'd ignore her stupid comments. But one thing I *wasn't* going to ignore was what she'd done to

Leo. No one fucks with my son's health and gets away with it.

'You put Leo's life at risk. He could have infections or viruses because of *you*. *Your* actions were selfish. Unforgiveable. And as for using formula, *damn*. Babies have been having it for years. Not all women can or want to breastfeed.'

'I give breast to both my sons,' she snapped again.

'*Vaffanculo!* Just because *you* did, it doesn't mean every woman has to. It's a personal choice and you should have respected my wishes. It's not me who is lazy or selfish. *You* are the selfish one. You want to keep Lorenzo trapped in this town forever just because you have no friends and no life. If you loved him as much as you say you do, you'd let him go. Let him live his own life and be happy. And anyway, shouldn't you be checking on your house? It'd be very awkward if Lorenzo stopped by there later and heard that you hadn't even been. Maybe then he'd start to wonder whether you were trying to delay things so you could stay here longer…'

Her face dropped. She'd been rumbled. Judging by the limited damage that Lorenzo had described, that house should have been fixed and ready for her to move back into ages ago. But Marta was clearly stalling. Some part of me even wondered if she had started the fire deliberately. That would be low, even for her.

'*Puttana*,' she spat, turning on her heels and leaving the room.

'*Baciami il culo!*' I shouted back, telling her to kiss my arse. The front door slammed. I rushed to the kitchen and looked out the window to check she'd really gone. I saw her walking towards the town centre, so the coast should be clear.

How dare she call me a whore. *Twice.* Geli was right to teach us those Italian swear words. I had been quite restrained. There were loads more insults I'd remembered and would have like to have used, but I'd stopped myself. She wasn't worth it.

Gosh. If only Lorenzo had come home early and heard her outburst. In English no less. Then he'd be able to see what she was *really* like. See for himself that his precious mamma really *did* hate me. I'd always suspected she thought I wasn't good enough and that she would have preferred Lorenzo to have shacked up with a good Italian woman. But now she'd confirmed it. It had come straight from the horse's mouth.

Trouble was, without any witnesses, it was just her word against mine. I couldn't prove it. Wish I'd known she was going to turn up at that time. Bollocks.

Anyway, there was no telling when she was coming back. Could be any minute now as she must have returned to pick up something. Either she'd come to get whatever she'd forgotten, or she had no intention of really going. I didn't want another run-in, because if she pushed my buttons again, I might not be able to control myself, so I needed to pack as quickly as possible.

As I walked back into the room, I spotted my phone. It was still on top of the drawers.

Hold on.

I just remembered. When Marta had come in, I'd been speaking to Geli. No, I hadn't been *speaking* to Geli. I'd been *recording a message* to Geli.

Recording.

I rushed over to the phone and looked down on the screen.

It was still running.

Holy shit.

That meant there was a good chance it had caught my conversation. The *entire* conversation with Marta. Where she'd called me lazy, selfish and a whore, not once but twice. Revealed that she wanted someone better for Lorenzo than me. That she had him under her thumb and he would never leave her. Where she'd pretty much confirmed she had lied to Lorenzo about there being a mix-up with the milk bottles.

The voice note would have captured every single word.

I had my proof.

Marta would finally get what was coming to her.

CHAPTER FORTY-ONE

I'd been standing here for almost five minutes.

The voice note was still recording.

My finger was hovering.

All I had to do was press the blue send button and like a bomb, Lorenzo's relationship with Marta would explode. It would be toast. Even *he* couldn't deny that she was manipulative with that kind of evidence. If I'd given her a script and asked her to read from it, she couldn't have screwed herself over any better if she'd tried.

It was so simple.

I just had to press *send* and it would go to Geli. Then I could forward or play it to him. Then he would see that I was right about his mother, come back to me and Leo and we'd be one happy little family all over again.

But if I pressed *cancel*, the evidence would be gone forever. It would just be Marta's word against mine and right now, if I was a betting woman, as much as I hated to admit it, I wasn't sure Leo and I would definitely win.

I paused again.

What was wrong with me? This was the perfect opportunity to take Marta down. Why wasn't I grabbing it? This is what I'd wanted.

I didn't know how or why, but it seemed like I'd been struck with a sudden crisis of conscience.

Half an hour ago, if I'd had a glimpse into the future and someone told me that this would happen, I'd have seen it as a victory. Been hanging the balloons and banners for a *get rid of Marta* celebration. Well, I probably wouldn't have gone that far as that'd be mean, but you catch my drift. I would have been relieved. Felt like a huge weight had been lifted from my shoulders. But yet somehow, this didn't feel like a happy moment. It felt sad.

If I sent Lorenzo the recording, then the perception he had of his mother being this wonderful woman would be erased. Gone forever. A bit like telling a five-year-old that Father Christmas didn't exist.

In the cold light of day, now that I had the chance to, I didn't want to be the one to ruin their relationship. As much as I didn't like Marta, I also wouldn't want to be responsible for breaking up a mother and a son.

Maybe I needed to take a step back and be more objective.

I thought about Leo and how I'd want him to feel about me when he was older. Naturally I'd hope he would love me and think that I was a great mother, as I'd always try to do my best by him. I wouldn't expect him to think I was perfect or worship the ground I walked on, but I'd hope that at least he would respect me. And whilst it would be up to him who he settled down with, I'd hope that I'd like them. That they would be worthy of my son. That even though he would go his own way, I would still be an important person in his life. So how would I feel if after changing his nappies, feeding and clothing him for years and all the sacrifices I'd made, some girlfriend breezed in and told him to kick me to the curb during my time of need? I'd be pretty pissed.

But this situation wasn't straightforward. Marta had done wrong. The whole lying thing and the stuff with the breast milk. That was unforgiveable.

Fuck it.

I couldn't decide what was best right now. Too many thoughts were racing through my head and I still had things I needed to get done before we caught our flight. I would send the recording to Geli—otherwise it would get lost—and then I'd think about what to do with it whilst I was away.

I clicked on the button, gluing my eyes to the screen until it was safely delivered.

Done.

I finished stuffing the bits for Leo in a bag, threw some of my clothes in a suitcase and then called Geli.

'Hey. Sorry I took so long to reply.'

'It is okay. I put Leo back to sleep. I saw you were recording a message. I tried to wait for you to finish but then I decided to just do it.'

'That's good. Thank you. About the message… do me a favour, please, and don't listen to it until I get there. You are not going to believe what just happened…'

CHAPTER FORTY-TWO

As Geli listened to the message her mouth fell open. Even though I was part of the conversation, I still couldn't believe it either.

The message ended.

'*Mio Dio!*' she shouted. '*Merda! Porca puttana!* You *have* to play this to Lorenzo.'

'I *can't.*' I winced. 'It will break his heart.'

'Well, this woman is happy to break up your relationship. You must not let her get away with it.'

'I know it's annoying, and as much as I believe Marta deserves to get her comeuppance, I have to take the higher ground. I want Lorenzo to choose me and Leo because he wants to. Not because I've proved that his mother is an evil cow.'

'I understand, but if I were you, I would go straight to the restaurant now and play it. *No.* I would want Marta to suffer. I would make her go to the restaurant, call Lorenzo out, then play the recording on speaker in front of the customers, so everyone can hear how disgusting she is.

And so she see Lorenzo's disappointed face when he realises his mother is a witch.'

'But that would crush him.'

'It would upset her more. Perhaps doing it in front of customers is too good for her. I would organise a party for the whole town and play it in front of them all.'

'That would just be evil,' I shook my head.

'*Sì*. Perhaps I go too far. But she is a bad woman.'

'She's lonely and sad. Lorenzo is all she has.'

What's wrong with you? screamed Reasanna. *Why are you sticking up for her all of a sudden?*

I know it sounds crazy, Reasanna. I'm just as surprised as you are.

'Look, what Marta did was unforgiveable, but like I said, I need Lorenzo to come to his own decision about our future. So promise me that you will not play that recording to him. Under any circumstances.'

Geli rolled her eyes and sighed.

'*Promise* me,' I said.

'Okay, *bene*. I will not play Lorenzo the recording.'

'Thank you.'

I hoped to God that Geli would keep her word…

∼

It felt strange being back in London. Never did I think I'd be here again so soon. I couldn't have predicted all of the things that had happened over the last few days either.

Life was funny. One minute everything seemed to be going well. After a long dry spell, you finally get your sexual mojo back, you have a relationship with a person you believed was the man of your dreams, are building a family with the beautiful baby you thought you'd never be able to have, and then someone like Marta comes along and steamrollers all over it. Just like that your happiness is sucked away. Gone. Kaput.

What with everything going on in my life with Lorenzo and worrying about Holly (even though she'd texted this morning to say she was holding up okay), the last few days had been a roller coaster of emotions.

Yesterday included. I'd completed the deal to sell the business. The contract was signed and the money was in my account. I should have been elated. I had my freedom and enough cash to live on for a little while without stressing about rushing out to work and paying bills. After all the ups and downs these past months with the clients, Robyn and the staff and the lack of personal life I'd had for years, this should have been a triumph. An achievement of epic proportions.

I should have been popping bottles of champagne, dancing in the streets, and have a giant smile plastered all over my face. But I didn't. I just felt empty. Deflated. Numb.

When I'd got the news, I breathed a sigh of relief, thanked my lawyer for letting me know, put the phone down, picked Leo out of his high chair, gave him a big hug and a kiss, put him back, then carried on loading the dishwasher. It was like it was just another ordinary day.

Pretty sad, really. But with everything that had gone on in Italy before I'd left, how could I feel like celebrating? How could I feel happy when my relationship was still hanging in the balance?

If Lorenzo was here, he would have made a big fuss. Made one of those homemade banners he loved creating for special occasions. Put up balloons, showered me with a thousand kisses, cooked my favourite meal or insisted he took me out to celebrate.

He would've congratulated me. Told me how proud he was and taken me in his arms, my favourite place in the world, for one of his amazing hugs.

But he wasn't here. He was hundreds of miles away, in Italy.

I missed him so much my body ached. I'd wanted to call him so many times, to tell him the news, but each time I'd resisted. I had to be strong. It was up to him now. He needed to come to me. To fight for us. For me and Leo. The ball was in his court.

The phone rang. As I walked over to the table to pick it up, my heart beat faster. Maybe it was Lorenzo?

I glanced down at the screen. It was Roxy. Calling rather than texting. This had to be important. I answered quickly.

'Hi, everything okay?'

'No! Not really!' she said sharply. I sat down to brace myself for bad news.

'What's up?'

'Well, I was just on Insta, you know, checking out the profile of some guy I've been chatting to online, *as you do*, in between working *very, very* hard of course, and I saw a post pop up from BeCome. It was of the team out celebrating last night. With the new owner. What's her name? Rhonda or something? It said the deal had been done. Is that true?'

'Yep.' Rhonda had invited me along, but I already felt like I'd said my goodbyes to everyone.

The day before the deal had gone through, I'd met the

team individually at the office to thank them for their hard work and answer any final questions they had about the takeover. Then I took them out for an all-expenses-paid slap-up meal at Sushisamba, which they'd loved. I'd also given them all cards and gifts. It was the least I could do. Even with all the ups and downs since I'd moved to Italy, without them I wouldn't have had a business to sell, so I wanted to show my gratitude. But last night was Rhonda's night. She was the boss now, so it was better to leave her to bond with the team without me. Plus, I didn't feel up to it...

'WTF!' Roxy screamed. 'That's *major*! Why the hell didn't you tell us?'

'I was going to... it's just...' If I told Roxy I was feeling down because I'd fallen out with Lorenzo, she'd think I was such a wet blanket and I wasn't in the mood for one of her strong-women feminist lectures. She'd see right through an attempt to use Leo as an excuse too as she'd know my parents would be chomping at the bit to babysit and spend time with their grandson, so that wouldn't work either. Sod it. 'I just didn't feel like it.' That was true. I didn't.

'You *just didn't feel like it*? For fuck's sake! What's wrong with you, woman? You know I've had my doubts about you giving up the business, *but* this is what you've been wanting for *ages*. You should be out. Celebrating. *Unless*... you better not have thrown a party without me and Bella!'

'Of course I didn't. I took the team out, but it wasn't a party.'

'That's work stuff. What did you do personally, for

yourself? Have a few drinks with your family? Have a heated phone-sex session with Lorenzo?' she cackled.

'No. I didn't do anything.'

Roxy sighed loudly. Thank God we were having this conversation over the phone. If she was here in person, although she's not normally violent, she would have made an exception and either clipped me around the ears, slapped my face, shaken me until I justified myself or all three.

'Wait there,' she snapped.

I heard her pressing some buttons on her phone. There was silence for a few seconds, then…

'Hi, Rox, what's up?' it was Bella. *Oh Jesus.* Roxy had added her to the call.

'Bella, listen up. We have an emergency situation on our hands. Whatever you have planned for tonight, cancel it. Whatever Mike has planned this evening, cancel it. He needs to babysit his son.'

'Why?' said Bella. 'What's happened?'

'Sophia is behaving like a lunatic. We need to take her out for an emergency FTA session and belated celebration…'

≈

Here we were, sitting in our favourite seats at one of our favourite restaurants in London, Hush, with a bottle of champagne in an ice bucket in front of us.

I knew that once Bella heard about the deal going through and the fact that I hadn't celebrated properly, there was no way either of them would let me get away with spending another night at home moping on my sofa. They immediately insisted we go out to celebrate. Even though, like yesterday I wasn't remotely in the mood, I knew that if I didn't go along willingly, they'd break down my door and drag me out kicking and screaming. So in the interest of keeping my house intact and my hair firmly on my scalp, I called Mum to ask if she could babysit. Then when Leo had his nap, forced myself to get ready, dropped him off at my parents' in a taxi and headed to the restaurant.

Bella and Roxy were there when I arrived with the champers already lined up and had jumped out of their seats to give me the biggest hug.

'Congratulations!!' they shouted.

'Thanks,' I replied, smiling half-heartedly, and then we all sat down on the banquette, which was just as comfy as I remembered. It felt good to be back.

'You did it, Soph!' said Bella. 'You sold the business! You're a free woman!'

'Yeah, you must be minted now! Dinner's on you tonight!' Roxy cackled.

'Not quite,' I said. 'The taxman and my lawyer take a chunk and I'll have to use it to live on until I figure out what to do for work.'

'I'm sure you'll be more than fine, darling. You've got your house here, which you can always rent out to get some extra cash,' said Roxy.

'Yeah, and Lorenzo's working,' said Bella, 'so it's not as if you have to do it alone or like you need to take any job to avoid being out on the streets.'

'I'll be okay financially for a little while, but if what's happened these past few days is anything to go by, I might become a single mum…'

Bella and Roxy gasped, then fell silent, their eyeballs

bursting out of their sockets.

'WTF? What drama has loverboy Lorenzo caused you now? If that bastard has cheated on you with some village floozy, there'll be hell to pay…'

I filled them both in on what had happened with Marta, my last conversation with Lorenzo and the accidental recording. Unsurprisingly, hot-headed Roxy was baying for blood.

'What's *wrong* with you, woman?' she shouted. 'Send Lorenzo the bloody message! Or send it to me. I won't waste any time worrying about Marta's feelings. I'll play it to him straight away. No, in fact, I'll put it on the internet and send him the link. Make it go viral. That'll teach her.'

Exactly the kind of thing Geli had said. Those two had more in common than Roxy wanted to admit. Humiliating Marta wasn't the answer, but clearly they disagreed. *Please, God, don't let Geli lose her cool, change her mind and play it to him.* I had to trust her…

'I can see where you're coming from, Soph,' said Bella. 'Sometimes it's best to be the bigger woman. It's normal to feel upset with Lorenzo. I would be too. But maybe he didn't really understand how dangerous Marta's actions were. Maybe even *she* wasn't aware of the severity, which is why she did it. Remember, back in the day, wet-nursing—getting milk from other women—was something people did. Obviously now, we know more about the risks, so it's not recommended anymore. But she's old-school. Even using formula probably wasn't the norm when she was bringing up Lorenzo, so maybe that's why she still has the view that "breast is best."'

'Bollocks! Big, giant, massive *bollocks*!' shouted Roxy. 'You're being too nice about it. Surely it's like giving blood. You have to be screened first. Otherwise if that person has an infection, they can pass it on. You're just making excuses for her Bella. His mum is an evil bitch! Lorenzo should kick her out. Pronto!'

'Look, I'm not excusing her behaviour completely,' said Bella, 'but surely she loves Leo, right? He's her only grandchild. So why would she do something she believed would cause him harm? It wouldn't make sense. Was she deluded? *Yes*. Was she disrespectful? *Of course*. Was it totally wrong for Marta to go behind Soph's back and against her wishes? *Absolutely*. But I don't think she did it maliciously.'

Roxy rolled her eyes. '*Whatever*. And as for Lorenzo, he should have stood up for Soph and Leo. Told Marta to sod off.'

'But again, I don't think it's quite that simple,' sighed Bella. 'You can tell a lot about a man and his attitude towards women by the way he treats his mother. Put yourself in Lorenzo's shoes. His mother is an old woman who has always been there for him. Made sacrifices. Then the one time she asks for his help, for a place to stay, he's supposed to turn her down? Of course he loves Soph, he wants to have her back, but she's given him a difficult ultimatum. *Kick your mum out or I'm leaving and taking your child with me*. Think about it. Honestly. Knowing that she has no one else to turn to, would you respect a man who immediately put his mum out on the street during her time of need?'

She had a point, but even if that were true, nothing could excuse Marta's behaviour during our showdown before I'd left. When Roxy read my mind and raised the same point, Bella had to admit that was harder to excuse.

In the end, she said that Marta was probably terrified of losing Lorenzo completely, and as I was the one person who could take him away from her, she was lashing out.

'So anyway, what you gonna do?' said Roxy.

'Wait, I guess. See what happens. I'll get Leo's results back from the doctor tomorrow, so of course I'll need to message Lorenzo to let him know. But apart from that, I just have to hope he sees sense.'

'Sounds sensible. But don't be too stubborn, Soph,' said Bella. 'Lorenzo is a good man and deep down, I'm sure you know that too. Don't let pride or his mother's actions ruin your relationship.'

'Personally, I wouldn't forgive him until he kicked her out and then begged you for forgiveness, but do whatever you think's best. Anyway, enough of this relationship, evil mother-in-law doom and gloom,' said Roxy, reaching in the bucket and taking out the bottle of champagne. 'We've got a big achievement to celebrate! Huge, huge, HUGE congrats to you, Soph,' she added, pouring champers into our glasses and then raising hers in the air. 'To freedom!'

'To freedom!' Bella and I clinked our glasses against Roxy's.

'Here's to a bright and happy future, Soph, with or without Lorenzo…'

CHAPTER FORTY-THREE

What a relief.

    I'd just got the results back from the doctor and Leo was fine. I plonked myself down on the bed. I'd been so worried. My doctor said he'd like to check him out again in a couple of months, just to be sure, but he was confident that Leo was okay.

I supposed I should call Lorenzo straight away. Let him know the good news. But it was still painful. I missed him.

The nights were the worst. The bed felt so cold without him. Lorenzo would always try and get under the duvet five minutes before me and lie on my side, so that it would be nice and warm when I climbed inside. *So sweet.*

I missed his smile, his crazy dancing, the way he looked at me and Leo like his heart was ready to burst. I missed his cooking. Nothing I'd eaten since I'd been in London was a patch on his food.

I wondered if he was missing us as much. No doubt

Marta was running around after him to make sure he wanted for nothing.

Just call him, Soph. Remember what Bella said. Don't let Marta's actions get in the way of your relationship.

I want to, but…

I was about to reel off a string of excuses about being scared to call him when my phone rang.

Speak of the devil.

Not that I was calling him a devil, but you know what I mean…

It was Lorenzo.

My heart skipped a beat.

'Hello?'

'Hello, Soph,' he said quietly.

'If you're calling about Leo, everything's fine. I just heard back from my doctor. I was… I was just about to call you…'

'Thank God. That is great. I am so happy to hear that. When Gloria call me last night, I ask her if there was news, but she said you will find out today.'

'My mum called you? Why?'

'To let me say goodnight to Leo. She did not tell you?'

'No, she didn't…' I had to admit it was a nice thing for her to do.

'I am glad Leo is okay. There is another reason that I call you. I wanted to know when you are coming back.'

The truth was, I didn't know. I'd only booked a single ticket. Not necessarily because I wasn't planning to return. I just… I wanted to see how I felt. Use this time away to decide what to do next…

'I ask because I made a decision,' said Lorenzo. 'And I want to talk to you about it.'

'Can't you just tell me now? On the phone?'

'No,' he said firmly. 'Is better I see you to explain.'

That sounded ominous.

'Okay. Hold on…' I launched my travel app and quickly checked flight availability. Maybe we could come back tomorrow? Everything was done and dusted with the business, Leo was okay, and now that Lorenzo had made a decision, if I stayed here, I'd only be twiddling my thumbs, overthinking about what he was going to say. There was a flight around noon with seats. That would be ideal. 'We can arrive at Pisa airport tomorrow around three?'

'*Perfetto*. I will take a break from the restaurant after lunch. Text me the flight details and I will wait for you at the airport.'

'Fine.'

'*Bene*. I see you tomorrow.'

I ended the call. It broke my heart to be formal, to act that hostile with the man I loved, but I was hurting too. I hoped that he'd come to his senses and would choose us, but I couldn't be so sure. Like Geli said, the bond between a mother and son could be strong. *Unbreakable*.

I supposed at least he'd made a decision. Only time would tell whether I thought it was the right one.

CHAPTER FORTY-FOUR

'You look beautiful.' Lorenzo smiled warmly as I got into the car and shut the door after putting Leo in the back. Luckily he was fast asleep.

'Thanks,' I replied reluctantly, hoping he wasn't just buttering me up before he dropped the news that he'd decided his mum should move in permanently or something. It was nice that he noticed, though, seeing as I'd made an extra effort.

Of course, Lorenzo looked as hot as ever. He was wearing his fitted blue jumper and dark jeans. *My favourite*. I still didn't know how it was possible. In all the time we'd been together, it didn't matter how little sleep he had, he'd never once looked terrible. I'd said this to him before and he'd said it was just my eyes seeing him like that.

Anyway, now wasn't the time to get distracted.

'So…you said you'd made a decision?' My heart began beating faster. I was anxious to hear what was coming next.

'*Sì.*' He reached for my hand and took a deep breath as if he was plucking up the courage to tell me something bad. Or maybe that was me just overthinking. Best to just let him speak before I started fretting. 'As I explain you before, my mamma is very important to me,' *Oh, here we go…* I resisted the temptation to roll my eyes. 'She has done many good things for me. Always been there to help me. Want the best for me…' *If only you knew the half of it*, I wanted to scream. Even though I'd let him hold my hand, I could already feel my finger twitching. I wanted to reach for the phone and play him that message so badly right now. Then he'd see that Mother Marta was about as sweet as vinegar… 'I know she can be difficult sometimes, but it hurt me that you did not want to welcome her into our home. That you would like that I put her on the street when she needed our help…'

'Now, hold on.' I pulled my hand away. 'I never said we should put her out on the streets. I just suggested that maybe she could stay with someone else.' At least he'd acknowledged she could be a pain and wasn't perfect, though, which was something I thought I'd never hear.

'I would never say that to you if it was your mother,' he said.

That was true and that's why I'd agreed. Because in the end I knew that even though I wasn't her biggest fan, it was the right thing to do. But equally, I'd said that having her there wasn't a good idea and look how it had turned out…

'Like I say before, Mamma is important to me. But'—he pulled my hand back and rested his on top of mine—'you and Leo are important to me too. *Voi siete tutto per me.* You are everything to me. You two are my life now.

These days without you and Leo have been some of the worst in my life. I do not want to spend another night without you next to me. Without our son with us.' He lifted my chin and stared into my eyes. 'I love you, Soph. I *need* you. I want you to come back home.'

I felt my heart flutter. Being away from Lorenzo had been unbearable for me too. It was reassuring to know that he missed us just as much and to hear we were important to him because after taking his mother's side, I'd begun to wonder. Speaking of which, what about the Wicked Witch of the West?

'And your mother?' I crossed my arms, making his hand drop.

It was all very well and good him saying he loved me and wanted us back, but as I'd said repeatedly, it wasn't going to happen if *she* was still there. Especially after what had happened before I went to London.

'I have prepared everything at Mamma's house. It is ready for her to go home. I will talk to her tonight. I am sure she will be happy to be back at her place.'

I wouldn't count on that. Marta would know that the longer she stayed with Lorenzo, the more she would drive a wedge between us. There was no way she'd leave without a fight.

'And if she refuses?'

'*Tranquilla.* It will be fine.'

Pff.

'If you say so,' I scoffed. 'And what about what she did? Do you at least acknowledge that she was wrong?'

'If that is what Mamma did, then yes. It is up to us to decide what is best for our son. We are the parents. *Sì*: we can ask Mamma for advice, but give Leo milk from another woman, is not good. I already tell her this.' *He did?* That was promising. 'But I am sure that there will not be problems with Mamma in the future.'

'Really?' I raised my eyebrow. 'How can you be so sure?'

'Like I tell you on the phone, I have made a decision.'

'Go on…' I thought us coming home and asking his mum to return to her place *was* his decision, so I was intrigued to hear what else he had in mind.

'I know you have been trying to make it work here. In this town. You do the lessons with Geli, make new friends. I am proud of you. But I also see sadness. This is not where you want to be. This town is too small for you. *For us*. For our future. So if you want, let us go. Make fresh start. Somewhere new.'

My jaw dropped. He was ready to move? That would be *amazing*. I'd felt for ages that this place wasn't right for either of us. And the same sadness he saw in me was what I saw when he worked at the restaurant. In a way, though, I was also surprised. I would have thought that after spending a week alone with Marta, she would have twisted him even further around her little finger and convinced him to stay here forever. *Unless…*

'Have you spoken to Geli today?'

I know she'd promised not to play him the recording, but if she had, that would explain his sudden change of heart.

'Geli? No. We have not spoken. Why?'

He sounded genuine. I believed him. And I trusted Geli.

'Nothing. Don't worry. Where were you thinking,

though?' I quickly changed the subject. 'Did you have somewhere particular in mind?'

'I have called some people. Some—how you say? *Contacts*? And there could be many opportunities for me. In cities in Italy and in other countries. You just tell me you are happy for us to move and I will make more calls to see where will be possible.'

I was stunned.

Good stunned, though. I'd be interested to hear which locations were on the table. Of course, they'd have to work for me and Leo too.

And what about Marta? *Oh, Jesus.* What if he suggested she come with us? When he said that we wouldn't have a problem with her in the future, I hoped that wasn't because she'd told him it wouldn't happen again and he just believed her.

Only one way to find out, Soph.

Yes, thanks, Reasanna. *Got it.* Obviously that was my next question...

'So we'll go somewhere new, just the three of us?'

I thought that was a more subtle way of asking whether the battleaxe would be joining us...

'*Sì.* You, me and Leo. Mamma is good woman, so I know she will understand. It will not be the first time I have left this town. And good mother should want the best for her son, for me. And that is to be with you and Leo.'

Wow.

That was a relief. He'd done it. Lorenzo had chosen us. Without the need to play that message. That's all I'd wanted. For him to commit to us fully. I didn't want it to feel like it was a 'competition'. There should be room for all of us in his life. But Marta had overstepped the mark, which made that difficult. At least for me anyway.

'This all sounds great. *In theory*. I have to see it all, though. See the action rather than just hear the words to believe it.'

'Of course. I understand. I have arranged to leave work early tonight. I thought, if Geli can have Leo, we can go home this evening and explain everything to Mamma. *Together.* And then come back and get Leo.'

'Okay,' I said, my mood lifting, but yet not entirely convinced it would be as simple as that. 'I'll ask Geli and text you later to confirm.'

'*Bene!* Will be great. You will see. I cannot wait to welcome you and Leo home, *mi amore*! Oh, Sophia. Tell me. What happen with the deal? Everything okay?'

Shit.

With all that was going on, I hadn't even mentioned it to Lorenzo. I'd wanted to. He was the first person I would've loved to call, but we'd fallen out, so…

'Yeah,' I said sheepishly. 'It went through a few days ago.'

'A few days? And you did not tell me? *Amore!* But this is important news! *Fantastico!*' He threw his arms around me. 'I wish you phone as soon as it happen so I could say congratulations. You did it! I am *so* proud of you. We must celebrate! Tonight we talk to Mamma and start plan our future and then tomorrow I take you somewhere to celebrate, *si*?'

'Great! Thank you!' I knew he'd be excited for me. I wished he could have been right there beside me when it had happened, but at least I could share the achievement with him now.

'I am so excited for us to be together again and start our new life,' he said, kissing me firmly on the lips.

The butterflies dancing in my stomach said it all. I was happy that he'd come back to me. I *wasn't* going to lose the love of my life. It would be a fresh start. Good times were on the horizon again. We had so much to look forward to as a family. Like Lorenzo, I was excited.

But something told me his precious mamma wouldn't feel the same…

CHAPTER FORTY-FIVE

'It sound like there is good promise,' said Geli, as she started chopping some onions. Like Lorenzo, she always said she'd like to be corrected if she got an English phrase wrong, but I often felt rude doing that. I knew she meant to say *it sounded promising*, so it was fine. 'But I still think you should have played Lorenzo the recording.'

'I know you do, and believe me, I was tempted at the beginning of the conversation, when he started harping on about what an angel his mum is, but it all worked out in the end. Well, now there's just the small hurdle of breaking the news to Marta, but apart from that...' I sighed.

'She should not be let free like this,' she huffed.

'I'm leaving it in the hands of fate. Karma will catch up with her. In a way, it already has. If she hadn't done what she did, I wouldn't have argued with her and left, and Lorenzo might not have wanted to leave town and have a fresh start so quickly. Now we'll be moving away, Marta won't get to see him or Leo as much, so that's surely punishment enough?'

Geli raised her eyebrow. She clearly didn't agree.

'What time will you meet Lorenzo tonight?'

'Around seven. That still okay?'

'*Sì*. Then I will make dinner earlier.'

'Do you need help? Leo should be asleep for a least another twenty minutes, so I don't mind.'

'It is okay.' She stopped chopping. 'I just need to poop out.'

'No problem. I didn't realise you needed to *pop* out,' I said, trying to correct her in the subtlest way possible. Whilst I was reluctant to tell her about her mistake before, I couldn't let her go around telling people she was *pooping* out. That had a totally different meaning. 'Sure you don't need me to do anything whilst you're gone?'

'Okay. Maybe you can chop the carrots and another onion? Is okay?'

'Of course!' I washed my hands and picked up the knife.

'*Grazie*,' she said, racing out of the kitchen.

～

'*Pronta?*' asked Lorenzo. We were parked outside our house, about to go inside and tell Marta our news.

'Yep. As ready as I'll ever be…'

Lorenzo opened the front door and stepped inside.

Even though I now knew Marta spoke and understood English, I would let Lorenzo lead the conversation. Made sense anyway as she was his beloved mother and he was her golden child. God only knew how she'd handle it. Maybe I should go around the house first and remove all sharp objects…

'Mamma?' he called out for her. She replied to say she was in the kitchen. We started walking towards it.

Here goes nothing...

'Mamma, I have got Sophia with me.' He translated what he said, then switched back to English. He started speaking Italian again and I understood that he was telling her that I was coming back home with Leo. He wrapped his arm around my waist and gave me a squeeze. 'I know that you and Sophia have had a disagreement'—*that was an understatement*—'but Sophia is the woman that I love. She is also Leo's mother and I need you to accept how she, how *we* decide to raise our son...'

Too right!

So glad to know he had my back. I studied Marta's face as he translated what he said. I almost wanted to scream, *There's really no need. She understands every word!* But I kept quiet. She was stony-faced, as usual, and just stood there saying nothing.

'We need time to learn how to be parents and of course, we will want your help, but at the moment we need this time alone... I have checked and your house, it is perfect. It is ready for you, I can help you to move back— whatever you want. You are my mamma and I love you very much, so of course I would want you to visit. For you to keep seeing Leo. But Sophia is important to me too and I need her to be comfortable, so it would help if you can apologise to her, please, Mamma, and for both of you try to and have better relationship...'

Oh, Jesus.

Could you imagine Marta apologising to *me*? There was more chance of hell freezing over. Although Marta stayed silent as Lorenzo translated, her face was getting redder by the second. This was bad. Not only had he told her that he wanted her to move out, he'd also asked her to suck up to me. That would be a lot for her to take in and if I knew Marta, any minute now she would probably explode like a pressure cooker. Anyway, if she did, I was ready for her...

I wondered if he was going to mention us moving away too. On the one hand, it'd probably be best to get it all out of the way in one go, but on the other, I wasn't sure if she could take that big bombshell on top of everything else.

'So? Mamma?' said Lorenzo.

Take cover, people. Marta's mouth is about to open...

'*Sì. Capisco, Lorenzo.*'

Hold up.

Even after Geli's lessons, I knew that my Italian wasn't the best, but I was pretty sure that Marta had just said *yes*, and that she'd understood?

*Now she's walking towards me...*I quickly glanced down at her hands to see if she was holding a knife or another instrument that could kill me.

Nope. All good. I didn't *think* I was about to get murdered.

Then again...

She opened up her arms. Was she going to strangle me instead? I'd like to see her try.

Don't be ridiculous, Sophia.

Button it, Reasanna. Stranger things have happened.

Suddenly she threw her arms around me and pulled me in for a hug.

What. The. Actual. Fuck...

Marta hugged me.

Marta was *still* hugging me.

Squeezing me even.

Well, knock me down with a feather.

Of all the things I was expecting, all the reactions that could have happened, I was not expecting *this*.

Even Lorenzo's eyes were popping out of his head. Marta's back was to him, so she couldn't see his expression.

After freezing for what felt like twenty-four hours due to the shock, I finally came to. Lorenzo did say that we both needed to make the effort, so even though I didn't want to, I guess I needed to be civil. Which meant I actually had to hug her back...

Having physical contact with a woman who I knew hated my guts? *Jeez.* This was going to be painful.

I slowly lifted both of my arms like they each had a ten-tonne weight attached, then gently wrapped them around her. But not completely. I didn't give Marta a full-on squeeze. It was more cautious. Like hugging someone with glue on their back. Making just enough contact to be polite, but not enough to risk becoming permanently affixed.

I still wasn't convinced that this wasn't a dream. *Or a nightmare.* At this stage, I couldn't quite work out which description was more accurate...

'I am sorry, Sophia,' said Marta in a stilted accent.

'Mamma?' Lorenzo beamed. 'You speak English!?'

'I try start to learn.' She pulled away and turned to face him. 'For Sophia.' She smiled back at me.

Hmmm.

Seriously. What the hell was going on?

'Thank you, Mamma!' Lorenzo threw his arms around

her. 'I am happy you apologise and is good you start to learn too. I am glad you use the books and CDs I give you.'

Books? Lorenzo had been giving Marta English books? *News to me.* Lorenzo explained he'd given them to her a while ago, when he'd moved to London as Marta had planned to visit, but she hadn't seemed interested in learning, so he hadn't mentioned it to me.

Pff. And after all the vile things she'd said to me before, there was no way she'd just started. As far as I knew, Geli didn't have an English clone teaching in this town. *Beginner my arse.*

That means as well as understanding when I'd asked her in English to babysit, the night she'd come to stay and I'd called out to Lorenzo, suggesting we have sex on the sofa, she'd understood too. That was why Marta had been funny when I'd asked her to sit down and she'd called it dirty. And that was why she'd huffed when I'd made a joke about us screwing on it the night before.

It was all making sense now…

'There is something else I must tell you.' He stepped back and took a deep breath. 'Sophia and I have decided to move away…'

Uh-oh.

Any minute now, I was expecting Marta's smile to fall and switch to a thunderous expression.

Instead, the grin stayed plastered to her face. It was so rigid, so definite, that I wondered if a mysterious gust of wind had blown in her direction and set it like that when I wasn't looking. Apart from when Leo was here, in all the time I had been in Chiorno, I'd never seen Marta look that happy around me. Did miracles really happen?

'Yes, son. You must go live your life.'

Lorenzo's eyes popped out of his head again. At least I wasn't the only one wondering if I was suddenly living in a parallel universe.

'It may not be in Italy, Mamma. Is possible we will go to live in another country. Me, Sophia and Leo.' Clearly he thought Marta didn't understand what he'd said and that was why she was being so cool about it.

'*Sì, sì. Capisco.* I understand.'

'Could be France, Spain or London... I will see where I find a job and then Sophia and me decide together.'

'*Sì.*' She patted his shoulder, reached for my hand, then took it in hers.

Enough now! I honestly needed to know what the hell was going on. Not so long ago, Marta was calling me a raggedy old whore and boasting that Lorenzo would stay with her forever. Now she'd apologised, hugged me and wanted to hold my hand?

I was tempted to slap my face with my other hand to wake myself up because this couldn't be real. All of the stress from the last few months must have finally gotten to me. I'd officially gone mad. It was the only explanation.

'Will be good for you. I hope you will allow me to visit Sophia?' she said, with her Joker-sized grin still plastered over her face.

Lorenzo turned to me, still beaming.

Come on, Sophia! shouted Reasanna. *Say something.*

Oh, oh, right. Yes.

'*Sì!*' I said, my voice so high-pitched that all of the cats in the neighbourhood probably heard. 'Yes, Marta. You can visit.'

I couldn't say no, could I, when she was being so nice.

But I would *definitely* need to find out what was happening before we moved and before she actually *did*.

'*Perfetto!* I am so happy everything is okay with you. The two most important women in my life. I *knew* you would understand, Mamma! That you are good mother!'

If only you knew the truth, I thought to myself. Then again, what *was* the truth? I still had no idea what was up with her tonight.

As far as I knew personality transplants hadn't been invented yet, so it couldn't be that. *Maybe she fell, hit her head and saw the errors of her ways?*

So strange.

The night got weirder still as, rather than accepting Lorenzo's offer to stay the night and go to her place in the morning, Marta said she'd leave straight away. She even had her suitcases packed.

Whaaat?

To be honest I was relieved, because by now, all sorts of crazy things were running through my head. That she was pretending to be nice now so I'd let my guard down but would sneak into our room in the middle of the night and murder me. I hadn't quite worked out how she'd do it with Lorenzo lying beside me, but after what I'd seen tonight, anything was possible.

Or perhaps Marta would go along with the charade and then, just before we were leaving to start a new life, she'd send a hitman to take me out, so that she could have Lorenzo and Leo all to herself. Maybe a tad far-fetched, but like I said, anything was possible.

After once again insisting that Lorenzo take her home so that we'd have more time alone in the house together (wtf?), Lorenzo started loading her cases in the car. We'd decided that he would drop me to Geli's on the way so I could get Leo and his things and then, after he'd got Marta settled, Lorenzo would come back to pick us up and we'd all finally go home together. I couldn't wait.

I was about to text Geli to tell her the plan when my phone pinged.

What a coincidence. It was her.

Geli

So how it go?

I quickly typed out a reply.

Me

Good...??!! Surprisingly! Marta apologised and miraculously seemed fine about us moving away??!! She's leaving tonight, so I'll be there shortly to collect Leo and our stuff.

Geli

Bene

Geli

I am glad she listened.

Geli

See you soon

She logged off.

Glad she listened?

Something told me there was more to this, and another reason why Marta had had a sudden change of heart...

CHAPTER FORTY-SIX

'You played it to her?'

'*Sì.*'

'But you promised not to!' I shouted.

'No. I promise not to play it to *Lorenzo*. I said nothing about Marta...'

'What exactly happened?'

'Not much.' Geli shrugged her shoulders. 'I went to see her this afternoon, play her the recording and said if she wanted to see her son and grandson again, would be good for her to agree to whatever you and Lorenzo want. Including to leave the house tonight and to give her blessing for you both to leave. That is all.'

Whoa. I'd love to have been a fly on the wall when Geli had rocked up. *Imagine Marta's face when she heard the recording.*

'Marta's face must have been a picture!'

'I do not understand?'

'Sorry, I mean, she must have been shocked.'

'Of course. But she is smart woman. She understand

that she did not have a choice. For me, playing the recording to her was perfect. You worry because you did not want to damage Lorenzo's relationship with his mother or upset him. *Sì?* But now Marta has said that she is happy about you and Lorenzo going away, Lorenzo still believes his mum is amazing and you get to live better life away from her with him.'

She was right. Wish I'd thought of the idea now. Then again, I reckoned it was better coming from Geli. Knowing that someone other than me had the recording would keep Marta on her toes.

Part of me worried if it was dishonest. Technically it was blackmail. I wondered if Lorenzo would just prefer to know the truth. But it wasn't me who had done anything. I was going to leave it, let the universe decide. It was Geli who'd intervened, so maybe that absolved me of any guilt. Anyway, like Geli had said, this way, Lorenzo and Marta got to keep their relationship intact. And surely that was more important to him.

'I suppose it's worked out for the best. And your heart was in the right place. You're a good friend, thank you. Honestly, I don't know how I would have got through this whole Marta drama without you.' I gave her a big squeeze. This time, a proper hug. One with conviction and genuine emotion. Not like that confusing embrace with Marta earlier.

'Okay, okay,' she said, pulling away. 'We must not get mooshy. You will have to get used to not having me here. I am leaving.'

'When?'

'Next week.'

'So soon?' My stomach sank.

'*Sì*. That is why I wanted to speak to Marta. To make sure everything was okay before I go.'

'I appreciate it. I'm really going to miss you, but I understand. You need to get out of here. I'll be fine. Hopefully, I won't be far behind you.'

'I know you will be okay. You are strong woman.'

'I didn't feel like that when I first arrived here, but I've got my confidence back again. Anyway, where are you going?'

'Vietnam.'

'Oh wow! You'll keep in touch, won't you?'

'*Sì!* You and Roxy will not lose me so easy.'

My eyes widened. I hoped to God Roxy had messaged her back. I didn't want any awkwardness.

'Don't worry. Roxy has message me to explain.' She read my mind. *That's a relief.* 'I know we will see each other again…' She smirked. I believed her. Something told me those two had unfinished business.

'Glad to hear it! And wherever Lorenzo, Leo and I move to, you have to come and visit.'

'I would like that. And you look out for Holly too? After I leave?'

'Yep. She texted earlier to say she'd be back tomorrow because there's something she needs to do. I really hope it's what I think it is…'

CHAPTER FORTY-SEVEN

It was almost time.

Time to leave this town. *For good.*

I was all packed and ready to go. Lorenzo would be back with Leo and Marta and then we'd be off. To have a fresh start.

It had been a busy time. Last week Geli had jetted off to Vietnam. She didn't like big goodbyes, so Holly and I and a few other people had gone round to her place the night before for a few drinks. There was no sign of Daphne. Apparently she'd already returned to England to start divorce proceedings.

Whilst I was sad that Geli was going, she was in great spirits. With her mother fully recovered and knowing she was about to leave Chiorno, Geli was more excited than an inmate being freed from prison. I didn't blame her.

Holly had also left. When she'd first messaged to say she was coming back to town because there was something she needed to do and asked if Geli and I could meet her,

I'd hoped that meant she was ready to report Silvestro. Little did I know that had already been done.

She'd explained that, after spending a couple of days crashing on her friend's sofa, beating herself up about what had happened, she'd finally taken Geli's advice and contacted a support group in Florence which helped women who had been victims of sexual violence. One of the workers who spoke good English spent a lot of time with Holly and helped her to see the light. Then Holly grew angry. And that anger sparked determination. She wasn't going to let Silvestro get away with it.

First, she tracked down the au pair who'd worked there before. Found her on Facebook apparently. They made contact and turned out, Silvestro had done the same to the previous girl. He'd tried to force himself on her, but she managed to escape before things had gone further. She was too scared to report him and so Silvestro had just called the agency and requested another au pair instead: that's how Holly had got the job.

Geli had also done some digging whilst I was away. Like she'd suspected, Silvestro had a history. He'd had affairs and regularly used prostitutes, until his wife had found out and threatened to leave him if he strayed again. So it seemed like he'd started using au pairs to get his cheap thrills instead.

Using her detective skills, Geli had tracked down another woman who used to work for Silvestro at his company in town. She said he'd flashed her before, but when she'd threatened to report him, he'd said it was an 'accident.' How can getting your dick out in the office be an 'accident'? The guy was a creep. She'd left shortly afterwards.

Armed with this information and the support of the two other women, Holly took the brave step of reporting Silvestro to the police. They were much more sympathetic than she'd thought and said they would investigate. That was one of the reasons Holly had come back. She wanted to be there when the police knocked on the door and took him in for questioning.

Geli and I had gone with her. We sat in the car across the road and watched it all unfold.

It wasn't nice to see his wife and kids there, as clearly they were upset, but they needed to know the monster they were living with. I especially feared for the children. None of us knew what he was capable of.

Holly had cried when it happened, but she assured us they were tears of relief.

Silvestro was charged, which was a step in the right direction. It would take a while for it to go to court, and of course, we didn't know what would happen, but at least he'd been called out for what he'd done.

Holly and the previous au pair had also reported him to their agency and they'd removed the family from their database. Geli said we should do a blanket email to all the agencies so that they could blacklist him, but we had to tread carefully. Even though Holly and the other women knew what he'd done, in the eyes of the law, he hadn't been convicted, so we had to make sure we didn't do anything rash that could affect the case.

At least the process had been started and hopefully no one else would be subjected to his perversion.

Holly had also seen the light and kicked Umberto to the curb. She realised as gorgeous as he was, looks weren't enough. Holly finally saw what I'd suspected early on, that he couldn't have loved her. In all the time she'd lived there, even though she'd taken the big step to move to Chiorno to be with him, Umberto hadn't shown her any form of commitment. And him blaming her for Silvestro's actions was the last straw.

Like me, we'd both made sacrifices for love. Giving up the lives we knew and travelling hundreds of miles to follow our hearts. But unfortunately, not all holiday romances could go the distance. This time, I was one of the lucky ones. Holly would be fine, though. She was young and still had her whole life ahead of her. There would be plenty of time to find someone who truly deserved her.

Holly was already back at home, planning her next move. She was thinking about returning to uni, but said she also might take some time out to go travelling. *Good for her*. The situation with Silvestro wasn't over yet, but she was prepared to see it through. Holly was stronger. More confident and happier. I was proud of her.

I also celebrated my birthday last week. Even though it was low-key, it was actually lovely. Lorenzo took the day off, made me breakfast in bed, then looked after Leo whilst I soaked in the bath. I FaceTimed my parents, and after lunch, we went for a drive in the Tuscan hills. When we came back, I did a group video call with Geli, who'd arrived safely in Vietnam, and Roxy and Bella, had dinner, put Leo to sleep, then enjoyed some *quality time* in the bedroom with Lorenzo. *Twice*. We were definitely getting back in the swing of things…

I looked around the house, then stepped out into the garden to take in the amazing views for the last time. Now we were in April, it was much warmer, and the countryside was even more lush and green with plenty of flowers and fruit trees in bloom. As much as I was happy to leave, it was strange knowing that I wouldn't live here again, and I'd definitely miss the scenery.

I'd had many highs and lows during my time in Chiorno. As weird as it may sound, I was glad I came. Glad that it was challenging. I'd grown a lot and I wouldn't be the person I was now if I hadn't gone through those difficulties.

When I'd arrived in Chiorno, I had been expecting perfection. But perfection didn't exist. Life wasn't a fairy tale. Wherever we lived, there were sure to be pros and cons. People I liked. People I didn't. Feeling homesick, missing family and friends. Struggling to get to grips with a different culture. It was all normal. The fact was, I'd lived in another country. So many people would love the chance to live abroad. Even though it wasn't all a bed of roses, it was an adventure. A new experience. And I was wiser for it.

I went back inside and reached in my bag to check the time on my phone. They should be here in about ten minutes. As I was putting it back, I spotted my notepad.

Ah, the list.

That notepad contained the magical plan that I thought would solve all of my problems. Back then I thought all I needed to do was take control and everything would fall into place. But actually, I should have realised that because I was going through so many changes, it was actually normal to feel out of control. It was okay that I didn't have my shit totally together.

Although the list had helped in some ways, I'd also learnt that even if you work hard and are more organised than a colour-coded spreadsheet, sometimes life happens and you just have to go with the flow.

Oh, what the hell.

I had some time to kill, so I may as well go through the list and see what I'd achieved. *Just for fun…*

I opened the page:

1) Learn Italian

Well, I was no Italian linguist, but thanks to Geli's lessons, Lorenzo and living here in general, I could get by. I understood a lot more than I did before and could communicate on a basic level. Including knowing how to ask for desiccated coconut and tell someone where to go if they tried to insult me. Who knew you could learn so much without structured lessons and textbooks? Mastering the language was never going to be something I could accomplish in just a few months. It would take *years* of practise. But I'd made a promising start and wanted to continue learning.

2) Make Some New Friends

Definite check. I know people always say they'll keep in touch, but I genuinely felt like in Geli, I'd made a friend for life. I was so glad I'd met her.

When I'd made the list, I wanted to make friends mainly to have someone to talk to so I didn't feel so isolated. But Geli had helped me realise not just the power of friendship but also the benefits of feeling like you had your own little community, which tied in with point number three…

3) Be More Independent

I'd always thought that to do better in this town I needed to be more independent. But actually, sometimes to be *independent*, you needed to *depend* on other people.

Whatever I thought of her, without Marta looking after Leo, I couldn't have gone to the Italian lessons. Without those lessons, I wouldn't have met Geli and found an amazing friend who did so much for me. I wouldn't have met Holly either and been around to help her. Holly was another friend I would *totally* stay in contact with.

4) Sort Out My Sex Life

Ooooh, *yes, yes, YES!* Lorenzo and I were back in business in the bedroom in a big way.

When I thought back to those early days, I'd put way too much pressure on myself to be some sort of sexual goddess. In the end, letting things happen naturally and going at my own pace was what worked for me.

It may have taken longer than expected for my mojo to return, but Lorenzo and I had definitely been making up for lost time. Ever since Marta had left, we hadn't been able to keep our hands off each other. Especially that night Geli babysat Leo and Lorenzo took me to Florence for a slap-up meal to celebrate the sale of the business. After dinner, we stayed at the same hotel we visited last time and let's just say we put that giant bed (in fact, the whole room) to good use…

Yep. When it came to getting jiggy, it had been just like old times. Leo had very considerately been sleeping through the night, which has given us time to enjoy each other. As Bella had reminded me, babies could be unpredictable, so these hours of freedom to frolic probably wouldn't be forever, but we were certainly going to enjoy them whilst they lasted.

5) Get Back Into Shape

When I'd written the list, I'd been obsessed with getting back my old body shape, when what I needed to do was learn to accept my new one. Now I found that taking a balanced approach and working out two or three times a week was a million times better than forcing myself to do it every day.

Was I always going to love what I saw in the mirror every single time? No. Of course I'd have my bad days, just like everyone else. But I was happy and healthy. I wasn't going to beat myself up about eating the things I liked. What was the point of living in bloody Italy if I couldn't enjoy a slice of my favourite crushed Florentine orange cake, a plate of pasta or some delicious gelato? It was all about *la dolce vita*, baby! And if I was really worried about the calories, there was always the option of doing an extra round of bedroom gymnastics with Lorenzo to help burn them off…

6) Have a Good Relationship with Lorenzo's Mum

Hmmm… when I'd put this on the list I had been determined to make Marta like me, but that was never going to happen. Some people just aren't meant to get along. *That's life.* I'd accepted that Marta and I would never be best buddies. For starters, there was no way I'd be able to forget all those bitchy things she'd said. But we had an understanding.

Since she'd moved back to her house, I'd made it clear that access to Leo was on terms that Lorenzo and I both agreed on. Any time she'd spent with Leo was deliberately 'supervised', so one of us was always with her. After what she'd done, that was *more* than reasonable. Even though she'd said sorry and done that awkward hugging stuff (which, let's face it, was only because of the recording), she couldn't expect me to trust her straight away. She would need to earn that back over time. But I had a heart. I knew seeing Lorenzo and Leo was important to her, even more so now we'd be moving away, so I'd *try* and be as civil as possible. Within reason…

7) Get the Business Back Under Control

Ha! Well, this one hadn't quite turned out as planned… I'd thought getting things back on track was the answer, when actually what I needed to do was let go of it altogether. Now I'd sold the business I was much happier. I wished I'd done it sooner rather than running myself ragged, trying to juggle all those balls, but everything happens for a reason. At the right time. In the right place. With the right person.

Rhonda seemed to be settling in well, and when I spoke to the clients and the team, they seemed to like and, most importantly, respect her. She had kept on most of the staff. Some took the sale as an opportunity to leave and pursue new career paths, including Harrison. He was getting ready to go travelling for a few months, which was something he'd never got to do as he had come to work with me straight after uni. Then once he returned, he'd consider his options.

Robyn was now working four days a week and was doing much better. She still had a while before she went on maternity leave. She wasn't sure yet whether she'd continue working in PR after the baby was born. Time would tell…

As for me and my professional future, I'd decided that for once, I wasn't going to overthink or make a formal plan. *I know, right? Miracles do happen.*

I'd spent so many years focusing on the business and now I wanted to take some time out to enjoy my son. I knew that wasn't an option for a lot of women. I was lucky. Like Mum had said, babies grow up so fast and I'd be silly not to make the most of my situation whilst I could. I'd finally decided to rent out my house in London, which would give us an income. I had the money from the sale of the business, and Lorenzo would also have a salary. Who knew what the future would bring and how long it would be possible for me not to work, but for the moment, that was what I was going to do.

In the meantime, to keep my brain ticking over, I'd approached an expat blog about writing some articles on finding my feet in Italy. There wasn't any money in it, but it wasn't about that. I wanted to give myself a little hobby and help others. If one of my tips could help another person coming here for the first time to avoid the challenges I'd had at the beginning, it would be worth it.

If I was being totally honest, though, I knew myself. At some point I would get itchy feet and want to dive back into having a career again. In fact, there were a couple of business ideas I'd been mulling over, which could be *really* exciting for me and Lorenzo…

8) Enjoy My Life in Italy

Although of course all of my experiences in Chiorno hadn't been perfect, I *did* have some really fun times. The lessons with Geli, Holly and even Daphne, the fun trip to Florence with Lorenzo, Roxy, Bella and Geli and a few other occasions.

Overall, if I did it all again, I'd relax more. Keep an open mind. Be more patient. Be kinder to myself. Prioritise based on what made me, Lorenzo and Leo happy and not worry about impressing Marta or hanging on to a business because I was too scared to let go.

I'd be less afraid to make mistakes. I'd get out there

and make friends sooner. Learning the language earlier would have helped too. But, *hey. It is what it is.* And it had all worked out how it was meant to, so I had no regrets.

In the end, I'd tried my best to make the most of my time in Chiorno and I was glad I stayed as long as I did.

But really, my time in this country was only just beginning.

Lorenzo had accepted a head chef role in Southern Italy, which started next week, so that would be our temporary home. We planned to drive there, stopping off at different places along the way. Rome, Naples and Puglia. Like a road trip. Our first holiday as a family. I couldn't wait.

The job was only for three to six months, but that suited us just fine as we still hadn't quite decided where we'd like to settle long-term. Offers in France, Spain and elsewhere in Italy were all still on the table. But we didn't want to rush or jump into anything permanent too quickly.

Whilst London was also a possibility, it was unlikely we'd go back. Even though I missed my family, friends and the familiarity massively, I'd spent most of my life there and wasn't ready to return just yet. As scary as it was, it was good to keep pushing myself out of my comfort zone. I'd learned that was often where the fun began. There was a whole world out there and I was looking forward to discovering a lot more of it with Lorenzo and our darling son.

'We are back,' shouted Lorenzo as he came through the front door. I closed my notepad, put it back in my bag and went out to meet them. '*Pronta?*'

'*Sì!* I'm ready. *Buongiorno*, Marta. Hello, Leo!' I lifted him from Lorenzo's arms and into the air.

'*Buongiorno, Sophia*,' said Marta. 'I come to say goodbye.'

'*Grazie*.' I smiled. She seemed genuine. I'd be sure to look out for a hitman when I stepped outside, though. Just in case…

Lorenzo loaded everything up into the car. I strapped Leo into his seat whilst Marta locked the front door. Lorenzo had arranged to rent the house to a young family to bring in some extra cash. As we knew we wouldn't come back to live here, he planned to either keep renting it out if the demand was there, or sell it altogether.

'*Ciao, Mamma*,' said Lorenzo, giving her a big squeeze and a kiss. Tears were now rolling down her face. She squeezed his cheeks like he was a baby and then hugged him again. I guess it didn't matter how old your child was. The love and that bond between mother and son was always strong. I was glad I hadn't broken it. Marta leant inside the car and kissed Leo on the forehead, then came and stood in front of me.

'Bye, Sophia. Please you look after my boys.' I could tell she was trying to be strong but was crumbling inside.

'I will,' I said. *Oh sod it*. I couldn't forget what she'd done, but I could take the higher ground for a few seconds. I wrapped my arms around her and patted her on the back. She seemed genuinely grateful. I slowly pulled away.

Lorenzo and I both got in the car and put on our seat belts. He took my hand.

'Ready for a fresh start?'

'Most definitely.' I smiled.

'Then let us go, *amore*.' Lorenzo leant forward and kissed me gently. 'Let you, me and Leo go and start our next adventure.'

Want more?

Join the Olivia Spring VIP Club and receive *The Middle-Aged Virgin in Italy Bonuses* for **FREE!** Get Sophia's **delicious apple crumble recipe**, check out **Geli's top Italian phrases**, and read **an exclusive interview with Olivia Spring**, where she reveals the inspiration behind the sequel, her favourite characters, whether there will be a third book and much, much more!

Get *The Middle-Aged Virgin in Italy Bonuses* FREE now, by signing up at: https://bookhip.com/HVMPAN

ENJOYED THIS BOOK? YOU CAN MAKE A BIG DIFFERENCE.

If you've enjoyed *The Middle-Aged Virgin in Italy*, I'd be so grateful if you could spare two minutes to leave a review on Amazon, Goodreads and BookBub. It doesn't have to be long (unless you'd like it to be!). Every review – even if it's just a sentence – would make a *huge* difference.

By leaving an honest review, you'll be helping to bring my books to the attention of other readers and hearing your thoughts will make them more likely to give my novels a try. As a result, it will help me to build my career, which means I'll get to write more books!

Thank you so much. As well as making a huge difference, you've also just made my day!

Olivia x

Only When It's Love: Holding Out For Mr Right

Have you read my second novel *Only When It's Love?* It includes the feisty character Roxy from *The Middle-Aged Virgin in Italy*, too! Here's what it's about:

Alex's love life is a disaster. Will accepting a crazy seven-step dating challenge lead to more heartbreak or help her find Mr Right?

Alex is tired of getting ghosted. After years of disastrous hook-ups and relationships that lead to the bedroom but nowhere else, Alex is convinced she's destined to be eternally single. Then her newly married friend Stacey recommends what worked for her: a self-help book that guarantees Alex will find true love in just seven steps. Sounds simple, right?

Except Alex soon discovers that each step is more difficult than the last, and one of the rules involves dating, but not sleeping with a guy for six months. Absolutely no intimate contact whatsoever. *Zero. Nada. Rien.* A big challenge for Alex, who has never been one to hold back from jumping straight into the sack, hoping it will help a man fall for her.

Will any guys be willing to wait? Will Alex find her Mr Right? And if she does, will she be strong enough to resist temptation and hold out for true love?

Join Alex on her roller coaster romantic journey as she tries to cope with the emotional and physical ups and downs of dating whilst following a lengthy list of rigid rules.

Only When It's Love **is a standalone, fun, feel-good, romantic**

comedy about self-acceptance, determination, love and the challenge of finding *the one*.

Praise For *Only When It's Love*

'**Totally unique and wonderful.** Olivia's book has a brilliant message about self-worth and brings to life an important modern take on the rom-com. Most definitely a five-star read.' - **Love Books Group**

'I guarantee **you will HOOT with laughter** at Alex's escapades whilst fully cheering her on. If you like romance, humour and a generally fun-filled read then look no further than this **gorgeous, well-written dating adventure**. Five stars.' - **Bookaholic Confessions**

'Such a uniquely told, **laugh-out-loud, dirty and flirty, addictive novel**.' - **The Writing Garnet**

'I've never read a story so quickly to find out who she would choose! Five stars.' - **Books Between Friends**

'Cool, contemporary, but still wildly romantic! Yet another smasher from Olivia Spring! There's something about the way she writes that really endeared me to the heroine of this story.' - **Amazon reader**

'WOW WOW WOW!!!! *Only When it's Love* is **a dynamite love fest**. I read the entire story with the biggest smile on my face. In case you might have missed the million hints I've dropped, download the book today and jump straight in.' **Stacy is Reading**

Buy *Only When It's Love* on Amazon today!

AN EXTRACT FROM ONLY WHEN IT'S LOVE

Chapter One

Never again.

Why, why, *why* did I keep on doing this?

I felt great for a few minutes, or if I was lucky, hours, but then, when it was all over, I ended up feeling like shit for days. Sometimes weeks.

I must stop torturing myself.

Repeat after me:

I, Alexandra Adams, will *not* answer Connor Matthew's WhatsApp messages, texts or phone calls for the rest of my life.

I firmly declare that even if Connor says his whole world is falling apart, that he's sorry, he's realised I'm *the one* and he's changed, I will positively, absolutely, unequivocally *not* reply.

Nor will I end up going to his flat because I caved in after he sent me five million messages saying he misses me and inviting me round just 'to talk'.

And I *definitely* do solemnly swear that I will *not* end up on my back with my legs wrapped around his neck within minutes of arriving, because I took one look at his body and couldn't resist.

No.

That's it.

No more.

I will be *strong*. I will be like iron. Titanium. Steel. All three welded into one.

I will block Connor once and for all and I will move on with my life.

Yes!

I exhaled.

Finally I'd found my inner strength.

This was the start of a new life for me. A new beginning. Where I wouldn't get screwed over by yet another fuckboy. Where I wouldn't get ghosted or dumped. Where I took control of my life and stuck my middle finger up at the men who treated me like shit. *Here's to the new me.*

My phone chimed.

It was Connor.

I bolted upright in bed and clicked on his message.

He couldn't stop thinking about me. He wanted to see me again.

Tonight.

To talk. About our future.

Together.

This could be it!

Things *had* felt kind of different last time. Like there was a deeper connection.

Maybe he was right. Maybe he *had* changed…

I excitedly typed out a reply.

My fingers hovered over the blue button, ready to send.

Hello?

What the hell was I doing?

It was like the entire contents of my pep talk two seconds ago had just evaporated from my brain.

Remember *being strong like iron, titanium and steel* and resisting the temptations of Connor?

Shit.

This was going to be much harder than I'd thought.

Want to find out what happens next? Buy *Only When It's Love* by Olivia Spring on Amazon now!

Losing My Inhibitions

Have you read my third novel *Losing My Inhibitions?* It includes Sophia and Roxy from *The Middle-Aged Virgin in Italy*, too! Here's what it's about:

Finally free and ready to have fun...

He's hot, single and off limits. She's just got her life together after a messy divorce. Should she risk it all for a forbidden fling?

A year after leaving her controlling ex, Roxy's divorce is finally official. She's got her confidence and career back on track and is ready to start enjoying some no-strings-attached fun.

But just when Roxy thinks she has her dating plan all mapped out, a hot younger single man unexpectedly appears. On paper, he sounds like exactly what Roxy's been looking for, until she's warned that he's strictly off limits. Getting involved with him will put her career, home and everything she's worked for in extreme jeopardy. There's a million reasons why Roxy shouldn't give into his charms. The trouble is, he's just too tempting...

Will Roxy take a chance and risk it all to pursue a forbidden fling? And if she does, can she find a way to let him rock her world, without turning it upside down?

Losing My Inhibitions is a sexy, laugh-out-loud romantic comedy with a modern twist. This story is about self-love, new beginnings, forging your own path in life and being true

to yourself. It can be read as a standalone novel or as a prequel to *The Middle-Aged Virgin* and *Only When It's Love*.

Here's what readers are saying about it:

"All hail the new queen of funny, sexy romantic fiction, Olivia Spring. A brilliant read with cringe worthy moments captured perfectly and **genius comedy that had me laughing out loud.** I can't wait to see what Olivia Spring conjures up next but I will snap it up. **All we need now is a movie deal for all three books. Five stars." Love Books Group**

"Oh my word. Ladies **if you haven't already read this, you are missing out. It's steamy, it's sexy and it's very funny.** There is a part in it, of which I can't repeat, that had me doubled up laughing. Totally loved it. **Five stars." Books Between Friends**

"*Losing My Inhibitions* is **the perfect mix of sexy, romance, drama and comedy. I would definitely recommend this book! It's perfect for a summer read**, chilled out in the garden with a glass of something lovely. Five stars." **Nicole's Book Corner**

"Well Olivia Spring, you've done it again. This modern girl's romcom is about self-love, self-discovery, and to always be true to who you are. **I devoured it!" Girl Well Read**

"I really enjoyed reading this - some of the situations Roxy finds herself in **had me laughing out loud!** Five stars." **Home Full Of Books**

"I read it in two evenings and it was brilliant!! **I couldn't put it down." Head In A Book 18**

Buy *Losing My Inhibitions* on Amazon today!

AN EXTRACT FROM LOSING MY INHIBITIONS

Chapter One

At last.

I thought it was never going to end.

He'd been pounding away for ten minutes, grunting like a pig, and I'd been listening to the radio playing in the background, trying to figure out what advert the song before last was from. Was it the one advertising car insurance or the one for those panty liners that are supposed to keep you *cotton fresh all day long*? *It'll come to me...*

We should have just called it a night when he'd first struggled to get his machinery working. Based on tonight, it seems like what I'd read about some older men finding it difficult to get it up was true.

It was only about half an hour after he'd popped a little blue pill that he'd been able to get his little soldier to stand to attention, if you catch my drift. Which, unfortunately for me, was around the same time I started to sober up and wonder what the hell I was doing.

But by then, he was really excited, and it had been so long since my last time that I'd got myself worked up and was just as keen as him to give it a go. I mean, when I start something, I like to see it through. *Yep, I'm dedicated like that.*

I'd also read that there are lots of benefits of sleeping with an older guy. Apparently, after years of experience in the sack, they know their way around a woman's body better than a gynaecologist, so I thought I may as well give it a try. *Purely in the name of research, of course.*

But now I was really wishing I hadn't bothered. It was about as exciting as watching a hundred-metre snail race. And this guy wouldn't know his way around my anatomy if I gave him a map.

Still, at least it was over now. I was back in the saddle. First time since I'd left my ex-husband. Frankly, I hoped it got better from here. *Please tell me it does?*

I opened my eyes slowly and glanced up at his crepey skin and flaky bald head, which had tufts of grey at the side. His droopy man boobs hung above my chest, whilst the weight of his large pot belly pressed down on my stomach.

Dear God.

I must have had a lot more to drink than I'd realised.

Don't get me wrong. If I was looking for a relationship and this was a man I'd fallen madly in love with, then I wouldn't be so shallow. It was just that right now, I was looking for fun. To make up for the years I'd wasted with my ex. When I was dreaming of the day that I'd be free from Steve and with another man, this wasn't exactly what I'd had in mind.

I'd pictured a young, hot, sexy guy with abs that would

give a Calvin Klein model a run for his money, with a full head of dark hair I could run my fingers through. A stud who would have me screaming for more, rather than wondering when it would all be over.

It was Colette, my boss, slash landlady, slash house-mate, slash friend, who'd set me up with him at my divorce party earlier this evening. Now that I was officially free, Colette said some male company might be good for me, so she'd invited Donald, her loaded sixty-two-year-old boyfriend, and he'd brought his fifty-five-year-old mate Terrence along.

I knew that I was ready to get back on the horse, and it was already under control. My cousin Alex had been helping me. She'd given me a crash course in online dating two weeks ago, and I wanted to set up my profile ASAP so I could get going on the whole swiping thing, but this big work exhibition kept getting in the way. I'd been burning the midnight oil every night and often over the weekends too, trying to get everything prepared, which didn't leave me with any time for extracurricular activities. And after another long, tiring and stressful day, a hook-up was the last thing I was thinking about. But I guess the booze I'd been drinking all night had made me relax a little too much, so when Terrence had started flirting, my libido had woken up, curiosity had got the better of me, and I'd hastily thought, *Why not just get it out the way now?*

Big Mistake.

Oh well. You live and you learn. We all do things in the heat of the moment that we regret. As long as I didn't do it again, then it was fine. Which meant I better start thinking about how I was going to get this big sweaty oaf of a man off me. *Now.* I'd heard the effects of those pills can last for hours, and I definitely couldn't endure another round.

No way.

Remind me never to drink alcohol again.

Want to find out what happens next? Buy *Losing My Inhibitions* by Olivia Spring on Amazon now!

ALSO BY OLIVIA SPRING

Love Offline

Have you read my fourth novel *Love Offline?* Here's what it's about:

Looking For Romance In Real Life…

Emily's Struggling To Find Romance Online. Will Ditching The Dating Apps Lead To True Love?

Online dating isn't working for introvert Emily. Although she's comfortable swiping right in her PJs, the idea of meeting a guy in person fills her with dread.

So when her best friend challenges her to ditch the apps, attend a load of awkward singles' events and find love in real life, Emily wants to run for the hills.

Then she meets Josh. He's handsome, kind and funny, but Emily's had her heart crushed before and knows he's hiding something…

Is Josh too good to be true? Can Emily learn to trust again? And if she does, will it lead to love or more heartache?

***Love Offline* is a fun, sexy, entertaining story about friendship, stepping outside of your comfort zone and falling in love the old-fashioned way**.

Here's what readers are saying about it:

"This book spoke to me on soooo many levels!! I loved the realness this book shows!!!! Five stars." **Once Upon A Book Review**.

"The perfect mix of a sexy, hot, modern day romance, wit and just an all out bloody fabulous book! Highly recommend. Five stars." **Nicole's Book Corner.**

"Fun, flirty and fabulous... I was laughing throughout the whole book. Five stars." **Reading In Lipstick.**

"Hilarious, sexy-romp with heart! I adored the relationship Emily has with her best friend Chloe." **A Girl With Her Head Stuck In A Book.**

"If you are a fan of Sophie Kinsella and Lindsey Kelk, then this book is for you! *Love Offline* is a romcom for the modern woman." **Girl Well Read.**

"This book just makes you feel good and all fuzzy inside, def one to curl up with on the sofa with a cup of tea. Five stars." **Barbs Book Club.**

"I loved the refreshing take on love and dating in this book....Definitely recommend!" **Nic Reads In Heels**

"A sexy little chick lit read...A lovely, modern story involving friendship and falling in love." **Mrs L J Gibbs**

"I loved Olivia's last book, but I think this one was even better. Five Stars" **Hayley Jayne Reads.**

"Pure Perfection. Five stars." **Head In A Book 18**

Buy *Love Offline* on Amazon today!

AN EXTRACT FROM LOVE OFFLINE

Chapter 1

Normally, I love social media.

The endless fancy food and envy-inducing holiday pics on Insta, the witty conversations on Twitter, the funny memes on Facebook—I adore it.

When I've got important designs to create for clients and deadlines to meet, I can often be found spending many minutes (truth be told, more like hours) scrolling through strangers' feeds rather than *actually* working. After all, who doesn't like staring at photos of cute kittens?

Like I said. Normally, I *love* social media.

Well, I *did* until precisely 9.29 a.m. today.

The day started off like any other Monday morning. Hitting the snooze button a dozen times before finally crawling out of bed. Having a shower whilst wondering why the weekend flashes by in what seems like five minutes, whereas Monday to Friday lasts for half a century. Throwing on whatever looked clean and didn't need ironing, then dragging myself to my local coffee shop to get the caffeine-and-sugar hit I needed to help me feel remotely human, or at least alert enough to start work.

I'd sat at my desk, taken a generous bite of my blueberry muffin, sipped on my steaming latte and switched on my computer. I had considered going through my emails but, in true procrastination style, decided to check Instagram first instead, because of course that was *much* more important than doing actual work.

And there it was.

That photo.

The picture, which had already amassed thirty-six likes.

The image that instantly made my head spin and my stomach sink.

Captioned with just three words that sent my world crashing down.

She said yes!

My ex-boyfriend Eric, who I always believed would be the man I'd spend the rest of my life with, had proposed to Nicole—the woman he'd been cheating with for the last six months of our relationship—and she'd said yes.

Great.

There they were on what looked like some tropical beach, waves crashing against the golden sand, gazing into each other's eyes, lips locked, her left hand strategically placed on his shoulder, showing off the giant rock adorning her ring finger.

Exactly what I *didn't* need to see on a miserable grey March Monday morning in South London.

After staring at my screen for longer than was healthy, I'd tried to do what any smart, sensible, level-headed, pragmatic woman would if she heard the news that her unfaithful ex was marrying the younger model she'd been traded in for. I'd told myself I couldn't care less, that it was his loss, there were plenty more fish in the sea, karma would catch up with them and to just get on with my day.

Did it work?

Of course it bloody didn't.

So instead I'd dragged myself the ten steps from my home study to my bedroom, put on the 'Life Sucks' Spotify playlist, curled up into a ball and sobbed until my mobile rang.

It was Chloe. She'd heard the news from a friend during the school run and was on her way over. *With cake.*

I'd told her I wasn't sure that even a Victoria sponge the size of the Atlantic Ocean could make me feel better, but she'd insisted. And now she had let herself into my flat using the key I'd given her for emergencies. I suspected that she was probably mentally preparing herself for the sight that was about to greet her.

Chloe knew how much I loved Eric and how I'd struggled to get over him, so she'd realise that this wasn't going to be pretty.

'Emily Robinson!' she shouted, bursting through the bedroom door. 'Up you get!'

I slowly peeled my head from the pillow and tried to gauge whether I really had to force myself off the bed and deal with the situation or if I could get away with lying here for the rest of the afternoon and convince Chloe to give me a bucketload of tea and sympathy.

Who am I kidding? This was my no-nonsense best friend. And she did *not* do self-pity. Especially over an unfaithful man.

'Come on, Em. We're not doing this again. Remember?' She picked up my iPad from the bedside table, frowning as she bashed away haphazardly at the screen before eventually managing to pause the playlist. 'No more listening to sad songs. No more tears over Eric. He's not worth it,' she said, edging closer to the bed. 'You can do *much* better than that tallywag.'

I slowly dragged myself upright, scraped my thick, dark curly hair off my face and tucked my knees under my chin.

'I know he's a loser, but seeing that picture, of *him*, with *her*, proposing after knowing her for all of two minutes, when he *knew* I'd wanted to get married for *years* and constantly fobbed me off, it just—it really hurt,' I said, using the sleeve of my grey jumper to wipe the tears streaming down my cheeks.

'I understand that,' said Chloe as she smoothed down the back of her 1950s-style polka dot dress and sat down on the plain magnolia duvet. 'But you really need to move on, Em. It's been seven months. It's time to start a new life. Unfollow the fool like I told you to ages ago and make new friends.'

'I make new friends all the time,' I scoffed. 'I'm up to almost six hundred on Facebook. Admittedly, Insta is lagging behind a little as I'm low on content, but—'

'For crying out loud!' Chloe crossed her arms. 'I don't mean friends on social media. That's nonsense. I'm talking about *proper* friends. You know, people that you speak to face-to-face in a restaurant, rather than clicking the stupid love heart button on a post of some person from Timbuktu that you've never met.'

Trust Chloe not to understand. She's so old-fashioned, she doesn't even own a smartphone. Can you imagine?

'I know you have an aversion to technology and anything online, Chloe, but social media has been my life-line. If you think I'm bad now, I would have been *much* worse without the support of my online community.'

'Your *online community*?' Chloe rolled her eyes. 'Good grief! Sounds like some sort of cult!'

'Laugh all you want, but their likes, comments and uplifting posts have kept me going.'

'*If you say so,*' replied Chloe, reaching in her bag and pulling out two forks, serviettes and a container before taking out a large slice of chocolate cake. The rich scent filled the room. *Mmmm*. It smelt delicious. 'Like I've said before, I really think you should venture out of these four walls and try new things. You work from home all day, and apart from coming round to mine, you never seem to go anywhere. If you had a load of hobbies and were out making new friends in real life, you wouldn't have time to think about what that idiot is doing. You'd be too busy having fun.'

Here we go again. It's the *you need to get out of the flat more* lecture. I love Chloe, I really do, but she just doesn't get it.

My whole social circle revolved around my life with Eric. His friends became my friends, and after the breakup, that disappeared overnight. Now it was almost impossible to find anyone to go out with. On the rare occasions that I *did* get invited out, all the people in the group were coupled up and I was the odd one out. I got treated like either a weirdo or a potential husband thief. That's when I wasn't getting pitied or being shown photos of other random single men they were convinced would be ideal for me, purely because we'd both been 'condemned' to a life of solitude. I shuddered just thinking about it. *No, thanks.* I'd rather sit at home and have conversations online than be subjected to that hell.

'It's not that simple,' I huffed as I reached for my own slab of sponge and took a large bite. I wasn't in the mood to use a fork and serviette like Chloe. 'Everyone I know is married and has kids and doesn't have time to go out.'

'I appreciate what you're saying,' said Chloe, stroking her raven bob, which she'd styled into her signature vintage waves. 'But you are not the only thirty-five-year-old singleton in London. There are *loads* of other people out there just like you, so if your old circle of friends doesn't fit your life anymore, make a new circle. Find new friends. Look.' She stood up. 'I hate to leave you like this, but I've been called into work today, so I've got to run. I'll call you later, but please—don't sit here moping. Go for a walk to clear your head and have a think about what I said. There's a whole world out there. So many exciting things you could be doing with your life, but you need to actually step outside of this flat to discover them. Promise you'll give it some thought?'

I looked up at her, fighting the temptation to roll my eyes after hearing her make the same suggestion for the millionth time.

'Yes, yes,' I said. 'I'll think about it.'

'And you'll stop thinking about Eric too?'

'Yes,' I muttered reluctantly. What was I supposed to say? It wasn't like I *wanted* to think about him. Eric was just always there. Right in the front of my thoughts.

'Excellent!' She smiled. 'You'll feel *so* much better

when you do. You don't need his toxic energy around you. Anyway, I'd better go.' She leant forward and hugged me tightly before rushing towards the door. 'Make sure you get stuck into the cake. Love you!'

I stretched over to the container and grabbed another helping of sponge, shamelessly stuffing it into my mouth, then wiped my fingers before wrapping the duvet tightly around me. Getting out of these four walls? Going for a walk? *Not a chance.* That was the last thing I felt like doing. I planned to stay right here in this flat until I ran out of food or was forced to evacuate due to a state of national emergency. Whatever happened first.

Want to find out what happens next? Buy *Love Offline* on Amazon now!

ACKNOWLEDGEMENTS

Novel number five! Whoop! This book wouldn't have been possible without a team of incredible people.

A massive *merci beaucoup* to my wonderful mum for always reading through my drafts and giving such fantastic feedback. Thanks for the apple crumble recipe too. It's still the loveliest I've ever tasted, so I *had* to give it a mention in this book.

My darling PD: *muchas gracias* for your support, encouragement and calming words of wisdom whenever I had one of my *will-this-book-be-ready-on-time?* moments. And of course for the generous supply of prawns, raffaellos and ice cream. You always know how to put a smile on my face!

Big thanks to my brilliant editor, Eliza, proofreader, Lily, cover designer, Rachel, and website designer, Dawn. You ladies are the best.

Grazie mille to my Italian consultants: Sergio for all the help with the Italian lingo (especially the phrases that were too cheeky for Google Translate…) and Beatrice at

Giambrone Law for providing such a useful insight into the Italian legal system.

Jo, Loz, Brad and Jas: thanks for being such awesome advance readers and offering suggestions on how to make the novel the best it could be.

Sending lots of love to all the fantastic book bloggers. Thanks for reading and reviewing my books and spreading the word to your followers.

And last but by no means least, a supersized shout out goes to my readers. I wrote this novel because of *you*. After *The Middle-Aged Virgin* was published, I received so many lovely messages from readers who were excited to find out what happened next with Sophia, Lorenzo and the baby and asking (well, in some cases, *demanding*, lol!) that I write a sequel. Now that you've reached the end of book two, I hope you enjoyed it as much as the first! Thank you for your continued support. It really does mean the world.

Until next time…

Olivia x

ABOUT THE AUTHOR

Olivia Spring lives in London, England. When she's not making regular trips to Italy to indulge in pasta, pizza and gelato, she can be found at her desk, writing new sexy romantic comedies.

If you'd like to say hi, email olivia@oliviaspring.com or connect on social media.

facebook.com/ospringauthor

twitter.com/ospringauthor

instagram.com/ospringauthor

Printed in Germany
by Amazon Distribution
GmbH, Leipzig